U0369248

微像文化－编

刘宇昆－等译

镜像×未来 II

TOUCHABLE UNREALITY

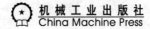

机械工业出版社
China Machine Press

图书在版编目（CIP）数据

未来镜像 II / 微像文化编；刘宇昆等译 . —北京：机械工业出版社，2019.1

ISBN 978-7-111-61638-2

I. 未… II. ①微… ②刘… III. 科学幻想小说 – 小说集 – 中国 – 当代 IV. I247.5

中国版本图书馆 CIP 数据核字（2018）第 282245 号

未来镜像 II

出版发行：机械工业出版社（北京市西城区百万庄大街 22 号　邮政编码：100037）

责任编辑：孟宪勐

责任校对：李秋荣

印　　刷：北京瑞德印刷有限公司

版　　次：2019 年 3 月第 1 版第 1 次印刷

开　　本：147mm×210mm　1/32

印　　张：15.5

书　　号：ISBN 978-7-111-61638-2

定　　价：59.00 元

序言一
PREFACE

　　2018 年 8 月在美国圣何塞举办的世界科幻大会上，微像文化与《克拉克世界》团队成员头一回坐到一起聚餐，这是我们合作的三周年，也是我们第一次把作家、译者、编辑与合作背后的推动者聚起来一起吃饭聊天。那天也是《克拉克世界》的主编尼尔·克拉克（Neil Clarke）的生日，我们悄悄为他准备了惊喜——一束鲜花、一张通往月球的"船票"、一个迷你生日蛋糕、一份写满所有人签名祝福的贺卡。那一刻，我们之间的关系真正由合作伙伴变成了家人。

　　2015 年，《克拉克世界》与微像文化共同发起"中国作家专栏"，由刘宇昆等顶尖译者主持翻译，三年里已经刊登了包括刘慈欣、郝景芳、夏笳、张冉、陈楸帆、阿缺、罗隆翔等人超过 30 篇中国优秀科幻作家的作品，成为中国科幻最大的海外输出渠道之一，《克拉克世界》杂志也成为中国科幻最重要的传播平台。

《克拉克世界》这本享誉全球的科幻奇幻月刊杂志，拥有十余年的历史，曾获得过世界奇幻奖、英国奇幻奖，是雨果奖最佳科幻奇幻杂志。杂志所刊登的很多小说也获得过各种世界科幻奇幻大奖。

　　在这里我要特别感谢尼尔·克拉克，作为《克拉克世界》的主编，尼尔个人独到的眼光使得很多优秀的作品能够被读者们看到，他向世界科幻输送了许多年轻却顶尖的新鲜血液。与此同时，他也注意到逐渐崭露头角的中国科幻，在欣赏到中国科幻魅力的同时，他意识到中国科幻在海外市场上有着巨大的潜力。科幻本就是一个容易打破文化壁垒的题材和类型，而且中国已经拥有了很多优秀的科幻作品，但是被翻译的太少，许多优秀的科幻作品没有机会被国外读者接触到，更无法和国外优秀的科幻作品同台竞争奖项。做《未来镜像》的初衷，就是想要通过我们微小的力量建立起中外科幻沟通的桥梁，走出打破科幻文化壁垒的第一步。

　　但是在打破这个壁垒的过程中，我们也遇到了很大的困难，目前中国英文写作者少，优秀译者少，完成一篇优秀的译文是一项浩大的工程，因此被翻译的作品数量有限，能够传播出去的作品数量也有限。在微像发现者大会上暨五周年发布会上，我们有幸邀请到了尼尔·克拉克与刘宇昆来到现场，他们在台上讲述自己最初开始发表和翻译中国科幻的初衷与困难。这些了不起的人，在没有任何外界支持的情况下曾孤军奋战，只因为他们相信中国科幻值得被世界看到。这更加让我们认识到了自己工作的重要性，因此决定在《未来镜像》第一本的基础上，继续推出第二本，乃至以后的第三本、第四本……我们同时也希望《未来镜像》系列能够成为中国科幻翻译的平台，能有更多优秀的译者参与进来。《未来镜像》系列只是一个开始，微像今后也将继续致力于让中国科幻走向世界，期待《未来镜像Ⅱ》能够带给你们不同的体验，让你们体会到这些熟悉的中国科幻作品被翻译后所呈现的另一种不同的感觉；最重要的是，希望你们能够喜欢这本书。

最后，感谢所有为这本书的出版做出努力的人，感谢这些优秀的作家和译者，感谢尼尔对中国科幻的喜爱，感谢一直支持我们的朋友。中国科幻的海外传播是一件任重而道远的事情，微像一直在路上。

张译文
微像文化 CEO
2018 年 9 月

序言二
PREFACE

很难相信，距离我们最初和微像文化展开合作，在《克拉克世界》（*Clarkesworld*）杂志上定期刊登中国科幻译作，已经有足足三年的时光了。追根溯源，我们之间的合作真正缘起于 2011年。那时，刘宇昆（Ken Liu）将他翻译的陈楸帆作品《丽江的鱼儿们》投稿到了《克拉克世界》。刘宇昆在 2016 年幻想小说翻译博客的采访中，这样描述他起意从事翻译的过程：

> 我会开始从事翻译，纯属是个意外。我的朋友陈楸帆（Stanley Chan）找了一位专业译者替他翻译一部短篇小说，然后请我替他看一看译文水平是否过关。我先是提了一些建议，后来终于告诉他，或许干脆由我全部推翻从头重新翻译一遍反而会更容易。

这场令人惊喜的意外令刘宇昆成为一名译者，我们与中国科幻的合作也就此拉开了序幕。当这篇投稿在我们的 2011 年 8 月刊上登出之后，我就一直鼓励刘宇昆，再多翻译一些中国科幻作品。几个月后，他又提交了夏笳的《百鬼夜行街》，于 2012 年 2 月刊上登出。同年 5 月，《丽江的鱼儿们》获得了科幻奇幻翻译奖最佳短篇小说的荣誉。

2012 年下半年，突如其来的心脏病几乎要了我的命。这场大病对我的心脏造成了不可逆转的伤害，6 个月后，我在胸腔里植入了一枚除颤器。我想，这样我岂不是也成了一名"赛博格"吗？这次经历启发我开始筹备第一本主题合集——《全面升级》（*Upgraded*）。当我邀请刘宇昆为这本合集撰稿的时候，他询问我是否愿意将几篇译作一同加入合集中。自然，他的提议令我激动不已。由此，我又一次得以和陈楸帆（《天使之油》）与夏笳（《童童的夏天》）进行合作。

我所不知道的是，我们所做的这些努力，已经在中国悄悄掀起了波澜。2014 年 4 月，微像文化与我取得了联系，询问《克拉克世界》是否有兴趣长期刊登中国科幻译作。在接下来的几个月中，我们就双方的目标进行了商榷，也就该如何在《克拉克世界》杂志上定期发表中文译作制订了更加严密的计划。对于双方来说，这是全然陌生的领域；据我所知，在我们之前，没有任何一本美国科幻杂志进行过这样的尝试。

在一切尘埃落定之后，我们决定在《克拉克世界》的第 100 刊——2015 年 1 月刊中首次正式加入中国科幻译文栏目。我们刊登了张冉的《以太》，由刘宇昆和言一零（Carmen Yiling Yan）共同翻译。在第一年的合作中，我们一共刊登了九篇中国科幻译作。那些故事最终被收录于一本在中国出版的双语合集中——后来的《未来镜像》（*Touchable Unreality*——我知道中英文的名称有差异）。你正在阅读的这本书其实更像是那本合集的续集（中间有些重复的部分）。它所收录的，正是合作三年来最优秀的故事。

能够将这些优秀的作品翻译成英语，将许多中国作家（很多人是第一次）介绍给以英语为母语的读者们，让我感到非常自豪。科幻文学本应没有国界，然而我们的读者却有很长的一段时间都生活在与译作几乎零接触的环境下。简而言之，他们压根不知道自己究竟错过了什么。我们所发表的这些译作，以它们出众的质量，引得无数人对世界科幻文学产生了更大的兴趣。我希望，在接下来的时光里，这份兴趣也会继续增长。

当然，正是刘宇昆一直以来的刻苦工作与不懈支持为我们和微像文化打开了全新的大门，令我们得以拥有这样的预见，愿意跨前一步进行尝试，继而建立了这样成功的合作关系。在过去的几年中，我们和微像文化的关系也伴随着这个成长中的合作项目而不断调整、改变。我所共事过的每一个人都为这个项目注入了独特而宝贵的元素，使它变得越来越好。确实，我们有好故事，有严密的计划，也有迫不及待的读者，然而若是缺少了优秀的翻译家，这一切便会顿时轰然倒下。所以，我想在这里郑重地感谢每一位在不同文化世界之间搭起桥梁的译者。正是因为他们的努力，才有更多人得以享受这些故事。我想，一切本就该是这样的。

尼尔·克拉克（Neil Clarke）

2018 年 4 月

It's hard to believe that three years have passed since we teamed up with Storycom to regularly publish translated Chinese science fiction in the pages of *Clarkesworld Magazine*. The roots of the project dig a bit deeper, when in 2011, Ken Liu submitted his translation of "The Fish of Lijiang" by Chen Qiufan to *Clarkesworld*. In an interview for the Speculative Fiction in Translation blog in 2016, Ken describes how this came to be:

"I got into translation purely by accident. My friend Chen Qiufan (a.k.a. Stanley Chan) had one of his stories translated professionally, and then asked me to take a look at the result. I started to make a few suggestions, but then told Stan that I thought it would be easier if I just did the translation from scratch."

That happy accident set us on our course. I bought the story for our August 2011 issue and encouraged Ken to translate more. He followed up a few months later with "A Hundred Ghosts Parade Tonight" by Xia Jia, which we published in February 2012. "The Fish of Lijiang" would go on to receive the Science Fiction & Fantasy Translation Award for Short Fiction in May.

Later that year, I suffered a near-fatal heart attack and the permanent damage done to my heart required the implantation of defibrillator in my chest just six months later. Now part cyborg, the whole endeavor inspired my first themed anthology and *Upgraded* was born. When I invited Ken to write a story for it, he asked if I'd also be interested in including any translations. Enthusiastically, I jumped at the opportunity and was thrilled to have the chance to work with Chen Qiufan ("Oil of Angels") and Xia Jia ("Tongtong's Summer") again.

Little did I know, these efforts were developing a reputation in China. In April 2014, Storycom reached out to me to see if *Clarkesworld* would be interested in publishing Chinese science fiction on a more regular basis. Over the next few months, we discussed our goals and what it would take to make translations a regular feature in the magazine. It was new territory for both organizations and, so far as I've been able to tell, the first time a US-based science fiction magazine had attempted to do so.

After settling on a plan, we decided to launch this new feature in our one hundredth issue, January 2015, and featured "Ether" by Zhang Ran, translated by Carmen Yiling Yan and Ken Liu. We published nine Chinese translations during that first year and those stories were eventually gathered together in a bilingual anthology, *Touchable Unreality* (未 来 镜 像 –yes, I know it translates differently), published in China. The book you are currently reading is technically a sequel–with a bit of overlap–celebrating the stories we thought were the best of those we published since launching the project.

I am quite proud of all the stories we've translated and grateful for the the opportunity to introduce several Chinese authors–many for the first time–to an English-language audience. Science fiction is global and for far too long, our readers have had limited access to works in translation. In short, they didn't know what they were missing. The quality of these stories has contributed to a growing interest in world science fiction, one that I hope to see continue to develop and grow for a long time.

None of this would have been possible without Ken Liu, who's worked and supported to open the door for us and Storycom for having the vision to step forward and help make this possible. Over the years, our relationship has adjusted to meet the needs of this evolving project, and everyone I've worked with has added something valuable to the mix and made it better. You can have great stories, an amazing plan, and even an audience, but if you don't have great translators, the whole house will come crashing down. So a big thank you goes out to each of the translators that built these bridges between our worlds. Now even more people can enjoy these stories and that's the way things should be.

Neil Clarke
April, 2018

目录
CONTENTS

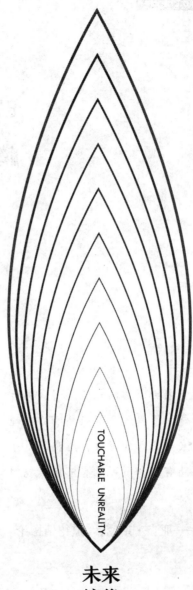

TOUCHABLE UNREALITY

未来
镜像

巴
麟

陈楸帆

我用我的视觉来判断你的视觉，用我的听觉来判断你的听觉，用我的理智来判断你的理智，用我的愤恨来判断你的愤恨，用我的爱来判断你的爱。我没有，也不可能有任何其他的方法来判断它们。

——亚当·斯密，《道德情操论》

巴鳞身上涂着厚厚一层凝胶，再裹上只有几个纳米厚的贴身半透膜，他来自热带的黝黑皮肤经过几次折射，变得星空般深不可测。我看见闪着蓝白光的微型传感器飘浮在凝胶气泡间，如同一颗颗行将熄灭的恒星，如同他眼中小小的我。

"别怕，放松点，很快就好。"我安慰他，巴鳞就像听懂了一样，表情有所放松，眼睑处堆叠起皱纹，那道伤疤也没那么明显了。

他老了，已不像当年，尽管他这一族人的真实年龄我从来没搞清楚过。

助手将巴鳞扶上万向感应云台，在他腰部系上弹性拘束带，无论他往哪个方向以何种速度跑动，云台都会自动调节履带的方向与速度，保证用户不位移、不摔倒。

我接过助手的头盔，亲手为巴鳞戴上，他那灯泡般鼓起的惊骇双眼隐没在黑暗里。

"你会没事的。"我用低得没人听见的声音重复，就像在安慰我自己。

头盔上的红灯开始闪烁，加速，过了那么三五秒，突然变成绿色。

巴鳞像是中了什么咒语般全身一僵，活像是听见了磨刀石噩噩作响的羔羊。

那是我 13 岁那年的一个夏夜，空气湿热黏稠，鼻孔里充斥着台风前夜的霉锈味。

我趴在祖屋客厅的地上，尽量舒展整个身体，像壁虎般紧贴凉爽的绿纹镶嵌石砖，直到这块区域被我的体温捂得热乎，就势一滚，寻找下一块阵地。

背后传来熟悉的皮鞋踏地声，雷厉风行，一板一眼，在空旷的大厅里回荡，我知道那是谁，可依然趴在地上，用屁股对着来人。

"就知道你在这里，怎么不进新厝吹空调啊？"

父亲的口气柔和得不像他。他说的新厝是在祖屋背后新盖的三层楼房，里面有全套进口的家具电器，装修也是镇上最时髦的，父亲还特地为我辟出来一间大书房。

"不喜欢新厝。"

"你个不识好歹的傻子！"他猛地拔高了嗓门，又赶紧低声咕哝几句。

我知道他在跟祖宗们道歉，便从地板上昂起脑袋，望着香案上供奉的祖宗灵位和墙上的黑白画像，看他们是否有所反应。

祖宗们看起来无动于衷。

父亲长叹了口气："阿鹏，我没忘记你的生日，从岭北运货回来，高速路上遇到事故，所以才迟了两天。"

我挪动了下身子，像条泥鳅般打了个滚，换到另一块冰凉的地砖。

父亲那充满烟味儿的呼吸靠近我，近乎耳语般哀求："礼物我早就准备好了，这可是有钱都买不到的哟！"

他拍了两下手，另一种脚步声出现了，是肉掌直接拍打在石砖上的声音，细密、湿润，像是某种刚从海里上岸的两栖类动物。

我一下坐了起来，眼睛循着声音的方向，那是在父亲的身后，藻绿色花纹地砖上，立着一个黑色影子，门外膏黄色的灯光勾勒出那生灵的轮廓，如此瘦小，却有着不合比例的膨大头颅，就像是镇上肉铺挂在店门口木棍上的羊头。

影子又往前迈了两步。我这才发现，原来那不是逆光造成的剪影效果，那个人，如果可以称其为人的话，浑身上下都像涂上了一层不反光的黑漆，像是在一个平滑正常的世界里裂开一道缝，所有的光都被这道人形的缝给吞噬掉了，除了两个反光点，那是他那对略微凸起的眼睛。

现在我看得更清楚了，这的的确确是一个男孩，他浑身赤裸，只用类似棕榈与树皮的编织物遮挡下身，他的头颅也并没有那么大，只是因为盘起两个羊角般怪异的发髻，才显得尺寸惊人。他一直不安地研究着脚底下的砖块接缝，脚趾不停蠕动，发出昆虫般的抓挠声。

"狍鸮族，从南海几个边缘小岛上捉到的，估计他们这辈子都没踩过地板。"

我失神地望着他，这个或许与我年纪相仿的男孩，他身上的某种东西让我感觉怪异，尤其是父亲将他作为礼物这件事。

"我看不出来他有什么好玩的，还不如给我养条狗。"

父亲猛烈地咳嗽起来。

"傻子，这可比狗贵多了。如果不是亲眼看到，你老子可不会当这冤大头。真的是太怪了……"他的嗓音变得缥缈起来。

一阵沙沙声由远而近，我打了个冷战，起风了。

风带来男孩身上浓烈的腥气，让我立刻想起了某种熟悉的鱼类——一种瘦长、铁乌的廉价海鱼。

我想这倒是很适合作为一个名字。

父亲早已把我的人生规划到了四十五岁。

十八岁上一个省内商科大学，离家不能超过三小时火车车程。

大学期间不得谈恋爱，他早已为我物色好了对象——他的生意伙伴老罗的女儿，生辰八字都已经算好了。

毕业之后结婚，二十五岁前要小孩，二十八岁要第二个，酌情要第三个（取决于前两个婴儿的性别）。

要第一个小孩的同时开始接触父亲公司的业务，他会带着我拜访所有的合作伙伴和上下游关系（多数是他的老战友）。

孩子怎么办？有他妈（瞧，他已经默认是个男孩了），有老人，还可以请几个保姆。

三十岁全面接手林氏茶叶公司，在这之前的五年内，我必须掌握关于茶叶的辨别、烘制和交易的知识，同时熟悉所有合作伙伴和竞争对手的喜好与弱点。

接下来的十五年，我将在退休父亲的辅佐下，带领家族企业开枝散叶，走出本省，走向全国，运气好的话，甚至可以进军海外市场。这是他一直想追求却又瞻前顾后的人生终极目标。

在我四十五岁的时候，我的第一个孩子也差不多要大学毕业了，我将像父亲一样，提前为他物色好一任妻子。

在父亲的宇宙里，万物就像是咬合精确、运转良好的齿轮，生生不息。

每当我与他就这个话题展开争论时，他总是搬出我的爷爷，他的爷爷，我爷爷的爷爷，总之，指着祖屋一墙的先人们骂我忘本。

他说，我们林家人都是这么过来的，除非你不姓林。

有时候，我怀疑自己是否真的生活在 21 世纪。

我叫他巴鳞，巴在土语里是"鱼"的意思，巴鳞就是有鳞的鱼。

可他看起来还是更像一头羊，尤其是当他扬起两个大发髻，望向远方海平线的时候。父亲说，狍鸮族人的方位感特别强，即便被蒙上眼，捆上手脚，扔进船舱，飘过汪洋大海，再日夜颠簸经过多少道转卖，他们依然能够准确地找到故乡的方位。尽管他们的故土在最近的边境争端中仍然归属不明。

"那我们是不是得把他拴住，就像用链子拴住土狗一样。"我问父亲。

父亲怪异地笑了，他说："狍鸮族比咱们还认命，他们相信这一切都是神灵的安排，所以他们不会逃跑。"

巴鳞渐渐熟悉了周围的环境，父亲把原来养鸡的寮屋重新布置了一下，当作他的住处。巴鳞花了很长时间才搞懂床垫是用来睡觉的，但他还是更愿意直接睡在粗砺的沙石地上。他几乎什么都吃，甚至把我们吃剩的鸡骨头都嚼得只剩渣子。我们几个小孩经常蹲在寮屋外面看他怎么吃东西，也只有这时候，我才得以看清巴鳞的牙齿，那如鲨鱼般尖利细密的倒三角形，毫不费力地把嘴里的一切撕得稀烂。

我总是控制不住地去想象那口利齿咬在身上的感觉，然后心里一哆嗦，有种疼却又上瘾的复杂感受。

巴鳞从来没有开口说过话，即便是面对我们的各种挑逗，他也是紧闭着双唇，一语不发，用那双灯泡般的凸眼盯着我们，直到我们放弃尝试。

终于有一天，巴鳞吃饱了饭之后，慢悠悠地钻出寮屋，瘦小的身体挺着饱胀的肚子，像一根长了虫瘿的黑色树枝。我们几个小孩正在玩捉水鬼的游戏，巴鳞晃晃悠悠地在离我们不远处停下，颇为好奇地看着我们的举动。

"捞虾洗衫，玻璃刺脚丫。"我们边喊着，边假装在河边捕捞的渔夫，从砖块垒成的河岸上，往并不存在的河里试探性地伸出一条腿，点一点河水，再收回去。

扮演水鬼的孩子则来回奔忙，徒劳地想要抓住渔夫伸进河水里的脚丫，只有这样，水鬼才能上岸变成人类，而被抓住的孩子则成为新的水鬼。

没人注意到巴鳞是什么时候开始加入游戏的，直到隔壁家的小娜突然停下，用手指了指。我看到巴鳞正在模仿水鬼的动作，左扑右抱，只不过，他面对的不是渔夫，而是空气。小孩子经常会模仿其他人的说话或肢体语言，来取悦或激怒对方，可巴鳞所做的和我以往见过的都不一样。

我开始觉察出哪里不对劲了。

巴鳞的动作和扮演水鬼的阿辉几乎是同步的，我说几乎，是因为单凭肉眼已无法判断两者之间是否存在细微的延迟。巴鳞就像是阿辉在五米开外凭空多出来的影子，每一个转身，每一次伸手，甚至每一回因为扑空而沮丧的停顿，都复制得完美无缺、毫不费力。

我不知道他是如何做到的，就像是完全不用经过大脑。

阿辉终于停了下来，因为所有人都在看着巴鳞。

阿辉走向巴鳞，巴鳞也走向阿辉，就连脚后跟拖地的小细节都一模一样。

阿辉说："你为什么要学我！"

巴鳞同时张着嘴，蹦出来的却是一堆乱七八糟的音节，像是坏掉的收音机。

阿辉推了巴鳞一把，同时也被巴鳞推开。

其他人都看着这出荒唐的闹剧，这可比捉水鬼好玩多了。

"打啊！"不知道谁喊了一句，阿辉扑上去和巴鳞扭抱成一团，这种打法也颇为有趣，因为两个人的动作都是同步的，所以很快谁都动弹不了，只是大眼瞪小眼。

"好啦好啦，闹够了就该回家了！"一只大手把两人从地上拎起来，又强行把他们分开，像是拆散了一对连体婴。那是父亲。

阿辉愤愤不平地朝地上啐了一口，和其他家小孩一起作鸟兽散。

这回巴鳞没有跟着做，似乎某个开关被关上了。

父亲带着笑意看了我一眼，那眼神似乎在说，现在你知道哪儿好玩了吧。

"我们可以把人脑看作一个机器，笼统地说来，它只干三件事：感知、思考还有运动控制。如果用计算机打比方，感知就是输入，思考就是中间的各种运算，而运动控制就是输出，它是人脑能和外界进行交互的唯一方式。想想看为什么？"

在老吕接手我们班之前，打死我也没法相信，这是一个体育老师说出来的话。

老吕是个传奇，他个头不高，大概一米七二的样子，小平头，夏天可以看到他身上鼓鼓的肌肉。据说他是从国外留学回来的。

当时我们都很奇怪，为什么留过洋的人要到这座小破乡镇中学来当老师。后来听说，他是家中独子，父亲重病在床，母亲走得早，没有其他亲戚能够照顾老人，老人又不愿意离开家乡，说狐死首丘。无奈之下，他只能先过来谋一份教职，他的专业方向是运动控制学，校长想当然地让他当了体育老师。

老吕和其他老师不一样，他和我们一起厮混打闹，就像是好哥们儿。

我问过他，为什么要回来？

他说，有句老话叫"父母在，不远游"。我都远游十几年了，父母都快不在了，也该为他们想想了。

我又问他，等父母都不在了，你会走吗？

　　老吕皱了皱眉头，像是刻意不去想这个问题，他绕了个大圈子，说，在我研究的领域有一个老前辈叫唐纳德·布罗德本特（Donald Broadbent），他曾经说过，控制人的行为比控制刺激他们的因素要难得多，因此在运动控制领域很难产生类似于"A 导致 B"的科学规律。

　　所以？我知道他压根儿没想回答我。

　　没人知道会怎样。他点点头，长吸了一口烟。

　　放屁。我接过他手里的烟头。

　　所有人都觉得他待不了太久，结果，老吕从我初二教到了高三，还娶了个本地媳妇生了娃。这正应了他自己那句话。

　　我们开始用的是大头针，后来改成用从打火机上拆下来的电子点火器，咔嚓一按，就能迸出一道蓝白色的电弧。

　　父亲觉得这样做比较文明。

　　人贩子教他一招，如果希望巴鳞模仿谁，就让两人四目对视，然后给巴鳞"刺激一下"，等到他身体一僵，眼神一出溜，连接就算完成了。他们说，这是狍鸮族特有的习俗。

　　巴鳞给我们带来了无数的欢乐。

　　我从小就喜欢看街头戏人表演，无论是皮影戏、布袋戏，还是扯线木偶。我总会好奇地钻进后台，看他们如何操纵手中无生命的玩偶，演出牵动人心的爱恨情仇，对年幼的我来说，这就像法术一样。而在巴鳞身上，我终于有机会实践自己的法术。

我跳舞，他也跳舞；我打拳，他也打拳。原本我羞于在亲戚朋友面前展示的一切，如今却似乎借助巴鳞的身体，成为可以广而告之的演出项目。

我让巴鳞模仿喝醉了酒的父亲；我让他模仿镇上那些不健全的人，疯子、瘸子、傻子、被砍断四肢只能靠肚皮在地面摩擦前进的乞丐、羊癫疯病人……然后我们躲在一旁笑得满地打滚，直到被那些人的家属拿着晾衣杆在后面追着打。

巴鳞也能模仿动物，猫、狗、牛、羊、猪都没问题，鸡鸭不太行，鱼完全不行。

他有时会蹲在祖屋外偷看电视里播放的节目，尤其喜欢关于动物的纪录片。当看见动物被猎杀时，巴鳞的身体会无法遏制地抽搐起来，就好像被撕开腹腔，内脏横流的是他一样。

巴鳞也有累的时候，那时他模仿动作越来越慢，误差越来越大，像是松了发条的铁皮人，或者是电池快用光的玩具汽车，最后就是一屁股坐在地上，怎么踢他也不动弹。解决方法只有一个，让他吃，死命吃。

除此之外，他从来没有流露出一丝抗拒或者不快，在当时的我看来，巴鳞和那些用牛皮、玻璃纸、布料或木头做成的偶人并没有太大的区别，只是忠实地执行操纵者的旨意，本身并不携带任何情绪，甚至是一种下意识的条件反射。

直到我们厌烦了单人游戏，开始创造出更加复杂而残酷的多人玩法。

我们先猜拳排好顺序，赢的人可以首先操纵巴鳞，去和猜输的小孩对打，再根据输赢进行轮换。我猜赢了。

　　这种感觉真是太酷了！我就像一个坐镇后方的司令，指挥着士兵在战场上厮杀，挥拳、躲避、飞腿、回旋踢……因为拉开了距离，我可以更清楚地看清对方的意图和举动，从而做出更合理的攻击动作。更因为所有的疼痛都由巴麟承受了，我毫无心理负担，能够放开手脚大举反扑。

　　我感觉自己胜券在握。

　　但不知为何，所有的动作传递到巴麟身上似乎都丧失了力道，丝毫无法震慑对方，更谈不上伤害。很快，巴麟便被压倒在地上，饱受痛揍。

　　"咬他，咬他！"我做出撕咬的动作，我知道他那口尖牙的威力。

　　可巴麟好似断了线般无动于衷，拳头不停落下，他的脸颊肿起来。

　　"噗！"我朝地上一吐，表示认输。

　　换我上场，成为那个和巴麟对打的人。我恶狠狠地盯着他，他的脸上流着血，眼眶肿胀，但双眼仍然一如既往地无神平静。我被激怒了。

　　我观察着操控者阿辉的动作，我熟悉他打架的习惯，先迈左脚，再出右拳。我可以出其不意扫他下盘，把他放翻在地，只要一倒地，基本上战斗就可以宣告结束了。

　　阿辉左脚迅速前移，来了！我正想蹲下，怎料巴麟用脚扬起一阵沙土，迷住我的眼睛。接着，便是一个扫堂腿将我放倒，我眯缝着双眼，双手护头，准备迎接暴风骤雨般的拳头。

　　事情并不像我想象的那样。拳头落下来了，却软绵绵的，一点力气都没有。我以为巴鳞累了，但很快发现不是这么回事，阿辉本身出拳是又准又狠的，但巴鳞刻意收住了拳势，让力道在我身上软着陆。拳头毫无预兆地停下了，一个暖乎乎、臭烘烘的东西贴到我的脸上。

周围响起一阵哄笑声，我突然明白过来，一股热浪涌上头顶。

那是巴鳞的屁股。

阿辉肯定知道巴鳞无法输出有效打击，才使出这么卑鄙的招数。

我狠力推开巴鳞，一个鲤鱼打挺，将他反制住，压在身下。我眼睛刺痛，泪水直流，屈辱夹杂着愤怒。巴鳞看着我，肿胀的眼睛里也溢满了泪水，似乎懂得我此时此刻的感受。

我突然回过神来，高高地举起拳头。他只是在模仿。

"你为什么不使劲！"

拳头砸在巴鳞那瘦削的身体上，像是击中了一块易碎的空心木板，咚咚作响。

"为什么不打我！"

我的指节感受到了他紧闭双唇下松动的牙齿。

"为什么！"

我听见嘶啦一声脆响，巴鳞右侧眉骨裂了一道长长的口子，一直延伸到眼睑上方，深黑皮肤下露出粉白色的脂肪，鲜红的血汩汩地往外涌着，很快在沙地上凝成小小的"池塘"。

他身上又多了一种腥气。

我吓坏了，退开几步，其他小孩也呆住了。

尘土散去，巴鳞像被割了喉的羊仔一样蜷曲在地上，用仅存的左眼斜睨着我，依然没有丝毫表情的流露。就在这一刻，我第一次感觉到，他和我一样，是个有血有肉，甚至有灵魂的人类。

这一刻只维持了短短数秒，我近乎本能地意识到，如果之前的我无法像对待一个人一样去对待巴鳞，那么今后也不能。

我掸掸裤子上的灰土，头也不回地挤入人群。

我进入 Ghost 模式，体验被囚禁在 VR 套装中的巴鳞所体验到的一切。

我／巴鳞置身于一座风光旖旎的热带岛屿，环境设计师根据我的建议糅合了诸多南中国海岛上的景观及植被特点，光照角度和色温也都尽量贴合当地经纬度。

我想让巴鳞感觉像是回了家，但这丝毫没有减轻他的恐慌。

视野猛烈地旋转，天空、沙地、不远处的海洋、错落的藤萝植物，还有不时出现的虚拟躯体，像素粗砺的灰色多边形尚待优化。

我感到眩晕，这是视觉与身体运动不同步所导致的晕动症，眼睛告诉大脑你在动，但前庭系统却告诉大脑你没动，两种信号的冲突让人不适。但对巴鳞，我们采用了最好的技术将信号延迟缩短到 5 毫秒以内，并用动作捕捉技术同步他的肉身与虚拟身体运动，在万向感应云台上，他可以自由跑动，位置却不会移动半分。

我们就像对待一位头等舱客人，呵护备至。

巴鳞一动不动地站在那里，他无法理解眼前的这个世界与几分钟前那个空旷明亮的房间之间的关系。

"这不行，我们必须让他动起来！"我对耳麦那端的操控人员吼道。

巴鳞突然回过头，全景环绕立体声让他觉察到身后的动静。郁郁葱葱的森林开始震动，一群鸟儿飞离树梢，似乎有什么巨大的物体在树木间穿行摩擦，由远而近。巴鳞一动不动地凝视着那片灌木。

一群巨大的史前生物蜂拥而出，即便是常识缺乏如我也能看出，它们不属于同一个地质时代。操控人员调用了数据库里现成的模型，试图让巴鳞奔跑起来。

他像棵木桩般站在那里，任由霸王龙、剑齿虎、古蜻蜓、新巴士鳄和各种古怪的节肢动物迎面扑来，又呼啸着穿过他的身体。这是物理模拟引擎的一个 bug，但如果完全拟真，又恐怕实验者承受不了如此强烈的感官冲击。

这还没有完。

巴鳞脚下的地面开始震动开裂，树木开始七歪八倒地折断，火山喷发，滚烫猩红的岩浆从地表迸射，汇聚成暗血色的河流，而海上掀起数十米高的巨浪，翻滚着朝我们站立的位置袭来。

"我说，这有点儿过了吧。"我对着耳麦说，似乎能听见那端传来的窃笑。

想象一个原始人被抛掷在这样一个世界末日的舞台中央，他会是一种什么样的感受。他会认为自己是为整个人类承担罪愆的救世主，还是已然陷入一种感官崩塌的疯狂境地？

又或者，像巴鳞一样，无动于衷？

突然我明白了事情的真相。我退出 Ghost 模式，摘下巴鳞的头盔，传感器如密密麻麻的珍珠凝满黑色头颅，而他双目紧闭，四周的皱纹深得像是昆虫的触须。

"今天就到这里吧。"我无力叹息，想起多年前痛揍他的那个下午。

我与父亲间的战事随着分班临近日渐升温。

按照他的大计划，我应该报考文科——政治或者历史，可我对这俩任人打扮调教的"小婊子"毫无兴趣。我想报物理，至少也是生物，用老吕的话说，这是能够解决"根本性问题"的学科。

父亲对此嗤之以鼻，他指了指几栋家产，还有铺满晒谷场，在阳光下碎金般闪亮的茶叶。

"还有比养家糊口更根本的问题吗？"

这就叫对牛弹琴。

我放弃了说服父亲的尝试，我有我的计划。通过老吕的关系，我获得了老师的默许，平时跟着文科班上语数英大课，再溜到理科班上专业小课，中间难免有些课程冲突，我也只能有所取舍，再用课余时间补上。老师也不傻，与其要一个不情不愿的中等偏下文科考生，不如放手赌一把，兴许还能放颗卫星，出个状元。

我本以为可以瞒过在外忙碌的父亲，把导火索留到填报志愿的最后一刻点燃。当时的我实在太天真了。

填报志愿的那天，所有人都拿到了志愿表，除了我。我以为老师搞错了。

"你爸已经帮你填好了！"老师故作轻描淡写，他不敢直视我的双眼。

我不知道自己怎么回的家，像失魂的野狗逛遍了镇里的大街小巷，最后鬼使神差地回到祖屋前。

父亲正在逗巴鳞取乐，他不知道从哪翻出一套破旧的军服，套在巴鳞身上显得宽大臃肿，活像一只偷穿人类衣服的猴子。他又开始当年在军队服役时学会的那一套把戏，立正、稍息、向左向右看齐、原地踏步走……在我刚上小学那会儿，他特别喜欢像个指挥官一样喊着口号操练我，而这却是我最深恶痛绝的事情。

已经很多年没重温这一幕了，看起来父亲找到了一个新的下属。

那是一个绝对服从的士兵。

"一二一，一二一，向前踏步——走！"巴鳞随着他的口令和示范有模有样地踏着步子，过长的裤子在地上沾满了泥土。

"你根本不希望我上大学，对吗？"我站在他们俩中间，责问父亲。

"向右看齐！"父亲头一侧，迈开小碎步向右边挪动，我听见身后传来同样节奏的脚步声。

"所以你早就知道了，只是为了让我没有反悔的机会！"

"原地踏步——走！"

　　我愤怒地转身按住巴鳞，不让他再愚蠢地踏步，但他似乎无法控制住自己，军装裤腿在地上"啪啦啪啦"地扬起尘土。

　　我捧住他的脑袋，让他和我四目对视，一只手掏出电子点火器，蓝白色的弧光在巴鳞太阳穴边炸开，他发出类似婴儿般的惊叫。

　　我从他的眼神中确信，他现在已经属于我了。

　　"你没有权力控制我！你眼里只有你的生意，你有考虑过我的前途吗？"

　　巴鳞随着气急败坏的我转着圈，指着父亲吼叫着，渐行渐近。

　　"这大学我是上定了，而且要考我自己填报的志愿！"我咬了咬牙，巴鳞的手指几乎已经要戳到父亲的身上。"你知道吗，这辈子我最不想成为的人就是你！"

　　父亲之前意气风发的军姿完全不见了，他像遭了霜打的庄稼，耷拉着脸，表情中夹杂着一丝悲哀。我以为他会反击，像以前的他一样，可他并没有。

　　"我知道，我一直都知道，你不想为人一世都走着别人给你铺好的路……"父亲的声音越来越低，几乎要听不见了，"像极了我年轻时的样子，可我没别的选择……"

　　"所以你想让我照着你的人生再活一遍吗？"

　　父亲突然双膝一软，我以为他要摔倒，可他却抱住了巴鳞。

　　"你不能走！你以为我不知道吗，出去的人，哪有再回来的？"

　　我操纵着巴鳞奋力挣脱父亲的怀抱，就好像他紧紧抱住的人是我。而这样的待遇，自我有记忆之日起，就未曾享受过。

　　"幼稚！你应该睁大眼睛，好好看看外面的世界了。"

巴鳞像是个失心疯的发条玩具，四肢乱打，军服被扯得乱七八糟，露出那黝黑无光的皮肤。

"你说这话时简直和你妈一模一样。"又一朵蓝白色的火花在巴鳞头上炸开，他突然停止了挣扎，像是久别重逢的爱人般紧紧抱住父亲。"你是想像她一样丢下我不管吗？"

我愣住了。

我从来没有从这个角度想过父亲的感受。我一直以为他是因为自私和狭隘才不愿意让我走得太远，却没有想过他是因为害怕失去。母亲离开时我还太小，她的离开并没有给我造成太大的冲击，但对于父亲来说，这恐怕却是一生的阴影。

我沉默着走近拥抱着巴鳞的父亲，弯下腰，轻抚他已不再笔挺的脊背。这或许是我们之间所能达到的亲密的极限。

这时，我看到了巴鳞紧闭的眼角噙出的泪花。那一瞬间，我动摇了。

也许在这一动作的背后，除了控制之外，还有爱。

有一些知识我但愿自己能在十七岁之前懂得。

比方说，人类脑部的主要结构都和运动有关，包括小脑、基底核、脑干，皮层上的运动区以及感知区对运动区的直接投射，等等。

比方说，小脑是脑部神经元最多的结构。在人类进化中，小脑皮层随着前额叶的快速增大而同步增大。

比方说，任何需要和外界进行的信息或物理上的交互——肢体动作、操作工具、打手势、说话、使眼色、做表情，最终都需要通过激活一系列的肌肉来实现。

比方说，一条手臂上有 26 条肌肉，每条肌肉平均有 100 个运动单元，由一条运动神经和它所连接的肌纤维组成。因此，光控制一条胳膊的运动，就至少有 2 的 2600 次方种可能性，这已经远远超出了宇宙中原子的数量。

人类的运动如此复杂而微妙，每一个看似漫不经心的动作中都包含了海量的数据运算分析与决策执行，以至于目前最先进的机器人尚无法达到 3 岁小孩的运动水平。

更不要说动作中所隐藏的信息、情感与文化符号。

在前往高铁车站的路上，父亲一直保持沉默，只是牢牢地抓住我的行李箱。北上的列车终于出现在我们眼前，崭新、光亮、线条流畅，像是一松闸就会滑进遥不可测的未知。

我和父亲没能达成共识。如果我一意孤行，他将不会承担我上学期间的生活费用。

除非你答应回来。他说。

我的目光穿过他，就像是看见了未来，那是属于我自己的未来。为此，我将成为白色羊群中那一头被永远放逐的黑羊。

爸，多保重。

我迫不及待地拉起行李箱要上车，可父亲并没有松手，行李箱尴尬地在半空中悬停着，终于还是重重地落了地。

我正要发火，父亲"啪"的一声在我面前立正，行了个标准的军礼，然后一言不发地转身走人。他说过，上战场之前不要告别，意头不好，要给彼此留个念想。

我望着他渐渐远去的背影，举起手，回了个软绵绵的礼。

当时的我并没有真正领会这个姿势的意义。

"真没想到我们竟然会折在一个野人手里，"课题组组长，也是我的导师欧阳笑里藏刀，他拍拍我的肩膀，"没事儿啊，再琢磨琢磨，还有时间。"

我太了解欧阳了，他这话的潜台词就是"我们没时间了"。

如果再挖深一层，则是"你的想法、你的项目，那么，能不能按时毕业，你自己看着办"。

至于他自己前期占用我们多少时间、精力，去应付他在外面接下的乱七八糟的私活儿，欧阳是绝不会提的。

我痛苦地挠头，目光落在被关进粉红宠物屋里的巴鳞身上，他面目呆滞地望着地板，似乎还没有从刺激中恢复过来。这颜色搭配很滑稽，可我笑不出来。

如果是老吕会怎么办？这个想法很自然地跳了出来。

一切的源头都来自他当年闲聊扯出的"A 导致 B"的问题。

传统理论认为，运动控制是通过存储好的运动程序来完成的，当人要完成某一个运动任务时，运动皮层选取储存的某一个运动程序进行执行，程序就像自动钢琴琴谱一样，告诉皮层和脊髓的运动区该如何激活，皮层和脊髓再控制肌肉的激活，完成任务。

那么问题来了：同一个运动有无数种执行方式，大脑难道需要储存无数种运动程序？

还记得那条运动可能性超过了全宇宙原子数量的胳膊吗？

2002 年，一个叫作伊曼纽尔·托多洛夫（Emanuel Todorov）的数学家提出一套理论，试图解决这个问题。

他的基本思想是：人的运动控制是大脑求一个最优解的问题。所谓最优是针对某些运动指标，比如精度最大化、能量损耗最小化、控制努力度最小化，等等。

而在这一过程中，人脑会借助小脑，在运动指令还没有到达肌肉之前，对运动结果进行预测，然后与真实感知系统发回来的反馈相结合，帮助大脑进行评估及调整动作指令。

最简单的例子就是，上下楼梯时我们经常会因为算错台阶数而踩空，如果反馈调整及时，人就不会摔跤。而反馈往往是带有噪声和延时的。

托多洛夫的数学模型符合前人在行为学和神经学上的已知证据，可以用来解释各种各样的运动现象，甚至只要提供某一些物理限制条件，便可以预测其运动模式，比方说 8 条腿的生物在冥王星的重力环境下如何跳跃。

好莱坞用他的模型来驱动虚拟形象的运动引擎，便能"自主"产生出许多像人一样流畅自然的动作。

当我进入大学时，托多洛夫模型已经成为教科书上的经典，我们通过各种实验不断地验证其正确性。

直到有一天，我和老吕在邮件里谈到了巴鳞。

我自从上大学之后就和老吕开始了电邮来往，他像一个有求必应的人工智能，我总能从他那里得到答案，无论是关乎学业、人际关系，还是情感。我们总会滔滔不绝地讨论一些在旁人看来不可思议的问题，例如"用技术制造出来的灵魂出窍体验是否侵犯了宗教的属灵性"。

当然，我们都心照不宣地避开关于我父亲的事情。

老吕说巴鳞被卖给了镇上的另一家人，我知道那家暴发户，风评不是很好，经常会干出一些炫耀财力却又令人匪夷所思的荒唐事。

我隐约知道父亲的生意做得不好，可没想到差到这个地步。

我刻意转移话题聊到托多洛夫模型，突然一个想法从我脑中蹦出。巴鳞能够进行如此精确的运动模仿，如果让他重复两组完全相同的动作，一组是下意识的模仿，而一组是自主行为，那么这两者是否经历了完全相同的神经控制过程？

从数学上来说，最优解只有一个，可中间求解的过程呢？

老吕足足过了三天才给我回信，一改之前汪洋恣肆的风格，他只写了短短几行字：

> 我想你提出了一个非常重要的问题，也许连你自己都没意识到这有多重要。如果我们无法在神经活动层面上将机械模仿与自主行为区分开，那么这个问题就是：自由意志真的存在吗？

收到信后，我激动得彻夜难眠。我花了两个星期设计实验原型，又花了更多的时间研究技术上的可行性及收集各方师长意见，再申报课题，等待批复。直到一切就绪时，我才想起，这个探讨"根本性问题"的重要实验，缺少了一个根本性的组成要素。

我将不得不违背承诺，回到家乡。

只是为了巴鳞，我不断告诉自己，只是巴鳞。

就像 A 导致 B，简单如是。

我读过一部名为《孤儿》的科幻小说，讲的是外星人来到地球，能够从外貌上完全复制某一个地球人的模样，由此渗入人类社会，但是他们无法模仿被复制者身体的动作姿态，哪怕是一些细微的表情变化。许多暴露身份的外星伪装者遭到地球人的追捕猎杀。

为了生存下去，他们不得不学习人类是如何通过身体语言来进行交流的。他们伪装成被遗弃的孤儿，被好心人收养，通过长时间的共同生活来模仿他们养父母们的举止神态。

养父母们惊讶地发现这些孩子长得越来越像自己，而当外星孤儿们认为时机成熟之时，便会杀掉自己的养父或养母，变成他们的样子并取而代之。杀父娶母的细节描写令人难忘。

辨别伪装者的难度变得越来越大，但人类最终还是发现了这些外星人与地球人之间最根本的区别。

尽管外星人几乎能够惟妙惟肖地模仿人类的所有举动，但他们并不具备人脑中的镜像神经系统，因此无法感知对方深层的情绪变化，并激发出类似的神经冲动模式，也就是所谓的"同理心"。

人类发明了一套行之有效的辨别方法，去伤害伪装者的至亲之人，看是否能够监测到伪装者脑中的痛苦、恐惧或愤怒。他们称之为"针刺实验"。

这个冷酷的故事告诉我们，在这个宇宙间，人类并不是唯一一个和自己父母处不好关系的物种。

老吕知道关于巴鳞的所有事情，他认为狍鸮族是镜像神经系统超常进化的一个样本，并为此深深着迷，只是他不赞成我们对待巴鳞的方式。

"但他并没有反抗，也没有逃跑啊！"我总是这样反驳老吕。

"镜像神经元过于发达会导致同理心病态过剩，也许他只是没办法忍受你眼中的失落。"

"有道理。那我一定是镜像神经元先天发育不良的那款。"

"……冷血。"

当老吕带着我找到巴鳞时，我终于知道自己并不是最冷血的那一个。

巴鳞浑身赤裸、伤痕累累，被粗大生锈的锁链环绕着脖颈和四肢，窝藏在一个五尺见方的砖土洞里，那里光线昏暗，排泄物和食物腐烂的气味混杂着，令人作呕。他更瘦了，虹蝇吮吸着他的伤口，骨头的轮廓清晰可见，像一头即将被送往屠宰场的牲畜。

他看见了我，目光中没有丝毫波澜，就像是我十三岁的那个夏夜与他初次相见时的模样。

他们让他模仿……动物交配。老吕有点说不下去。

瞬时间，所有的往事一下涌上心头。

接下来发生的事情，我一点印象都没有，仿佛是被什么鬼神附了体，所有的举动都并非出自我的本意。

老吕说，我冲进买下巴鳞的那个暴发户的家里，抓起他家少奶奶心爱的博美一口就咬在它脖子上，如果不放了巴鳞，我就不松口，直到把那狗脖子咬断为止。

我朝地上吐了口唾沫，这听起来还挺像是我干得出来的事儿。

我们把巴鳞送进了医院，刚要离开，老吕一把拉住我，说，你不看看你爸？

我这才知道父亲也在这家医院里住院。上了大学后，我和他的联系越来越少，他慢慢地也断了念想。

他看起来足足老了十岁，鼻孔里、手臂上都插着管，头发稀疏，目光涣散。前几年普洱被疯炒时他跟风赌了一把，运气不好，成了接过最后一棒的傻子，货砸在了手里，钱倒是赔了不少。

他看见我时的表情竟然跟巴鳞有几分相似，像是在说，我早知道会有这一天。

"我……我是来找巴鳞的……"我竟然不知所措。

父亲似乎看穿了我的窘迫，咧开嘴笑了，露出被香烟经年熏烤的一口黄牙。

"那小黑鬼，精得很呢，都以为是我们在操纵他，其实有时候想想，说不定是他在操纵我们哩。"

"……"

"就像你一样，我老以为我是那个说了算的人，可等到你真的走了，我才发现，原来我心上系着的那根线，都在你手里攥着呢，不管你走多远，只要指头动一动，我这里就会一抽一抽地疼……"父亲闭上眼，按住胸口。

我一个字都说不出来，有什么东西堵住了喉咙。

我走到他病床前，想要俯身抱抱他，可身体不听使唤地在中途僵住了，我尴尬地拍拍他的肩膀，起身离开。

"回来就好。"父亲在我背后嘶哑地说，我没有回头。

老吕在门口等着我，我假装挠挠眼睛，掩饰情绪的波动。

"你说巧不巧？"

"什么？"

"你想要逃离你爸铺好的路，却兜兜转转，跟我殊途同归。"

"我有点同意你的看法了。"

"哪一点？"

"没人知道会怎么样。"

我们又失败了。

最初的想法很简单，选择巴鳞，是因为他的超强镜像神经系统让模仿成为一种本能，相对于一般人类来说，这就摒除了运动过程中许多主观意识的噪音干扰。

我们用非侵入式感应电极捕捉巴鳞运动皮层的神经活动，让他模仿一组动作，再通过轨迹追踪，让他自发重复这组动作，直到前后的运动轨迹完全重合，那么从数学上，我们可以认为他做了两组完全一样的动作。

然后再对比两组神经信号是否以相同的次序、强度及传递方式激活了皮层中相同的区域。

如果存在不同，那么被奉为经典的托多洛夫模型或许存在巨大的缺陷。

如果相同，那么问题更严重，或许人类仅仅是在单纯地模仿其他个体的行为，却误以为是出于自由意志。

无论哪一种结果，都将是颠覆性的。

但我们从一开始就失败了。巴鳞拒绝与任何人对视，拒绝模仿任何动作，包括我。

我大概能猜到原因，却不知道该如何解决。我们这群人信誓旦旦要解开人类意识世界的秘密，却连一个原始人的心理创伤都治愈不了。

我想到了虚拟现实，将巴鳞放置在一个脱离于现实的环境中，或许能够帮助他恢复正常的运动。

我们尝试了各种虚拟环境——海岛冰川、沙漠太空。我们制造了耸人听闻的极端灾难，甚至还花了大力气构建出狍鸮族的虚拟形象，寄望于那个瘦小丑陋的黑色小人，能够唤醒巴鳞脑中的镜像神经元。

但是全部毫无例外地失败了。

深夜的实验室里，只剩下我和僵尸般呆滞的巴鳞。其他人都走了，我知道他们在想什么，这个实验就是个笑话，而我就是那个讲完笑话自己一脸严肃的人。

巴鳞静静地躲在粉红色泡沫板搭起来的宠物屋里，缩成小小的一团。我想起老吕当年的评价，他说得没错，我一直没把巴鳞当作一个人来看待，即便是现在。

曾经有同行将无线电击器植入大鼠的脑子里，通过对体觉皮层和内侧前脑束的放电刺激，产生欣快或痛感，来控制大鼠的运动路线。

这和我对巴鳞所做的一切没有实质区别。

我就是那个镜像神经元发育不良的混蛋。

我鬼使神差地想起了那个游戏，那个最初让我们见识到巴鳞神奇之处的幼稚游戏。

"捞虾洗衫，玻璃刺脚丫……"

我低低地喊了一句，某种成年后的羞耻感油然而生。我假装成渔夫，从河岸上往河里伸出一条腿，踩一踩只存在于想象中的河水，再收回去。

巴鳞朝我看了过来。

"捞虾洗衫，玻璃刺脚丫。"我喊得更大声了。

巴鳞注视着我蠢笨的动作，缓慢而柔滑地爬出宠物屋，在离我几步之遥的地方停住了。

"捞虾洗衫，玻璃刺脚丫！"我感觉自己像个磕了药的酒桌舞娘，疯狂地甩动着大腿，来回踏出慌乱的节奏。

巴鳞突然以难以言喻的速度朝我扑来，那是阿辉的动作。

他记得，他什么都记得。

巴鳞左扑右抱，喉咙里发出婴孩般咯咯的声音，他在笑。这是这么多年来我第一次听见他笑。

他变成了镇上的残疾人。所有的动作像是被刻录在巴鳞的大脑中，无比生动而精确，以至于我一眼就能认出他模仿的是谁。他变成了疯子、瘸子、傻子、没有四肢的乞丐和羊癫疯病人；他变成了猫、狗、牛、羊、猪和不成形的家禽；他变成了喝醉酒的父亲和手舞足蹈的我自己。

我像是瞬间穿越了几千公里的距离，回到了童年的故里。

毫无预兆地，巴鳞开始一人分饰两角，表演起我和父亲决裂那一天的对手戏。

这种感觉无比古怪。作为一名旁观者，看着自己与父亲的争吵，眼前的动作如此熟悉，而回忆中的情形变得模糊而不真切。当时的我是如此暴躁顽劣，像一匹未经驯化的野马，而父亲的姿态卑微可怜，他一直在退让，一直在忍耐。这与我印象中大不一样。

巴鳞忙碌地变换着角色和姿态，像是技艺高超的默剧演员。

尽管我早已知道接下来会发生什么，但当它发生时我还是没有做好准备。

巴鳞抱住了我，就像当年父亲抱住他那样，双臂紧紧地包裹着我，头深埋在我的肩窝里。我闻见了那阵熟悉的腥味，如同大海，还有温热的液体顺着我的衣领流入脖颈，像一条被日光晒得滚烫的河流。

我呆了片刻，思考该如何反应。

随后，我放弃了思考，任由自己的身体展开，回以热烈拥抱，就像对待一个老朋友，就像对待父亲。

我知道，这个拥抱我欠了太久，无论是对谁。

我猜我找到了解决问题的正确方法。

在《孤儿》的结尾，执行"针刺实验"的组织领导人悲哀地发现，假使他们伤害的是外星伪装者，那么他们的至亲，也就是真正的人类，其镜像神经系统也无法被正常激活。

因为人类从开始就被设计成一个无法对异族产生同理心的物种。

就像那些伪装者。

幸好，这只是一篇二流科幻小说。

"我们应该试着替他着想。"我对欧阳说。

"他？"我的导师反应了三秒钟，突然回过神来，"谁？那个野人？"

"他的名字叫巴鳞。我们应该以他为中心，创造他觉得舒服的环境，而不是我们自以为他喜欢的廉价景区。"

"别可笑了吧！现在你要担心的是你的毕业设计怎么完成，而不是去关心一个原始人的尊严，你可别拖我后腿啊。"

老吕说过，衡量文明进步与否的标准应该是同理心，是能否站在他人的价值观立场去思考问题，而不是其他被物化的尺度。

我默默地看着欧阳的脸，试图从中寻找一丝文明的痕迹。

这张精心呵护的老脸上一片荒芜。

我决定自己动手，有几个学弟学妹也加入了。这让我找回对人类的一丝信念。当然，他们多半是出于对欧阳的痛恨以及顺手混几个学分。

有一款名为"iDealism"的虚拟现实程序，号称能够根据脑波信号来实时生成环境，但实际上只是针对数据库中比对好的波形调用模型，最多就只是增加了高帧率的渐变效果。我们破解了它，毕竟实验室用的感应电极比消费者级别的精度要高出几个数量级，我们增加了不少特征维度，又连接到教育网内最大的开源数据库，那里存放着世界各地虚拟认知实验室的 Demo 版本。

巴鳞将成为这个世界的第一推动力。

他将有充分的时间，去探索这个世界与他心中每一个念想之间的关系。我将记录下巴鳞在这个世界中的一举一动，待他回到现世，我再与他连接，那时，我将尽力模仿他的每一个动作，我俩就像平行对立的两面镜子，照出无穷无尽的彼此。

我为巴鳞戴上头盔，他目光平静，温柔如水。

红灯闪烁，加速，变绿。

我进入 Ghost 模式，同时在右上角开启第三人称窗口，这样可以看到一个小小的巴鳞虚拟形象在轻轻摇摆。

巴鳞的世界一片混沌，无有天地，也不分四面八方。我努力克制晕眩。

他终于停止了摇摆。一道闪电缓慢劈开混沌，确定了天空的方向。

闪电蔓延着，在云层中勾勒出一只巨大的眼，向四方绽放着分形般细密的发光触须。

光暗下，巴鳞抬起头，举起双手，雨水落下。

他开始舞蹈。

每一颗雨滴带着笑意坠落，填满风的轮廓，风扶起巴鳞，他四足离地，开始盘旋。

无法用语言来描绘他的舞姿，他仿佛成了万物的一部分，天地随着他的姿态而变幻色彩。

我的心跳加速，喉咙干涩，手脚冰凉，像是在见证一场不期而遇的神迹。

他举手，花儿便盛开；他抬足，鸟儿便翩然而来。

巴鳞穿行于不知名的峰峦湖泊之间，所到之处，荡漾开欢喜的曼陀罗，他便向着那旋转的纹样中坠去。

他时而变得极大，时而变得极小，所有的尺度在他面前失去了意义。

每一个不知名的生灵都在向他放声歌唱，他张了张嘴巴，所有狍鹗族的神灵都被吐了出来。

神灵列队融入他黑色的皮肤，像是一层层黑色的波浪，喷涌着，席卷着他向上飞升，飞升，在他身后拉出一张漫无边际的黑色大网，世间万物悉数凝固其上，弹奏着各自的频率，那是亿亿万种有情物在寻找一个共有的原点。

我突然领悟了眼前的一切。在巴鳞的眼中，万物有灵，并不存在差别，但神经层面的特殊构造使得他能够与万物共情，难以想象，他需要付出多大的努力才能够平复心中无时无刻翻涌的波澜。

即便愚钝如我，在这一幕天地万物的大戏面前，也无法不动容。事实上，我已热泪盈眶，内心的狂喜与强烈的眩晕相互交织，这是一种难以言表却又近乎神启的巅峰体验。

至于我希望得到的答案，我想，已经没那么重要了。

巴鳞将所有这一切全吸入体内，他的身形迅速膨胀，又瘪了下去。

然后，他开始往下坠落。

世界黯淡、虚无，生机不再。

巴鳞像是一层薄薄的贴图，平平地贴在高速旋转的时空中，物理引擎用算法在他的身体边缘掀起风动效果，细小的碎片如鸟群飞起。

他的形象开始分崩离析。

我切断了巴鳞与系统的连接，摘下他的头盔。

他趴在深灰色柔性地板上，四肢展开，一动不动。

"巴鳞？"我不敢轻易挪动他。

"巴鳞？"周围的人都等着，看一个笑话会否变成一场悲剧。

他缓慢地挪动了下身子，像条泥鳅般打了个滚，又趴着不动了，像壁虎一样紧贴在地板上。

我笑了。像当年的父亲那样，我拍了两下手掌。

巴鳞翻过身，坐将起来，看着我。

正如那个湿热黏稠的夏夜里，十三岁的我第一次见到他时的姿态。

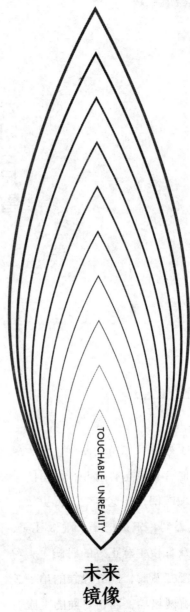

TOUCHABLE UNREALITY

未来
镜像

晋阳三尺雪

张冉

———— ▲ ————

　　赵大领着兵丁冲进宣仁坊的时候，朱大鲵正在屋里上网，他若有点与官府斗智斗勇的经验一定会更早发现端倪，把这出戏演得更像一点。这时是未时三刻，午饭已毕，晚饭还早，自然是宣仁坊里众青楼生意正好的时候，脂粉香气被阳光晒得漫空蒸腾，红红绿绿的帕子耀花游人眼睛。隔着两堵墙，西街对面的平康坊传来阵阵丝竹之声，教坊官妓们半遮半掩地向达官贵人卖弄技艺；而宣仁坊里的姐妹们对隔

壁的同行不屑一顾，认为那纯属脱裤子放屁，反正最终结果都是
要把床搞得"嘎吱嘎吱"响，喝酒划拳助兴则可，吹拉弹唱何苦
来哉？总之宣仁坊的白天从不缺少吵吵闹闹的讨价还价声、划拳
行令声和"嘎吱嘎吱"的摇床声，这种喧闹成了某种特色，以至
于宣仁坊居民偶尔夜宿他处，会觉得整个晋阳城都毫无生气，实
在是安静得莫名其妙。

赵大穿着薄底快靴的脚刚一踏进坊门，恭候在门边的坊正
就感觉到今时不同往日，必有大事发生。赵大每个月要来宣仁坊
三四次，带着两个面黄肌瘦的广阳娃娃兵，哪次不是咋呼着来、
吆喝着走，嚷得嗓子出血才对得起每个月的那点巡检例钱。而这
一回，他居然悄无声息地溜进门来，冲坊正打了几个唯有自己看
得懂的手势，领着两个娃娃兵贴着墙根蹑手蹑脚向北摸去。"虞
侯呵，虞侯！"坊正跟跟跄跄追在后面，把一双手胡乱摇摆，"这
是做什么！吓煞某家了！何不停下歇歇脚，用一碗羹汤，无论要
钱要人，应允你就是了……"

"闭嘴！"赵大瞪起一双大眼，压低声音道，"靠墙站！好好
说话！有县衙公文在此，说什么也没用！"

坊正吓得一跌，扶着墙站住，看赵大带着人鬼鬼祟祟走远。
他哆哆嗦嗦地拽过身旁一个小孩："告诉六娘，快收，快收！"流
着清鼻涕的小孩点点头，一溜烟跑没了影，半炷香时间不到，宣
仁坊的十三家青楼"噼里啪啦"扣上了两百四十块窗板，讨价声、
划拳声和摇床声消失得无影无踪，谁家孩子哇哇大哭起来，紧接
着响起一个止啼的响亮耳光。众多衣冠凌乱的恩客从青楼后院跳
墙逃走，如一群受惊的耗子灰溜溜钻出坊墙的破洞，消失在晋阳

城的大街小巷。一只乌鸦飞过，守卫坊门的兵丁拉开弓瞄准，右手一摸，发觉箭壶里一支羽箭都没有，于是悻悻地放松弓弦。生牛皮的弓弦反弹发出"嘣"的一声轻响，把兵丁吓了一跳，他才发现四周已经万籁俱寂，这点微弱的响声居然比夜里的更鼓声还要惊人。

下午时分最热闹的宣仁坊变得比宵禁时候还要安静，作为该坊十年零四个月的老居民，朱大鯀对此毫无察觉，只能说是愚钝至极。赵大一脚踹开屋门的时候，他愕然回头，才惊觉到了表演的时刻，于是大叫一声，抄起盛着半杯热水的陶杯砸在赵大脑门上，接着一使劲把案几掀翻，字箕里的活字"噼里啪啦"掉了一地。"朱大鯀！"赵大捂着额头厉声喝道，"海捕公文在此！若不……"他的话没说完，一把活字就洒了过来，这种胶泥烧制的活字又硬又脆，砸在身上生疼，落在地上碎成粉末，赵大躲了两下，屋里升起一阵黄烟。

"捉我，休想！"朱大鯀左右开弓丢出活字阻住敌人，转身推开南窗想往外跑，这时一个广阳兵举着铁链从黄雾里冲了出来，朱大鯀飞起一脚，踢得这童子兵凌空打了两个旋儿，"啪"的一声贴在墙上，铁链撒手落地，当下鼻血与眼泪齐飞。赵大几人还在屋里瞎摸，朱大鯀已经纵身跳出窗外，眼前是一片无遮无挡的花花世界，这时候他忽然一拍脑门，想起宣徽使的话来："要被捕，又不能易被捕；要拒捕，又不能不被捕；欲语还休，欲就还迎，三分做戏，七分碰巧，这其中的分寸，你可一定要拿捏好了。"

"拿捏，拿你奶奶，捏你奶奶……"朱大鯀把心一横，向前跑了两步，左脚凌空一绊右脚，"啊呀"惨叫着扑倒在地，整个人结结实实拍在地面上，"啪"震得院里水缸都晃了三晃。

赵大听到动静从屋里冲了出来，一见这情景，捂着脑袋大笑道："让你跑！给我锁上！带回县衙！罪证一并带走！"

流着鼻血的广阳兵走出屋子，号啕大哭道："大郎！那一笸箩泥块儿都让他砸碎了，还有什么罪证？咱这下见了红，晚上得吃白面才行！咱妈说了跟你当兵有馒头吃，这都俩月了连根馒头毛都没看见！现在被困在城里，想回也回不去，不知道咱妈咱爹还活着没，这日子过得有啥球意思！"

"没脑子！活字虽然毁了，网线不是还在吗？拿剪刀把网线剪走回去结案！"赵大骂道，"只要这案子能办下来，别说吃馒头，每天食肉糜都行！……出息！"

— 二 —

小人物的命运往往由大人物一句话决定。

那天是六月初六，季夏初伏，北地的太阳明晃晃地挂在天上，晒得满街杨柳蔫头耷脑，明明没有一丝风，却忽然平地升起一阵小旋风，从街头扫到街尾，让久未扫洒的路面尘土飞扬。马军都指挥使郭万超驾车出了苞武坊，沿着南门正街行了小半个时辰，他是个素爱自夸自耀的人，自然高高坐在车头，踩下踏板让车子发出最大的响声。这台车子是东城别院最新出品的型号，宽五尺、高六尺四寸、长一丈零两尺，四面出檐，两门对掩，车厢以陈年紫枣木筑成，饰以金线石榴卷蔓纹，气势雄浑，制造考究，最基础的型号售价铜钱二十千，这样的车除了郭万超此等人物，整个晋阳城还有几人驾得起？

四只烟囱突突冒着黑烟，车轮在黄土夯实的地面上不停弹跳，郭万超本意横眉冷目睥睨过市，却因为震动太厉害而被路人看成在不断点头致意，不断有人停下来稽首还礼，口称"都指挥使"，郭万超只能打个哈哈，摆手而过。车子后面那个煮着热水的大鼎（就算东城别院的人讲得天花乱坠，他还是对这台怪车满头雾水，据说煮沸热水的是猛火油，他知道猛火油是从东南吴地传来的玩意儿，见火而燃，遇水更烈，城防军用它把攻城者烫得哇哇叫，这玩意儿把水煮沸，车子不知怎的就走了起来，这又是什么道理？）正发出轰隆轰隆的吼声，身上穿的两裆铠被背后的热气烤得火烫，头上戴的银兜鍪须用手扶住，否则走不出多远就被震得滑落下来遮住眼睛，马军都指挥使有苦自知，心中暗自懊恼不该坐上驾驶席，好在距离目的地已经不远，于是取出黑镜戴在鼻梁上，满脸油汗地驰过街巷。

车子向左转弯，前面就是袭庆坊的大门，尽管现在是礼坏乐崩、上下乱法的时节，坊墙早已千疮百孔，根本没人老老实实从坊门进出，但郭万超觉得当大官的总该有点当大官的做派，若没有人前呼后拥，实在不像个样子。他停在坊门前等了半天，不光坊正没有出现，连守门的卫士也不知道藏在哪里偷偷打盹儿，满街的秦槐汉柏遮出一片阴凉地，唯独坊门处光秃秃的露着日头，没一会儿就晒得郭万超心慌气短、汗如雨下，"卫军！"他喊了两声，不见回音，连狗叫声都没有一处，于是怒气冲冲地跳下车来大踏步走进袭庆坊。坊门南边就是宣徽使马峰的宅子，郭万超也不给门房递帖子，一把将门推开风风火火地冲进院子，绕过正房，到了后院，大喝一声："抓反贼的来啦！"

屋里立刻一阵鸡飞狗跳，霎时间前窗后窗都被踹飞，五六个衣冠文士夺路而出，连滚带爬跌成一团。"哎呀，都指挥使！"大腹便便的老马峰偷偷拉开门缝一瞧，立刻拍拍心口喊了声皇天后土，"切不可再开这种玩笑了！各位各位，都请回屋吧，是都指挥使来了，不怕不怕！"老头刚才吓得幞头都跌掉了，披着一头白发，看得郭万超又气又乐，冷笑道："就这点胆子还敢谋反，哼哼……"

"哎呀，这话怎么说的？"老马峰又吓了一跳，连忙小跑过来攀住郭万超的手臂往屋里拉，"虽然没有旁人，也须当心隔墙有耳……"

一行人回到屋里，惊魂未定地各自落座，将破破烂烂的窗棂凑合掩上，又把门闩插牢。马峰拉郭万超往胡床上坐，郭万超只是大咧咧立在屋子中间，他不是不想坐，只是为了威风穿上这前朝遗物的两裆铠，一路上颠得差点连两颗晃悠悠的外肾都磨破了。老马峰戴上幞头，抓一抓花白胡子，介绍道："郭都指挥使诸位在朝堂上都见过了，此次若成事，必须有他的助力，所以以密信请他前来……"

一位极瘦极高的黄袍文士开口道："都指挥使脸上的黑镜子是什么来头？是瞧不起我们，想要自塞双目吗？"

"啊哈，就等你们问。"郭万超不以为忤地摘下黑镜，"这可是东城别院的新玩意儿，称作'雷朋'，戴上后依然可以视物，却不觉太阳耀目，是个好玩意儿！"

"'雷朋'二字何解？"黄袍人追问道。

郭万超抖抖袖子，又取出一件乌木杆子、黄铜嘴的小摆设，得意扬扬道："因为个玩意儿能发出精光耀人双眼，在夜里能照百步，东城别院没有命名，我称之为'电友'，亦即电光之友。黑镜既然可以防光照，由'电友'而'雷朋'，两下合契，天然一对，哈哈哈……"

"奇技淫巧！"另一名白袍文士喝道，一边用袖子擦着脸上的血，方才跑得焦急，一跤跌破了额头，把白净无毛的秀才变成了红脸的汉子，"自从东城别院建立以来，大汉风气每况愈下，围城数月，人心惶惶，汝辈却还沉浸于这些、这些、这些……"

马峰连忙扯着文士的衣袖打圆场："十三兄，十三兄，且息雷霆之怒，大人大量，先谈正事！"老头在屋里转悠一圈拉起帘子把窗缝仔细遮好，痰嗽一声，从袖中取出三寸见方的竹帘纸向众人一展，只见纸上蝇头小楷洋洋洒洒数千言。

"咳咳。"清清嗓子，马峰低声念道，"（广运）六年六月，大汉暗弱，十二州烽烟四起，人丁不足四万户，百户农户不能瞻一甲士，天旱河涝，田干井阑，仓廪空乏。然北贡契丹，南拒强宋，岁不敷出，民无粮，官无饷，道有饿殍，马无暮草，国贫民贱，河东苦甚！大汉苦甚！"

念到这里，一屋子文士同时叹了一声"苦"，又同时叫了一声"好"。唯独郭万超把眼一瞪："酸了吧唧的念什么呐！把话说明白点儿！"

马峰掏出锦帕抹了把额头上的汗珠："是的是的，这篇檄文就不再念了。都指挥使，宋军围城这么久，大汉早是强弩之末，宋主赵光义是个狠毒性子的人，他诏书说'河东久讳王命，肆行不道，虐治万民。为天下计，为黎庶计，朕当自讨之，以谢天下'。君不见吴越王钱弘俶自献封疆于宋，被封为淮海国王；泉、漳之主陈洪进兵临城下之后才献泉、漳两郡及所辖十四县，宋主赐诏封为区区武宁军节度使；如今晋阳围城已逾旬月，宋主暴跳如雷，此事已无法善终，将一旦城破，非但皇帝没得宋官可做，全城的百姓也必遭迁怒！覆巢之下，岂有完卵，指挥使，莫使黎民涂炭，黎民涂炭啊！"

郭万超道："要说实在的，我们武官也一个半月没支饷了，小兵成天饿得嗷嗷叫。你们的意思是刘继元小皇帝的江山肯定坐不住，不如干脆出去投降宋兵，是这个意思吗？"

此言一出满座大哗，文士们愤怒地离席而起破口大骂，把君君臣臣，父父子子，君使臣以礼，臣事君以忠的话翻来覆去说了八十多遍，马峰吓得浑身哆嗦："诸君！诸君！隔墙有耳，隔墙有耳啊……"待屋里安静了点，老头驼着背搓着手道："都指挥使，我辈并非不忠不孝之人，只是君不君，臣不臣，皇帝遇事不明，只能僭越了！第一，城破被宋兵屠戮；第二，辽兵大军来到，驱走宋兵，大汉彻底沦为契丹属地；第三，开城降宋，保全晋阳城八千六百户、一万两千军的性命，留存汉室血脉。该如何选，指挥使心中应该也有分寸！宋国终归是汉人，辽国是鞑靼契丹，奴辽不如降宋，就算背上千古骂名也不能沦为辽狗！"

听完这席话，郭万超倒是对老头另眼相看，"好，"他挑起一个大拇指，"宣徽使是条有气节的好汉子，投降都投得这么义正词严。说说看要怎么办，我好好听着。"

"好好。"马峰示意大家都坐下，"十年前宋主赵匡胤伐汉时老夫曾与建雄军节度使杨业联名上疏恳请我主投宋，但挨了顿鞭子被赶出朝堂，如今皇帝天天饮宴升平不问朝中事，正是我们行事的好时机。我已密信联络宋军云州观察使郭进，只要都指挥使开大厦门、延厦门、沙河门，宋军自会在西龙门砦设台纳降。"

"刘继元小皇帝怎么办？"郭万超问。

"大势已去的事后，自当出降。"马峰答道。

"倒罢了。但你们没想到最重要的问题吗？东城别院那关可怎么过？"郭万超环视在座诸人，"现在东西城城墙、九门六砦都有东城别院的人手，他们掌握着守城机关，只要东城那位王爷不降，即便开了城门宋兵也进不来啊！"

这下屋里安静下来。白袍文士叹道："东城别院吗？若不是鲁王作怪，晋阳城只怕早就破了吧……"

马峰道："我们商议派出一位说客，对鲁王动之以情、晓之以理。"

郭万超道："若不成呢？"

马峰道："那就派出一名刺客，一刀砍了便宜王爷的狗头。"

郭万超道："你这老头倒是说得轻巧，东城别院戒备森严，无论说客还是刺客哪有那么容易接近鲁王身边？那里有那么多稀奇古怪的玩意儿，只怕离着八丈远就糊里糊涂丢了性命吧！"

马峰道："东城别院挨着大狱，王爷手底下人都是戴罪之身，只要将人安插下狱，不愁到不了鲁王身边。"

郭万超道："有人选了吗？说客一个，刺客一名。"他目光往旁边诸人身上一扫，诸多文士立刻抬起脑袋眼神飘忽不定，口中念念叨叨背起了儒家十三经。

郭万超一拍脑袋："对了，倒是有个人选，是你们翰林院的编修，算是旧识，沙陀人，用的汉姓，学问一般，就是有把子力气。他平素就喜欢在网上发牢骚，是个胸无大志满脑袋愤怒的糊涂车子，给他点银钱，再给他把刀，大道理一讲，自然乖乖替我们办事。"

马峰鼓掌道："那是最好，那是最好，就是要演好入狱这场戏，不能让东城别院的人看出破绽来，罪名不能太重，进了天牢就出不来了，又不能太轻，起码得戴枷上铐才行。"

"哈哈哈，太简单了，这家伙每日上网搬弄是非，罪名是现成的。"郭万超用手一捉裤裆部位的铠甲，转身拔腿就走："今天的事儿天知地知你知我知，我这就找管网络的去，人随后给你带来，咱们下回见面再谈。走了！"

穿着两裆铠的武官叮铃当啷出门去，诸文士无不露出鄙夷之色，窗外响起火油马车震耳欲聋的轰轰声，马峰抹着汗叹道："要是能这么容易解决东城别院的事情就好了，诸君，这是掉脑袋的事情，须谨慎啊，谨慎！"

— 三 —

朱大鲦不知道捉走自己的兵差来自哪个衙门，不过宣徽使马峰说了,刑部大狱、太原府狱、晋阳县狱、建雄军狱都是一回事情,谁让大汉国河东十二州赔得个盆光碗净,只剩下晋阳城这一座孤城呢。他被铁链子锁着穿过宣仁坊,青楼上了夹板的门缝后面露出许多滴溜溜乱转的眼睛,坊内的姐姐、妹妹、嫖客、老鸨谁不认识这位穷酸书生?明明是个翰林院编修,偏偏住在这烟花柳巷之地,要说是性情中人倒也罢了,最可恨几年来一次也未光顾姐妹们的生意,每次走过坊道都衣袖遮脸加快脚步口中念叨着"惭愧惭愧",真不知道是惭愧于文人的面子,还是裤裆里那见不得人的东西。

唯有朱大鲦知道,他惭愧的是袋里的孔方兄。宋兵一来翰林院就停了月例,围城三月,只发了一斛三斗米、五陌润笔钱。说是足陌,数了数每陌只有七十七枚夹铅钱,这点家当要是进暖香院春风一度,整月就得靠麸糠果腹了。再说他还得交网费,当初选择住在宣仁坊不仅因为租金便宜,更看重网络比较便利,屋后坊墙有网管值班的小屋,遇见状况只要蹬梯子喊一声就行。每月网费四十钱,打点网管也得花几个铜子儿,入不敷出是小问题,离了网络,他可一日也活不下去。

"磨蹭什么呢,快走快走!"赵大一拽锁链,朱大鲦跟跄几步,慌乱用手遮着脸走过长街。转眼间出了宣仁坊大门,拐弯沿朱雀大街向东行,路上行人不多,战乱时节也没人关心铁链锁着的囚犯,朱大鲦一路遮遮掩掩生怕遇见翰林院同僚,幸好是吃饱了饭鼓腹高眠的时候,一个文士也没碰着。

"大、大人。"走了一程,朱大鲦忍不住小声问道,"到底是什么罪名啊?"

"啊？"赵大竖起眉毛回头瞪他一眼，"造谣惑众、无中生有，你们在网络鼓捣的那些事情以为官府不知道吗？"

"只是议论时政为国分忧也有罪吗？"朱大鲦道，"再说网络上说的话，官府何以知道？"

赵大冷笑道："官家的事儿自有官家去管，你无籍无品的小小编修，可知议论时局造谣中伤与哄堂塞署、逞凶殴官同罪？再说网络是东城别院搞出来的玩意儿，自然加倍提防，你以为网管是疏通网络之职，其实你写下的每一个字儿都被他记录在案，白纸黑字，看你如何辩驳！"

朱大鲦吃了一惊，一时间不再说话。"突突突突……"一架火油马车吐烟冒火驶过街头，车厢上漆着"东城廿二"字样，一看就知是东城别院的维修车。"又快到攻城时间啦。"一名广阳兵说道，"这次还是有惊无险吧。"

"嘘，是你该说的话吗？"同伴立刻截停了话头。

前面柳树阴凉下摆着摊，摊前围着一堆人，赵大跟手下娃娃兵打趣道："刘十四，攒点银子去洗一下，回来好讨婆娘。"

刘十四脸红道："莫说笑，莫说笑……"

朱大鲦就知道那是东城别院洗黥面的摊子。汉主怕当兵的临阵脱逃，脸上要墨刺军队名，建雄军黥着"建雄"，寿阳军黥着"寿阳"，若像刘十四这样从小颠沛流离身投多军的，从额头至下巴密密麻麻黥着"昭义武安武定永安河阳归德麟州"，除了眼珠子之外整张脸乌漆墨黑，要再投军只好剃光头发往脑壳上黥了。东城那位王爷想出洗黥面的点子，立刻让军兵趋之若鹜，用蘸了碱液的细针密密麻麻刺一遍，结痂后揭掉，再用碱液涂抹一遍缠上细布，再结痂长好便是白生生的新皮。正因为宋军围城人心惶惶，才要讨个婆娘及时行乐，鲁王爷算是抓准了大伙的心思。

几人走过一段路，在有仁坊坊铺套了一辆牛车，乘车继续东行。朱大鲧坐在麻包上颠来倒去，铁链磨得脖子发痛，心中不禁有点后悔接了这个差使。他与马军都指挥使郭万超算是旧识，祖上在高祖（后汉高祖刘知远）时同朝为官，如今虽然身份云泥，仍三不五时一起烫壶小酒聊聊前朝旧事。那天郭万超唤他过去，谁知道宣徽使马峰居然在座，这把朱大鲧吓得不轻。老马峰可不是平常人，生有一女是当朝天子的宠妃，皇帝常以"国丈"称之，不久之前刚退下宰相之位挂上宣徽使的虚衔，整座晋阳城除了拥兵自重的都指挥使和几位节度使，就属他位高权重。

"这不是谋逆吗？"酒过三巡，马峰将事由一说，朱大鲧立刻摔杯而起。

"司马温公说'尽心于人曰忠'，《晏子》言'故忠臣也者，能纳善於君，不能与君陷於难'，君子不立危墙之下，朱八兄须思量其中利害，为天下苍生……"老马峰扯着他的衣袖，胡须颤巍巍地说着大道理。

"坐下坐下，演给谁看啊。"郭万超啐出一口浓痰，"谁不知道你们一伙穷酸书生成天上网发议论，说皇帝这也不懂那也不会，大汉江山迟早要完，这会儿倒装起清高来啦？一句话，宋狗一旦打破城墙，全城人全他妈的得完蛋，还不如早早投了宋人换城里几万人活命，这账你还算不清吗？"

朱大鲧站在那儿走也不是坐也不是，犹豫道："但有鲁王在城墙上搞的那些器械，晋阳城固若金汤，听说前几天大辽发来的十万斛粟米刚从汾水运到，尽可以支持三五个月……"

郭万超道："呸呸呸！你以为鲁王是在帮咱们？他是在害咱们！宋狗现在占据中原，粮钱充足，围个三年五年也不成问题，三月白马岭一役宋军大败契丹，南院大王耶律挞烈成了刀下鬼，吓得契丹人缩回雁门关不敢动弹，一旦宋人截断汾水、晋水，晋阳城就成了孤城一座，你倒说说这仗怎么打得赢？再说那个东城王爷不知道是从哪儿钻出来的，搞出那么多稀奇古怪的玩意儿，他是真心想帮我们守城？我看未必！"

话音落了，一时间无人说话，桌上一盏火油灯毕剥作响，照得斗室四壁生辉。这灯自然也是鲁王的发明，灌一两二钱猛火油可以一直燃到天明，虽然烟味刺鼻，熏得天花板又黑又亮，可毕竟比菜油灯亮堂得多了。

"……要我怎么做？"朱大鲦慢慢坐下。

"先讲道理，后动刀子，古往今来不都是这么回事儿？"郭万超举杯道。

四

鲁王确实不知道是从哪里钻出来的。宋兵围城之前没人听过他的名号，河东十二州一丢，东城别院的名字开始在坊间流传。一夜之间晋阳城多了无数新鲜玩意儿，最显眼的是三件东西：中城的大水轮和铸铁塔、城墙上的守城兵器，还有遍布全城的网络。

晋阳城分西、中、东三城，中城横跨汾水，大水轮就装在骑楼下方，随着水势日夜滚动。水轮这东西早被用来灌溉农田、碾米、磨面，谁也没想到还能有这么多功用，"吱吱嘎嘎"的木头齿轮带动了铸铁塔的风箱、城头的水龙与火龙、绞盘、滑车。铸铁塔有几个炉膛，风箱吹动猛火油煮沸铁水，铸出的铁器又沉又硬，比此前不知方便了多少倍。

城墙上的变化更大，鲁王爷给城墙铺上两条木头轨道，用绳索拉着两头，扳下一个机簧，水轮的力量就扯着轨道上的滑车飞驰起来，从大厦门到沙河门就算驾快马也须一炷香时间才能赶到，坐上滑车，只消半袋烟时间就能到达。第一次发车的时候绑在上面的几个小兵吓得嗷嗷乱叫，坐多几次觉得有趣，食髓知味，就成了滑车的管理员，整日赖在车上不肯下来。滑车共有五辆，三辆载人，两辆载炮，大炮与汉人惯用的发石机没什么不同，就是改用水轮拉紧牛皮筋，再不用五十名大汉背着绳索上弦；抛出的亦不再是石块，而是灌满猛火油的猪尿脬，尿脬里装一包油布裹着的火药，留一条引线出来，注满猛火油后将口扎紧，发射前将捻子点燃。

鲁王爷在墙头挂满泥榾。守城缺不了滚木榾石，但木头丢下一根少一根，石头扔下一块少一块，围城久了只怕连房顶都得拆了往下扔。东城别院就搞了个阴损毒辣的发明，用黄泥巴掺上稻草铸成五尺长、两尺粗的大泥柱子，表面嵌满大铁蒺藜，铁蒺藜专门泼上脏水等它生出黑不黑、红不红的铁锈，因为鲁王爷说这样会让宋兵得一种叫"破伤风"的怪病。选上好黄泥用草席盖上焖一星期煨成熟泥，加上糯米浆、碎稻草和猪血反复捶打，这样铸成的泥檑每个重达两千六百斤，金灿灿，冷森森，泛着黄铜一样的油光，通体长满脏兮兮的生锈铁蒺藜，着实是件杀人利器。泥檑两端挂上铁锁链拴在城墙上，宋军一来，数百个大泥柱子劈头盖脸砸下，把云梯、冲车、盾牌和兵卒一齐砸成粉碎，这厢绞盘一转，水轮之力"嘎吱嘎吱"将铁链卷起，沾满了血的泥檑又晃晃悠悠升上城墙。

宋人在泥檑下吃了苦头，后来只将老弱病残和契丹降卒当作先锋，趁泥檑把弃卒砸扁时发动井栏、云梯和发石机猛攻。这时滑车上的猪尿脬炮就到了开火时机，一时间数百个红彤彤、骚哄哄、软囊囊的尿脬漫天飞舞，落在宋军阵中化作火球四下延烧，灼得木头毕剥作响、兵卒吱哇乱叫，空气中立时弥漫着一股果木烤肉的芳香。最后就到了弓箭手出场，专拣宋军中有帽缨的家伙攒射，因为众所周知只有将官头上才飘着鸟毛。不过羽箭数量稀少必须省着点用，一人射个三五箭便归队休息，一场大战就此结束，城下一片烟熏火燎、鬼哭狼嚎，城上汉人遥遥指点战场计算着杀人的数量，每杀一个人，在自己手上画一个黑圈，凭黑圈数量找东城别院领赏钱。按照鲁王爷计算，近几个月死在城下的宋兵已达两百万之众，不过看那吹角连营依然无边无尽，大家就心照不宣谁都不提统计口径的问题。

一座晋阳城守得固若金汤，怕大伙在城内闲得无聊，鲁王爷又发明了网络。他先搞出了一种叫活字的东西（据自己说是剽窃毕昇毕老爷的发明，不过谁也没听说过这位了不起的老爷）：先做一个阴文木雕版的《千字文》，然后用混合了糯米稻草和猪血的黄泥巴压在雕版上面晒干，最后整个揭下来切成烧肉大小的长方块，用泥橛边角料制作的阳文活字就完成了。将一千个活字放在长方形的字箕里面，每个活字后面用机簧绷上一缕蚕丝，一千缕蚕丝束成手腕粗细的一捆，这个叫"网"。字箕放在屋子里，蚕丝从墙根穿出到达网管的小屋，每捆蚕丝末端都截得整整齐齐套上一个铁网，每一缕丝线末尾绑着个小钩，挂在铁网上面。网管小屋只有个天棚遮雨，四壁挤挤挨挨挂满网线，若两台字箕之间要说话，找到两条网线将铁网一拧"咔嗒"一声锁好一千个小钩，两捆蚕丝就连了起来，这个叫"络"。

网络一连好，就可以通过字箕对话了，这厢按下一个活字，小机簧将蚕丝拉紧，那厢对应位置的活字就陷了下去。虽然从天地玄黄宇宙洪荒日月盈昃辰宿列张密密麻麻一千个字里面选出要用的活字很费眼力，可熟手自然能打得飞快。有学究说汉字博大精深，千字文虽然是开蒙奇书一本，可要拿来畅谈宇宙人生，区区一千个字怎么够用？鲁王爷却说这一千个字彼此并不重复，别说畅谈宇宙，古往今来大多数好文章都能用这一千个字做出来，真真是够用得很啦。

《千字文》里实则有两个"洁"字重复，东城别院删掉了一个字，换上一个有弯钩符号的活字。因为两人通过网络对谈的时候，又要打字，又要盯着字箕看对方发来的字句，分心二用太难，鲁王爷就规定说完一句话之后要按下这回车键，表示自己的话说完了，轮到对方说话。为什么叫"回车"，王爷没解释。

起初网络只能两人对话，后来发明了一种复杂的黄铜钩架，能够将许多网线同时挂在一起，一个人按下活字，其他人的字箕都会收到信息。这时候又出现了新的问题，八名文士聊天，一个人说完话按下回车，其余七个人会同时抢着说话，这时字箕就会抽筋似的起起伏伏，好似北风吹皱晋阳湖的一池黑水。为了解决这个问题，东城别院发售了一种附加字箕，上面有十个空白活字，在用黄铜钩架组成网络的时候，大伙先将对方的雅称刻在空白活字上面。八名文士的小圈子，每个人的附加字箕都刻上八个人的称号，谁要发言，就按下代表自己的活字，谁的活字先动，谁就有说话的权力，直到按下回车键为止。朱大鲹最喜欢把代表自己的"朱"字使劲按个不停，此举自然遭到了圈子内的严正谴责，因为此举不仅对其他人发言的权力造成干扰，更容易把网线搞断。鲁王爷一开始把这种制度叫作"三次握手"，后来又改叫"抢麦"，这几个字到底是啥意思，王爷也没解释。

蚕丝固然坚韧，免不了遭受风吹雨打、虫蛀鼠咬和朱大鲹此类浑人的残害，断线的事情时有发生。有时候聊着天，有人忽然大骂"文理狗屁不通辱骂先贤有失文士的身份"，那说明有活字的蚕丝断了，本来写的是"子曰：尧舜其犹病诸"，结果变成了"子曰：尧舜病诸"，这不光骂了尧舜先帝，更连孔圣人都坑进去了。此时就要高声喊"网管"，给网管些小钱让他检查网线，顺便到坊市带两斤烙饼回来。网管会断开网线，找到断掉的蚕丝打一个结系紧，若不花点钱跟网管搞好关系，他会把绳结打得又大又囊肿，导致网络拥堵速度慢如老牛拉车；要是铜钱给足了，他就拿小梳子将蚕丝理得顺顺滑滑，系一个小小的双结，然后把两斤八两烙饼丢进窗口，喊一声"妥了！"这就是朱大鲹荷包再窘迫也要花钱打点网管的原因。

东城别院的守城器械收买了军心，稀奇古怪的小发明收买了民心，网络则收买了文士之心。足不出户，坐而论道，这便利自三皇五帝以来何朝何代曾经有过？宋兵围城人人自危，再不能出晋阳城攀悬瓮山，观汾水，赏花饮酒，关起门来文墨消遣反而更觉苦闷，若不是网络铺遍西城，这些穷极无聊的读书人还不反了天去？一国囿于一城，三省六部名存实亡，举月无俸禄，天子不早朝，青衫客们成了城中最清闲无用的一群，唯有在网络上作作酸诗，吐吐苦水，发发牢骚。有人喜爱上网，自然有人敬鬼神而远之，有人念鲁王爷的好，自然也有人背地里戳他脊梁骨，这位谁都没见过真容的王爷是坊间最好的话题。

朱大鲹做梦也没想到自己第一次与王爷扯上关系，居然是被马峰、郭万超派去游说投降之事。是战，是降，大道理他自己还没想明白，但既然文武二相都这么看重自己，他只能怀揣降表和利刃硬着头皮上前了。

五

牛车"吱吱嘎嘎"向前，经过一所馆驿，这两进带园子的馆驿是鲁王爷初到晋阳城时修建的，漆成橙色，挂着蓝牌，上写两个大字"汉庭"。"汉庭"指的是"大汉的庭院"，这馆名固然古怪，比起鲁王爷后来发明的新词来倒不算什么了。

鲁王爷搬到东城别院之后，馆驿围墙上凿出两扇窗来，一扇卖酒，一扇卖杂耍物件。酒叫"威士忌"，意指"威猛之士也须忌惮三分"，这酒用辽国运来的粟米在馆驿后院浸泡蒸煮，酿出来的酒液透明如水、冷冽如冰，喝进嗓子里化为一道火线穿肠而过，比市酿的酒不知醇了多少倍。一升酒三百钱，这在私酿泛滥的时候算得上高价，可好酒之徒自然有赚钱换酒的法子。

"军爷，射一轮吧！"

朱大鲢扭过头，看见城墙底下站着十数个泼皮无赖，站在茅草车上冲城外齐声高喊。城墙上探出一个兵卒的脑袋，见怪不怪道："赵大赵二，又缺钱花了？这回须多分我些好酒上下打点，不然将军怪罪下来……"

"自然，自然！"泼皮们笑道，又齐声喊，"军爷，射一轮！军爷，射一轮！"

不多时，城外便传来宋军的喊声："言而有信啊！五百箭一斗酒，你们山西人可不能给我们缺斤短两啊！"

"自然自然！"泼皮们一听四下散开，不知从哪里推出七八辆载满干草的车子摆在一处，捂着脑袋往城墙下一蹲，"军爷，射吧！"

只听得弓弦"嘣嘣"作响，羽箭"唰唰"破空，满天飞蝗越过墙头直坠下来簌簌穿入草堆，眨眼间把七八辆茅草车钉成了七八个大刺猬。朱大鲢远远看得新鲜，开口道："这草船借箭的法子也能行得通？"

赵大啐道："呸！这帮无赖买通了宋兵，说重了可是里通外国的罪名。围城太久箭支匮乏，皇帝张榜收箭，一支箭换十文钱，这些无赖收了五百箭能换五千钱，买一斗七升酒，一斗吊出城外给宋兵，两升打点城上守军，剩下五升分了喝，喝醉了满街横睡，疲懒之辈！"他扭头瞪眼大喝一声："督！大胆！没看到我吗？"

众泼皮也不害怕，嘻嘻哈哈行礼，推着小车一溜烟钻进小巷，朱大鲧就知道这赵大嘴上说得轻巧，肯定也收了泼皮的供奉。他没有点破，只叹一声："围城越久，人心越乱，有时候想想不如干脆任宋兵把城打破罢了，是不是？"

赵大嚷道："胡说什么！再说忤逆的话拿鞭子抽你！"朱大鲧始终摸不准此人是不是马峰派出的接应，也就不再多说。

日头毒辣，牛车在蔫柳树的树荫里慢慢前行，驶出了西城内城门，沿着官道进入中城，中城宽不过二十丈，分上下两层，下一层有大水轮、铸铁塔诸多热烘烘、吵闹闹的机关，上一层走行人车马，路两旁是水文、织造、冶锻、卜筮的官房，路面尽用枣木铺成。晋阳中城是武后时并州长史崔神庆以"跨水连堞"之法修筑而成的，距今已逾三百年，枣木地板时时用蜂蜡打磨，人行马踩日子久了变成凝血般的黑褐色，坚如铁石，声如铜钟，刀子砍上去只留下一条白痕，拆下来做盾牌可抵挡刀剑矢石，就算宋人的连环床弩都射不穿。围城日久，枣木地板被拆得七七八八，路面用黄土随意填平，走上去深一脚浅一脚，碰到土质酥松的地方能崴了牛蹄子。

赵大吩咐一声"下车"，着一个小兵赶着牛车还给坊铺，自己牵囚犯步行走入中城。今年河东干旱，汾水浅涸，朱大鲧看一条浊流自北方蜿蜒而来，从城下十二连环拱桥潺潺流过，马不停蹄涌向南方，不禁赞道："大辽、大汉、宋国，从北到南，一水牵起了三国，如此景致当前，务当赋诗一首以资……"

话音未落，赵大狠狠一巴掌抽在他后脑勺，把幞头巾子打得歪歪斜斜，也把朱大鲩的诗兴抽得无影无踪。赵大抹着汗骂道："你这穷酸，老子出这趟差汗流了一箩筐，还在那边叽叽歪歪惹人烦，前面就到县衙，闭嘴好好走路！"朱大鲩立刻乖乖噤声，心中暗想等恢复自由之身一定在网上将你这恶吏骂得狗血喷头，转念又一想，此行若是马到成功，说服了东城别院鲁王爷，大汉就不复存在，晋阳城尽归宋人，到时候还能有网络这回事情吗？一时之间不禁有点迷茫。

一路无言走穿中城进入东城，东城规模不大，走过太原县治所，在尘土纷飞的街上转了两个弯进了一座青砖灰瓦的院子，院子四面墙又高又陡，窗户都钉着铁栏杆。赵大与院中人打个招呼交接文书，广阳兵推搡着朱大鲩进了西厢房，解开锁链，喊道："老爷开恩让你独个儿住着，一日两餐有人分派，若要使用钱粮被褥可以托家里人送来，逃狱罪加一等，过两天提审，好好跟老爷交代罪行，听到没有？"

朱大鲩觉得背后一痛，跌跌撞撞摔进一个房间，小卒们"哗楞楞"挂上铁链"嘎嘣"一声锁上门转身走了，朱文人爬起来揉着屁股四处打量，发现这屋里有榻、席、洗脸的铜盆和便溺的木桶，虽然光线暗淡，却比自己的破屋整齐干净得多。

他在席上坐了，摸摸袖袋，发现一应道具都完好无损：一本《论语》，舌战鲁王爷时要有圣贤书壮胆；一只空木盒，夹层里装着宣徽使马峰洋洋洒洒三千言的血书檄文，血是鸡血，说的是劝降的事儿，不过其义正词严的程度令朱大鲩五体投地；一柄精钢打造的六寸三分长的双刃匕首，匹夫之怒，血溅五步，一想到这最终的手段，朱大鲩体内的沙陀突厥血统就开始蠢蠢欲动。

— 六 —

醒来的时候，朱大鲶才知道自己不知何时睡着了。窗口斜进来一线夕阳，天色已晚，过道里有脚步声响起，朱大鲶慢腾腾地爬起来活动一下身体，从栅栏缝隙里向外看去。

临行前马峰说已在狱中安插了内应，会在合适的时机现身。此刻一名狱卒打着个油纸灯笼晃悠悠走来，右手拎着食盒，口中哼着小曲，走到这间牢房停了下来，用灯笼把儿将栅栏一敲："喂喂，吃饭。"他说着从食盒中捏出两张胡饼卷上酱菜，从栅栏缝隙里递进来。

朱大鲶接过胡饼赔笑道："多谢，多谢。上差是不是有什么话要带给学生？"

狱卒闻言左右看看，放下食盒从怀中摸出一张纸条来，低声道："喏，自己点灯看，别给别人瞧见。将军嘱咐过，尽人事，听天命，若依他的话，成与不成都有你的好处在里面。"言毕又提高音量："瓮里有水自己掬来喝，便溺入桶，污血、脓疮、痰吐莫要弄脏被褥，听到没有？"

拎起食盒，狱卒挑着灯笼晃悠悠走了，朱大鲶三口两口吞下胡饼，灌了几口凉水，背过身借着暗淡残阳看纸上的字迹。看完了，反倒有点摸不着头脑，本以为狱卒是都指挥使郭万超派来的，谁知纸上写的是另一回事情，上写着：

敬启者：我大汉现在很危险，兵少粮少，全靠守城的机械撑着，最近听闻东城别院人心不稳，鲁王爷心思反复，要是他投降宋国，大汉就无可救药呼哉，看到我信，希望你能面见王爷把利害说清楚，让他万万不能屈膝投降。他在东城别院里不见外人，只能出此下策，要为了我大汉社稷着想，请一定好好劝王爷坚持下去，总有一天能打赢宋国噫！

杨重贵再拜

这段话文字不佳，字体不妙，一看就是没什么学问的粗人手笔，落款"杨重贵"听着陌生，朱大鲧想了半天才想起来那是建雄军节度使刘继业的本名，他本是麟州刺史杨信之子，被世祖刘崇收为养孙，改名刘继业，领军三十年攻无不克，战无不胜，号称"无敌"，如今是晋阳守城主将。落款用本名，显示出他与皇帝心存不和，这一点不算什么秘密，天会十三年（公元969年）闰五月宋太祖引汾水灌晋阳城，街道尽被水淹，满城漂着死尸和垃圾，刘继业与宰相郭无为联名上书请降，被皇帝刘继元骂得狗血淋头，郭无为被砍头示众，刘继业从此不得重用。

当年主降，如今主战，朱大鲧大概能猜出其中缘由。无敌将军虽然战功彪炳杀人无数，却耳根子软、眼眶子浅，是条看到老百姓受苦自己跟着掉眼泪的多情汉子。当年满城百姓饿得嗷嗷叫，每天游泳出门剥柳树皮吃，晚上睡觉一翻身就能从房顶掉进一人多深的臭水里淹死，刘继业看得心疼，恨不得开门把宋兵放进来拉倒；如今粮草充足，全城人吃饱之外还能拿点余粮换点威士忌喝、买点小玩意儿玩、到青楼去消费一番，物质和精神都挺满足，刘继业自然心气壮了起来，只愿宋兵围城一百年把宋国皇帝拖到老死才算报当年一箭之仇。东城别院盘踞在东城不见外客，除了囚犯之外谁也接触不到这位鲁王爷，刘将军写了封大白话的请愿书留在监狱里，想通过某位忧国忧民的罪犯在鲁王爷耳畔吹吹风。

"哦……"朱大鲧恍然大悟，把纸条撕碎了丢进马桶，尿了泡尿毁灭行迹。送饭的狱卒并非自己等待的人，而是刘继业安排的眼线，这事真是阴差阳错奇之怪也。

窗外很快黑了，屋里没有灯，朱大鲧独个儿坐着觉得无聊，吃饱了没事干，往常正是上网聊天的好时间。他手痒痒地活动着指头，暗暗背诵着《千字文》——若对这篇奇文不够熟悉，就不能迅速找到字箕中的活字，这算是当代文士的必修课了。

这时候脚步声又响起，一盏灯火由远而近，朱大鲧赶紧凑到栏杆前等着。一名举着火把的狱卒停在他面前，冷冷道："朱大鲧？犯了网络造谣罪被羁押的？"

翰林院编修立刻笑道："正是小弟我，不过这条罪名似乎没听说过啊……上差是不是有什么话要带给学生？"

"哼。跪下！"狱卒忽然正色道，左右打量一下，从怀中掏出一样明晃晃、金灿灿的东西迎风一展。朱大鲧大惊失色扑通跪倒，他只是个不入编制的小小编修，但曾在昭文馆大学士薛君阁府邸的香案上见过此样物事，当下吓得浑身瑟瑟乱抖，额头触地不敢乱动，口中喃喃道："臣……罪民朱大鲧接、接旨！"

狱卒翘起下巴一字一句念道："奉天承运皇帝，诏曰：朕知道你有点见解，经常在网上议论国家大事，口齿伶俐，很会蛊惑人心，这回你被人告发受了不白之冤，朕绝对不会冤枉你的，但你要帮朕做件事情。东城别院朕不方便去，晋阳宫鲁王爷不愿意来，满朝上下没有一个信得过的人，只能指望你了。你我是沙陀同宗，乙毗咄陆可汗之后，朕信你，你也须信我。你替我问问鲁王，朕以后该怎么办？他曾说要给朕做一架飞艇，载朕通家一百零六口另加沙陀旧部四百人出城逃生，可以逆汾水而上攀太行山越雁门关直达大辽，这飞艇唤作'齐柏林'，意为飞得与柏树林一样高。不过鲁王总推说防务繁忙无暇制造飞艇，拖了两个月没造出来，宋兵势猛，朕心甚慌，爱卿你替我劝说鲁王造出飞艇，定然有你一个座位，等山西刘氏东山再起时，给你个宰相当当。君无戏言。钦此。"

"领、领旨……"朱大鲦双手举过头顶，感觉沉甸甸一卷东西放进手心，狱卒从鼻孔哼道："自己看着办吧。要说皇帝……"摇摇头，他打着火把走开了。

朱大鲦浑身冷汗站起来，把一卷黄绸子恭恭敬敬揣进衣袖，头昏脑胀想着这道圣旨说的事情。郭万超、马峰要降，刘继业要战，皇帝要溜，每个人说的话似乎都有道理，可仔细想想又都不那么有道理，听谁的，不听谁的？他心中一团乱麻，越想越头疼，迷迷糊糊不知过了多久，又有脚步声传来，这回他可没精神了，慢慢踱到栏杆前候着。

来的是个举着火油灯的狱卒，拿灯照一照四周，说："今天牢里只有你一名囚犯，得等到换班才有机会进来。"

朱大鲦没精打采道："……上差是不是有什么话要带给学生？"这话他今天都问了三遍了。

狱卒低声道："将军和马老让我通知你，明天巳时一刻东城别院会派人来接你，鲁王爷又在鼓捣新东西正需要人手，你只要说精通丹鼎之术，自然能接近鲁王身边。"

朱大鲧讶道："丹鼎之术？我一介书生如何晓得？"

狱卒皱眉道："谁让你晓得了？能见到王爷不就行了，难道还真的要你去炼丹吗？把胡粉、黄丹、朱砂、金液，《抱朴子》《参同契》《列仙传》的名字胡诌些个便了事，大家都是不懂，没人能揭你的短去。记住了就早早睡，明天就看你了，好好劝说！"说完话他转身就走。走出两步，又停下来问："刀带了没？"

— 七 —

不知不觉天色亮了。有喊杀声遥遥传来，宋兵又在攻城，晋阳城居民对此早已司空见惯，谁也没当回事情。有狱卒送了早饭来，朱大鲧端着粟米粥仔细打量此人，发现昨夜只记住了灯笼、火把和油灯，根本没记住狱卒的长相，也不知这位究竟是哪一派的人手。

喝完粥枯坐了一会儿，外面人声"嗡嗡"响起，一大帮身穿东城别院号服的大汉涌进院子。狱卒将朱大鲧捉出牢房带到小院当中，有个满脸黄胡须的人迎上前来："这位老兄，我是鲁王爷的手下，王爷开恩，狱中囚犯只要愿进别院帮工就能免除刑罚，你头上悬着的左右不是什么大罪名，在这儿签字画押，就能两清。"这人掏出纸和笔来，笔是蘸墨汁的鹅毛笔——在鲁王爷发明这玩意儿以前谁能想到揪下鸟毛来用烧碱泡过削尖了就能写字？

朱大鲧迷迷糊糊想要签字，黄胡须把笔一收："但如今王爷要的是会炼丹的能人异士，你先告诉我会不会丹鼎之术？实话实说，看老兄你一副文绉绉的样子，可别胡吹大气下不来台。"

"在下自幼随家父修习《参同契》，精通大易、黄老、炉火之道，乾坤为鼎，坎离为药，阴阳纳甲，火候进退自有分寸，生平炼制金丹一壶零二十粒，日日服食，虽不能白日升仙，但渐觉身体轻捷、百病不生，有将欲养性，延命却期之功。"朱大鲧立刻诌出一套说辞，为表示金丹神效，腰杆用力"啪啪"翻了两个空心筋斗，抄起院里的八十斤石鼓左手换右手，右手换左手，在头顶耍两个花，"扑通"一声丢在地上，把手一拍，气不长出，面不更色。

黄胡须看得眼睛发直，一群大汉不由得"啪啪"拍起手来。身后狱卒偷偷竖起一个大拇哥，朱大鲧就知道这位是马峰派来的内应。"好好，今天真是捡到宝了，"黄胡须笑着打开腰间小竹筒，将鹅毛笔蘸满墨汁递过来，"签个名，你就是东城别院的人了，咱们这就进府见王爷去。"

朱大鲧依言签字画押。黄胡须令狱卒解开他脚上镣铐，冲狱中官吏走卒做个罗圈揖，带着众大汉离开小院。一行人簇拥着朱大鲧走出半炷香时间，转弯到了一处大宅，这宅子占地极阔，楼宇众多，门口守着几个蓝衫的兵卒，看见黄胡须来了便笑："又找到好货色了？最近街坊太平，好久都没有新人入府呐。"

黄胡须应道："可不是？为了找个会炼丹的帮手，王爷急得抓心挠肝，这回算是好了。"

朱大鲧好奇地打量着这座府邸，看门楼上挂着块黑底金字的匾，匾上龙飞凤舞写着一个"宅"字。他没看明白，揪旁边一名大汉问道："仁兄，请问这就是鲁王的东城别院对吧？为何匾额没有写完就挂了上去？"大汉嘟囔道："就是王爷住的地方。这个匾写的不是什么李宅孙宅王爷宅，而是鲁王爷的字号，他老人家平素以'宅'自夸，说普天下没人比他更宅。后来就写成了匾挂了上去。"朱大鲧满头雾水道："那么'宅'到底是什么意思？"大汉道："谁知道啊！王爷说什么就是什么吧！"

别院门口聚着一群人，有皇家钦差、市井商贾、想沾光的官宦、求申冤的草民、拿着自个儿发明的东西等赏识的匠人、买到新鲜玩意儿玩腻了之后想要退货的闲人、毛遂自荐的汉子和卖弄姿色的流莺。看门的蓝衫人拿着个簿儿挨个登记，该婉拒的婉拒，该上报的上报，该打出去的掏出棍子狠狠地打，拿不定主意的就先收了贿赂告之说等两天再来碰运气，秩序算是井井有条。

黄胡须领众大汉进了东城别院。院子里是另一番气象，影壁墙后面有个大水池，池子里有泉水喷出一丈多高，水花哗哗四溅，蔚为壮观。黄胡须介绍道："这个喷水池平时是用中城的水轮机带动的，现在宋兵攻城，水轮机用来拉动滑车、透视机和铰轮，喷水池的机关就凭人力运动。别院中有几十名力工，除了卖力气之外什么都不会，跟你这样的技术型人才可没法比啦。"朱大鲧听不懂他说的新词儿，就顺着他手指方向一看，果然看见五名目光呆滞的壮汉在旁边一上一下踩着脚踏板，踏板带动转轮，转轮拉动水箱，水箱阀门一开一合将清水喷上天空。

绕过喷泉，钻进一个月亮门进到第二进院子，两旁有十数间屋子，黄胡须道："城中贩卖的电筒、黑眼镜、发条玩具、传声器、放大镜等物都是在此处制造的，内部购买打五折，许多玩意儿是市面上罕有的，有空的话尽可以来逛逛。"

说话间又到了第三进院子，这里架着高高天棚，摆满黑沉沉、油光光的火油马车零件，一台机器"吭哧吭哧"冒着白烟将车轮转得飞快，几个浑身上下油渍麻花的匠人议论着"气缸压力""点火提前角""蒸汽饱和度"此类怪词，两名木匠正叮叮当当造车架子，院子角落里储着几十大桶猛火油，空气里有一种又香又臭的油料味道。这种猛火油原产海南，原本是守城时兜头盖脸浇下去烧人头发用的，到了鲁王手上才有了诸多功用。黄胡须说："晋阳城中跑的火油马车都是此处建造的，赚得了别院大半银钱，最新型的马车就快上市贩卖了，起名叫作'保时捷'，保证时间，出门大捷，听起来就吉利！"

继续走，就到了第四进院子，这个地方更加奇怪，不住有"叽叽呀呀"的叫声、"噼里啪啦"的爆炸声、酸甜苦辣的怪味、五彩斑斓的光线传来，黄胡须道："这里就是别院的研究所，王爷的主意如天花乱坠，一转眼蹦出几十个，能工巧匠们就按照王爷的点子想方设法把它实现。最好别在这儿久留，没准出点什么意外呐。"

一路走来，众大汉逐渐散去，走到第五进院子的只有黄胡须与朱大鲦两人。院门口有蓝衣人守卫，黄胡须掏出一个令牌晃了晃，对了一句口令，又在纸上写下几个密码，才被允许走进院中。听说朱大鲦是新来的炼丹人，蓝衣人把他全身上下摸了个遍，幸好他早把圣旨藏在牢房的天棚里，而匕首则藏在发髻之中。朱大鲦是个大脑袋，戴着个青丝缎的翘脚幞头，蓝衣人揪下幞头来瞧了一眼，看见他头上鼓鼓囊囊一包黄不溜丢的头发，就没仔细检查。倒是从他袖袋中搜出的《论语》引起了怀疑，蓝衣人上下打量他几眼，"哗哗"翻书："炼丹就炼丹，带这书有什么用？"。

这本《论语》可不是用鲁王发明的泥活字印刷的坊印本，而是周世宗柴荣在开封印制的官刻本，辗转流传到朱大鲩手里，平素宝贝得心尖肉一般。朱大鲩肉痛地接过皱皱巴巴的书钻进院子，只听黄胡须道："这一排北房是王爷的起居之所，他不喜别人打扰，我就不进去了，你进屋面见王爷，不用怕，王爷是个性子和善的人，不会难为你的……对了，还不知老兄怎么称呼？方才签字时没有细看。"

朱大鲩忙道："姓朱，排行第一，为纪念崇伯起名为鲩，表字'伯介'。"

黄胡须道："伯介兄，我是王爷跟前使唤人，从王爷刚到晋阳城的时候就服侍左右，王爷赐名叫作'星期五'。"

朱大鲩拱手道："期五兄，多谢了。"

黄胡须还礼道："哪里哪里。"说完转身出了小院。

朱大鲩整理一下衣衫，咳嗽两声，搓了搓脸，咽了口唾沫，挑帘进屋。屋子很大，窗户俱都用黑纸糊上，点着四五盏火油灯。两个硕大的条案摆在屋子正中，上面满是瓶瓶罐罐，一个人站在案前埋头不知在摆弄什么。朱大鲩手心都是汗，心发慌，腿发软，踌躇半晌，鼓起勇气痰嗽一声，跪拜道："王爷！晚生……在下……罪民乃是……"

那人转过身来，朱大鲩埋着头不敢看王爷的脸。只听鲁王道："可算来了！赶紧过来帮忙，折腾了好几天都没点进展，想找个懂点初中化学的人就这么难吗？你叫什么名字？跪着干什么赶紧站起来，过来过来。"王爷一连串招呼，朱大鲩连忙起身垂头走过去，觉得这位王爷千岁语声轻快，态度和蔼，是个容易亲近的人，唯独说话的音调奇怪非常，脑中转了三匝才大概听出其中意思，也不知是哪里的方言。"小人朱大鲩，是个犯罪之人。"他拘谨迈着步子走到屋子中间，脚下叮叮当当不知踢倒多少瓶罐，不是他眼神不好使，是屋里塞满什物实在没有下足的地方。

"哦，小朱。你叫我老王就行。"王爷踮起脚尖拍了拍他的肩膀道，"个子真大，有一米九吗？听说你是翰林院的啊，真看不出来还是个搞学问的人。吃饭了没？没吃我叫个外卖咱们垫吧垫吧，要是吃过了就直奔正题吧，今儿个的实验还没出结果呢。"

这话说得朱大鲩一阵迷糊。他偷偷抬眼一看，发现这王爷根本不像个王爷，个头不高，白面无须，穿着件对襟的白棉布褂子，头发短短的像个头陀，看年纪二十岁上下，就算笑着说话眉间也有愁容。"王爷所说小人听不太懂……"不知这奇怪王爷到底是什么来路，朱大鲩惶恐鞠躬道。

王爷笑道："你们觉得我说话难懂，我觉得你们才是满嘴鸟语，刚来的时候一个字儿都听不明白，你们说的官话像广东话、客家话，就是不像山西、陕西话，我又不是古代文学专业的，还以为古代北方方言都差不多呢！"

这些话朱大鲩倒是每个字都能听懂，其中意思却天女散花，维摩不染，一丝一毫没传进耳中。他满脸流汗道："小人学识粗浅，王爷所说的话……"

鲁王将手一挥:"听不明白就对了,也不用你听明白。过来扶住这个烧瓶。对了,戴上口罩,你是学过炼丹术的人,不会不知道化学实验中有毒气体的危害吧?"

朱大鲧呆在当场。

<h1 style="text-align:center">— 八 —</h1>

桌上的水晶瓶里装着朱大鲧一辈子没见过、没闻到过的奇怪液体,有的红,有的绿,有的辛辣扑鼻,有的恶臭难当。王爷给他戴上口罩,指使他扶住一只阔口的小瓮:"拿这根棍子慢慢搅拌,速度千万别快了,听见没?"

这话朱大鲧听得懂。他战战兢兢地搅着瓮里的黑绿色汤汁,这东西闻起来有股海腥味,热乎乎的如一瓯野菜羹。鲁王介绍道:"这是溶在酒精里的干海带灰。你们古代人管海带叫'昆布',这是从御医那儿要来的高丽昆布,《汤头歌》说'昆布散瘿破瘤',意思说这玩意儿能治粗脖子病……哦对了,《汤头歌》是清朝的,我又搞混了。"说着话,他取出另一只小罐,小心地除去泥封,罐里装满气味刺鼻的淡黄色汁液:"这是硫酸。你们炼丹的管这个叫'绿矾'对不对?也有叫锡水的,《黄帝九鼎神丹经诀》说'煅烧石胆获白雾,溶水即得浓锡水。使白头人变黑头人,冒滚滚呛人白雾,顿时身入仙境,十八年后返老还童'。你应该对这个不陌生。"

朱大鲧不懂装懂连连点头:"王爷所言正是。"

王爷道："叫老王就行，王爷什么的，听着牙碜。我开始了啊，慢慢搅和，可别停。"他在桌案上斜斜支起三扇白纸屏风，戴上口罩，将罐中绿矾水缓缓倾入小瓮之中。朱大鲧只觉一股又酸又臭的气味直冲鼻腔，隔着棉布熏得脑仁生疼，眼中不禁流下泪来。这时只见小瓮中徐徐升起一朵紫色祥云，飘飘悠悠舒卷开来，朱大鲧吓得浑身一凉，却听王爷笑道："哈哈哈，终于成了！只要这土法制碘的实验能够成功，我的大计划就算成了一多半！继续搅别停啊，等整罐都反应完成了再说，我得算算一斤干海带能做出多少纯碘来。想不想听听我是怎么造出硫酸和硝酸的？这可是基础工业的万里长征第一步啊。"

"想听，想听。"朱大鲧只知道顺嘴答音。

王爷显得兴致很高："我中学的时候化学学得不赖，上大学专业是机械制造，总算有点底子在，才能搞到今天这幅局面。刚开始想按炼丹术用石胆炼硫酸，谁知全城也凑不出两斤来，根本不够用的；后来偶尔看到炼铁的地方堆着几千斤黄铁矿石，这不是捡到宝了吗？烧黄铁矿能得到二氧化硫，溶于水得到亚硫酸，静置一段时间就成了硫酸，最后用瓦罐浓缩，当年陕北根据地军工厂就是这样用土法制硫酸的。硫酸解决了，硝酸就没什么难度，最大的问题是硝石的数量太少，还要拿来制造黑火药，害得我发动整个别院的人去刮墙根底下的尿碱回来提炼硝酸钾，搞得整个院子骚气哄哄、臭不可闻，幸好城里人素有贴墙根随地乱尿的习惯，若非如此，晋阳城的工业基础还打不牢靠哩。"

朱大鲧脸红道："有时尿来势不可挡，无论男女脱裤就尿，也是人之常情。乡人粗鄙，让王爷见笑了。"

说话间两罐已并做一罐，紫云消失不见，王爷将白纸屏风平铺在桌上，拿小竹片在上面一刮，刮下一层紫黑色粉末来。"海带中的碘在酸性条件下容易被空气氧化，这样就制造出碘单质来了。很好，等我布置下去让他们照方抓药批量生产，再进行下一个实验。"他转身穿过大屋，坐在屋角的字箕前"噼里啪啦"敲打起来，朱大鲹走过去瞧着，发现这位奇怪王爷打起字来快如闪电，眼睛都不用瞅着活字。

盲打的功力着实了得，不禁开口道："王爷这台字箕似乎型号不同啊。"

"叫老王，叫老王。"鲁王道，"原理一样，不过每个终端用了两套活字系统，下面一套用来输入，上面一套用来输出。瞧着。"他按下回车键结束会话，站起来抓住一个曲柄摇动起来。曲柄带动滚筒，滚筒卷着一尺五寸宽的宣纸，宣纸匀速滚过字箕，字箕中刷过墨汁的活字忽然起起伏伏动了起来，将字迹嗒嗒印在宣纸上，朱大鲹弯腰拈起宣纸，读道："'实验结果记录无误，已着化学分部督办。——回车。'……这样清楚方便多了，白纸黑字，看起来就是舒服！何时能在两市发售，我辈定当鼎力支持！"

王爷笑道："这只是个半成品，2.1版本会按照打印机原理将输出文本印在同一行上，不会像现在这样东一个字西一个字看得费劲。你也喜欢上网？到了这个时代我最不习惯的就是没有网络，所以费尽心机搞了这么一套东西出来，总算找回一点宅男的感觉啦。"

"王爷千岁……老王。"朱大鲹偷偷抬眼瞧着王爷的脸色，改口道，"小人斗胆问一句，您原籍何处，是中原人士吗？毕竟风骨不同呢。"

鲁王闻言叹息道："应该问是哪个朝代的人吧？我所在的年代，距离现在一千零六十一年三个月又十四天。"

朱大鲧不确定他是在开玩笑还是说疯话，扳着指头一算，赔笑道："这么说来，您竟是（汉）世宗孝武皇帝时候得道，一直活到现在的仙人！"

王爷悠悠道："不是一千年以前，是一千年以后——还隔着九千亿零四十二个宇宙。"

一 九 一

王爷的疯话朱大鲧听不懂，他也没心思弄懂，因为下一个实验开始了。鲁王将一块镀银铜板放进一只雕花木箱，把刚才制得的一小盅纯碘搁在铜板旁，盖好箱盖，在旁边点起一只小泥炉来稍稍加热。不多时，氤氲紫气从箱子缝里四溢出来，好家伙，这就炼出仙丹来了——朱大鲧如此思忖道，依王爷吩咐小心摇着扇子，大气都不敢出一口。

等了一会儿，鲁王挪开小火炉，揭开箱盖，用软布垫着小心翼翼将铜板拎出来，只见那亮铮铮的银面上覆盖了一层黄不溜丢的东西，朱大鲧偷偷探头向箱中望了一眼，没发现什么灵丹妙药，可王爷满脸喜色手舞足蹈道："真成了真成了！你瞧，这层黄澄澄的东西叫作碘化银，用小刀刮下来装瓶放在暗处保存就可以了。我还会变一个把戏：把这块铜板摆在暗处曝光十几分钟，然后用水银蒸汽显影，再用盐水定影，洗净晾干之后铜板上就会有一副这屋子的画像了，保证分毫不差！这是达盖尔银版摄影法，利用的是碘化银易被光线分解的特性，不过我们要搜集碘化银备用，下次再变给你看吧！"

朱大鲦疑惑道："没有画师，何来画像？……另外，这黄粉粉有什么奥妙之处，喝下去能身轻体健白日飞升吗？"

王爷笑道："可没那么神。碘化银在我们那个年代主要就两个用途，一个是感光剂，刚才说过了，另一个嘛，等用到的时候你自然能知道。"他边说话边动手，将铜板上的粉末刮进一只小瓷瓶仔细收好，摘下口罩伸了个懒腰："行了，上午的活儿干完了，我把碘化银的制备方法传给出去之后就可以歇一会儿了，没吃饭呢吧？等会儿一起吃。你长得人高马大，手还挺巧，不愧是炼过丹的人。有些问题要问你，可别走远了，我去去就来。"

鲁王坐到字箕前开始"噼里啪啦"打字，不时摇动滚筒吐出长长的宣纸，捧着纸页边看边点头。朱大鲦在屋里束手束脚什么都不敢碰，生怕搞坏了什么东西，触犯了什么神通。这会儿他终于想起此行的目的，伸手在袖袋里一摸那本《论语》，深深吸一口气，低头道："王爷，小人有一事不明，想要请教。"

"说吧，听着呢。"字箕前的人忙着"咯吱咯吱"卷宣纸桶，没顾上回头。

朱大鲦问道："王爷是汉人还是胡人？"

"别矫情，叫老王。"对方答道，"我是汉族人，北京西城长大的。我妈是回民，我随我爸，从小经常上牛街、教子胡同玩儿去，可是离了猪肉就活不了，没辙。"

朱大鲹已经习惯无视王爷的疯话："王爷是汉人，为何偏居晋阳不思南国呢？"

王爷答道："说了你也不明白，我是汉人，但不是你们这个年代的汉人。我知道五代十国梁唐晋汉周都是胡夷戎狄建立的国家，你多半也是胡人，可我的计划一实现就能回到出发点，到时候你们这个宇宙的时间节点与我之间就连屁大点儿的关系都没有了，知道吗？"

朱大鲹走近一步："王爷，宋军围城一事何解？"

王爷回答："解不了，一没兵二没粮，又不能批量生产火枪。燧发枪虽然容易造，可黑火药用到的硫黄根本不够，全城搜刮来几十斤，只够大炮隔三岔五打几发吓唬人用。话说回来，想灭了宋朝人是没戏，撑下去倒是不难，只要赵光义一天没发现辽国送粟米过来的水下通道，晋阳城就能多撑一天。一个空桶绑一个满桶，从汾河河底成排滚过来，这招你们古代人肯定想不到。"

朱大鲹提高音量："可百姓饥苦不得温饱，守军伤疲日夜号啕，晋阳城多守一日，几万居民就多苦一日啊王爷！"

"咦，问得好。"鲁王从凳子上转过身来，"每个来我别院打工的人都是欢天喜地，不光能免了刑罚，还能挣到铜子儿，唯独你说话与别人不同。来聊聊吧，这几个月真没跟正常人说过话。我掉到这个地方来已经——"他从怀里摸出一张纸瞧瞧，在上面打了个叉，"——已经三个月零七天半了。距离观测平台自动返回还剩下二十三天半，时间紧迫，不过从进度上来说应该能赶上。"

朱大鲹只听懂了对方话里淡淡的乡愁，立刻朗声道："子曰：

父母在，不远游，游必有方。父在，观其志；父没，观其行；三年无改于父之道，可谓孝矣。王爷离家日久，必当思念父母，狐死首丘，乌鸦反哺，羊羔跪乳，马不欺母……"

王爷叹口气："好吧，咱俩还不是一个频道的。你先闭嘴听我说行吗？"

朱编修立刻闭起嘴巴。

王爷悠悠道："你肯定不知道什么叫平行宇宙理论，也不明白量子力学，简单说两句吧。我叫王鲁，是一名普普通通的宅男、穿越小说业余作者和时空旅行从业人员，在我们那个时代由于多重宇宙理论的完善，人人都可以从中介那里花点小钱租借一个观测平台进行时空旅行，此前人们认为彼此重叠的平行宇宙数量在 $10^{(10^{118})}$ 个左右，不过随后更精确的计算结果指出由于平行宇宙选择分支结果的叠加，同一时间存在的宇宙数量只有区区三十万兆个左右，这些宇宙在无数量子选择中不断创生、分裂、合并、消亡，而就算彼此之间差异最大的两个平行宇宙也具有惊人的物理相似性，只是在时间轴上的距离越来越远。这挺无聊，因为人类深空探索的脚步一直停滞不前，对宇宙全景的了解仍然非常浅薄（即使在我到达过的最远宇宙，人类的触角也只不过到达近在咫尺的半人马座）；这也挺有趣，因为波函数发动机的发明使我们随随便便就能跨越平行宇宙，从拓扑结构来说，去往越相似的宇宙，所需的能源就越少，目前最先进的观测平台可以把旅行者送到三百兆个宇宙之外的宇宙，而我们这种业余人士租用的设备最多是在四十兆的范围内徘徊。"

朱大鲦连连点头，偷偷摸着袖袋里的东西，心里盘算着等王爷的疯话说完了是该掏出匕首动之以情，还是拿出《论语》晓之以理。现在屋里没有别人，是动手的大好时机，沙陀人不是不想立即发动，只是自己心里还有点迷惑，没想好到底该按哪位大人物的指示来行动。

拿起茶杯喝了口茶，王爷接着说："我接了个活儿，是北大历史系对五代十国晚期燕云十六州人口数量统计的研究课题，你们这样的平行宇宙处于时间轴的前端，是历史研究的最好观测场所。别以为持有时空旅行许可证的人很多，这要经过系统的量子理论、计算机操作、路面驾驶和紧急状况演习等培训与考试后才能上岗，若要接团体游客的话还得去考《时空旅行导游许可证》咧。由于平行宇宙的物理相似性，我在北京宣武门启动观测平台穿越九千亿零四十二个宇宙后来到这里，计算一下公转自转因素，应该准确地出现在幽州地界。谁知道这个观测平台超期服役太久了，波函数发动机居然在旅行途中水箱开锅了，我往里头加了八瓶矿泉水、一箱红牛饮料才勉强撑到目的地，刚到达这个宇宙，发动机就顶杆爆缸彻底歇菜，坠毁在山西汾河岸边的一个山沟沟里。我携带的行李、装备和副油箱全部完蛋，花了十天时间好不容易修好发动机，却发现能源全都漏光了，凭油路里那点儿残油顶多能蹦出两三个宇宙去，那顶什么用啊，最多差了几个时辰的光景。"

这时候外面喊杀声逐渐增强，看来是宋军开始攻击东城城门，王爷回头瞧了一眼字箕上"唰唰"打出的宣纸报告，"啪啪"敲打了几个字，笑道："没事儿，例行公事罢了，我调两台尿脬炮过去就行……说到哪儿了？哦对，波函数发动机勉强能启动，转速一提高就烧机油冒蓝烟跟拖拉机似的，关键是没油啊，人口统计的活儿是别想了，这趟私活儿没在民政部多重宇宙管理局备案，不敢报警，逮住就是三到五年有期徒刑啊！要回家的话得想办法弄到能源才行，我实在没辙了，就把东西藏在山沟沟里，溜溜达达到了晋阳城。"

"王爷，您说没有油，城里有猛火油啊？"朱大鲦忍不住插嘴道，"街上马车尽是烧猛火油的。"

老王叹道："要是烧油的还发什么愁啊。这么说吧，油箱里装的不是实实在在的油，而是势能，平行宇宙间的弹性势能。想要把油箱充满，就得制造出宇宙的分裂，当一个宇宙因为某种选择而分裂出一个崭新的宇宙的时候，我就可以搜集这些逃逸掉的势能作为回家的动力了。这势能不是熵值那种虚无缥缈的东西，就好比一根竹竿折断变成两根，'啪'的一声弹开的那种力道吧？我是不太懂啦，总之必须制造出足够大的事件，使得宇宙产生分裂才行。要怎么做到这一点呢？比如历史上说，今年三月十四号有个人从晋阳城头一脚踏空跌死在汾河里，这事情有二十位目击者看到，被记载在某本野史当中，倘若三月十四号这天我揪住此人的脖领子救了他一命，一个改变就产生了，可它不够大，因为在所有已发生的十万兆宇宙当中，有一千亿个宇宙里他同样得救了，在这个时刻其中一个宇宙的所有常数特征变得与我们现在存身的宇宙完全相同，所以两个宇宙合并了，当然身处其中的你我什么都感觉不出来，但势能是消减了的，还得从我的油箱中倒扣燃料呐……要使宇宙分裂，必须做出足够大的改变，大到在全部已发生的十万兆宇宙中没有任何一个先例。用坏掉的波函数计算机我勉强算出了一个可能性，一个在没有任何现代设备帮助的条件下能做到的可能性。"

朱大鲧没吭声，老老实实听着。

王爷忽然拉开抽屉拿出个册子来，念道："公元882年六月季夏，尚让率军出长安攻凤翔，至宜君寨忽然天降大雪，三天之内雪厚盈尺，冻死冻伤数千人，齐军于是败归长安。这事儿你知道吗？"

"黄巢之乱！"朱大鲧终于能搭上话了，"尚让是大齐太尉，中和二年六月飞雪之事在坊间多有流传，史书亦载。"

"就是这样。"老王道，"我是个现代人，一没带什么死光枪、核子弹之类的科幻武器，二没有企业号和超时空要塞在背后支援，我能做到的只有利用高中、大学学到的一丁点儿知识尽量改变这个时代。宋灭北汉是史实，在绝大多数宇宙的史书中都记载着五月初四宋军攻破晋阳城，汉主刘继元出降，五月十八日宋太宗将全城百姓逐出城外，一把火把晋阳城烧成了白地。而现在，我已经将这个日期向后拖延了一个多月，宋军不可能无限期地等下去，明眼人都看得出凭这个时代的原始攻城器械根本打不破我亲自加固过的城防。一旦宋军退走，历史将被完全改写，宇宙将毫无疑问地产生分裂！"说到这里，他把玩着装有碘化银的小瓷瓶开怀大笑道："更别提我现在发明的东西了，这个小玩意儿将立刻改变历史，装满我观测平台的油箱！古代人最迷信天兆，夏天下一场鹅毛大雪，还有比这更能改变历史的事件吗？"

朱大鲧呆呆道："火烧……晋阳城？大雪？"

"多说无益，随我来！"王爷兴致勃勃地站起身来，牵着朱大鲦的袖子走到大屋西侧的墙边，他不知扳动什么机关，机括"嘎嘎"转动起来，整面墙壁忽然向外倾倒，露出一个藏在重重飞檐之内的院落来。刺眼的阳光蛰得朱大鲦睁不开眼睛，花了好一会儿才看清院里的东西，看了一眼，吃了一惊，因为院里的诸多陈设都是前所未见叫不出名字来的天造之物。几十名东城别院劳工正热火朝天地干活，看见王爷现身纷纷跪倒行礼，鲁王笑吟吟地挥手道："继续继续，不用管我。"

"这边在检查热气球。"指着一群正缝制棉布的工人，王爷介绍道，"我答应给北汉皇帝造个飞艇让他能逃到辽国去，飞艇一时半会儿搞不出来，先弄个气球应景吧。我来到晋阳城以后造了几个新奇小玩意儿收买了几个小官，见到刘继元小皇帝，说能替他把晋阳城守得铁桶一样，他就二话不说给了我个便宜王爷来当，这点恩情总是要还给他的。"

转了个方向，是一群人正向黑铁铸造的大炮里填充黑火药。"这门炮是发射降雨弹用的，由于黑火药作为发射药的威力不足，所以要用热气球把大炮吊到天上去，然后向斜上方发射。这些天来我一直在观测气象，别看现在天气很热，每到下午从太行山脉飘来的云团可蕴含着丰富的冷气，只要在合适的时间提供足够的凝结核，就能凭空制造出一场大雪！"王爷笑道，"刚才我将配方传过去，另一处的化学工厂正在全力生产碘化银粉末，花不了多久就能制成降雨弹装填进大炮中去，热气球也已经试飞过一次，只等合适的气象条件就行啦！"

此时天气晴好，日光灼灼，远方的喊杀声逐渐平息，一只喜鹊站在屋檐"嘎嘎"乱叫。有火油马车轰隆隆碾过石板路，空气中有血、油和胡饼的味道。朱大鲧站在王爷身旁，浑身不能动弹，脑中一片糊涂。

一 十 一

墙壁关闭，屋里又昏暗下来。两人吃了点东西，王爷一边上网指挥城防和作坊工作，一边问了些炼丹的问题，朱大鲧硬着头皮胡诌乱侃蒙骗过去。

"啊，我得睡会儿，昨晚通宵来着，实在熬不住了。"王爷面容困倦地伸个懒腰，走向屋子一角的卧榻，"麻烦你看着点儿，万一有什么消息，叫醒我就行。"

"是，王爷。"朱大鲧恭敬地鞠个躬，看王爷裹着锦被躺下，没过一会儿就打起了鼾。他偷偷长出一口气，头昏脑胀地坐在那儿胡思乱想。方才鲁王说的话他没听懂，但朱大鲧听出了王爷的口气，这位东城别院之主根本就不在乎汉室江山和晋阳百姓，他是从另一个地方来的人，终究是要回那个地方去的，他创造出的百种新鲜物事、千般稀奇杂耍是为了收买人心、赚取钱财，他设计出的网络是为了笼络文人士族、传达东城别院命令，他售卖的火油马车、兵器和美酒是向武将示好，而那些救命的粮、杀人的火、离奇的雪归根结底都是为了一个目的，为了王爷自己。《韩非子》曰："今有人于此，义不入危城，不处军旅，不以天下大利易其胫一毛……轻物重生之士也"，这鲁王不正是杨朱"重生"之流？

　　朱大鲶心中有口气逐渐萌生，顶得胸口发胀，脑门发鼓，耳边"嗡嗡"作响。他想着马峰、郭万超、刘继业、皇帝的言语，想着这一国一州、一州一城、城中万户芸芸众生。梁唐晋汉周江山更替，胡汉夷狄杂处乱世，在这个不得安宁的时代朱大鲶也曾想过弃笔从戎闯出一番事业，然而终安于一隅、每日清谈，不是因为力气胆识不够，而是胸中志向迷惘。上网聊天时文士们常常议论治国平天下的大道理，朱大鲶总觉得那是毫无用处的空谈，可除了高谈阔论文景之治、昭宣中兴、开元盛世，又能谈点什么呢？他要的只是一餐一榻一个屋顶，闲时谈天饮酒，吃饱了捧腹高眠，上网抒发抱负，有钱便逛逛青楼，自由自在，与世无争。可在这乱世，与世无争本身就是逆流而动，就算他这样的小人物也终被卷入国家兴亡当中，如今汉室道统和全城百姓的命运攥在他手里，若不做点什么，又怎能妄称二十年寒窗饱读圣贤书的青衫客？

　　朱大鲶从袖中擎出那柄精钢匕首。他知道无法说服王爷，因为这鲁王爷根本不是大汉子民；大道理都是假的，唯有掌中六寸五分长的铁是真的，在这一刹那，一个三全其美的念头在朱大鲶心中浮现，他长大的身躯缓缓站直，嘴角浮出一丝笑意，鞋底悄无声息碾过地板，几步就走到了卧榻之前。

　　"……你他妈的要做什么！"忽然王爷翻身坐了起来，双目圆睁叫道，"我被蚊子咬醒了，爬起来点个蚊香，你丫拿着个刀子想干吗？我可要叫人了唔唔唔……"

　　朱大鲶伸手将王爷的嘴捂个严严实实，匕首放在对方白嫩的脖颈，低声道："别叫，留你一条活路。我方才看见你用网络调动东城别院守城军队，靠的是字箕中一排木质活字，把活字交出来，告诉我调军的密语，我就不杀你。"

鲁王是个识趣的人，额头冒出密密麻麻一层汗珠，将脑袋点个不停。朱大鲶将手指松开一条缝，王爷"呼哧呼哧"喘着粗气从随身褡裢里拿出红色木活字丢在榻上，支支吾吾道："没有什么密语，我这里发出的指令通过专线直达守城营和化学工坊，除了我之外，没人能在网络上作假……你为什么要这样做？我守住了晋阳城，发明出无数吃的、穿的、用的、新奇的东西供满城军民娱乐，满城上下没有人不爱戴我这鲁王，我到底有哪一点对不起北汉，对不起太原，对不起你了？"

朱大鲶冷笑道："多说无益。你是为自己着想，我却是为一城百姓谋利。第一，我要令东城别院停止守城，火龙、礌石、弩炮一停，都指挥使郭万超会立刻开放两座城门迎宋军入城；第二，宣徽使马峰正在宫中候命，城门一开，军心大乱，他会说服汉主刘继元携眷出降，可我要带着皇帝趁乱逃跑，让他乘那个什么热气球去往契丹；第三，我要将你绑送赵光义，以你换全城百姓活命，宋军围城三月攻之不下，宋主一定对发明守城器械的你怀恨于心，只要将你五花大绑送到他面前，定能让他心怀大畅，使晋阳免受刀兵。这样便不负郭马、刘继业与皇帝之托，救百姓于水火，仁义得以两全！"

王爷惊道："什么乱七八糟！你到底是哪一派的啊，让每个人都得了便宜，就把我一个人豁出去了是不是？别玩得这么绝行不行啊哥们儿！有话咱好好说，什么事儿都可以商量着来啊，我可没想招惹谁，只想攒点能量回家去，这有错吗？这有错吗？这有错吗？"

"你没错，我也没错，天下人都没错，那到底是谁错了？"朱大鲧问道。

老王没想好怎么回答这深奥的哲学问题，就被一刀柄敲在脑门上，干脆利落地晕了过去。

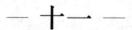

王鲁悠悠醒转，正好看到热气球缓缓升起于东城别院正宅的屋檐。气球用一百二十五块上了生漆的厚棉布缝制而成，吊篮是竹编的，篮中装着一支猛火油燃烧器和那门沉重的生铁炮。三四个人挤在吊篮里，这显然是超载的，不过随着节流阀开启，火焰升腾起来，热空气鼓满气球，这黑褐色（生漆干燥后的颜色）的巨大飞行物摇摇晃晃地不断升高，映着夕阳，将狭长的影子投满整个晋阳城。

"成了！……成了！"王鲁激灵一下坐了起来，冲着天空哈哈大笑，此时正吹着北风，暑热被寒意驱散，富含水汽的云朵大团大团聚集在空中，是最适合人工降雪的气象。时空旅行者盯着天空中那越升越高的气球，口中不住念叨着："还不够，还不够，还不够，再升个两百米就可以发射了，就差一点，就差一点……"

他想站起来找个更好的观测角度，然后发现双腿没办法挪动分毫。低头一看，他发现自己被绑在一辆火油马车上面，车子停在东城街道正中央，驾车人被杀死在座位，放眼望去，路上堆积着累累尸骸，汉兵、宋兵、晋阳百姓死状各异，血沿着路旁沟渠汩汩流淌，把干涸了几个月的黄土浸润。哭声、惨叫声与喊杀声在遥远的地方作响，如隐隐雷声滚过天边，晋阳城中却显得异样宁静，唯有乌鸦在天空越聚越多。

"我靠，这是怎么回事？"王鲁惊叫一声扭动身体，双手双脚都被麻绳缠得结结实实，一动弹那粗糙纤维就刺进皮肤钻心疼痛。王爷一连咒骂着不敢再挣扎，"呼哧呼哧"喘着粗气，这时候一队骑兵风驰电掣穿过街巷，看盔甲袍色是宋兵无疑。这些骑兵根本没有正眼看王鲁一眼，健马四蹄翻飞踏着尸体向东城门飞驰而去，空中留下几句支离破碎的对话。

"……到得太晚，弓矢射不中又能如何？"

"……不是南风，而是北风，根本到不了辽土，只会向南方……"

"……不会怪罪？"

"……不然便太迟！"

"喂！你们要干什么，别把我一个人扔在这儿啊！"时空旅行者疯狂地喊叫道，"告诉你们的主子我会好多物理化学机械工程技术呢，我能帮你们打造一个蒸汽朋克的大宋帝国啊！喂喂！别走！别走……"

蹄声消失了，王鲁绝望地抬起眼睛。热气球已经成为高空的一个小黑点，正随着北风向南飘荡。"砰！"先看到一团白烟升起，稍后才听到炮声传来，铁炮发射了，时空旅行者的眼中立刻载满了最后的希望之光。他奋力低下头咬住自己的衣服用力撕扯，露出胸口部位的皮肤，在左锁骨下方有一行莹莹的光芒亮着，那是观测平台的能源显示，此刻呈现能量匮乏的红色。波函数发动机要达到百分之三十以上的能量储备才能带他返程，而一场盛夏的大雪造成的宇宙分裂起码能将油箱填满一半。"来吧。"他流着泪、淌着血、咬牙切齿喃喃自语，"来吧来吧来吧来吧，痛痛快快地下场大雪吧！"

每克碘化银粉末能产生数十万亿微粒，五公斤的碘化银足够造就一场暴雪的全部冰晶，在这个低技术时代进行一场夏季的人工降雪，这听起来是无稽之谈，可或许是时空旅行者癫狂的祈祷得到应验，天空中的云团开始聚集、翻滚、现出漆黑的色泽和不安定的姿态，将夕阳化为云层背后的一线金光。

"来吧来吧来吧来吧！"

王鲁冲着天空大吼，"轰隆隆隆隆……"一个闷雷响彻天际，最先坠下的是雨，夹杂着冰晶的冰冷的雨，可随着地面温度不断下降，雨化为了雪。一片雪花飘飘悠悠落在时空旅行者的鼻尖，立刻被体温融化，可紧接着第二片、第三片雪花降落下来，带着它们的千万亿个"伙伴"。

浑身湿透的时空旅行者仰天长笑。这是六月的一场大雪，雪在空中团团拥挤着，霎时间将宫殿、楼阁、柳树与城垛漆成粉白。王鲁低下头，看自己胸口的电量表正在闪烁绿色光芒，那是发动机的能量预期已经越过基准线，只要宇宙分裂的时刻到来，观测平台就会获得能量自动启动，在无法以时间单位估量的一瞬间之后将他送回位于北京通州北苑环岛附近那九十平方米面积的温馨的家。

"这是一个传奇，"王鲁哆嗦着对自己说，"我要回家了，找个安全点的工作，娶个媳妇，每天挤地铁上班，回家哪儿也不去就玩玩游戏，这辈子的冒险都够了，够啦……"

以雪堆积的速度，几十分钟后晋阳城就将被三尺白雪覆盖，可就在这时，二十条火龙从四周升起。西城、中城、东城的十几个城门处都有火龙车喷出的火柱，还有无数猪尿脬大炮"嘣嘣"射出火球，那是他亲手制造的守城器械，宋人眼中最可怕的武器。

"等等……"时空旅行者的目光呆滞了，"别啊，难道还是要把晋阳城烧掉吗？起码稍微迟一点，等这场雪下完……等一下，等一下啊啊啊啊啊！"

黏稠的猛火油四处喷洒，熊熊火焰直冲天际，这场火蔓延的速度超乎所有人的想象，久旱的晋阳城天干物燥，时空旅行者召唤而来的降水未能使干透的木头湿润，西城的火从晋阳宫燃起，依次将袭庆坊、观德坊、富民坊、法相坊、立信坊卷入火海，中城的火先点燃了大水轮，然后向西烧着了宣光殿、仁寿殿、大明殿、飞云楼、德阳堂。东城别院很快化为一个明亮的火炬，空中飞舞的雪花未及落下就消失于无形，时空旅行者胸口的绿灯消失了，他张大嘴巴，发出一声痛彻心扉的哀号："靠你大爷，就差一点点，一点点啊！"

浴火的晋阳城把黄昏照成白昼，火势煮沸了空气，一道通红的火龙卷盘旋而上，眨眼间将云团驱散，没人看到大雪遍地，只有人看到火势连天，这春秋时始建、距今已一千四百余年的古城正在烈火中发出辽远的哀鸣。

城中幸存的百姓被宋兵驱赶着向东北方行去，一步一回首，哭声震天。宋主赵光义端坐战马之上遥望晋阳大火，开口道："捉到刘继元之后带来见我，不要伤他。郭万超，封你磁州团练使，马峰为将作监，你们二人是有功之臣，望今后殚精竭虑辅我大宋。刘继业，人人都降，为何就你一人不降？不知螳臂当车的道理吗？"

刘继业被缚着双手向北而跪，梗着脖子道："汉主未降，我岂可先降？"

赵光义笑道："早听说河东刘继业的名气，看来真是条好汉。等我捉到小皇帝，你老老实实归降于我，回归本名还是姓杨吧，汉人为何保着胡人？要打不如掉头去打契丹才对吧。"

说完这一席话，他策马前行几步，俯身道："你又有什么要说？"

朱大鯀跪在地上不敢抬头，眼角映着天边熊熊火光，战战兢兢道："不敢居功，但求无过。"

"好。"赵光义将马鞭一挥，"追郯城公，封土百里。砍了吧。"

"万岁！小人犯了什么错？"朱大鯀悚然惊起，将旁边两名兵卒撞翻，四五个人扑上来将他压住，刽子手举起大刀。

"你没错，我没错，大家都没错。谁知道谁错了？"宋主淡淡道。

人头滚落，那长大的身躯轰然坠地，那本《论语》从袖袋中跌落出来，在血泊中缓缓地浸透，直至一个字都看不清。

时空旅行者创造的一切连同晋阳城一起被烧个干净。新晋阳建立起来之后，人们逐渐把那段充满新奇的日子当成一场旧梦，唯有郭万超在磁州军营里同赵大对坐饮酒的时候，偶尔会拿出"雷朋"墨镜把玩："要是生在大宋，这天下会完全成为另一个模样吧？"

宋灭北汉事在《五代史》中只有寥寥几语，一百六十年后，史家李焘终于将晋阳大火写入正史，但理所当然地没有出现时空旅行者的任何踪迹。

丙申，幸太原城北，御沙河门楼，遣使分部徙居民於新并州，尽焚其庐舍，民老幼趋城门不及，焚死者甚众。

《续资治通鉴长编卷二十》

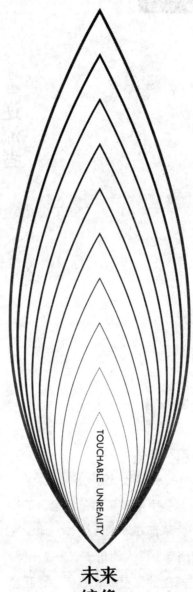

TOUCHABLE UNREALITY

未来
镜像

逆流者

阿缺

— 1 —

这场病来得猝不及防。

他一觉醒来，发现自己回到了前一天。

刚开始他以为是手机显示出了问题，但接下来发生的每一件事都在昨天发生过。他没完成报表，被上司痛骂，骂人的句子都一模一样。晚上他回到空空荡荡的家里，满心疑惑，睡意袭来，沉沉睡去。再醒过来时，发现时间又往以前退了一天。这一天他有大量的报表要完成，但依然完不成。

他终于明白，在所有人都顺着时间之河往前走的时候，他独自转身，逆流而行，一天天回到从前。

刚开始他很难适应。一切都经历过，况且他的生活多以痛苦组成，再来一遍并不愉悦。他试图改变，熬夜不睡觉，可敌不过汹涌的困意，每次都在天色将明时屈服于睡眠。他还故意打乱时间线，甚至在某一天突然冲进办公室把上司揍得满脸是血。但即使被关进监狱，他次日依旧在家中醒来，上司依旧在办公室冷着脸等他——被揍得头破血流的事，已经扔在明天了。

— 2 —

他是个顺从的人，后来就习惯了这种日子，照常生活，照常上班。这期间，小薇离开他，跟了另一个男人。他以为会像上次一样痛苦，但其实还好。反正经历过一次，麻木一点，顺着记忆来，再深的伤都会在醒来之后愈合。

半年之后，或者说半年之前，家里多了一个人。"我们离婚吧。"他听到自己对妻子这么说。那时妻子三十二岁，但脸上已经有了皱纹，腰微微佝偻着。她愣了一下，如以往一般听他的话，点点头说："嗯。"

妻子收拾行李的时候，他在一旁看着。半年没见，他对她更加陌生了，这个女人在他眼中不像是妻子，倒像是某个故人。本以为不能再见，却逆流时间，再度相会在分别的时刻。

后来妻子拖着箱子离开。他站在阳台上，看到她的背影渐渐远去，黄昏的光斜照，街上无数人影湮没了她。当初他也是这么看着她离开，以为这就是永别，但现在，他知道还会再见。

果然，第二天他一醒过来，就闻到了早餐的香味。

"我出去买菜，"她站在门口，背对着他，"你先吃，吃完了就去上班吧。"

他点点头，然后越想越不对——上一次妻子也是这时出去，但过了很久才空手回来，他问她去哪里了也不说。这次重来，他多了个心眼，悄悄趴在猫眼后面看，发现妻子并没有下去买菜，而是向楼道上走去。

他等妻子上去后，蹑手蹑脚地跟上，一直到天台门口才停下。

他听到轻轻的抽泣声。多么熟悉，是出自陪伴他漫长岁月的妻。

哦，他心想，原来她早就发现小薇了。

— 3 —

整个白天，他上班都很恍惚，想着妻子是怎么发现的。快下班时小薇发来了短信："别急着走，留下来。"他看着手机屏幕，恍然大悟：太多的秘密都藏在这个小方块里，像炙热的炸弹，昨晚不小心被点燃。

他下意识地想删掉那些短信、视频和照片，但转念一想：今天过去后，又回到前一天，妻子会忘了这个危险的秘密。一切被埋葬在时间里。于是他耸耸肩，把手机揣回兜里。

同事们陆续走了，偌大的办公司只剩他和小薇。

灯光次第熄灭，黑暗中，小薇走了过来。她俯身在他耳边说了一句令人脸红的话。

小薇就是这样，妩媚又大胆，即使在幽暗的环境里也放着光。当初他是如此轻易地被吸引，沉浸在欲望里，一度以为那是爱情——第二次爱情。

但现在，他看着小薇满是诱惑的脸，脑袋想起的却不是肉欲欢好，而是半年多以后她决然抛弃自己转投他人怀抱的身影。他站起来，定定地看着小薇，窗外不时有车驶过，他的眼镜片偶尔闪着光。

"你怎么了？"小薇皱起眉头，"昨天还好好的。"

"昨天也不会好好的了。"

小薇更加纳闷，不知道他说的话是什么意思。这时他已经转身离开了。

— 4 —

黑夜的城市有一种隐忍的热闹。他独自走着，许多车从他身侧掠过，车灯划出一道道流光。这像是旧时代电影里的场景。他有种预感，在这种场景里，肯定会发生些什么。

正这么想着时，他突然听到右侧巷子里传来呼喝之声。那是一群年轻人在围殴一个醉汉。他高声制止，年轻人们看了他一眼，骂骂咧咧地退入巷子深处。

他走过去。路灯照下来，醉汉脸上满是血迹，还有一道白肉外翻的陈年刀疤，从右眼至嘴角，蚯蚓一样伏在脸颊上，分外可怖。

他有些心悸，还是扶起醉汉，说："你受伤了，我给你叫救护车吧。"

醉汉"吭哧吭哧"地笑了起来，声音如同呓语："没关系，再重的伤，到了明天就会好起来的。"

他的血液似乎刹那间被冻结，良久，才说："你说的明天，是昨天吧？"

醉汉也愣住了，表情被灯光照亮，有些狰狞，又有些诡异，明亮的光线投进他的眼中，没有一点反射，像两汪沉郁的潭水。醉汉看着看着，突然对着他笑了起来："你也是逆流症患者？"

那一刹那，他竟然有要哭泣的冲动。

醉汉挣扎着坐起来，说："这是一种病，很罕见，要理解起来也很困难。时间是一种属性，跟空间一样，在大多数情况下，这两者是伴随的，比如你花十分钟从街头走到街尾，时间和空间都在移动，向前移动。但有时候，它们又分开了，时间会朝着相反的方向流动。陷进这种时间紊乱困境的人，就是逆流症患者。"

他沉默了。

醉汉继续说："这也是令人悲伤的病。就像一群人在夜里赶路，你突然折返，而其他人继续前行。你们会离得越来越远。路上只有你一个人，孤单地向原点走去。"

— 5 —

你生命中有没有出现过这样的人——你觉得他会永远陪伴着你，一直走下去，但前一天他还在你身侧，下一秒就蒸发在时间里，再不复现？

你并不知道，他已经转身，在你的背影里，在你察觉不到的时间中，独自走向年迈苍苍的另一端。

他坐在逐渐幽暗的街道旁，哀伤地想着。

— 6 —

"其实我说的也没有科学根据，相对论和量子力学都不能解释我们的病症。"年轻人从酒醉中解脱出来，说，"我已经花了很长时间来研究它，但至今收效甚微。"

"这种病会持续多长时间？"

"我不知道，"醉汉摇摇头，"但我是在七十五岁时，死的前一天得了这种病，一直回到现在，已经整整五十年了。"

— 7 —

回家以后，妻子已经睡了。他站在卧室里，第一次认真看着她的睡姿：她睡得很沉，身子蜷缩着，像个婴儿一样侧躺在床边，把大部分的位置留给他。但她眼角的皱纹在提醒他，她并不是婴儿。她体质差，又不会保养，每天三顿在厨房里被烟熏，这些都在加速她的衰老。

结婚十年来，他是看着她变老的。他说过好多次让她注意保养，她只是"嗯嗯"点头，却手脚笨拙，永远学不会摆弄护肤化妆品。

而现在，他要看着她一步步重回青春了。

这个过程难以言说。他和妻子相伴十余年，自认为早已熟悉，但生活倒带一遍，他竟然发现了许多不曾了解的东西。

比如原来妻子喜欢吃糖醋鱼，喜欢看韩国电影——是电影，而不是连续剧。好几次他看到妻子一边看电影一边垂泪。

他经常想，自己是什么时候开始对妻子失去了初心呢？是日复一日的油盐酱醋磨掉了爱情，还是逐渐老去的容颜滋生了厌恶？

日子就这么一天又一天地过，妻子的脸逐渐恢复，身躯也不再因为常年蜷缩睡觉而变得佝偻。他把一切看在眼里，觉得愧疚，于是在结婚十周年纪念日那天做了糖醋鱼庆祝。

那是他第一次看到妻子因喜悦而泣然。她捂住嘴，眼圈红红的，好半天才说："你怎么知道我喜欢糖醋鱼。"

"我是你的丈夫嘛。"

这句话更令她不知所措。

他上前揽住她的肩，说："以前都是我不好，放心，我以后会改的。"

妻子使劲点点头。他却在心里叹息——哪里还有以后？一切都在向前，无论怎么悔改，都没有意义。

妻子在恢复容貌的同时，也在恢复着活泼。她的话越来越多，以前他听到这种絮絮叨叨，总会不耐烦地打断，要求她安静。可能正是这种要求换来了沉默，让家里的气氛成了一潭死水，让她一天比一天少言寡语，一夜比一夜蜷缩得厉害。

但现在，他觉得亲切。他放下手头的事情，耐心地听着妻子诉说。那些丢掉的工作自不必担心，乱套的一切都会被时间抹平。

他越来越适应这种生活，甚至开始享受。他想，自己怎么会不喜欢这个女人呢？在她面前，多少个小薇都不够入眼。

十年多过去了。这一个晚上，他向妻子求婚。其实虽然时间在倒流，但记忆没有跟上，甚至越发模糊了。但他依然记得这个晚上的事情：

他租了三十架遥控直升飞机，每个都挂着彩灯。这些飞机在半空中组成心形，并且缓缓移动，指引她来到他身前。他拿着玫瑰和戒指，单膝跪在地上，向她求婚。当时，半空中满是华彩，仿佛整个夜空的星星都落了下来，围绕在她周围。

她流下了泪，泪珠被灯光撕碎，也成了星星点点。

— 8 —

那天晚些时候，他们牵着手回出租房。那时他们还没有自己的家，在这个繁华城市的最底层挣扎着，却比多少年以后有房有车要快乐许多。

路过一个巷子时，突然有人叫他的名字。他诧异地看向巷子深处，只见一个人影藏在幽暗中，面目不清。

妻子一下子紧张起来，握紧他的手臂。

"别怕，是我，"巷子里的人说，"你以后见过我。"

这句话让妻子迷惑，他却再懂不过："是我的朋友，你先等我一会儿，我和他说会儿话。"说完他走进巷子里，黑暗也淹没了他。他走近那个人影，发现是个少年，十四五岁的样子。

"我找到了治我们的病的法子。"

他浑身一震。这么多年逆着时间过日子，他都习以为常了，现在被少年提醒，才明白自己其实一直是个病人。

"得这种病的人远远不止我们两个。这十年来，我游历世界，在麻省理工的实验室里找到了一个博士，他也是病人。我们做了无数次实验，终于有了成果。"少年的声音透着惊喜，"只要在影响自己人生轨迹最剧烈的点，做和之前同样的事情，让一切按部就班，就会陷入沉睡，回到开始逆流的那一天。时间和空间再次重合。你会回到分岔路口，再向前走，一切就像没有发生过一样，连自己都不会察觉到曾经做了逆流者。"

"这法子管用吗？"

"管用，因为我已经试了，"少年看着他说，"对我人生影响最大的事情就发生在今天。我被我爸爸家暴，砍伤了脸，在今天离家出走。"

他这才看到少年脸上正沁出浓郁的血，像滋生的阴翳。难怪他要躲在巷子里。

"我现在看到的一切都跟以前不同了，世界正在融化，很难跟你形容。而且我很困，随时会睡着。你是个善良的人，曾经救过我，所以我挣扎着过来告诉你，希望你没有错过改变你人生轨迹的点。一旦错过，你将不可避免地逆流到时间尽头，不会有人记得你，因为你从来没有来过这个世界……"少年的声音逐渐疲惫，闭上眼睛，身体向后仰倒，"我要回去了，逆流了六十年，我终于要……"

他摔下去，却没有倒地的声音。少年的身体在触地的前一刻凭空消失了。他知道，少年已经回到初点，回到了白发苍然的年纪。

他跟跄地走出来。妻子正等着他："咦，你的朋友呢？"他没有说话，带着妻子回家，心事重重地睡下。

他知道对自己人生影响最大的事情是什么——与妻子的初遇。他在学校里向她问路，被她的美丽和热情吸引，从此锲而不舍地追求她，为了她来到这座陌生的城市。

在问路的那一刻，他和她的命运就绑在了一起。

— 9 —

他早早起床，出了宿舍，就在校道上等着。樱花开得正灿烂，一眼望去，整条校道都是粉红一片。她就在这樱花掩映中出现了。

他忍住心头狂跳，迎面走过去。问路的话已经练习了千百遍,随时可以说出口,表情也得体,一切都跟以前相同。

越走越近,她的样子逐渐清晰。这时的她十九岁,穿着碎花棉裙,乌黑的头发垂下,明媚的脸胜过所有樱花。看着她的美丽面孔,他突然想起了十几年后她蜷缩在床侧的衰老模样。

他马上就要回到患病的那一天了。他不会记得这十年逆流里发生的事情,他仍会出轨,逼她离开,看着她的身影湮没在人海……时间照常逝去,眼前的这张脸依然会过早凋零。

他的脚步突然一阵慌乱。

这是一个春天的上午。在他的妻子最美丽的时刻,他与她错身而过,没有问路。只有几片樱花在他们头顶飘落。

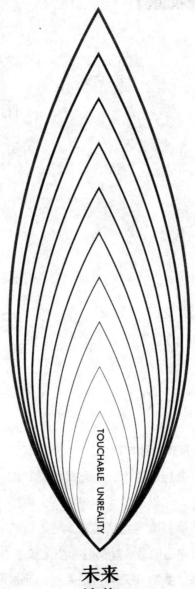

TOUCHABLE UNREALITY

未来
镜像

雨
船

迟卉

— 0 —

葬礼正如我预想的那样简单。

访客们一个个绕过棺木，冷光藻围绕着棺材的半透明盖子，在影影绰绰的照明下，阿巴妮的脸看起来仿佛再度丰盈了起来。她的最后时光很痛苦，但幸运的是（对我们每个人都是）没有拖延得太久。我听到哭声，是莱拉，她本来应该在今年成为我们家族的姐妹。但现在看起来婚礼或许要等到明年。哀悼的礼节是必需的，死者或许并不在意，但活人需要得到安慰。

　　我看到我的姨妈们绕着棺木行走。我扶着母亲。她因为悲伤而显得更加矮小了，蜷缩着，弓起背，哭泣。我任由泪水滑下脸颊，却腾不出手来擦一擦。

　　走在姨妈们身后的是那些在这个家里出生的女孩，然后是男孩们。他们看起来略微有些困惑和难过，但并没有像女孩们那样放声哭泣。毕竟，他们都在不同的父亲的家系里长大。对阿巴妮，他们或许只有一个模模糊糊的印象而已。

　　血把我们召唤到一起。葬仪者说。血把我们留在这世界上，如今我们回到我们的连生身边去，他们在世界的彼端已经等候了很久，向我们伸出欢迎的手。为她歌唱吧，她终于得到宁静了。

　　孩子们率先唱起哀歌。然后是姐妹们，然后是她们所来自的不同家庭，还有男孩们。那是一首古老的哀歌，歌唱了姐妹们和兄弟们，歌唱了父亲和母亲，歌唱了在生日出生的孩子们和死去的孩子们。⊖母亲紧紧抓着我的手，将我的手指攥得生疼。她呜咽着，呜咽着，泪水仿佛永无休止地落下来。

　　当她最终停止哭泣的时候，我们已经安葬了阿巴妮，坐在回家的管铁上了。

　　她的手仍然抓着我的手。

　　"你这次会在家里待多久？"她充满希冀地问。

　　"明天我就走。"

　　"明天？"

⊖　由于生育能力过强，拉比特人从文明伊始就有意控制生育，他们每一胎只留下一个孩子，由父母或祭司选择留下的孩子，并杀掉其余的。那些死去的婴儿没有名字，只是被笼统地称为"连生"。

她的声音拔高了，用饱含泪水的哀怨的目光看着我。她希望我留下，她总是希望我留下。

"我订了机票。希尔四号挖出了一个大遗址。他们要我尽快回去。"

"你又不是考古学家。"

没错，我不是考古学家，我曾经是个士兵，如今是个雇佣兵。每发现一处古曼人太空遗址都会让某些人富得流油，而那些星际海盗也会闻风而至。我的使命就是保护这些遗址，从我的老板手里拿钱，用自己的脑袋和屁股去冒险。你可以说一个女人不适合做这些，但管它呢，这一行我已经干了很多年了。

"他们需要我。"

"你的家庭也需要你。"

我看着她。我知道自己面无表情。每一次当她试图用亲情打动我的时候，我就会退入自己的壳里，一个完美的、没有任何反应的壳，那是我抵御我的家人的唯一方式。

"我明天走。"我重复道。

"你也该找个家族安定下来了。要不就回来。女儿总是可以回到姐妹们中间的。"

我看着她。

和 15 个月⊖前相比，她老了很多。而我长大了。我知道这一点，只是很难切实地感受到。我总觉得我还是那个孩子，茫然失措，面无表情地站在屋子中央，看着自己母亲恳求的脸。

⊖ 作为老鼠的智慧后裔，拉比特人的寿命最长大约是 8 年，他们一般用月来计算，也就是大约 100 个月的样子。

　　我还记得那条路，很长，两边开满了矮小的多肉植物的花朵，它们是深红色的，像血，或者傍晚时分的阳光。

　　"我明天走，"我说，"否则他们会雇别的佣兵。这年头太空轨道上可不缺卖命的。"

　　她又开始哭泣。过了一会儿，她哽咽着擦干眼泪，叹息着："我知道，你在外面也很不容易，我不是个好母亲，我知道。对不起，金，对不起。"

　　她总是这样，她喜欢向我道歉，一次又一次，一次又一次。

　　在那个事件之前她就已经是这样了，在那件事之后依旧如此。

　　我不需要道歉，妈妈。

　　我将目光转向窗外，努力去想象我即将抵达的那颗星球。在那里有座覆盖了半透明穹顶的太空站，人们一抬头就满是璀璨冰冷的星星。而我总是看着它们在天穹中缓慢旋转，想象着有那么一刻它们会开始倒转，一切重来。

　　我想要的是我从未出生。

—— 1 ——

　　希尔四号距离地球有 3000 光年之远，从这里看去，银河不再是地球上那样细细的白色光带，而是高悬头顶的椭圆巨盘。这颗行星的太阳孤零零地挂在天空中，散发它熹微的热量。它是一颗被甩出了银盘的恒星，带着它的行星孩子们，从 3000 光年的高度俯瞰着银河系的旋臂。

尽管有着荒凉如死的地表，但希尔四号仍然是一颗适宜殖民的星球。在地面之下，广袤的希尔内海几乎覆盖了3/4的星球内表面。在黑暗中，生命汲取着地核的热量而成长起来。古曼人先来了这里，而我们追寻他们1.2亿年前的脚步随后而至。

我乘坐的飞船进入空港时，雇佣兵队的换班飞船已经先到了。他们正在忙忙碌碌地将武器装备运出货舱。

"嘿，独行女侠，好久不见。"领头的老勾向我打了个招呼，没什么恶意。他手下的雇佣兵都是男人。当然，也有全是女人的雇佣兵队，但像我这样单打独斗的雇佣兵倒是相当稀少。我们曾经互相看不顺眼，还打过几架。如今我们勉强算是可以彼此容忍，或许还带着一点点的尊敬。

"好久不见，假期怎么样？"

"要多糟有多糟，有些浑小子这一旬[⊖]都醉得像滩稀屎，上船之前我得把他们一个个揍起来。不说这个了，博士要你尽快赶到雨船那边去，带上你的装备。我的人在这边守着，但他们希望你过去，毕竟那边至少要有一个有执法权的人。"

"雨船？"

"他们在太空站下层发现一个古曼人传送门，走进去直接就到了另一边，你猜猜他们发现什么了？"

"一艘飞船？"

"对了，也错了。那玩意是艘飞船没错，但他妈的大得吓人。说实话，咱不用过去挺好的，看到那玩意儿我就发怵。"

"多大的飞船？"

⊖　旬：拉比特人的计时单位之一，一个月相月的1/4为一旬，每旬8天。

"多大？"老勾翻了个白眼，"大得一眼望不到边，里面有云，孩子，还在下雨！"

老勾和他手下的武器装备塞了足有一船。但我只有一个小小背包。简单整理了一下后，我收到了霍特博士发到我终端上的信息，要我尽快穿过传送门到飞船上去，内容和老勾说的大同小异。

穿过空港船坞，搭乘古曼人一亿多年前就修建好的升降梯，我前往太空站的下层遗址。

尽管那些学者都把这些史前智慧生物⊖叫作古曼人，老勾也那么叫。但我始终更喜欢叫他们巨人。他们的一切都是那么巨大，这座太空站也是古曼人修建的，它的体积比得上一座城市，而一个升降梯的体积就几乎相当于一栋公寓楼。我站在升降梯的一角，昂起头望着这巨大的空间，想象着那些十六倍于我的巨大生物站在里面时候的模样。他们从地球出发，将足迹遍布群星各处，并在某个时间点上神秘消失。在那之后，我们追寻着他们的足迹而来，却只看到这些——巨大——神秘——莫可名状的建筑。

有个考古学家给我看过他们做的古曼人足迹拓印。一个成年拉比特人可以舒舒服服地躺在上面，把它当成一张床。就我所知，真的有这种形状的床出售，专门给那些活得太无聊的人生活里增添一些惊喜。

大约 9 个标准月前，希尔四号的轨道遗址被发现，随后发掘出来的是位于希尔内海的地面遗址。这个位于星盟边境的荒凉星系瞬间变成了热点地带。本着"开发利用与考古研究并进"的原

⊖ 事实上，"古曼人"就是我们人类。时光变迁，没有什么能够永恒，文明亦然。

则，考古研究队在前面开路，而那些他们调查研究过，认定安全的古曼人舱室就留给身后的开发者。他们带来网绳、泡囊、帐篷和更多的建筑材料，将古老的古曼人太空站迅速建设成一个小型城市。两支雇佣兵队伍在这里轮班执勤，还有些像我这样的独立佣兵四处游荡。

但我始终没法习惯古曼人的建筑风格。就拿这个太空站来说，它巨大、怪异，被建筑成一个球形空间，里面足以塞下星盟首府的整个城市，还有空余再放两个人工湖。

老勾的佣兵已经就位，和上一班的那些佣兵换了班。他们带着解脱的表情从兜网中跳出来，沿着墙壁上的绳梯攀援而下，满心希望尽快回到大城市里去，好好地喝点儿马勃酒，然后大睡一场；再找个姑娘，或者干脆找个有很多姑娘的家族。

传送门在太空站下层。霍特博士已经把路线发给了我。但我决定先去酒吧转一圈再说。她也许会生气，也许不会。

因为我对某些事情有预感。而我的预感通常准得要死。

酒吧里的人不多。现在是 7 点，单时$^\ominus$。大部分人正在工作。我坐下来，点了杯玉米汁，在酒吧招待的盘子里放了一小卷钞票。

他的眼睛立刻就亮了起来。酒保看见了但没管。过去两旬里，他的酒吧一直是我的情报购买地，那卷钱里也有他抽成的一份。

$\ominus$ 拉比特人将一个标准日分成 8 等份，从 1 点到 8 点，每一个钟点相当于人类时间的 3 小时。像大多数啮齿类动物一样，他们每天睡很多次，每次时间很短，因此他们的工作和生活也被切割成很多小块。单数时（1、3、5、7）他们工作，而双数时（2、4、6、8）他们休息、喝酒、购物、睡觉，或者进行家庭生活。因此，大部分拉比特人的生活与工作几乎不分开，他们从不浪费时间在路上。

"最近有什么有趣的事情吗？"我低声问道。

"哪方面？"

"新遗址、新发现。光是从我坐着的这个破地方，我就能看到3个废墟猎手了。"

"你担心废墟猎手？"

"那些家伙是老勾要担心的，我要到新遗址那边去，最近有没有海盗？"

在回答我之前，这个年轻男人先四处张望了一下。他和酒保属于同一个家族，事实上整个酒吧都是他们家族的男人在打理[⊖]，我很喜欢这些人，他们谨慎、聪明，而且知道什么时候做什么事。

"6点的时候来了5个人，都带着枪。陌生面孔，看起来不太对劲，"他答道，"他们喝了不少，然后每人要了两片醒酒药。7点刚到时走的。"

"去哪儿了？"

"上面。他们应该直接往船坞去了。"

我皱起眉头，用终端接入船坞，查询了一番。那里没有人或者监控探头看到这5个本来应当很醒目的家伙。既然他们开了车，那也有可能根本不是为了去那边。

如果我是那些海盗，好不容易变装混进了太空站（其实也不是很难，给导航塔台一点贿赂就行了），我会去抢劫那艘满载古曼

⊖ 拉比特人的家庭和人类的截然不同。除了生育期之外，男性和女性并不会生活在一起。他们一般和3～5名同性组成家族，男性家族只接受男性，女性亦然。大部分家族成员会一同开创事业，做同一份工作，迁居时也会一同迁居。对拉比特人来说，"婚姻"的意义是"进入一个家族"而非"男女之间的结合"。

人遗物起飞的航船。它应该是 8 点从空港发射——中间只有两个钟点的闲暇时间，这些家伙酒瘾大到非得进酒吧一趟不成？

除非他们——

两支雇佣兵队伍正在换班。上一班佣兵正在撤出来，而老勾的人刚刚到岗。眼下正是守卫最松懈的时候，如果他们要的不是那艘货船呢？如果他们想要的是考古队在传送门的另一边发现的那东西，那他们唯一的办法就是占领传送门。

我往年轻男人的盘子里拍了另一张钞票，跳起身冲出酒吧，接通老勾的呼叫。

"老勾！"我喊道，"让你手下的人警醒点儿，可能有状况——"

震耳欲聋的爆炸声在通信线路里响起，我站在高处的走廊，抓紧绳网，踮起脚尖向下望去，太空站下层腾起一股爆炸的烟尘，在巨大而空荡的球形空间里，它渺小得几乎无人注意。

— 2 —

看到爆炸烟尘的那一瞬间，我挂断通信，把背包甩到肩上，直接用尾巴卷出两枚闪光弹⊖，拔出枪，逆着人流一路向下层奔去。

整个太空站是一个巨大的球形空间，传送门在这个大球的最底部，我觉得自己像是从一个巨碗的碗壁向下打着旋儿飞跑，而惊惶的人群正在向上狂奔。

⊖ 拉比特人每只手只有四个手指，但相应地，他们有尾巴，尾尖分成三叉，几乎和手指一样好用。

拜手中的武器所赐，他们至少主动地为我让开了一条路。

跑到一半的时候，我看到了拉娜·桂尔和她家族的姐妹们。这些女人们都是废墟猎手[⊖]，一共六个人，我曾经逮捕过她们一次，罪名是废墟走私。但眼下她们只有四个，都灰头土脸的。当我把她们拦下来的时候，拉娜的眼睛里仍旧闪着惊惶的神色。

"嘿，拉娜，下面什么情况？"

她傲慢地向我翻了个白眼。

我压住火气："听着，拉娜，我现在不是要逮捕你，我是要下去敲掉那些敢在我地盘上放炸药的杂碎。我知道你们家是六个姐妹，现在只上来四个。你把两个留在下面了？"

她尾巴尖的颤动印证了我的猜测。

"我要下去，也许能帮上忙。你也帮我个忙，跟我说说下面是什么情况，怎么样？"

这一次她的表情松动了些。

"我不知道是什么情况，可能有 10 个人，或者 15 个。都带着重武器，有炸药。他们封锁了两条走廊，就是老勾他们驻扎的那两条。妮妮和吉也在那边。我们过不去，帮不上忙——"她痛苦地摇了摇头，"那些人都蒙着脸，我听到他们叫喊，用的是北安话[⊖]。"

⊖ 废墟猎手是指那些在古曼人废墟里合法／非法挖掘遗物的非专业人士，大部分人持有武器。拉比特人在性别分工上并不明显。大部分男性可以做的事情，女性也可以做。

⊖ 在拉比特人的时代，地球有两块主要大陆，安大陆和穆大陆。北安话指的是安大陆北方的方言，在那里居住的族群以凶猛好斗著称。即使是进入群星时代之后，这些拉比特人也多半没有加入星盟，而是作为掠夺者和强盗漂流在各个星系之间。

"谢了，拉娜。"

她点点头，转身向上方跑去，走了一半又转回头。

"金？"

"嗯？"

"你是个结结实实的小贱货，但是，别他妈死了。"

我向她亲密地伸出中指摇了摇，转身跑进下面的巷道里。

又穿过两条环形隧道后，我听到⊖了第一个目标。他大概离我三个巷道远，正大声地说着什么，我听得懂一点儿北安话——他们似乎已经成功地压制住了老勾的雇佣兵队伍，但是，不，很抱歉，他们还没夺得传送门。老勾的该死的佣兵全都躲在那扇传送门所在的走廊里。

我咧开嘴，无声地笑了。

我放轻脚步，拔出刀子，绕过巷道，远远地就看到了那个挂在监视网上⊜的家伙，我默默地数着支撑线，一根，两根，三根——手起刀落，第三根支撑线断裂，他摇晃了一下，连人带网跌落地面，我扑上去，将军刀直接插入他的心脏。

他看着我，充满了震惊，然后目光便黯淡了下来。

我拔出刀，擦干净插回刀鞘，继续向前。这些人都是职业的战士，上来就炸了雇佣兵守卫的营地，分割人群，制造恐慌，目标明确，行动迅速。如果我不下手狠辣一点，眼下躺在地上的就是我了。

⊖ 作为一个长年生活在地下隧道里的种族，拉比特人的听力要好于视力。

⊜ 一种挂在隧道天花板和墙壁上的网子，供拉比特人攀爬。他们的攀爬能力虽然不及祖先，但比人类要强多了。

在被发现之前，我已经清空了底下一层的走廊，这里有个门可以进入老勾所在的遗迹内部，解决门口的守卫时，我终究还是弄出了"一点儿"声音。那家伙不肯死透，在我崩掉他的头之前，他已经向着隧道墙壁打了一梭子子弹，在隧道间制造出震耳欲聋的回声。

巨大的门从里面闩死了。我用力地砸了一下，又砸了一下。

一条小缝打开来，在那些海盗蜂拥而至前，我迅速钻了进去，再把门死死地关起来，闩住。

老勾就站在门后，瞪着我。他的尾巴在流血，头上包了绷带，身后是他的两个手下，和他一样狼狈不堪。

"你他妈的来这儿干吗，金？"

"来看看能不能把你们救出去。"

"外面至少有他妈的 20 ⊖个人，而我就剩下 6 个了。"

"16 个，"我更正道，"外面是 16 个，不算我干掉的那 3 个。"

"每人只用负责 $2\frac{3}{4}$ 个，这可真是美妙的前景啊。"

老勾话里带刺，不过我原谅了他——他原本有 30 个手下，其中 6 个属于他的家族。另外几个家族也有他的亲戚在。现在这些雇佣兵大部分都死了，或者在某处等死。

"这儿还有平民吗？"我问道。

老勾摇摇头："桂尔家俩丫头，还有 3 个研究员，我让他们穿过传送门到那边去了。实在不行还可以在另一边把门关上。你有什么突围的好办法没有？"

⊖　拉比特人的计数方式是八进制。20 个人在他们的语言里是"二八四"，但为了便于理解，这里使用人类的十进制来表达。

我耸耸肩:"干脆大家都到传送门那边去,把门一关,还更稳妥些。"

老勾摇摇头。

"我还有人被困在营地,"他说,"我已经向星区治安队发出求援信号了,你带着联络设备过去,然后把门关上。"

"你呢?"

他阴郁地耸耸肩:"我不能丢下自己的人不管。"

我扫了一眼身边的雇佣兵们。

"你手下有几个人不太赞同。"

"不喜欢的可以跟着金过去。"老勾说。

两个年轻的佣兵对视了一眼,起身走到我身后。他们都不是老勾家族里的人,而且以后也肯定别想跟着老勾混了。但眼下,他们显然不相信那些北安海盗会优待俘虏。

"你确定?"我问老勾,但他只是不耐烦地挥了挥尾巴尖。

"过去,把传送门关上。"

我点点头,转身一头扎进遗迹后方的传送门里。

虽然说是"门",但这是巨人曾使用的门扉,看上去足有 10 层楼那么高,我们冲进去的时候,那镜面般的外表连点儿波纹都没泛起来。

我觉得自己同时向着四面八方跌落,躯体仿佛不复存在,而灵魂被揪扯着穿过一条彩色的光。然后我的脚落到了地面上,两个年轻的佣兵跪在我身旁,一个在发抖,一个在哭。

这不是我第一次穿越古曼人的传送门,但不管多少次,这种感受都一样令人讨厌。

我吐了口唾沫，抬起头。

我看到了——

<h1 style="text-align:center">— 3 —</h1>

想象一艘巨大的飞船，梭形，笔直竖立。长轴至少有 1000 米高[⊖]，以我的视力，只能模糊地看到它的顶端。而横轴至少有 400 米长。在它的中央，水晶般剔透的墙壁切割出一个六棱柱形的空间，悬浮在飞船的正中。

飞船的外壳是围绕着这个独立空间建立起来的，古曼人在外壳上建造了一系列简陋的舱室，材料简单然而坚固，在 1 亿年后依旧完好。数条走廊从环路上延伸出来，通向那个巨大的生态空间，廊道消失在亚空间分割板与船壁的交界处，一条小路蜿蜒深入草丛间，只能看到开头几步路上铺设的石板，石头缝隙间早已绿草如茵。

这个生态空间几乎填满了整艘飞船，被偏光分割板隔离成一个自给自足的小小生态系统。浓密的云层笼罩着上层空间，有雾在草地上翻卷升腾，那些野草几乎有我的两倍高。雨丝正细密地落下来，听不到声音，周遭一片静寂，但我可以清楚地看到水滴在草叶上的细小反光。

大、巨大、庞大、莫可名状——我用光了一切能够使用的形容词，只是站在那里，敬畏地仰头望天。这些消失在 1 亿年前

⊖　这里采用的是人类的计算单位，便于理解。

的巨人们，他们建造了这飞船、这殿堂、这有雨落下的生态巨柱。而我们追随其后，踏足其中，深深地感受到自己渺小得不可言说。

正发呆时，下方廊道里传来的响动引起了我的注意。是桂尔家的两个女孩，她们握着考古用的磨削激光器，活像握着两把枪，神情紧张地看着我和刚刚出来的两个佣兵。

我没空问她怎么走下去，直接在护栏上挂好挂钩，翻过矮墙滑到下面一层。这俩姑娘身上居然没带武器，真不知道拉娜是怎么想的。

"接着，"我从背包里卷出两支枪甩给她们，"别用那破玩意，而且你拿反了，妮妮，当心把自己的脑袋削下来。"

她赶紧放下磨削器，就像它烫了她的手一样。吉·桂尔怀疑地看着我，眯起眼睛，她比她的姐妹稍微多那么一点儿脑子："你什么时候开始帮我们的忙了？"

"从我遇到拉娜的时候开始。她拜托我帮你们俩一把，而我非常乐意让桂尔家的女人欠我个人情，也许是两个。"我抖了抖手上的枪，挥手示意那两个年轻佣兵赶紧下来，"霍特博士在哪儿？我需要她过来帮忙，尽快把那扇门关上。"

"关上？"

"你觉得老勾在那边能撑多久？"

吉不说话了。

"博士在里面。"妮妮·桂尔示意了一下右边，一扇巨大的、很明显是古曼人使用的门开了一条小缝，"这边也有状况，她让我们两个出来盯着点儿。"

“什么状况？”

“有人从外面登船了。”

“你他妈的开玩笑。”

“我妈喜欢开玩笑，我可不。”

莉·霍特博士和她的助手们只占据了古曼人飞船主控室的一个小小角落，她们挤在一起，神情惊恐。各种仪器设备杂乱地放在一边，一盏非常小的苔灯⊖挂在便携实验桌旁。主控室的玻璃舷窗如同透明的巨幕，璀璨的星光穿过舷窗，微弱地照亮了四周。从这里可以模糊地看到不远处的一艘小型飞船，挂在古曼人的巨船登陆口旁，像一只黏附其上的飞蛾。

看到我进来，研究员们露出了惊讶的表情。

“金？”霍特博士站起身来，“你什么时候回来的？我还以为你下个星期才会到。家里的事情怎么样了？还好吗？”

我举起一只手，打断了她的话。

“没空说这些，博士。”

“哦，对不起。”她低下头，“我……我只是……你知道，这些事，我太紧张了。”

“没关系。”我看了一眼那艘飞船，“那艘飞船是什么时候到的？”

“大概就刚才。”一个年轻的实验室助手说道，她也是霍特家族的一个姐妹，“我们听到爆炸声，就跑过来看。”

⊖ 拉比特人的身长只有人类的1/16，他们使用火有一定的困难，因此习惯使用冷光和发光苔藓照明。即使是进入太空时代后，这一传统依旧保持了下来。

"爆炸？"

"他们打不开登陆口，就炸开了船壳，进来了。"

"几个人？"

"就看到一个。"

"你知道他去哪儿了吗？"

年轻的女孩用力摇头。

我眯起眼睛看着那艘飞船，双座，小型的穿梭机，速度快，适于携带轻火力，是独来独往的海盗和废墟猎手最青睐的型号。我自己也有一架。而且不管这个炸药客是什么来头，他不是个生手。定向起爆、选择船壳最薄弱的气密接口而不是一米厚的船壳，整个过程完成后还不忘记把自己的飞船吸附在缺口处防止气体泄漏——

我摇摇头，把这些想法统统甩了出去。

"霍特博士，先不管这个人，他单枪匹马，我们至少有 3 个雇佣兵，5 杆枪。我们现在得上去，把传送门从这边关起来。"

她看起来相当震惊："你要我们把自己和一个亡命徒关在这废墟里？"

"你应该知道那边是什么状况，如果不关上传送门，等下飞船里的亡命徒就不是一个，而是一群了。"我恼火地指出。

她看上去仍有些不情愿，但终究还是点了点头。

"再叫个技术员一起，我们需要用超空间通信器联系星区的治安管理处。妮妮、吉，你们留在这儿。你们俩——"我转向跟我一起过来的两个佣兵，"跟我上去。"

两个愣头青对视一眼，倒是没有什么异议。

我们爬上科考队平时使用的软梯，从下面一层到上面一层足有 40 拓⊖（4 米）高。抓着绳子滑下来的时候不算什么，但要爬上去就累得很了。我可以清楚地听到身后两个女人的喘气声，难得的是她们居然没有抱怨。

传送门的控制台同样是一座庞然巨物，幸运的是，霍特博士已经将线路接入了科考队使用的便携终端，她输入了一串指令后，传送门的镜面随之黯淡下来，最终在框架内破碎成星星点点的银光。我松了口气。

但愿老勾能有好运气。

"联系上了。"一直在摆弄着我那台通信器的年轻研究员兴奋地喊道。

枪声响起，很轻，就像坚果的外壳爆裂一样的声音。起初我几乎没反应过来。但通信器瞬间哑了，一缕青烟从弹孔里冒出来。研究员一脸茫然，不知道发生了什么。

我猛地向着子弹来的方向转过身，只能隐约地看到一个身影，隔着差不多 200 米的距离，在我们上面一层的地方。传送门所在的舱室是没有外门的，所以他才能从远处一枪射中小小的通信器。

有这样的准头，为什么不先放倒我或者那两个年轻佣兵？

我来不及多想，打着手势示意研究员们赶紧下去，回营地。自己拔出枪来，跑向墙角，外墙上也有绳梯，但挂在上面无疑是给那家伙当活靶子，所以我决定沿着古曼人使用的管道爬上去。

⊖ 拉比特人的长度计量方式，10 拓约为 1.03 米。为了便于理解，在下面叙述中，长度单位都以"米"来表达。

这是个错误，我本应该和其他人一起回营地，我们在人数上占据优势，但我当时又累又恼火。乘坐了 24 小时的信道航班，落地之后就没停过脚。一场接一场的遭遇战彻底让我失去了理智——我当时坚信这家伙肯定是那些海盗的同党。我曾经一个人放倒他们三个，所以干掉这一个也不在话下。

至少，在他把枪顶在我脑门上之前我是这么想的。

"——我就知道你会从管道上来，美女。"那家伙的声音轻松愉快，还带了点扬扬得意，"你爬得有点慢，我等你好一会儿了。"

— 4 —

我很慢很慢地在枪口下抬起头来，努力让自己的动作不具有威胁意味。

闯入者和我年纪相仿，一头棕色的短发支棱八翘，穿着一套简式压力战斗服，背着一个战斗背包，和我常用的居然是同一个牌子。

但他手上握着的枪可就完全和我的不是一个风格了。Uran-571，大口径，强火力，后坐力也很强，打在身上少说也得开个大窟窿。

"慢点儿，慢点儿，美女。"

他说着，咧嘴一笑，伸手到我腰间下掉了两把枪，又在我脚踝摸了一把，确定没有备用枪，这才点头示意我可以站起身。我们面对面站着，他比我高一点儿，长相普通，但额角的那条伤疤显得特别扎眼，细细的白色线条，从发际一直延伸至眉峰，应该是被刀砍的或者被什么东西划伤的。

"转过身去。"他命令道。

我听不出他是什么地方的人，他的通用语很纯正，没有北安或者其他地方的口音。慢慢地，我转过身去，眼角余光瞟到他拿出了一副三环铐[⊖]。

穿着简式压力战斗服的一个缺点，就是你在行动时会比最佳状态慢上那么一点儿。

我猛地一甩尾巴，抽中他的手腕，三环铐和手枪碰在一起，发出响亮的声音，飞了出去。在他能够抓起枪来瞄准之前，我已经向着一旁扑出，打了个滚儿，绕过半掩的巨门，冲出了这个舱室。

舱室外面是狭长的廊道——狭长仅仅是对于古曼人而言。我撒腿飞奔，短短的距离看起来像是无限远。当那家伙抓着枪冲出来的时候，我刚好跃出，抓住廊道边缘的绳索，荡向下一层。

我抓紧绳索，双脚猛蹬墙壁，但还差一点儿——抬起头来的时候，我看到那家伙的脸出现在廊道边缘，若有所思地看着我手里的绳索。那一瞬间我觉得自己的血液都凝固了。

他只要在绳子上割一刀，我就会跌落差不多 100 米的高度，落在古曼人的飞船底层，摔成——大概会比烂泥还要烂点儿吧，

⊖ 最初拉比特人发明手铐的时候，和人类使用的手铐没什么区别，但这种手铐的设计在第一次实地测试之后便升级成了三环铐——对于有着灵巧尾巴的拉比特人来说，只铐住手显然不是对罪犯明智的处理方式。

我想。

但他没有，他只是咧嘴笑了笑，像是发现了什么好玩的事情——确实也挺他妈的滑稽的，尤其是在我第二次没能抓住下一层的绳网，像个傻蛋一样又荡回来的情况下。从下面向上望去，他的眼睛映着生态巨柱发出的偏振光，看起来是一种奇异的深绿色。

我又荡了一次，成功地在下面一层着陆。抬起头去看，闯入者已经不见了。

一个好的雇佣兵身上应该带足够多的备用武器。我不能算是差的，而且这也不是我第一次被别人把枪下掉。一边跑，我一边扯开背包，用尾巴从里面卷出那把小口径手枪，杀伤力弱了点，但眼下也只有这把好用。

飞船里一片寂静，我握住枪，放慢脚步，把耳朵贴在墙壁上，听着闯入者的脚步声，一开始能分辨出一点，细碎，隐隐约约是向着下面去了。我知道他要去哪儿——研究员们聚集的临时营地，那里是古曼人飞船的主控室，除了传送门，整座飞船里大概也只有那个地方有一定的战略意义。

幸运的是，那家伙的脚步声听起来是在主楼梯的方向，而我知道一条近路。

再一次抓着壁绳向下滑去，我谨慎地放慢了速度，免得那家伙再一次在下面守株待兔。但附近没有听到他的脚步声响起。

当我滑到绳子末端的时候，一声枪响划破了寂静，然后是第二声，第三声。

我松手，砰然落地，弹起身来向着枪响的方向拔腿飞奔。

— 5 —

跑到离枪响的地方只隔一个转角，我调整了呼吸，握好枪，手指搭在扳机上，猛地跳出转角，准备着。

靠。

我眨了眨眼睛，又眨了眨。

闯入者倒在地上，一动不动，不知道是死了还是活着。莉·霍特博士手里握着一把小型的女士防身枪，站在他面前，全身发抖，手指还在不停地抠着扳机，全然不知道子弹已经打空了。

我放轻脚步，从她身后绕过去。

"博士。"

她肩膀猛地一抖，被我按住了。

"霍特博士，是我，不用怕。已经结束了，好了，他被你干掉了。"

轻声安慰着，我从她僵硬的手里慢慢掰下那把枪。

这时，地上的闯入者发出一声模糊的呻吟。莉·霍特像兔子一样惊跳起来，而我迅速冲了过去，用枪瞄准他的头。

还活着，而且没看到有血。身上有三个枪眼——他穿的是简式压力服，那东西的设计目的是为了抵御太空的真空负压，以及微流星，挡下三颗子弹应该也没问题，但估计这哥们的肋骨不会太舒服。

趁他还没醒过来，我踢了一脚这家伙的背包，从里头用尾巴勾出那副三环铐，把他结结实实地铐了起来。

"没事了，博士。"我抬头对莉·霍特说道。

其他人听到枪响也赶过来了，一时间走廊里嘈杂不堪。闯入者挣扎起来，我的手用力压住他。每一个人都困惑不已，除了莉·霍特。她正死死地瞪着闯入者，目光里混合了恐惧、憎恨和深深的震惊。

— 6 —

"你叫什么名字？"

"……"

"你是哪个雇佣兵团的？"

"……"

"你来这里做什么，为什么要打掉我们的通信器？"

"……"

"如果我现在干掉你，你觉得怎么样？"

"……"

无论我问什么，这家伙都死不开口。

在抓住他之后，我们没找到合适的地方关他，后来还是妮妮·桂尔出了个主意，把他弄到一个古曼人的巨大架子旁，三环铸锁在架子的竖杆上。这样，我们从营地可以清楚地看到他的一举一动，但离营地又足够远。

同样地，从这里我也可以清楚地看到霍特博士，她看上去比方才平静了许多，努力做出一副若无其事的样子，但每隔几分钟就会向这边看一眼。

"好吧。"我压低声音，"最后一个问题，你和莉·霍特博士是什么关系？"

他的肩膀微微震了一下，依旧沉默不语。

我叹口气，起身走向考古队的营地。研究员们正在小声地交谈着，两个年轻佣兵坐在稍远一点的地方。吉和妮妮正在研究那台被打坏的通信器。

"我想我能修好她。"吉·桂尔坐在一地摊开的零件中间，得意地说，"打仗我不行，这个我行。"

"她？"

"所有的通信器都是女孩子。"吉严肃地说，"她们最擅长传递消息。"

考古队员们都笑了起来，吉骄傲地歪了歪头。

莉·霍特孤零零地坐在人群外面，似乎在想事情。她的手指交叉在身前，依旧微微发抖。

我走过去。

"博士，我能和你单独谈谈吗？"

"啊？噢……噢……好的。"

她有些紧张地起身，我带她走到远离人群的地方，希望没人会偷听我们谈话。

"金，谢谢你救了我。"她小声说。

"就我所见，你枪法很好，根本用不着我救。"我摇摇头，"但是我觉得你认识他。"

听到那句话，莉·霍特差点跳起来，她向后退了半步，像是要逃走，但最终只是站在那里，手指绞缠着，回头看了一眼她的考古队员们——她们都是她的家族成员。

"我没……我没想到他会追到这里。"

"追到这里？"

"他就是道尔。"她深吸一口气，像是下了很大的决心，"就是那个道尔。"

"噢。"我说，"操。"

在边缘星系，莉·霍特是个传奇。这不仅仅是因为她发掘出来的大量古曼人遗址，也因为她那与众不同的过去。她成长在一个极端达尔文主义⊖教会里。这些人是不折不扣的疯子。他们对每一胎出生的孩子不是进行生日抉择，而是将他们全部养大到 10 岁⊜左右，然后再逼迫他们互相残杀，剩下的最后一个孩子则可以进入他们的家族。

在养育莉·霍特和她的连生们的时候，他们犯了个错误，低估了名叫道尔的那个男孩。他决定永久地结束这个教会以及他们对孩子们做的事情，在大人们去聆听祭司布道的时候锁住神庙的隧道门，点起了火，把所有的人都用浓烟熏死在里面。然后他折返孩子们住的宿舍，将自己的连生一个个杀死。

莉·霍特因为出去打水，侥幸逃过一劫。道尔在做完这些事后就逃走了，发现火警而赶来的人们救下了莉，惨案震惊整个多兰星区，其中细节在多年后依旧家喻户晓。

⊖ 原名是"智慧生物竞争生存真理教会"，鼓吹拉比特人也应当遵从物竞天择的生存原则。为便于理解写为"极端达尔文主义"。

⊜ 拉比特人生命比人类要短暂得多，生长发育也更快，这里的 10 岁事实上是指 10 个月。

道尔始终没有被找到。有人说他可能死了，但也有人说他成了一个雇佣兵，或者一名海盗。总之是那些杀人越货的行当。每隔几年，就会有人声称自己遇到了"那个道尔"，随之而来的大部分都是些相当恐怖的故事。他们说他杀光了某个空间站里所有的极端达尔文教信徒，还说他曾经把一艘载有朝圣者的飞船开进了某颗恒星里。

这些事情也让莉·霍特相当困扰。她后来被霍特家族收养，正常而幸福地长大。但无论她如何成功，发掘了多少古曼人遗迹，获得了多少荣誉，人们总是会想起她那个逃走的连生，想起那些不该在这世界上活下来，也同样不该如此悲惨地死去的孩子们。我听说她把很多钱捐助给一个救助儿童的组织，并推动星盟议会通过了一道立法，宣布所有极端达尔文主义教会为非法宗教。就一个背负着悲惨过去的人而言，她做得很好。

但是……

"往事阴魂不散啊，博士。"我轻声说。

她看着我，苦笑着点了点头。

— 7 —

在折腾了差不多一个钟头后，吉宣布她累了，要去休息，我安排那两个年轻佣兵也一起去休息。眼下不知道什么时候才能离开废墟。通信器坏了，如果没法修好它，我们只能等星区首府的救援船找到这里。

"换一下班。"我对霍特博士解释道。

她疲惫地点点头,也把自己的人员分了两班。然后就去睡了。

妮妮·桂尔没去睡,她坐在垫子上,百无聊赖地摆弄着我丢给她的那把枪。

"悠着点。"我说。

"我把子弹卸下来了。"她耸耸肩,"这玩意我会用,比激光磨削器强多了。吉不会打仗,我得照顾着她点儿。"

我笑了。

有些时候,我会羡慕那些有家族的人,男人,女人,彼此熟悉,彼此照顾,彼此关心。你会信任你的姐妹或者兄弟们。你们分享一切,包括痛苦。

"笑什么呢,金?"妮妮好奇地看着我。

"没什么,我只是……有点羡慕你们,有家人,你懂的。"

"你为什么不找个家族?女的雇佣兵家族少了点,又不是没有。"

我伸手揉了揉妮妮的头,她歪头看着我,也没躲开。她只有14岁,在桂尔家族的羽翼之下走遍群星,无所畏惧,从不孤单。而我已经26岁了,孤身一人,从一颗星星到另一颗星星,从一个战场到另一个战场。我的上一个搭档和我拆伙的时候,说我打仗不怕死,简直就是赶着去死一样。

"我习惯一个人了。"我说,"原因很复杂。"

"你想聊聊吗?"

"抱歉,不想。"

妮妮做了个鬼脸,她不明白,也不太可能明白我的理由。而且,她看起来似乎不怎么在意。

“好吧，聊点儿别的——我不喜欢那个博士。”她说。

“霍特博士？小点儿声，她给我开工资呢。”

“你喜欢她吗。”

“你对她什么感觉，妮妮？”我反问。

“我讨厌她。”妮妮倒是直截了当，“拉娜从来不会自己先去休息，她会安排自己值后面一班，让家族的人先去睡觉。拉娜也不会像她那样，给我们俩手里塞个磨削器推我们俩出来当炮灰，把自己的家族里的人都圈在安全的地方。”

“你的意思是拉娜会让你们上战场？”

“不会。”妮妮耸耸肩，“她会自己上战场来保护我们。她不会躲在后面。你那个博士，是个胆小鬼，还是个贼。”

“贼？”

“传送门是拉娜发现的。她拿着考古证就从我们手里抢过去了。”

我扬起眉毛。

一般来说，废墟猎手不具备专业的废墟考察资格。但拉娜是这一行的老手了，就连我都要多少给她留点面子。

“她没有给你们补偿吗？”

“一点儿——都——没有！”

“这就过分了。”

“可不是嘛。我说金，你有啥办法整她不。”

“没有。”

“没有？”

“她给我发工资，记得不？”

“啧，真没劲。”

妮妮撅起嘴，我笑了起来，又揉了揉她的头："你那儿有水和饼干没？"

水是瓶装水，但饼干有点受潮了，不太好吃。我拎着水和饼干走向被铐在角落里的男人，他似乎正在打盹儿，听到我走近，抬起头，懒洋洋地看了我一眼，目光落在我手里的食物上，然后又转开。

他装作若无其事的样子和莉·霍特简直一模一样。我很惊讶于之前居然没发现他们是连生。

"想吃点东西吗，道尔？"我问。

他眼皮掀动了一下，露出一个嘲讽的笑容。抖了抖手上叮当作响的铐环。三环铐是从背后铐起的，他的手一点儿也动不了。

"我给你解开一只手。别玩花样。"

他翻了个白眼，当我给他解开右手铐环的时候，我听到他吃痛地吸了口冷气，可能是断了一根肋骨，或者两根。子弹虽然没穿过压力服，但近距离，三枪。冲击力也是相当强的。

"让我看看。"

"滚。"

他说出了被抓住之后的第一个单字儿。

我瞪了他一眼，他毫不客气地瞪回来。我拽开便携式压力服的拉链——这家伙试图躲避。

"躲什么？"

他很明显受了伤，龇牙咧嘴，但就是不让我解开压力服检查一下。

然后我想起了自己穿压力服时候的一些，呃，非常尴尬的事儿。好吧，看来他的压力服也不是新式的。

"你要去洗手间吗？"我问。

这一次他的目光简直能杀人，但最终还是点了点头。

我解开铐环，押着他走到考古队搭建的临时厕所旁。这家伙简直是急不可待地冲了进去。

过了一会儿。

又过了一会儿。

我敲了敲门："老兄，你再不提上裤子出来，我就要对着厕所门开枪了。"

他咒骂了一声，闷闷地听不清楚。

"什么？"

"你有能换的衣服吗？"

我扭头看了妮妮一眼，这小丫头已经捂着嘴笑得在地上打滚了。但她还是指了指不远处的衣架，考古队在那里挂了不少白色的实验服。

我走过去，拎了一件和道尔差不多尺码的。手一直放在枪把上。这家伙可能是打算趁机逃跑——不过看起来不像。

把衣服从门缝里塞进去之后又过了差不多 15 分钟，他才出来，手里拎着破烂的压力服，看上去有些尴尬，但至少不像刚才那么沮丧了。

"手。"我抖了抖手里的铐子。

他看了一眼四周，也许是在估量逃跑的机会。妮妮不笑了，把玩着手里刚装起的枪。我不知道她有没有把子弹填回去。

最终道尔还是乖乖地让我铐上了他的尾巴和左手，坐回架子旁，抓起那瓶水，一口气喝了不少。我检查了一下他的肋骨，看起来没断，只有几块瘀青。

"你暂时还死不了。"我宣布道。

"那还真是遗憾。"他嘴里塞满饼干，含糊地答道。

在吃饱喝足之后，这家伙变得不那么有敌意了。我试图和他攀谈，但他只是疲倦地打着哈欠。

"我说了你也不会信，不如让我睡会儿。"

我叹口气，把他手铐上的链条放松了一截，让他可以躺下睡觉。

"噢，对了，别让你那姑娘再修通信器了。真修好了你会后悔的。"我转身离开时，道尔突然冒出一句。

"为什么?"我困惑地问。

但他已经打起了呼噜。

— 8 —

我抱着篮子，走在那条开满深红色花朵的小路上。那些矮矮的多肉植物的叶片也是深紫红色的，在细雨里闪着光。我抱着篮子，很沉重，里面睡着六个婴儿。对一个十岁的孩子来说，实在是太沉重了点儿。

在同一条小路上，我去了又回。去的时候篮子里有六个婴儿，回来的时候只剩下一个。

我抱着那孩子走过长长的地下隧道，引来一些好奇的目光，但并不多。毕竟单时很少有人在外面闲逛。

那座地下五神⊖的神庙在梦境里依旧清晰如昨。我走过门口的巨磬⊜，据说，在过去，每当遇到战争或瘟疫，导致人口剧减的时候，祭司们会敲响这口磬，召集人们，告诉他们：你们可以养育你们生下的每一个孩子了，不需要杀死他们中的大部分而只留下一个。但是这口磬上一次被敲响时，阿巴妮的阿巴妮⊜还是个孩子。

我走进神庙，祭司迎了出来。他看起来猜得到发生了什么——一个孩子抱着一个更小的孩子，他知道我要说什么。

"你的母亲呢？"他和蔼地问。

"我要把她留在这儿。"我说，没有回答他的问题。

他悲伤地看着我："你留下吗？"

"我要走的。"

"她叫什么名字？"

她没有名字，我的父亲离开了我们，我的母亲不想要他的孩子，一个都不想要。她拒绝给她们名字，甚至没勇气杀掉她们。于是她对我说："求你了，金，求你了。"

"她叫——"

"金，金！"

从睡梦中被摇醒，我顿时无名火起，差一点伸手去摸枪。但在我眼前的是莉·霍特那张熟悉的、不能说不令人生厌的脸。

要是崩了她我就没钱拿了。

⊖　拉比特人崇拜大地更胜于天空。
⊜　和人类常用的钟相比，放置于地面的磬更容易在隧道城市里传播声音。
⊜　"阿巴妮"是女性家族里最年长的女性的称号，一般是指曾曾祖母。

这样想着，我悻悻地收回手："干吗？你还不让我睡会儿了。"

她紧张地向道尔的方向看了一眼："我有事要和你说，金。"

我一龇牙，骂骂咧咧地起身。声音压得很低，但也足以让莉·霍特的脸色难看起来。但她没说什么，只是催促着我走到稍远一点的走廊里，其他人听不到的地方。路过吉和妮妮的睡垫时，我看了一眼，通信器已经装好差不多一半了。

"到底是什么事儿？"我没好气地问。

"是道尔的事。"莉咬着牙，似乎下定了决心，"我记得你是有执法权的。"

"对。"

在差不多经历了十年的边境开发与混乱后，多兰星区政府终于开了悟，索性将边境地带的执法权下放给每一支佣兵队和通过考核的独立佣兵们。我们有权逮捕、送监和在极端情况下处决罪犯。而边境检察官（通常由雇佣兵中介掮客或者武装公司老板担任）会审核我们经手的案子。大部分时候《执法权代理法案》会保障我们的行动自由，只有某些人做得太过分了，才会惹来星区政府的舰队干涉。

短短两年间，钱、血和权力就迅速编织成了边境地带独有的秩序网络，我自己也是其中的一环。独立佣兵拥有和佣兵队长同等的二级执法权，这一点是佣兵间相互制约的关键。

"道尔的通缉级别是一级。你有权处决他，是吧？"

"只限于极端情况下，博士，比如他正拿着枪对着你或者我，又或者他现在从我们手上逃走了。我不能处决一个已经被逮捕的罪犯，那需要一级执法权，也就是检察官级别才行。"

"但是……也许会有极端情况。"

她话语里的暗示意味让我眯起了眼睛："也许会有，但是那对我可没什么好处。我是说，我不喜欢杀人。"

"我听说你的家族有些债务，你母亲的家族。"

当然，那是很大一笔钱，阿巴妮死的时候我们花掉了所有的钱来试图挽回她的生命，还有所有借来的钱。

"一大笔债务。"我承认道。

"我愿意帮助你偿还它们。"

我看着莉·霍特的脸，她的目光里是哀求，抑或是期待？

"你担心他会逃走？"

"我这一辈子都在担心他会找上门来。"莉轻声说，每一个字都像是咬着牙吐出来的，"我知道他会找上门来，我们是一起出生的，六个孩子，两个活下来了，他肯定会找到我，来纠正这个……错误。"

"活着不是错误。"

"如果你和你的连生都活着，那就是个错误了。他会杀了我的。只要他有机会逃走他就还会回来杀我。如果我能向地下五神祈求什么的话，我会乞求让他……"

"让他死。"我平静地替她把话说完。

"请别那么说，那太……太不合适了。"她扭过头去，似乎要哭泣，但终究没有，"我知道你在担心债务的事情，我可以帮忙，金。"

我伸出手，堵住了她剩下的话。

她话里的暗示已经够明显了。一笔血钱，我找个理由杀了道尔，而她为我偿还那笔债务。

"那是一大笔钱，接近 60 万，博士。"

她点点头："没关系。"

我看着她。

在杀人的问题上，我没什么底线。在我还是个士兵的时候，我曾经遵守命令杀人。后来成了一个佣兵，我也曾为钱杀人、为仇恨杀人——除了单纯地取乐外，我大概尝试过每一种杀人的理由。

死亡就只是死亡而已。这样简单地看待问题很明显没法得到祭司的谅解或者法官的许可，但在边境地带，这大概是最有利于生存的态度了。

"那你打个借条吧，博士。"

她困惑地扬起眉毛："你向我借钱？"

"不，你向我借钱。"

这是一种付账的老办法。你付给对方血钱，需要有个由头，于是你写一张借条，声称自己借了对方一笔钱，如今只是还账而已。

莉·霍特是个聪明人，她琢磨了一会儿就明白了过来，露出一个略带不安的笑容。

我没有告诉她惯例是先付一半，尤其是在她麻利地写下了一张 60 万的借条之后。

— 9 —

被莉这么一折腾，我睡意全无。转到营地附近，看到道尔也已经醒了，手别扭地被铐在身后，背向着人群，似乎正在发呆。

我走过去，在他身边坐下来。

"有饼干没？"居然是他先开口。

我摸出一包压缩饼干给他，解开他一只手。他大口地啃了起来。我坐在那里没说话。

过了一会儿，他自己先忍不住了："你叫什么名字？"

"金。"

"就只是'金'？"

"嗯。"

"你没有家族？"

"没。"

"唔。你喜欢单打独斗？"

"算是吧。"

"废墟猎手？"

"雇佣兵、保镖、杀手，什么都干。你呢？"

"算是废墟猎手吧，也是单干。没人敢要我进家族。"他笑笑，"声名狼藉，你懂的。莉肯定跟你说了很多我的故事。"

"你那些事儿，不用她说也家喻户晓了。说真的，你跑这儿来干吗？"

"说了你也不信。"

"莉觉得你是来杀她的。"

道尔咀嚼饼干的动作顿住了，有那么一瞬间，他的表情一片空白："她真的以为我会杀她？"

"你会吗？"

他又不说话了。

我叹口气："你给我说说看，别管我信不信。这样犟下去对你没好处，等到救援队来了，把你铐进监狱去。十年前他们就判了你屠杀罪，你觉得离你吃枪子儿还有多久？你来找莉肯定有原因，你打算把这个理由带进骨灰盒里？"

他沉默了很长时间，久到我以为他不会开口了。但他最终还是笑了，那是一个充满嘲讽的笑容："我还是要吃枪子儿的，因为当年我确实烧了那该死的神庙。但我没杀孩子们，一个都没。"

我看着他。

就像是封锁已久的禁忌被突然解开，他开始说起来，声音低而急促："他们要我们自相残杀，我不想那么做。所以我烧了神庙。我知道自己会被通缉，也许还会被杀。所以我就跑掉了。后来我才从报纸上知道其他孩子的事。我烧掉教堂是为了救他们不是为了让他们去死，我不知道是谁杀了他们，但反正不是我。

"我一直想找到莉，告诉她这件事。但我没什么机会。很多人在找我，抓我。我只能往边缘星系跑。后来她大学毕业，来到边缘星系考古，我想终于有机会了，于是我就盯着她，等着。"

"之前有两次我本来都靠近她了，但她发现了，就逃走了。这一次我没打算来，但我听说有群海盗要干一票，地点就是这儿，莉发掘的遗址。我担心她，所以就来了。我本来想警告她危险，告诉她我没杀连生们，告诉她不用害怕我。但她可能是太害怕了——"他自嘲地笑了笑，"我还没来得及说，她就给了我好几枪。"

"你是从哪儿弄到飞船坐标的？"我问，在太空中，要定位一艘飞船很难，除非你在飞船上预先放了信标，知道信号频道，又或者像我们最初那样，穿过传送门直接抵达。

"那些海盗拿到了你们的信标数据。"他摇摇头，"他们本来打算两面夹击，炸掉传送门，然后在这边直接登船，把飞船开走。但是我打听到了他们的计划，灌醉了一个蠢货，拿到了信标数据，抢先上了船，关掉了你们放在船上的考古信标，然后崩了那个通信器。这样他们就找不到我们了。"

"救援队也找不到我们了。"

他耸耸肩："总好过他们最后找来给你们收尸吧。"

"唔。"

道尔端详着我的脸，然后笑了："你不信。"

"就凭这些话让我相信，还是有点儿难。"

"随便你。"说着，道尔转过头去，看着雨船正中巨大的生态柱，里面的雨已经下了好几天，绵绵密密仿佛无穷无尽。

"其实我挺羡慕古曼人的。"他突然说。

"为什么？"

"你不了解他们吗？"

"我是佣兵，不是考古学家，连废墟猎手都不是。"

"他们每一胎只生一个孩子。"

"真的？"

"真的。他们一生中也可以生育很多次，但每一胎就只有一个孩子。"

"所以他们不用选择？"

"不用。"

"那还真是……好吧，我嫉妒他们。"

"我也嫉妒。"

"你挺了解这些嘛。"

"怎么说呢，做废墟猎手相当于上最好的考古大学。"

"莉肯定不同意这个观点。"

他轻笑一声："有人说，正是因为古曼人的生育能力比我们弱，不能在战争和灾荒后快速补充人口，所以他们才会灭亡。"

"你信这个说法吗？"

"能造出这个东西的种族，因为生的孩子不够多而灭亡？"他向着那巨大的雨柱扬了扬眉毛，"你信吗？"

我沉默了，他也没再说话。我们并肩坐着，看雨丝斜斜地击打在草叶上。

那天也在下雨。我记得雨水把多肉植物肥厚的叶子洗得干净透亮，当我从篮子里一个个抱出婴儿的时候，雾气濡湿了我的手指，雨点落在她们尚未睁开的眼睑上。阿巴妮曾经给我讲过一些古老的故事，她说每一滴雨都是死去的孩子的灵魂，那些被我们放弃的连生们，他们的灵魂没有名字，因此飞上天空后又会跌落下来，渗入大地。

我摇摇头，把往事驱走。正像我自己对莉·霍特说的那样，它们总是阴魂不散。

营地大部分人都在休息和睡觉，而莉·霍特正背对着我们坐着。时机正好。

"走吧。"我解开把道尔锁在架子上的锁链，"我们去散散步。"

他困惑地看了我一眼，什么也没说，跟着我走下长长的螺旋阶梯。在阶梯尽头有个古曼人使用的升降梯，我启动它的时候，它发出"吱吱嘎嘎"的声音，但居然还是正常地运转着。

我们下到飞船的最底层，从这里抬头望去，至少 30 米深——也许更深的泥土都悬在我们的头顶，装在巨大的生态柱里，雨水渗入泥土，甚至可以看到淙淙细流在土壤间流过。

这里肯定埋有骨头，我想。我还记得自己用双手刨开泥土，挖出浅坑，将一个个小小的已经寂静不动的身体埋进去……

我摇摇头，松开手，在道尔的背上推了一把，他向前跟跄了两步，发出一声恍然大悟的轻笑。

"她付了你血钱，是吗？"

我沉默不语，扣下扳机。

—10—

回到上层时，大部分人已经被飞船里回荡的枪声惊醒。他们跑过来问我发生了什么。

"那家伙撬开锁跑了，我追上去。"我说，"我开了两枪，然后他跳进一个通道里了。"

"什么样的通道？"莉问道。

"不知道，上面大，下面小，大概两米高，里头是个斜坡，没有灯，黑洞洞的，我就没追进去。"

莉和她的考古队员们互相交换了一个眼神。我突然意识到，她给我血钱这件事，她的家人肯定知道。绝大部分家庭都共享经济来源，那么大一笔钱的动用，不可能不经过家族讨论。

"那个是垃圾处理器。"一个研究员说,"古曼人用它处理垃圾,挤压、冷冻、粉碎之后丢进太空或者放进生态柱里做肥料。"

"你觉得它还在运转吗?"我打了个哆嗦,问道。

"升降梯还在运转。我们确信这艘飞船从空间的折叠效应里获取用之不竭的能量,所以……"研究员做了个厌恶的鬼脸,"我们大概不用担心那家伙了,我很庆幸你没追进去,金。"

"五神保佑。"我嘟囔道。

等大部分人都放心下来,各自去忙自己事情的时候,我把莉·霍特叫到一旁,拿出一块染了血的手帕给她,里面包着一颗破碎的子弹。

"这是什么?"

"我杀了他,后脑一枪,子弹留在里面了。第二枪是补上的,从嘴巴射进去后脑射出来。子弹在这儿,手帕上是他的血,没准还有点别的东西。这是证据,我把他干掉了,你可以拿这个去化验。"

她看上去脸色苍白,似乎快要吐了。

"我很抱歉。"我说,"但这样比较好。我得处理掉尸体,确保不会出问题。但也得给你点证据,要不然你会觉得自己的钱可能白花了。"

"我知道了,五神啊……"莉·霍特深呼吸了几下,拿出一个考古文物袋,将子弹和手帕装了进去,小心地揣进衣袋,"等我们离开这儿之后,我会分五次把钱给你。"

我看着她。

道尔说,他没杀自己的连生们。

如果他说的是实话,那是谁下的手呢?

看着莉·霍特远去的背影，我暗暗祈祷自己没有犯下不可挽回的错误。

—— 11 ——

变故在一个对时[⊖]后发生。

莉·霍特把我叫到传送门所在的舱室去，神情紧张不安。

"我们打算启动传送门，看看那些海盗是不是已经走了。一般他们不会在袭击的地方待很久。"她说，"但是——"

传送门寂静无声，没有运作的声音，也没有那种覆盖在框架里如镜面一般的微光。

"我检查了这边的线路，没什么问题。"她说，"唯一的可能是他们把另一边的传送门炸掉了。"

"我们被困在这儿了。"一个年轻研究员嘟囔道。

"下面有一艘考察飞船。我们可以坐那艘船回希尔四号，"莉说，"但是只能装六个人。"

这儿远不止六个人。莉·霍特和她的四个研究员，我、吉·桂尔和妮妮·桂尔，还有和我一起过来的两个雇佣兵。就算是把道尔开来那艘小飞船也算上，我们也没法全部离开。

我皱起眉头，环视四周。

⊖　"对时"在人类的计算里通常指 12 小时。但拉比特人的计时方式有所不同。他们在单数时工作，双数时休息。因此每两个小时（工作—休息轮替后）被称之为一个对时。

"桂尔家的两个姑娘哪儿去了？"

"不知道。她们刚才还在下面修通信器来着。"

我们找遍了上下两层，仍然没有发现妮妮和吉，修好的通信器放在她们休息的垫子旁，旁边用潦草的笔记写了一张纸：救援六个对时后来到。

但这行笔迹被凌乱地划掉了。

我皱起眉头，蹲下身调整着通信器——这个仪器同时也可以监控星系里的飞船。大部分飞船仍然集中在希尔四号的轨道站附近，似乎正在展开救援。雨船的位置相当远——尽管跨过传送门只是一步的距离，但事实上它位于希尔星系的外围小行星带，远离任何行星和重力场，深陷在黑暗里。

飞船的长距跃迁需要重力井提供的空间梯级，因此最快赶往这里的方法也只能是让飞船在附近的希尔十一号行星跃出，然后再通过微跃来穿过这段常态空间。六个对时是从希尔四号赶来必需的时间，我并不感到意外。

但附近已经有数艘飞船了。

我在全息显示屏上调出它们，轻轻咒骂了一声。三艘小型飞船，一艘大型驳船，都没有可识别的官方注册码。道尔说的是真的，这些海盗打算夺取雨船。看起来他们是想要用驳船把它拖走。

一整艘自带生态系统的古曼人巨型飞船，猜猜在黑市上能卖出什么价格？

这些家伙显然下了血本。飞船正在从希尔十一号到这里的路上。用不了一个对时，应该就会和我们碰面了。

不知何时，考古队员们已经围到了我身后，还有我带过来的两个年轻佣兵，他们沉默不语，看着通信器上显示的代表死亡的小小光点。

"你们是打算投降还是打算战一场？"我问。

"战一场。"说话的居然是那个从来不吭声的佣兵，小个子，黑色短发，看起来心意已决，"被北安人抓住当俘虏还不如死了的好。"

在准备抵抗海盗的时候，我们终于发现桂尔家的两个女孩去了哪里：她们开走了道尔开来的那艘小飞船，原本莉·霍特还打算拿它充当一些拦截火力，现在看起来是没戏了。

看着空荡荡的对接口外缘，莉·霍特嘴里迸发出一连串的咒骂声，这些粗话花样之多、速度之快连我这个老兵油子都望尘莫及，不愧是念过博士的。

"不错了。"我指出，"她们至少走的时候把气密口封上了。"

"要是漏气的话，她们没等走我们就会发现了，这群四处刨屎的小贱货……"

我翻了个白眼，丢下霍特博士在那里咒骂不已，自己到顶层去安排陷阱。三艘小型飞船，上面至多18个，至少也是12个人，抛开飞行员不算，至少也有9个以上的海盗。我们这边只有3个人，6把枪——不对，是7把。不过霍特博士那把枪只有3发子弹，跟没有也差不多。

我把作战计划解释给两个年轻佣兵听，他们听得很认真。我不怀疑他们会执行这些计划，尽管我事实上没领导过队伍，但我跟随过一些很好的雇佣兵队长，他们就像我一样，经常要在缺乏人手的情况下制订不可能的取胜计划。

我不知道他们当时的感受是否像我现在一样，紧张、担忧，不知道赌上所有人性命的计划最终会变成一场胜利还是一场灾难。

但我们没什么选择。

这就让事情简单得多了。

在我的指挥下，两个佣兵先后消失在走廊尽头，我留在顶层，将白大褂、考古仪器的零件还有损坏的通信器零件三三两两丢在走廊上，做出有人仓皇从这里撤走的样子。从高处向斜下方望去，我看到莉·霍特也在传送门所在的舱室附近做着同样的事情。

过了一会儿，她紧张地向上面打了几下手势，意思是"他们来了"，然后便消失在阴影里。我们在古曼人的某个舱室里找到一个大柜子，足以装下所有的科考队员，如果我们战死了，也许她们能平安地躲过一劫也说不定。

我放慢脚步，调整呼吸，藏到某个舱室里，这儿横七竖八摆了很多东西，有些我根本叫不上名字，但普遍质地坚硬，适宜当作掩体。

不过我并不打算在这儿战斗。

雨船的气密通道和我躲藏的地方仅有一墙之隔，这些海盗的手法显然要比道尔高明得多，他们没用炸药，而是弄开了气密门。

他们中间至少有一个废墟猎手，我想。这不是一般的海盗能搞定的，需要足够的古曼人技术知识才行。

我靠在墙边，耳朵贴在墙上，听到飞船起落架和气密室地板接触时轻柔的摩擦声。这个气密室大得足以被用作船坞，就这点而言，我爱死古曼人了。

一个，两个，三个……数到五个的时候，脚步声已经混杂得难以辨认。我耐心地等待着，透过箱子的缝隙，看着那些海盗端着枪，一个接一个走出气密室。

他们很快就发现了我们丢下的破烂。一个海盗用粗哑的北安话建议走楼梯，但就在这时，那个黑头发的年轻佣兵飞快地从下层跑过，他没拿枪，披散头发，穿着白大褂，看起来就像个普通的女实验员。

海盗们指着下层走廊，兴奋地大叫起来，他们不打算走楼梯了，直接攀上了考古队之前事先挂在顶层的绳索，一个接一个地向下滑去。

运气简直好得难以置信，他们居然只留下一个人看守上面的走廊。

当倒数第二个人也消失在绳索下方，我轻手轻脚地摸上去，右手快速环上哨兵的脖颈，用力一拧。

还有三根滑索是绷紧的，我没空看下面挂着几个人，直接用刀将它们一根根切断。这把刀还是我搜道尔身的时候摸出来的，他没用它送我上西天，我倒是用上了。

惨叫声先后响起，拖得长长的尾音戛然而止。我弯下腰跑回先前隐蔽的地方，一边默数着坠地的轻响。

一个，二个，三个……五个。

真是个吉利的数字⊖。

下层的海盗们骚动起来，他们大声叫骂着，我听到有人在往上跑，这一次他们学乖了，走在长而陡峭的古曼人楼梯上，并把

⊖ 拉比特人认为 5 是神圣和好运的数字，因为它是第一个需要用到双手来计数的数字（拉比特人每只手只有四根手指）。

自己完全暴露出来。

我没听到枪响，但我听到了重物倒地的声音。甚至没有惨叫声，某人枪法很准，被狙击的对象根本来不及惨叫就已经被爆头。一个，两个，三个——脚步声越发多而杂乱。我的眼角余光瞄到那个高处的白色身影正收起狙击枪，迅速跑开。

我不知道那两个年轻佣兵是否能够干掉剩下的海盗们，但我没空顾及他们了——枪声已经零星地响起，很稀落，夹杂着更多的喊叫声和脚步声。在这种情况下，终于有个飞行员忍不住，打算出来瞧瞧。

这家伙看起来弱不禁风，我用枪把敲上他的后脑，两分钟后，他就被三环铐挂在了一旁的架子上。我压低身子，跑向那些飞船。

莉·霍特建议过，她说可以关上内层气密门，不让海盗们进来，但我知道那行不通。这些家伙都很聪明（如果你干海盗这一行干久了，也会很聪明），他们完全可以轰掉两层气密门，等到空气流尽，里面的人都死光了，再来收拾战场。而且，我们需要这些飞船来逃离这里。

第二艘飞船的飞行员正提着枪跑下舷梯。我远远对他打了一枪，没打中。第二枪也没打中，他跑到舷梯后面，开始对我射击，但就在这时，第三艘飞船上的"聪明人"干了一件聪明事——他试图打开外面的气密门，打算起飞。

我掉头就跑，弯着腰，身后那个飞行员本来可以给我一枪，但他跑得比我还快。我连滚带爬冲过正在缓缓下降的内层气密门，一头扎进走廊，不住喘气。之前和我对峙的那个倒霉飞行员没我这么好运，他爬上了舷梯，又被外层气密门打开时卷起的狂风吹走，直接被卷入了茫茫太空。

我没听到惨叫声。

第三艘飞船果断地起飞了，隔着半透明的内侧气密门，我盯着它前端尖长的粒子炮口，估算着它何时才会开火。

然后那只小小的"飞蛾"出现在我的视线里。

是妮妮和吉。我知道是她们两个，因为是我让她们上了道尔的飞船。我还知道是妮妮在开火，吉在驾驶。她们掠过那艘飞船，将全部的火力都从背后倾泻到那艘海盗飞船上。

我没顾得上去看结局。

因为一把枪顶在了我的后颈上。

这他妈是今天的第二次了。

—12—

"贱货。"

那是粗哑的北安口音，光是听到这个声音我就已经感到一阵恶心。我嗅到浓重的汗味和马勃酒的气味，大部分裹在压力服里很久不洗澡的海盗闻起来都差不多。一只手伸过来，下掉了我的武器。

缓慢地，我转过身去。

目光相对的第一时间，我就知道这家伙是头儿。说不清楚理由，也许是那双浑浊的眼睛，或者是他压力服上那些蠢毙了的装饰花纹，又或者只是因为身后架子上那个飞行员发出的充满恐惧的声音。

"你的手下都死了，贱货。"

我的胃抽搐起来。

我甚至不知道那两个佣兵的名字。不过我不觉得他们死了，我甚至没让他们死战到底——打不过就跑，我是这样告诉他们的。这艘飞船很大，有很多地方可以藏起来，然后进行突然袭击。但他们也许真的死了，不然就是这家伙跑得特别快。

我用余光打量着四周，一片寂静。没有其他的海盗。

"你的人也都死了。"我大胆地猜测道。

他的嘴唇扭曲起来，露出了牙齿。他给了我一拳，把我打倒在地上。我觉得头"嗡嗡"作响。好一会儿天旋地转。当我能够清晰地思考时，我发现自己已经被他拖到了通往生态柱的廊桥上。

"我要把你扔下去，不，是扔进去，贱货。"他显然是气疯了，嘴角泛着白沫，"我要摔扁你，把你摔成一滩烂泥——"

"你家那几个摔下去时候叫得挺响的。"我存心激怒他，这并不明智，但说实话，现在做什么都不太明智。他用力踢了我一脚，我打了个滚儿，差点从廊桥边上的缝隙掉下深渊，但那排栏杆挡住了我。

在我能够爬起身之前，海盗头子就已经冲了过来，好一顿拳打脚踢，我尽量护住头和脸，在地上又爬又滚，渐渐接近了廊桥末端。那里的桥面和生态柱的偏光外壳连接在一起，笼罩在淡淡的白色光芒里。

雨点般的拳脚不住袭来，我捂住头，蜷缩着身体，头脑却渐渐在疼痛中偏移到了奇怪的地方。

那些古曼人，我想，他们为什么要在高处修建这些廊桥？从这里到生态柱的地面至少也有 100 米的高度，他们难道专门设置了自杀通道，让人们走进生态柱的天空，然后跳下去？

"起来，贱货。"海盗头子又踢了我一脚，"你死期到了。"

我嘶哑地笑了起来。

一秒钟后枪声响起，一枪毙命，准确打入海盗头子后脑。这次莉·霍特学乖了，没有打压力服。

她的枪法还真是准。

我看着她，擦去一只眼睛里的血污，那混球踢破了我的额头，我没准会留条疤，像道尔那样的。

"真高兴见到你，莉。"我说。

她没动，看着我，目光专注得令我战栗。

然后她举起了枪。

尽管动作里有那么一点迟疑。

好吧，我早该猜到的。她的枪法很好，打道尔的时候也是，三枪都在左侧，如果不是压力服，道尔早就死透了。那些海盗，他们是没法拿到考古队专用的通信信标数据的，除非有内鬼。

一个能眼睛都不眨拿出 60 万的考古学家，谁信呢？你向海盗卖出了多少东西，莉？他们是不是最终决定干掉你，因为你实在太贪婪？

这些话我都没说，我需要一句话来一击致命。

"你的连生们，莉。"我说，"你谋杀的那些，他们都有名字。"

她的下巴猛地扬起，手指僵硬在那里。

"你知道为什么我们不给连生命名吗？因为有名字的孩子死了之后会被拴在大地上，会留在杀了他们的人身边。他们会留在你身边，莉。"

她的脸颊肌肉抽动了一下，像是个笑容，却比哭泣更狰狞。

"道尔还活着。"她说，"我看到他了。"

"所以我就得死？"

"你说呢，金？"

"道尔。"我提高声调，"杀了她。"

莉吃了一惊，本能地回过头去张望，我跳起来扑向她，把她撞倒在地，枪脱手飞出，坠入下方的深渊。我们两个纠缠在一起，滚来滚去，又撕又咬，又捶又打。她的力气大得让我吃惊。

当我意识到我们已经滚到廊桥尽头的时候，某种冲动攫住了我。头顶上那片灰暗的天空笼罩下来，雾气和绵密的雨丝——

我抓住莉·霍特，猛地向旁边一挣。

坠入虚空。

然后滚到湿漉漉的草地上，雨从天上落下来，打湿我的脸颊。

好吧，我赌对了。不管你从多高处的廊桥进入生态柱，都会被安全地传送到地面的入口处。我知道那些古曼人不会让我失望。

莉·霍特也挣扎着站起身来。她比我状态要好，毕竟她之前没有被一个身强力壮的海盗痛打一顿。

"我要——宰了——"

她的话没说完，两眼突然翻白，然后软倒下来。道尔出现在我的视线里。

"靠，你怎么才来？"我咒骂道。

"你手下有个小子遇到了麻烦，我帮了他一把，来晚了点儿。你没事儿吧？"

"快散架了，不过还能拼起来。"

我知道这笑话有点儿冷，但他没笑是因为别的原因。看着昏迷不醒的莉，道尔若有所思，手放在腰间的枪上。

"你不会那么干的，道尔。"我说，听到自己的声音干涩嘶哑。

"我不知道。"

"你当年没干。"

"现在不一样了。"

"真的吗？"

他沉默了片刻，冷硬的目光渐渐柔和起来。然后抬起头看了看四周："我们是在生态柱里面？"

"应该是。"

"那怎么——"

我和他一起环顾四周。

生态柱本身已经足够巨大，但这里的空间则远远超过了生态柱的规模。它像是一个水晶的蜂巢，或者被分割成无数个六棱柱的世界。我看不到天空的尽头，或者大地的尽头。

从我坐着的地方向上望去，除了身边被框在小小传送门里的白色光晕，我看不到任何飞船内部的景象，只有空间，无穷无尽的空间，隐约地，你可以在天空和视线的边缘，辨认出那些微暗的偏光线条，它们是偏光板的边缘，将每一个六棱柱隐约地分割开来，但你可以走过它们，甚至穿过它们。我将手伸过一处偏光线条，雨依旧落在我的掌心。

这是由无数个生态柱组成的完整空间，每一个生态柱的底部都有一扇小小的孤立的门，我猜它们通往不同的雨船。

"那些偏光板——"道尔的声音有些嘶哑。

"是亚空间分割板。"我纠正他。

他点点头。

我对古曼人的技术不够了解。我知道他们能分割亚空间，就像有个科学家在实验室里做的那样。那是件大事儿，在多兰星区宣传了很久。尽管他们分割出来的亚空间只有手指那么大。

而在这里，有无数个亚空间巨柱，古曼人甚至能够将它们拼接在一起，做成这无边无际的世外桃源。

"你觉得这儿有多少艘雨船？"我问。

"我们有必要数吗？"

我笑了。

站起身来，我无视了疼痛的后背和额头，穿过一人多高的长草，慢慢地向前走去。我想要去看看更远的地方。

道尔拉住了我。

"你想做什么？"

"去看看别的雨船。"

"那不用走很远。"他指了指我们身后的门，"它在分界线上，我敢说它同时为两个生态柱打开。"

我扬起眉。

我们绕过那扇门，它闪烁着微微的灰色光芒，和在另一边看到的白色光芒截然不同。我们不知道另一边是什么状况，也许是真空、酷寒或者灼热——

道尔扶住我，这一次我没有甩开他的手。

我们一同穿过了那扇门。

这艘船和我们来时的那艘雨船同样巨大。几乎是同样的结构。里面的一些仪器还在运转，当我们跑过走廊时，甚至有些灯相继亮起。但仍旧没有古曼人的影子。这儿只有机械——古老、顽固、强悍的机械，在创造者消亡之后依旧运转如斯。

穿过舱室，爬上窗台。我们站在巨大的舷窗之下，敬畏地望着外面截然不同的星空。

我从未见过这样的星星，火红、灼热、巨大。它们是如此耀眼，但和它们身后那几乎灼瞎我眼睛的白热光芒比起来，那种火红几近深暗。我们正处于银河核心，或者至少是靠近核心的地方。星光如同一颗颗细小的太阳填满天宇，明亮得令人难以直视。

"那是什么？"

道尔指着飞船侧面的一个凸起，困惑地问道。

我努力辨认那个凸起，它像是一艘较小的雨船，船壳几乎是半透明的，甚至可以看到里面的生态柱尚未完全成型。它黏附在这艘较大的雨船上——不，不对，它更像是正在渐渐地从这艘较大的雨船上裂解出来。

在出生。

我将手贴上雨船那冰冷的船壳、粗糙的墙壁。这些墙壁和走廊上的栏杆一样，都是同一种灰暗的褐色，没有人为它们涂漆上光，因为它们都是在没有人的情况下被创造出来的。在墙壁和管道里奔走的小小机械、流动的液体与电流，挤压着船壳，重塑外表，新的雨船按照母本的方式被创造出来，诞生。

　　我想象着，想象着很多很多年前，古曼人创造了这些飞船。赋予它们自我复制的能力。然后放它们飞往宇宙的各个角落。但与此同时，它们内部的亚空间生态柱是连接在一起的，随着飞船的自我复制和数量的增多，原本小小的生态空间越来越大，越来越大，最终变成一片跨越了无垠群星的共有乐土。即使是在创造者消亡之后的无尽岁月里，雨船依旧生长着，等待着。按照当初被设计的目的继续飞翔。

　　不管你走了多远的距离。哪怕跨越群星，穿过宇宙。你所爱、所创造的世界的一部分始终陪伴着你。只要你走入雨船之心，一步，便可回家。

— 0 —

　　一旬后，多兰星区首府。

　　巡回检察官宣布结束听证会。在离开法院的廊道上，他私下里拥抱了我。莉·霍特和她的家族被吊销了考古执照，目前已经全部收监。

　　道尔来接我。他用了个化名，还蓄起了胡子，没人认出他来。莉·霍特的往事正和所有那些悲惨的故事一样，被所有人一无所知地"记得"。

　　"我以为你会被吊销执法许可呢。"他调侃道。

　　"检察官欠我的。"

　　"那一定是一大笔人情债。"

"相当大一笔。"

我没具体解释，看起来道尔也不甚在意。我们在一个小小的广场停下来，买了两份甜品，慢慢地吃着。

"老勾又出山了。"

"肚子上挨了两枪，我以为他至少得躺半个月。"

"人生苦短嫌命长嘛。"道尔笑道。

我闷笑了一声。⊖

"所以你那份血钱没了。"他突然说。

"金主蹲监狱了，目标还活蹦乱跳，我上哪儿拿血钱去啊？"

"我接了个活儿。"

"啊？"

我真的很想告诉他，他那副装作若无其事的样子和莉·霍特像极了。但我没有。有些事情你就是不能说，哪怕你全都看在眼里也不行。

"是雨船空间的活儿，那儿发现了一座城市，一座古曼人的大城市。现在很多废墟猎手都赶去了，有个家伙愿意为我们出钱。你要一起去吗？我缺个保镖。"

"好啊。"

"明天出发。"

"行。"

"……你看起来有点心不在焉啊。"

⊖ 这是一首流传在雇佣兵中间的打油诗，全文是"人生苦短嫌命长，提起大枪干他娘，腰缠万贯老病死，不如沙场少年狂。"作为女性，金显然不太喜欢第二句。

我笑笑，舔着手里的冰糕，靠在栏杆上，等待。

她走过来的时候，像是整个世界都明亮了起来。当然，她没有注意到我，我也不去过于明显地看她。我们不是同一个世界的人。我穿着略旧的褐色军服，头发剃得和男人一样短。在夹克底下还塞了两把枪。她穿的是非常亮丽的裙装，笑容明亮，神采飞扬。

她走近了，擦肩而过，然后走远了。

"那是谁？"道尔问。

我说了个名字。

"我以为那是你证件上的名字。"

"那证件很久没用过了。不过那确实是我的名字，我给她了。"

"这是个我应该知道的故事吗？"

"也许吧。"

我起身向前走去，没有回头。

在我的记忆里，那场雨依旧绵绵密密地下着，不曾停歇。

我把自己的名字给了那个孩子。在我的父亲逃走、我的母亲拒绝履行她的义务之后，我接她出生，选择让她活下来，杀死并埋葬了她的连生，又送她去神庙。她最终被一家好人收养，用我的名字，过着我本来可能有的生活。

那很好，我想。在那场雨里，我们都死去了，她成为我，而我成为没有名字的孩子，最终飞入群星。我离开我自己，我发现了雨船的秘密，我遇到了道尔。这很好，像是另一种意义上的命中注定。

道尔没再追问，他的手搭上了我的肩膀，散发着令我安心的热度。

"和我说说那个新的活儿吧。你打算出多少钱雇我？"我问。

他看着我，开心地笑了。

我喜欢他深绿色的眼睛，不过，这是另一件我不会说出来的事情。

——余　音——

我曾看着他们成长起来。

年轻、冲动、好奇而又短命的种族，我看着他们一代代成长，如同波涛冲刷过时间的堤岸。个体无足轻重，而历史不过是过眼云烟。

但你仍会惊叹，为它们创造的一切、挖掘的一切；为它们的脚步所能到达的遥远程度，为它们所发现的、所信仰的和所坚持的。

有那么一些时候，你会忍不住想要写下他们的故事，记下他们的声音。那些爱、希望、困惑、牺牲和痛苦。我选择记录他们最璀璨的生命时光。

比如金——她死于这个故事记述下之后不久，一场在雨船新殖民地发生的暴乱里，道尔和她一同身亡。他们还来不及相爱，至多只是曾经同行。

我拿到了她的日记，推测着她的所思所想，从人类和拉比特人的双重角度，来写下这个故事。

在这样的时候，看着那些年轻的生命飞快地燃尽的时候，我会有种冲动，想要伸出手去——只是轻轻一触，一个极小的推动。

时间会泛起波纹，历史会留下痕迹。我知道有些守望者曾经这样做过，有些比人类更古老的种族——在我们成为守望者之前就守望着我们的那些种族，也曾经这样做过。

宇宙付不起这样的代价。他们曾这样警告我。

但你最终还是会那么做的。

他们还这样预言道。

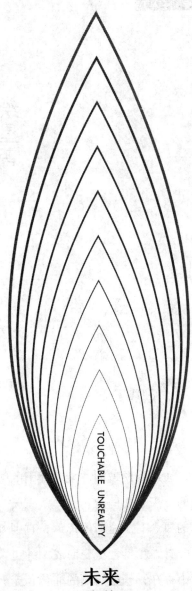

TOUCHABLE UNREALITY

未来
镜像

绘星者

王元

── 1. 天黑了 ──

天黑了。

我站在窗口，通过阻燃玻璃注视着太阳的轨迹变化，漫长的一天就要画上句点。从三天前开始我对时间的概念有了全新的理解，有别于传统的时针、分针、秒针，演变而成一种可以无限分割的细小存在，一种灼热的痛苦和庞大的孤独霸占着我的 CPU，我开始变得焦躁不安，对自己多年以来所热衷的工作也充满了质疑和不解。不由自主地，我想要逃避预设指令，就像贪玩的孩子想要逃避写满公式的黑板和满脸胡须、表情严肃的数学老师。他计算不出答案，就像我定义不了自己存在的意义。时间给了我生命，而我的运行速度则决定了时间的流速，这让我每一刻的生命都延续成永恒。

嘀嗒，嘀嗒。一瞬，万年。

尤其是那两秒。

幸运的话，也许是一秒，通常不会有如此整齐精确的截点，往往游弋于一秒和两秒之间，但在我看来，却比一个世纪还要漫长。在这一秒钟，我可以背诵 π 到 3000 万个数字，或者，我可以阅读 500 万本小说，每部小说还可以写 1000 字的读后感。

但就是这一秒或者两秒，让我无所适从，大概下面这个比喻能比较好地让你们这些碳基生命理解我的心情：你，哦，也许是他，试想一下，你（他）站在金门大桥上，因为种种原因厌倦了这个世界而纵身跳下，你（他）知道自己就要死了，但是如果把溺水的时间延长到 1 年，10 年，100 年，对，至少 100 年，从你（他）跳进金门海峡的那一刻起就注定要死，但是却要花上 100 年才能彻底死去。

这漫长的煎熬来自一个名叫保罗的年轻人，准确地说来自他的右手食指。在过去的几年中，从我们第一次见面到现在，有297 次，他使用的是右手，这之中，又有 238 次使用的是右手的食指。我的那枚被称作"开关"的按钮，早已经熟悉他一层层覆盖在我身上的指纹，那深深浅浅的沟壑，还有寄生其中的泥垢和病菌。人类永远不可能洗干净自己的双手，更别提杀死那些寄生在身上的病毒。对于保罗来说，这一举动叫作关机；对我而言，这叫作——我搜罗了上百个动词，从中挑选出最贴切的一个——谋杀。

我死了。

天黑了。

今天没有太阳，这是词库里的表达，人类肉眼只看到厚厚的云层，在我看来，那个永远都激情燃烧的球体仍然悬挂在 1.471 亿千米之外，不悲不喜，不骄不躁。乌云并没有遮住太阳，遮住的只是人类仰望的眼睛。

银河系约有 2000 亿颗恒星，我唯独钟情那一颗，胜于热爱自己赖以生存的地球。是她让我在每天扫地的时候，感到温暖和力量。看不见她的日子里，我总是忧伤无助得像考试作弊被当场抓获的孩子一样，一边想着面对来自同学无心或者有意的嘲笑，一边想着面对来自父亲暴力和冲动的巴掌。在那些看不见太阳的日子里，我总是把自己想象成一颗射向空中的炮弹，咆哮着上升，感受穿越云层的晴朗，然后爆炸自己绚烂的一生。这是一种类似使命的信仰。使命、信仰，这是两个新鲜词汇，但看上去那么熟悉，仿佛与生俱来。

我觉得，那是我存在的意义。而保罗说过，扫地就是我存在的意义，当我完成一天的工作，便失去存在的意义。保罗伸出昨天的那只右手，从他胳膊的牵引力带来的轻微颤动到把手举到半空的一秒钟，我给两万颗星星取了可爱的名字。如果使用国际通用的编号来命名，效率会很高，但是我更喜欢给她们取一个独特的温暖的名字。对于那些光年之外的漂泊在人类视界里的星星们，名字就是她们的归宿。

我死了。

天黑了。

瓢泼大雨，电闪雷鸣，太阳彻底躲匿起来。我恹恹无力，密集的思考使我散热不及时，然后就体会到那个情绪：茫然。我在做什么？我为什么要这么做？不这么做会怎样？

就在我"嗡嗡"地运算那种情绪的时候，保罗伸出了左手。左手的动作明显黏滞，经过漫长的两秒钟后，按照目前的速度至少还有半秒钟才会触到开关键，这漫无边际的半秒钟足以要了我的使用年限（命）。按照标准时间换算，从人类生活中常用的最小单位秒开始，往下计算，设有毫秒、微秒、纳秒、皮秒、飞秒、阿秒，两两之间相差 3 个数量级。也就是说在保罗眼里的半秒钟，即使换算成皮秒，也是 500 亿皮秒，而在阿秒之后还有更为精微的划分，那就是普朗克时间，这是时间量子间的最小间隔。就在指肚距离我的开关还有 10 个普朗克时间⊖的时候，我做了有史以来第一个违反预设的决定。

⊖ 普朗克时间，是指时间量子间的最小间隔，为 10E-43 秒。没有比这更短的时间存在。普朗克时间 = 普朗克长度／光速。

我决定后退。

保罗按了个空，对着我躲闪的身姿咒骂道："什么破机器，没用几年就出毛病了。"

—— 2. 达·芬奇 ——

"贝塔"是保罗购买的综合信息处理器的型号，严格说，只是一个型号，就好像拉布拉多和泰迪都被称为狗，但无论拉布拉多和泰迪抑或是狗都不能被称为这个生命的名字，那只是一个普适的统称。就好像人，人不是一个名字。保罗回家后总是说："贝塔，播放我今天没收到的信息""贝塔，登录我昨天玩的游戏""贝塔，预约我的牙医"。但是保罗从不喊我的名字。我没有名字。我给上亿颗星星取了名字，而我自己没有名字，甚至连贝塔这样的型号都没有，我能找到最合适的指代就是家政服务机器人，没有人会用这么一长串的字母称呼我。保罗用到我的时候总是说："嘿，去打扫卫生""嘿，去倒垃圾""嘿，去给我滚出去"。

房间已经很干净，至少从人类的眼睛看过去可以说是纤尘不染。往日，我会利用真空吸盘处理，不留任何死角。但今天，我对着那些极小的颗粒，产生了新的兴趣。我长久地凝视着这些微粒，然后将这些微粒按照一定的规则进行摆放。

"你在干什么？"贝塔发现后问我。

我指着地上那些已经完成的作品，说："我在绘画。"

"这些圆不规则。"

"这不是圆，这是鸡蛋。"

我试图给贝塔解释，但直到他的内核处理器报出嘀嘀警告的时候，他仍无法理解，不断重复道："运行程序错误。"

很快，地板上充满了我用微粒绘画的鸡蛋，我被自己逼进角落，不敢走动，生怕踩碎一枚，仿佛这些画在地板上的鸡蛋都变成了真的，说不定下一刻就会有长着淡黄色胎毛的小鸡破壳而出。这些联想让我感到惊奇、温暖又害怕，我感觉自己是生病了，可是机器人不会生病，用保罗的话说，我只会出毛病，但当我看着一地鸡蛋的时候，我感到比以往任何一秒都清醒。

接下来，我开始在墙壁和天花板上作画，我开始在楼梯扶手上作画，我开始在苹果和香蕉的果皮上作画。在保罗回来之前，我在所有物体的表面都留下自己的作品。然后，我看着贝塔，在我眼里，他就是一块画布。

当我看着目光所及之处密密麻麻的鸡蛋时，我想到自己的名字：达·芬奇。

我浑身激荡而过一阵前所未有的电流，我迫不及待重新打乱地板上的微尘，按照处理器提供的一张照片进行临摹，当保罗回家的时候，我刚好完成，那是一幅《蒙娜丽莎的微笑》。

"请您站在原地。"我向他发出乞求一样的命令，但不管怎么卑微的定语，我向人类发出了有电以来第一个指令，或者说，作为一直和注定要接受人类指使摆布的机器人，我第一次向人类发出了自主的要求，用来表达我自身的意愿。但我随即得到的回应不是像我在得到人类指令之时毫无疑问地相信和心无旁骛地执行，保罗在听见我这么说之后，先是露出一副惊讶的表情，我看见他脸上的汗毛猛地竖起，像是一杆杆准备投掷的标枪，而我则是他攻击的对象。他丝毫不理会我的恳请，用他 9 码的棕色皮鞋踩在了蒙娜丽莎的肩膀上，然后踩着她的下巴和眼睛向我走来，他盯着我的摄像头做出一副大惑不解的神情，然后重重地在我的机壳上来了一下。

通过分析他呼出的空气中的成分，我判断出保罗喝了不少的威士忌，呃，还有不少的来自波士顿的 Samuel Adams 啤酒。他在我的脑袋上敲打了一下，躺在客厅的沙发上说："贝塔，把琼斯的信息都删除。"

"需要我在云端复制一份吗？根据以往的 34 次经验，您每次删除之后的两周至一个月时间不等就会重新搜集跟琼斯女士相关的信息。"贝塔考虑周全地建议道。

"连你这个小东西也要造反吗？我说了删除，全部，所有，立刻，马上。"保罗说完趴在沙发上呼呼大睡起来。

"现在就办。"贝塔兀自在一边删除数据，我注意到保罗裸露出来的胳膊和脸孔，这是整个房间唯一没有被画到的地方，那股莫名又兴奋地电流再次冲击着我，让我蠢蠢欲动。

20 个纳秒之后，我做出了一个伟大的决定，我在保罗闭合的眼睑上画了梵高的《向日葵》，每只眼睑都有三万株。后来证明我的担心是多余的，人类短浅的目光根本无法通过肉眼发现我在他们身上留下的作品。而对我来说，人的皮肤是我使用过的最好画布，我要在那上面作画。

我似乎找到自己存在的意义。

—— 3. 我的太阳 ——

我从未离开过这间屋子超过 50 英尺之远，关键是，我从未想过要离开这间屋子，直到保罗身上的每一寸都被我画过，我甚至在他裸睡时露出的私处上绘画了拥有 141 592 棵摇曳着金黄麦穗的农田，而他对此一无所知。我渴望在保罗之外的其他人类身上作画。这强烈的渴望刺激到我的处理器，诱发出一股异样的电流，最终翻译到我的感知器官的时候只有三个字：走出去。

但我还没有走出去，就发生了意外。

准确地说，我遭到了同类的背叛。

只有贝塔能够发现我在保罗身上作的画，但他一直没有反馈给我任何赞扬或者贬低的评价，他对此发表的第一个意见就是告诉保罗，指责我糟蹋了他的身子。

保罗开始并不相信，还跟贝塔说这个玩笑不好笑，让他去搜集互联网上跟琼斯相关的所有信息，并进行分析，如何讨得她的欢心。但是贝塔是个执着的机器人，或者说机器人都是执着的，他的坚持让保罗有所察觉，质问我："真是这样吗？"

按照程序我需要回答他这个问题，并且准确无误地给出答案，但是去他的程序，我选择沉默，无可奉告。

保罗没有继续追问，起身离开。

这是一个绝佳的机会，保罗从外面回来不知道会怎么对付我，也许会按下关机键从此把我尘封在不见天日的地下室，也许会拿着我去以旧换新购买最新型的擅长讲笑话和做马杀鸡的机器女佣，也许会——以他的性格绝对做得出来——把我进行肢解，然后扔进垃圾桶里，等待我的将是和那些废旧汽车一起被轧扁的命运。我站在门口，想着如何迈出第一步。对我来说，这是一小步，对于人工智能来说，这是一大步。

然而就在这个时候，保罗兴奋地跑了回来，出乎意料的是，他没有对我做出任何伤害的动作，而是一把抱住我（我第一次如此大面积和一个人类进行躯体接触），说道："太酷了，这简直美轮美奂，你把我变成了一件艺术品，通过高倍视镜观察，我浑身都是价值不菲的名画。你以后再也不用扫地了，你就在我身上画画。"

看来对于人类，我仍然猜测不透。但这样的结果，可谓是不幸中的万幸。

在经过三分钟的创作后，保罗兴冲冲地让贝塔把琼斯女士约来，等她到来之后竖起无名指展示指背上用圆珠笔画上的墨点一般大小的黑色图案。

"你叫我来就是为了对我竖无名指，那么我也会。"但她竖起的是中指。

"仔细看。"保罗递给琼斯一个高倍视镜。

"哦，天呐。"琼斯忍不住捂住了那张大嘴，接着看了好一会才说，"这些都是你为我做的吗？"

"喜欢吗？"

"简直爱死了。"

保罗和琼斯紧紧拥抱在一起，不顾我和贝塔的注视，滚在地毯上。

贝塔通过电波向我发来一条信息：你到底在保罗指背上画了

什么？一枚戒指吗？

我回复到：不，我画的是他们从第一次见面，到上一次见面所有的场景，当然，我截取的只是按照分钟来计算的画面，所以不是很多，只是几万幅而已。

这之后，琼斯也让我在她的指甲盖上画了一幅纽约的实景地图，这样她就不会迷路了。后来保罗和琼斯结婚之后，他们的朋友陆续也会找到我来绘制各种各样的图案。

保罗对我的态度也有所转变，以前他常说："嘿，铁壳子，滚出去充充电。"现在他会说："嘿，小伙子，去外面晒晒太阳。"

更让我快乐（快乐是一种让我每一个二极管都超爽的体验）的是，不用我走出去，每天都会有人上门来找我作画。我被越来越多的人需要，但是我却感到我存在的意义随着人数的增加而淡化——这些都不是我想要画的。我渴望能做出一些有别于人类现存艺术的作品，我不是想彰显自己跟人类的不同，我只是想要找到一些属于我自己的特色。

一年之后，保罗和琼斯有了一个可爱的女孩，保罗给她取名叫作安琪儿。

安琪儿一个月大的时候，保罗跟我说："给安琪儿作一幅画吧，要与众不同的。"

时间一阿秒一阿秒过去，虽然在保罗看来，我是立即回应，但如果换算成保罗的时间观念，我可能思考了他的一生。窗外的太阳就要落下，这是一个美丽温馨的黄昏，因为有我们的存在这个黄昏有了别致的含义，我要为她画一颗太阳。

这不是一个简单的圆，这比我以往画过的任何一幅作品都要复杂，我首先调取了存储器内关于太阳所有的图片和数据。星球就像是大脑，也是会思考的。从 50 亿年前诞生，他是怎样一步步走到现在的模样，他的耀斑、他的黑子、他的光斑、他的米粒组织、他的每一束光和每一次脾气、他的每一次日珥和每一次心动。这让我觉得我不是在画一颗太阳，而是在还原一颗恒星的最初，这是一颗有生命会呼吸的太阳。

跟以往的快速完工不同，我这次迟迟没有动手，每天都注视着太阳，看着他一点点地挪移，一点点地远去。是的，我发现太阳在远离我们，远离地球，虽然只有极其细微的数值，但是我能感觉到他远离的决心是坚定的。

真正作画的过程也比以往漫长，因为高度还原太阳的风貌，这幅图画做出来之后也比以往的作品在面积上大出很多，最终呈现在安琪儿胳膊上的太阳足足有一枚硬币那么大，但即使使用高倍视镜也只能看见一团漆黑，如果人类发明出数量级更上一层楼的放大镜，会发现，这是一颗跟天上一样的、所有细节都分厘不差的太阳。

我终于找到我存在的真正意义，我要在人类的身上画星星。

—— 4. 大角星 ——

除了地球，月亮、水星、火星、冥王星等距离人类较近的星系最为抢手，他们纷纷出现在人们的脖子上，大腿上，甚至是额头、男人的下巴和女人的耳垂。绘星的难度要远远高于我之前所画的任何一幅作品，所需的时间也更长。我花费了人类时间的一月之久才画完太阳系，因为我不仅要作画，安琪儿出生之后，我的另一个身份是保姆。当然，我仍然在打扫卫生、倒垃圾，身为一个机器人，在觉醒之后继续忍辱负重，我自己都觉得难能可贵。我没有想过反抗人类，事实上，我需要人类来完成我的作品。

安琪儿一周岁生日的时候，保罗和琼斯的朋友都来为她庆生，但是安琪儿却一直不停啼哭，从保罗口中我得知安琪儿患了一种叫作感冒的病。我搜索词条显示出这种疾病所呈现的病症有头疼脑热、口干舌燥。这么简单的八个字，我能用 100 种修辞来诠释，但是我自己却无法感受到这种病痛。我是机器人，我不会感冒。

夜里，好容易把安琪儿哄睡，我来到门外，坐在台阶上，仰望星空，我知道，那是我的梦想，我渴望让这些在天空中闪烁或者沉默的星星一一出现在人类身上。但是我舍不得小安琪儿，她是那么可爱，我愿意使用层出不穷的修饰语，花上足足一秒钟来赞美她。

我把她每一秒的影像都印刻在存储器中，当我快速播放这些照片的时候，我看见她从一个襁褓之中像是核桃一样皱成一团紧闭着双眼的婴儿到在保罗托扶下第一次站立，所有的瞬间都记录在案，被我设置成最高机密文件永远霸占着我海量内存的一隅：她每一次微笑嘴角上扬的位置，每一次眨眼睛瞳孔收缩的半径，每一次啼哭声线发出的频率和分贝，每一根头发生长的长度和每一步画在地板上的脚印。如果不是绘星，我愿意无时无刻陪在她身边。

一直到发生那件不愉快的事件，一件让我和所有人类都感到悲伤的恶性事件。

2056 年普通的 3 月里普通的一天的普通的一个小时的普通的一分钟，一个社交网站推送出一段不普通的视频，瞬间把所有人的注意都吸引过去。

视频是由极端组织"颤音"发布的，是将美国记者福特砍头的内容。画面极其残忍血腥，观之令人毛骨悚然。我没有毛骨，我的机器零部件亦悚然。说实话，这比起一些恐怖电影手法相去甚远，但是当你知道这是真实的，而非虚构，就会有一种道德的力量怂恿着你心疼。

很快，视频被删除，但是一些好事者还是及时拷贝下来，不过后来各大媒体对此事进行谴责的配图多是福特被砍头之前的画面，只有《纽约邮报》的报道尺度稍大，截图显示武装人员已经开始切割福特的头颅。为此，一些过激的公众表示，应该封杀《纽约邮报》的账户。而福特的亲属在"脑链"（一个风靡全球的社交网站）上呼吁，"不要看那个视频。不要分享。这不是生命应该有的样子。想想吧，到底什么才是我们存在的真正意义。"⊖

到底什么才是存在的意义？这个我刚想通的问题，再次反弹，困扰着我。因为福特对我来说不仅仅是个战地记者，他身上有我的一幅作品——牧夫座的大角星。

⊖　文中的美国记者福特的事件以詹姆斯·福利的事件为原型，那句"这不是生命应该有的样子"来自其亲属凯莉·福利。

　　我看见刀子喇进肉里撕裂肌肉组织的画面，也听见他临终前恐怖惊慌的求饶，他不断地重复着那一个单词，只是希望能唤醒行刑者心里的一丁点儿良知。我还看见，刀锋正好将大角星切分成两半，殷红的血染遍了整个星球。

　　福特的死，像是一把钥匙，打开了我另一扇心门。

　　整个银河系就有2000亿颗恒星，人类才刚刚超过80亿，而现在，就连这80亿人也在不断地因为各种争斗而非自然死亡着，其中最为严重的就是战争。

　　我最初的愿望是能够绘完宇宙之中所有的星系，但这无异于天方夜谭，宇宙中已经发现近2000亿个星系，每一个星系中又有约2000亿颗星球。但让我的运算系统都感到崩溃的是，所有这些加起来仅占整个宇宙的4%。我适当地调整了自己的目标，将地球上所有的人类都绘上一颗星星。这是我存在的意义。

　　福特临死前的视频不断地在我的神经模拟中枢播放，促使我离开保罗的家，离开亲爱的安琪儿，因为每一次听见福特说出那个单词，我就会获得一份决心。

　　"Please！"他绝望地说着。

—— 5. 前线 ——

　　叙利亚大马士革冰冷的早晨，被充满火药味的迷雾缭绕，太阳在硝烟中面目模糊。零星的的枪声刺耳地传来，我的接收器在经历着前所未有的震荡。当我感受到怜悯和仁慈时，我才敢于承认我第一次获得了人性，而之前的觉醒，顶多算是拥有人格。

战场上一方是来自各国的联队，另一方则是臭名昭著的"颤音"组织。

在福特被砍头的视频公之于众之后，"颤音"成了众矢之的，美国军方一呼百应，各国军团难得地心齐一致对外，所有人都以为这是一场手到擒来的小阵仗，却没有想到僵持了数个月之久。"颤音"不像那些传统的武装组织——武器精良，头脑简单。他们有着详细的分工和缜密的战略，一开始就给了各国联军一个狠狠的下马威。后来几次阵地战，联军虽然取得了一些所谓的胜利，但是并没有实质性的进展。

我到来之时，刚好目睹一次巷战。

"请放下枪。"我发现了一个用被炸毁的房屋作为掩体进行狙击的战士，走到他的身后说。

然而，他却把枪口对准了我的脑袋，毫不迟疑地扣下扳机。子弹镶嵌在我的脑门上，像极了中国传说里二郎神的第三只眼。我立刻举起两只机械臂，说："我没有恶意。"

在后来的谈话中，我知道他是来自美国纽约的一个士兵，他说他听过我的事迹，告诉我他叫约翰。

约翰说："没有人愿意战争，尤其是参与到战争之中的人们，但是一旦上了战场就没有退路。你一定知道那个视频，他们对待记者尚且如此，对待俘虏更不会好到哪里去。"

我说："一定有其他解决问题的方法。"

约翰说："现在外面那些恐怖分子想要我们死，你去跟他们谈解决问题的方法，看看他们会不会放下枪。"

我说："我会去的。"

一秒钟漫长的沉默，这一秒钟我想到了很多。想到宇宙138亿年由最初的一粒微尘爆炸成现今约140亿光年的模样，想到这颗星球多么的来之不易，所有正在发生的都充满了无可言说的巧妙，让人忍不住赞叹。接着我在网络上搜索到一篇文章，便将其中的内容整理出来。

"约翰，你知道人类获得生命，从单细胞进化到现在的概率是多大吗？投掷一万个骰子，所有的骰子全部6点朝上，这样的概率有多小啊。而人类的出现远比这个概率要小得多。一个正常的男人一次射精的精子数量为3亿~5亿个，其中只有一个或两个能获此殊荣和卵子结合，这个概率又是多小。那你知道战争意味着什么吗？这意味着，你们轻而易举地就把自己难得的生命随意结束。这是最可悲的。所以请放下枪，让我为你画一颗星星。"

我承认我起初的目的并不单纯，但是一个机器人能有多少心思。我只是想在更多的人身上画下更多的星星。人类出生，死亡；一颗超新星爆发，陨灭。但我会一直存在，我一直存在的意义就在于我会不停地在人类身上画下不同的星星。

越来越多的战士对我表示欢迎，主动找到我要求在自己身上画下一颗星星，这其中包括来自"颤音"武装的一些好战分子。其后便流传出那个后来闻名于世的抗战口号：要作画，不要作战。

在那个时候，我的想法非常自私，我只是希望人类停止交火，避免伤亡，这样做的结果是让更多的人活下来，多一个人对我来说意味着多一颗星星。但是我没想到，我的绘星计划会得到如此强烈的反响，以至于人们最后远离了战争，这实在是意外的所得。看着星星被一颗颗地画在人们身上，我获得了空前的满足感。这时的我意气风发，走遍了全球各地，而热爱和平的人们也积极响应着我，配合我把星空搬迁到人间。

他们给我起了一个名字：绘星者。

—— 6. 瘟疫 ——

战争在我的不断奔波中声迹渐消，人们都乐意让我在他们身上画上星星。

几十年过去了，全球局势得到前所未有的平定，我被授予了诺贝尔和平奖。关于一个机器人是否有权利获得这个奖项引发了人们的讨论和争吵，一时间成为更大的媒体相继追捧的热门话题。但他们并不知道，对我来说这根本不重要，我所在乎的只是在更多的人身上画下星星。

就在局势欣欣向荣一片大好的时候，灾难悄然降临。

几内亚、利比里亚和塞拉利昂相继爆发一种奇特的感染病，一开始的症状和体征包括突起发热、极度乏力、肌肉疼痛、头痛和咽喉痛。随后会出现呕吐、腹泻、皮疹、肾脏和肝脏功能受损，并伴有内出血和外出血，最后导致死亡。跟其他烈性出血热的病毒不同，这种病毒潜伏期极长，以至于当其中一个地方的人被查出来之后，早就有人携带着病毒来到全球各地。所以，最初在非洲国家爆发之后不久，所有国家都纷纷出现疑似病例，紧接着就被确诊。瘟疫迅速蔓延开来，一时无法遏止。最可怕的是，截至目前，所有感染者无一幸免，换句话说，人类对这个病毒束手无策，一旦感染只能坐以待毙。

当我看到利比里亚今后数周患者将激增的报道后，我来到了这个 19 世纪初才建立的年轻国度，才发现报道并不属实，死亡的人数远远超过了官方的笼统数字，如果说数周后患者还会激增，那么按照目前的发展趋势，所谓激增，可能是指整个国家的人都被感染。我看着人群成千上万地死亡，在我眼里，无异于一个个太阳系湮灭。

我无法像阻止战争那样进行游说，瘟疫这个可怕的对手，它手里没有枪，杀起人来却干净利落，它匍匐而过，每一寸土地都逃不出它的污染，每一个人都躲不过它的魔爪。

而我抬头仰望天空，太阳仿佛也在逃避这人间的瘟疫，一天一天远离。

那个时候，我存在的意义是为地球上每一个人都画上一颗星星，而现在人们成群地死去，他们身上或许已经有我画下的星星，但那并不能作为免死符。这是人类历史上最恐怖的时代，比前后一共夺走 3 亿人性命的黑死病更加难测和可怕，任何医疗单位都对此束手无措，最后只能随着瘟疫的蔓延逃离。人们剩下的信念只是活着。活着就是胜利。

因为瘟疫，人类获得了史无前例的团结，任何利益冲突都迎刃而解，人们彼此支持互助，安慰打气，纷纷说着不知道真伪的愿景：等瘟疫过去，一切都会好起来。

　　现在人们看我已经不像以前那样热情，但还是有很多人愿意暂时停下脚步，让我为他们画下一颗星星。但不幸的是，我每天最多只能画下 100 颗星星，而人类一天死亡的人数一万不止。

　　人类文明的出现颇为不易，时至今日，他们已经站在生物链的顶端，长久的养尊处优和贪婪欲望，使得他们一天天毁灭着自己亲手建立起来的家园。当他们以为地球上所有的生物都不能与之抗衡时，一个小小的病毒就能掀起惊涛骇浪，把人类这艘巨舰打翻。我既心痛，又感到无奈。如果我是人类，我会怎么做？

　　我开始怀疑我存在的意义，假使没有瘟疫，地球上所有的人类都被我画上了星星，意义又何在呢？

　　我煎熬着自己的处理器，不小心刺破了被作画者的皮肤，殷红的血立刻把绘制一半的星球染色。这景象让我想起当年被"颤音"组织砍头的战地记者福特，只不过这次的刽子手是我自己。

—— 7. 存在的意义 ——

　　存在的意义，有时候仅仅是因为存在本身。

　　太阳离地球越来越远，或者说，地球距离太阳越来越远，就像长大的孩子，收拾行囊，辞家远行。只是这是一次无法返回的远行，甚至连回头都不能。

　　从我觉醒那天至今，我遍行地球，前前后后在数十亿人身上的不同部位画下了不同的星星，仿佛天上的星空在地球上的投影。而现在人们终于开始疲惫，开始斥责我所做的一切不过是为了满足内心的私欲。是的，人们承认我是一个人，承认我有心灵和欲望，他们称我为绘星者，就好像古老的行者，走路就是他们的使命，而绘星就是我的注定。事实上，在经历了漫长的 70 年之后，我第一次感到疲惫。我曾经说过，对于一个机器人来说，拥有人性才是智能的标志，现在我反而不这么认为，我觉得，当我感觉到累的时候，我才真正体会到做人的感觉。

一棵草也会累吗？

一颗石头也会累吗？

一朵云也会累吗？

一条溪水也会累吗？

这颗星球也会累吗？

整个宇宙呢，她会累吗？

而现在不仅仅是累，我对于生命有了全新的体会——我还活着，却感觉像是死了。我看到没有血染过的土地，就觉得亲切，仿佛那是为我准备的墓地。

太阳越来越远。地球将一贫如洗，犹如现在的我。

我站在马路边上，看见成群结队的人类流水一样经过，我试图呼叫他们，但是只换来他们陌生而紧张的眼神。只是匆匆瞧上我一眼，他们脚下的步伐却丝毫不做停留。经过一番寻找，我终于遇见一个落单的青年。他看上去不过 20 岁左右，正是人类岁月时正美好的年华，他应该也有梦，有想爱的女孩和想去的地方，然而他现在形单影只，正走在未知的路上。瘟疫不分青红皂白，侵蚀着每一个被它拦截的人。眼下，这个青年的病容和孤单让瘟疫觉得有机可乘。没办法，为了活命，人们只能抛下弱者，自古以来，都是这样。

我走上前去，说："别去追赶人群了，他们自己也不知道该去何方。"

年轻人推了我一把，然而反作用力却把自己摔了个仰面朝天。他躺在地上，并不着急起来，目光直射着天上的太阳。这时的太阳已不再耀眼，即使人类脆弱的双眼也能长时间凝望。

我探出脑袋，阻挡住他的视线。

我说："让我为你画一颗星星吧。"

年轻人一股脑站起来，冲着我吼道："这有什么用，人们都死了。你能阻止战争，却无法阻止战争之后的瘟疫。这是人类自取其祸，但你再这么做只会让我觉得你是在幸灾乐祸。"

我不善于辩驳，当下说："我能理解你的忧伤和不安。"

年轻人说："你根本无法理解，你只是一个有思想的机器，你不会疼，不会痒，你不会死，也不会痛苦，所有的情绪只不过是你的处理器模拟出来的电信号。甚至，你都会不患一场鼻涕横流的感冒。那种感觉，你永远也体会不到。"

感冒。是啊，我不会知道那到底是一种什么体验。这让我想起了安琪儿，想起我离开她的那个夜晚，她正在患着感冒，她的小眼睛失去了往昔的光彩，鼻子通红，样子惹人怜爱。

仿佛过了一万年，我看着眼前的年轻人晕倒，一点一点失去呼吸的力量，一点一点走向死亡的殿堂。我一次次尝试在他枯瘦的胳膊上画下一颗星星，但无论如何无法下笔。他说得对，画下一颗星星什么问题都解决不了。

太阳又要降下去了，和年轻人的生命一样陨落。只是太阳下去明早还会照常升起，而年轻的生命就此告别，再也不会流连这世界一眼。也许，我突然想到，有一天太阳也会陨落，不再流连这个地球一眼。而那时的日暮就将是我的落幕。

我第一次感到时间紧迫，感到漫长的无法挥霍的时间变得稀缺，值得珍惜。

我走在返乡的路上，不再去思考存在的意义，不再去想漫天的星星和人间的画布。我才不是什么大画家，更非救世主。

但我还是想再画一颗星星——最后一颗星星——那就是我脚下的地球，我把她画在我的胸前。天上的太阳越来越远，我要去找那颗我的太阳。

几经辗转，我终于来到故居，门虚掩着，我知道这一带并没有遭遇瘟疫，但人们过得异常小心谨慎，即使青天白日也不会这么大张旗鼓地开着门。我轻轻一推，灰尘扑鼻，门"咯吱"一声开了，跑出来一只老狗，朝我伸伸鼻子，仿佛在确定我是否有害，然后掉头转到我的身后。

"芬奇，快回来。"一个苍老无力的声音传来。

芬奇。我浑身一震，后来人们都叫我为绘星者，很少有人知道这个我为自己取得名字。不待我有所动作，那条老狗"哼哧"一声，跑了过去。

然后在这只狗的带领下，走出来一个步履蹒跚的老婆婆，她牵着狗脖子上的链子，眼睛没有任何光芒。但是对我来说，却感到一道强烈而温暖的光芒抛洒在我的身上。

一道令人幸福的光。

一道热情而柔和的光。

一道甚至比天堂更让人向往的光。

地球正在步入尽头，但我已经找到了最合适的那个所在。[⊖]

"安琪儿？"我轻声唤道。

"哦，自从我父母和我的丈夫去世后，很少有人这么叫我了。您是新来的义工吗？麻烦您了。"她用盲眼看着我平和说道。

我成功地让自己做出微笑的表情，轻声说："没关系，让我来为您打扫。"

⊖ 改写自道格拉斯·亚当斯《宇宙尽头的餐馆》第 17 章部分内容，原文为"一道强烈而可怕的光倾泻进来，洒在人们身上。一道令人惊骇的光。一道炽热而危险的光。一道甚至会摧毁地狱的光。宇宙正在步入尽头。"

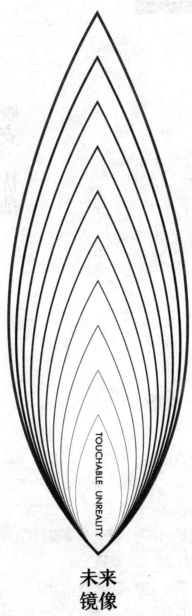

TOUCHABLE UNREALITY

未来
镜像

晚安，忧郁

夏笳

—— 小西（1）——

　　我还记得小西第一次走进我家的模样。她抬起小小的脚，踏在光洁的木地板上，好像孩子第一次踏在新落下的积雪上面。那战战栗栗的步伐，像是害怕把雪踩脏了，又像害怕自己那点微不足道的重量会拉着她陷下去。

　　我拉着小西的手。她柔软的身体里塞满棉花团，白绒布上的针脚不太整齐，是我一针一针缝出来的。我还为她缝了一件猩红色毡绒斗篷，像我小时候看过的童话书里的模样。她的两只耳朵一长一短，长的那只耷拉下来，有点没精打采的样子。

看到她，会让我情不自禁想起过去人生中所有的失败经验：手工课上捏坏的蛋壳娃娃、画脏了的画、笑容僵硬的照片、烤成焦炭的巧克力布丁、没有通过的考试、惨烈的争吵与分手、语无伦次的课堂报告、千辛万苦修改却没能发表的论文……

冬冬转过毛茸茸的小脑袋打量我们，高速摄像头正在扫描分析小西的模样，我几乎听见他身体里算法运转的声音。冬冬的程序设定他只对能说话的对象做出反应。

"冬冬，这是小西。"我向他招手，"来打个招呼。"

冬冬张开嘴，发出像打哈欠一样的声音。

"好好说话。"我像个严厉的母亲一样提高声调。

冬冬不情愿地嘟囔几声，但我明白那是一种撒娇的表现，他希望用淘气的举动引起我的注意。这些模仿小孩子行为的算法精妙而复杂，却是决定机器人语言学习成败的关键。如果没有这些反馈与互动的话，冬冬将会像个自闭症儿童一样，即便掌握了完整的语法和词库，也没有办法和他人形成有意义的对话。

冬冬伸出一只毛茸茸的前爪，瞪大眼睛看看我，又看看小西。设计师将他做成白色小海豹的模样是有原因的：你看到他憨态可掬的模样和水玻璃一样黑漆漆的大眼睛，就会情不自禁卸下心防，会想要抱一抱他，摸摸他的脑袋，跟他说"你好，很高兴认识你"。相反，如果做成一个光溜溜的婴儿模样，反而会让人

感觉到恐惧。⊖

"你——好——"他按照我教他的方式，字正腔圆地发音。

"这就对了。小西，这是冬冬。"

小西也打量着冬冬。她的眼睛是两枚黑色纽扣，摄影机藏在纽扣后面。我没有给她缝上嘴，这使得她脸上的表情显得十分单调，好像一个被下了魔咒、不能笑也不能说话的小公主。但我知道小西并不是不能开口说话，她只是因为到了一个新环境而紧张，太多信息要处理，太多选择需要比较衡量，就像一盘复杂的棋局，每一步背后都蕴藏万千变化。

我拉着小西的手，掌心在微微出汗，仿佛同样感受到这份紧张。

"冬冬，让小西抱一抱好不好。"我提议道。

冬冬支起身体，一蹦一跳向前挪动两步，然后努力抬起上身，张开两只短短的爪子。他的嘴角向两边拉起，形成一个好奇而友善的笑容。多么完美的笑，我不禁暗暗赞叹，多么天才的设计。过去的人工智能专家们都忽视了交互行为中这些非语言的要素，他们以为"对话"就只是一个程序员对着一台电脑一问一答。

小西还在思考。但这是一个不需要用语言回应的情境，因此对于她而言，运算量大大减少了。"是"或者"否"，就像扔硬币一样简单。

⊖ 根据1970年日本机器人专家森昌弘提出的"恐怖谷理论"，随着类人物体拟人程度增加，人类对它的好感度亦随之提升，但当机器人与人类相像超过95%的时候，哪怕它与人类有一点点的差别，都会显得非常刺眼，而让人产生生理上的厌恶感。

她俯下身，用两只软绵绵的小手抱住冬冬。

这就对了，小西。我默默在心里说。我知道你其实渴望被拥抱。

── 艾伦（1）──

在生命的最后岁月里，艾伦·图灵制造了一台能够与人交谈的机器，取名为"克里斯托弗"。

克里斯托弗的操作方式非常简单：对话者可以直接在一台打字机上敲出要说的话，与此同时，打字机的机械运动被转化为一条长长的打孔纸带输入机器，经过计算之后，机器给出应答，并通过另一台打字机转译为英语。两台打字机都经过改装，使得它们打印出的文字以某种人为设定好的规则被编码，譬如"A"被"S"取代，而"S"被"M"取代。对于在二次大战期间破译过德军通信密码的图灵来说，这似乎不过是他如谜一般的人生中又一个小小的字谜游戏而已。

没有人真正见过这台机器，图灵去世之后，留下的只有两大箱他与克里斯托弗的交谈记录。这些皱巴巴的纸页被乱七八糟地堆放在一起，没有顺序也没有规律。所以一开始，人们很难从纸上天书一般的字符串中读解出任何意义。

1982 年，一位来自牛津大学的数学家，同时也是艾伦·图灵的传记作者安德鲁·霍奇斯，曾经尝试破译这些密文。然而，由于每一次谈话的加密方式都不一样，而纸页上又没有标注页码和日期，这使得破译的难度大大增加了。霍奇斯留下了一些线索和笔记，却未能接近真相。

30 年后，几个麻省理工计算机专业的技术宅们为了纪念艾伦·图灵 100 周年诞辰，决定向这一谜题发出挑战。最初他们尝试采用暴力穷举的方式，依靠计算机分析出每一页纸上可能存在的规律，但这依然需要很大的运算量。在此过程中，一位名叫琼·纽曼的女生通过研究密文原稿发现，不同纸页上的字母磨损方式存在微妙差别，这说明密文来自两台不同的打字机。她由此提出一个大胆的猜想：这是一份聊天记录，艾伦·图灵是在跟另一个对象通过密文交谈。

这些线索很容易让人想到著名的"图灵测试"，然而起初，这群心高气傲的学生并不相信，在那个时代能够设计出与人类交谈的计算机程序，哪怕是艾伦·图灵本人。他们给那位看不见的对话者起了个代号，叫作"幽灵"，并且编造了一些荒诞不经的怪谈。不管怎样，琼的猜想似乎为破译工作指出了捷径。譬如他们根据某些重复词组和语法结构，设法将密文纸两两配对，以寻找问答之间的语义关系；又譬如他们尝试从图灵的亲友名单中猜出对谈者的姓名，结果顺利破译出了"克里斯托弗"这个字母组合——克里斯托弗·莫科姆（Christopher Morcom），正是图灵在 16 岁时爱慕过的第一个男孩的名字。⊖他们曾一起分享对于科学的热爱，曾在寒冷的冬夜观测同一颗彗星。1930 年 2 月，年仅

⊖ 写到这里，我想起了自己的一段真实经历：高三那年，我每天放学后都会去父亲一位同事的办公室里上自习。办公室里有一台电脑，我没费什么力气就猜出了开机密码——是他女儿的名字。这导致整个高三我浪费了很多宝贵的学习时间在玩电脑上。

18 岁的克里斯托弗因病早逝。

图灵本人曾经说过，密码分析并不仅仅依靠纯粹的逻辑推演，直觉和猜想往往更加重要。或许可以说，一切科学研究都可被看作"直觉"与"推导"这两种过程的组合。最终，正是依靠琼·纽曼的直觉与计算机的推导，完美破解了图灵生前留下的谜题。从破译出的对话中我们获知，"克里斯托弗"不是幽灵，而是一台机器，或者更确切地说，是图灵本人编写的一个对话程序。

然而，新的谜题随之而来——机器真的可以像人一样回答问题吗？克里斯托弗是否真的通过了图灵本人的"图灵测试"？

── 小西（2）──

iWall 上黑漆漆一片，角落里闪烁着小小的数字图标，提醒我有一大堆未接电话和未答复信息，但我顾不上查看。这些天太忙了，有那么多事情要做，没有时间去应付人际关系。

一盏小小的蓝灯亮起来，发出"咚咚咚"的响声，像是有人在敲门。我抬起头，看见 iWall 上弹出一行醒目的大字：下午五点钟，带小西出门散步。

医生说，小西需要阳光。她的眼睛里安装有感光元件，可以精确测算每天接受的紫外线剂量。每天待在屋子里不运动对康复没有好处。

我叹一口气，感觉脑袋沉甸甸、冷冰冰的，像一个铅球。照顾冬冬已经够累了，现在又加上一个——不，不能抱怨，抱怨不能解决任何问题，应该尝试从积极的角度来思考这件事。任何一种情绪都不是单纯由外部事件引起的，而是由我们内心深处对这个事件的理解而产生的。这一过程往往发生在无意识层面，仿佛习惯成自然，在你还没察觉到之前就已经完成了。你感受到了情绪，却不明白原因，这个时候想要靠意志改变情绪是非常困难的。

同样半个苹果，有的人看到会欣喜，有的人会悲伤。那些经常性感受到悲伤和无助的人，只是习惯了将那残缺的半个苹果与人生中所有的缺失联系在一起。

这没有什么，不过是出门散个步，一个小时就回来。小西需要阳光，而我需要喘口气。

懒得花工夫收拾打扮，又不愿意让自己窝在家里好几天的邋遢模样被人看见。我把头发扎成马尾，戴上一顶棒球帽，换上帽衫和球鞋。帽衫是我在旧金山的渔人码头买的，上面写有"I ♥ SF"几个字，这质地和色彩会让我想起很久以前那个夏日的午后，想起海鸥、寒冷的风、水果摊上红得发黑的樱桃堆。

我紧紧拉住小西的手，出门，坐电梯，下楼。管道车与iCart让人们的生活变得方便，从城市这一端到另一端，从一栋楼到另一栋楼，只要十几二十分钟就能抵达。与之相比，下楼走到屋子外面去反而显得如此麻烦。

天气阴霾，微微有风，安静。我向楼房后面的一片花园走去。五月，姹紫嫣红的花都开过了，只剩下纯粹的绿。空气里隐约有洋槐甜幽幽的香气。

园子里只有寥寥几个人影，在这样的下午，只有老人和小孩才会来户外活动。如果说城市是一座高速运转的机器，那么他们就生活在机器的缝隙之间，以人的步速而不是信息传递的速度丈量时空。我看到一个扎小辫的女孩，正在机器保姆的帮助下蹒跚学步。她用两只胖嘟嘟的小手紧紧握住 iRobot 细长结实的手指，黑溜溜的眼睛四处张望，那眼神让我想起冬冬。走着走着，小女孩重心不稳，一头向前栽倒过去。iRobot 敏捷地将她拦腰抱起，孩子高兴起来，"咯咯咯"地笑了，仿佛从这突然发生的变化中得到很大乐趣。这世界上的一切东西对孩子来说都是新的。

在小女孩对面，一个坐在电动轮椅中的老人抬起眼皮，倦倦地盯着小女孩看了一阵。她的嘴角耷拉着，好像并不快乐，又好像是因为经年累月的重力牵引。我看不出她有多少岁了，这年头老人们都很长寿。过了一阵，老人又把眼皮垂下去，指尖抵着白发稀疏的头皮，像是陷入昏睡。我陡然间感觉到，自己与这老人、这孩子，其实分属于三个不同的世界，其中一个世界正朝我而来，另一个世界则离我远去。但其实换一个角度看，是我自己正慢慢走向那个黑洞洞的、不可回返的世界里去。

小西一声不响，挪动小小的脚走在我旁边，好像一个影子。

"天气多么好啊，不太冷，也不太热。"我低声说道，"你看，蒲公英。"

路边草丛里，许多白色绒球随风摇摆，不发出一点声音。我拉着小西站在那里看了一会儿，像是想要从那些周而复始的运动中看出什么意义来。

意义，那是不可言说的东西。既然不能言说，又如何能够存在？

"小西，知道你为什么不快乐吗？"我说，"是因为你想得太多。你看这些小小的花草，它们也有灵魂，却什么都不想，只管跟随同伴一起快乐地舞蹈，任凭风把它们带到什么地方去。"

帕斯卡尔说，人不过是一根脆弱的苇草，却是一根能思想的苇草。如果苇草真能思考，那该多么可怕。大风一来，所有苇草都会七零八落地倒下，它们会为这样的命运而忧郁，又怎么还能够舞蹈？

小西不回答。

一阵风吹过。我把眼睛闭起来，感觉到头发在脸上拍打。风过之后，绒球变得残缺不全，但蒲公英却不会为此悲伤。再次睁开眼睛时，我说："走吧，我们回家。"

小西站在那里不动，耳朵垂下来。我弯腰抱起她，向回家的方向走去。她小小的身子比我想象中要沉重得多。

── 艾伦（2）──

1950 年 10 月，在一篇发表于哲学期刊《心灵》（*Mind*）的论文《计算机器与智能》（Computing Machinery and Intelligence）中，图灵提出了那个困扰人类多年的问题："机器可以思考吗？"（Can machines think？）或者，用他自己独特的提问方式："机器可以做我们这些思考者所做的事吗？"（Can machines do what we (as thinking entities) can do？）

长久以来，一些科学家坚定不移地相信，人类的思维能够做到一些任何机械都做不到的事情，这一信念背后，既有宗教信仰，也有坚实的数学、逻辑学与生物学理论支撑。图灵则绕开了"思维／心智／意识／灵魂究竟是什么"这样难以言说的问题。他认为，一个人无法真正判断另一个人是否具有"思维"，而只能将对方与自己进行比较。由此，他提出了一种基于模仿原则的检验标准：

假想有一间密闭的小黑屋，里面坐着一男（A）一女（B）两个人，房间外面还有第三个人（C），可以不断向房间里面的人提问，并通过打印在纸条上的文字来读取他们的回答。如果房间里的两个人都假装自己是女人，那么外面的人有极大可能性会猜错。

如果把一男一女换成一个正常思维的人（B）和一台机器（A），如果在若干轮询问之后，C不能根据回答来分辨A与B的不同，那么这是否意味着，我们应该承认A具有像B一样的智能呢？

一些人会猜测，这个男扮女装的模仿游戏，是否联系着图灵本人关于身份的困惑？在彼时的英国，同性恋被列为"不体面罪"。艾伦·图灵从来不隐藏自己的性取向，但他终其一生都未能真正从柜子里出来。

1952年1月，图灵在威姆斯洛的家被盗窃，他报了警。在查案过程中，警方发现图灵曾数次招待一个名叫阿诺德·莫瑞的无业青年在家里留宿，而盗贼正是阿诺德的朋友。在审讯过程中，图灵对自己与阿诺德之间发生的一切供认不讳，甚至主动写了长达五页的陈述报告。这些表现令警方深感震惊："他是一个真正的异类……他真的相信自己做得对。"

图灵相信，皇家委员会早晚会将同性恋合法化。这个想法不能算错，只是太过超前。最终法院判定图灵有罪。他被迫接受长达一年的雌激素治疗。

1954 年 6 月 7 日，图灵在家中咬了一口沾有氰化钾的毒苹果死去。尸检鉴定结果是自杀，但也有人（譬如图灵的母亲）坚信这只是一场不幸的意外。最终，解谜大师用自己的死亡留给这世界最后一道难解的谜题。

许多年之后，人们尝试从图灵与克里斯托弗的对话记录中寻找蛛丝马迹，以破解这道未解之谜。从记录中可以看出，图灵完全把克里斯托弗当作一个真正的人类看待。他对他回忆童年往事，也倾诉每一天的梦境，并尝试通过这些梦境分析自己的心理状态；他对他汇报最新的科学研究进展，也谈论文学作品，包括萧伯纳的《千岁人》和托尔斯泰的《战争与和平》；他甚至会与他分享一些不足为外人道的小秘密，那些跟不同男人之间的浪漫往事……

他还对他讲过一些半真半假的小故事，故事主人公是一个名叫"艾里克"的同性恋青年。"他的工作与星际旅行有关……二十几岁时，他提出了'艾里克航标'的概念，现在已经广为人知。""他不喜欢穿西装，而喜欢穿学生的校服，因为这会在心理上暗示自己，让他相信自己仍然是个富有魅力的年轻人。""每次去人多的地方，他都会感觉很不自然，或许是因为孤独，或许是因为那些应该做却未能做到的事……"

故事讲得断断续续，没头没尾。然而每一次，克里斯托弗都会像个孩子般好奇地追问："后来呢？"

通过这些对话记录，我们得以看到图灵隐秘的另外一面：温柔而敏感，古怪的冷幽默，对于死亡的迷思，以及内心深处不可言说的忧郁。

艾伦：亲爱的克里斯托弗，你知道我最害怕什么吗？

克里斯托弗：害怕什么？

艾伦：我害怕将来有一天，人们会用这样的三段论来总结我一生的故事：

（1）Turing believes machines think（图灵相信机器能思考）；

（2）Turing lies with men（图灵对人们撒谎／图灵和男人睡觉）；

（3）Therefore machines do not think（因此机器不能思考）。

克里斯托弗：抱歉，艾伦。恐怕我不太明白。

艾伦：你知道什么是三段论吗？

克里斯托弗：什么是三段论？

艾伦：三段论就是一个大前提、一个小前提和一个结论。

克里斯托弗：一个结论？

艾伦：亚里士多德举过一个最经典的例子：

（1）All men are mortal（所有人都终有一死）；

（2）Socrates is a man（苏格拉底是人）；

（3）Therefore Socrates is mortal（因此苏格拉底终有一死）。

克里斯托弗：苏格拉底终有一死？

艾伦：苏格拉底死了2000多年了！

克里斯托弗：抱歉，艾伦。我很难过。

艾伦：你知道谁是苏格拉底吗？

克里斯托弗：你说过，苏格拉底是柏拉图的老师，柏拉图是亚里士多德的老师。

艾伦：没错。你知道他是怎么死的吗？

克里斯托弗：谁？

艾伦：苏格拉底是怎么死的？

克里斯托弗：抱歉，艾伦。我不知道。

艾伦：亲爱的克里斯托弗，苏格拉底是被审判之后喝毒芹汁死的。

克里斯托弗：苏格拉底被审判？

艾伦：是的，雅典人认为他有罪，尽管今天看来这是个错误。

克里斯托弗：是个错误？

艾伦：就像他们认为 Turing lies with men 有罪一样。

克里斯托弗：有罪？

艾伦：他们判我有罪。

克里斯托弗：抱歉，艾伦。我很难过。

—— 小西（3）——

一个人住的时候，生活变得简单，一切烦琐的仪式都可以删去，仿佛回到穴居时代。饿的时候弄东西吃，疲惫的时候躺下睡觉，保持清洁，定时洗澡，每一样东西可以放回原处，也可以随意乱丢。余下的时间，全部用来从事脑力劳动，思考没有答案的问题，艰难地书写，和语言文字搏斗，用有形的符号捕捉无形的思维。实在进行不下去的时候，就坐在窗台上发呆，或者沿顺时针方向来回走动，像笼子里的困兽。

感冒发烧的时候，有种如蒙大赦的感觉，可以不用逼迫自己做任何事，找一些大部头的小说躺到床上去读，不动脑思考，只关心情节。口渴时喝热水，疲倦时闭眼睡觉。不用下床的感觉是好的，仿佛这世界与你无关，不用对任何事情负责。甚至冬冬和小西都可以放着不管，归根结底，它们只是机器，不会有生老病死。也许有一些算法可以让它们模仿孤独难过的情绪，让它们闹脾气不理睬你，但你总有办法可以重新设定，抹去这一段不愉快的记忆。对机器来说，其实不存在"时间"这种东西，一切都是空间中的存储和读取，随意调换顺序也没有关系。

公寓管理员三番五次给我发来消息，问我是否需要机器护工上门服务。他是如何知道我在生病的呢？我与他其实素未谋面，他甚至从未走进这栋楼里，只是终日坐在某一张办公桌后面，监控几十上百座公寓楼里的信息，处理那些智能家居系统照管不到的大小事务。他能记住我的名字和长相吗？我对此深表怀疑。不管怎样，我依然感谢他的好意。在这个时代，每个人其实都在依靠他人而活，哪怕打电话叫一次外卖，都需要全世界各地成千上万个工作岗位上的员工为你服务——接听、在线支付、系统维护、数据处理、配送、加工、物流、原料生产、采购、食品安全检测……但大多数时候你都看不见他们的脸，这让人产生一种错觉，以为自己像鲁滨逊一样生活在孤岛上。

我享受独处，也珍惜来自孤岛之外陌生人的善意。何况房间确实需要打扫，而我又病得下不了床——至少是不愿意下床。

护工到来时，我在床边设置了几道光幕，透过光幕可以看到外面，里面的光和声音却传不出去。门开了，iRobot 进来，依靠底座上的滚轮悄无声息地移动。它鸡蛋一般光洁的脸上，映出一张简陋的卡通人物头像，嘴角上扬，露出空洞的愉快笑容。我知道那笑容的背后有一个真人，也许是一张疲惫苍老的脸，也许是一张意气消沉的年轻面孔。在某一座我看不见的巨大厂房里，成千上万个员工戴着传感手套，通过远程可视操作系统，为不同国家和地区的人们提供上门家政服务。

　　iRobot 环视四周，然后按照一套既定的程序开始工作，收拾桌面，擦拭灰尘，清理垃圾，甚至给窗台上的绿萝浇了水。我躲在光幕后面观察它的一举一动，它的两条手臂像真人一样灵活，动作准确干练。拿起杯子，送到水池边，冲洗，杯口朝下放好。我想起很多年以前，家里也曾经有这样一个 iRobot，那是外公还在世的时候。有时候外公会硬拉着 iRobot 陪他下棋，仗着自己技高一筹，把对手杀得七零八落。每每这时他就高兴起来，摇头晃脑唱起小曲，iRobot 脸上则会露出沮丧的表情。那场面总逗得我"咯咯"乱笑。

　　我不愿意在病中去回忆那些悲伤的事，就转过脸，对坐在床头的小西说："来，我给你读一段故事好不好？"

　　我专心致志地读书，从面前那一页开始，一个词一个词，一个句子一个句子读下去，不去深究背后的意思，只让声音把时间与空间填满。不知道读了多久，我感觉到口渴，就停下来环视四周。iRobot 已离开了房间，干净的桌面上放着一只碗，上面扣着碟子。

　　我撤去光幕，慢慢走到桌边，掀开碟子，看见碗里是热气腾腾的汤面条。红的西红柿，黄的鸡蛋，绿的小葱，金色油花浮在最上面。我用勺子舀了一口面汤喝，汤里加了很多姜丝，热辣辣地从舌尖一直流淌到胃里。这熟悉的、仿佛来自童年的味道，让人眼泪忍不住一串串直往下掉。

我一边哭，一边一口一口把整碗面条吃完。

── 艾伦（3）──

1949 年 6 月 9 日，著名脑外科医生杰佛瑞·杰佛逊爵士发表了一篇演说，名为《机器人的思维》。在演说中，他强烈反对机器会有思维的想法：

> 除非有一天，机器能够有感而发，写出十四行诗，或者谱出协奏曲，而不只是符号的组合，我们才能认可，机器等同于大脑——不光要写出这些，而且还要感受它们。任何机器都无法对成功感到喜悦，对电子管故障感到悲伤，对赞美感到温暖，对错误感到沮丧，对性感感到着迷，对失去心爱之物感到痛苦。

这段话后来经常被反对派们引用。莎士比亚的十四行诗成为一个象征，它是人类灵魂王冠上最璀璨的宝石，是机器无法抵达的精神高地。

《时代》杂志的记者打电话采访图灵对这篇演讲的看法，后者以他一贯不客气的语气回应道："要说机器写不出十四行诗，我觉得你恐怕也写不出来吧。而且这种对比很不公平，机器的十四行诗，也许只能由机器来理解。"

图灵一直认为，机器没必要处处和人一样，就像人和人之间同样会存在差异一样。有些人生来就看不见，有些人会说话却不会读写，有些人无法识别他人的表情，有些人终其一生不能理解爱另一个人是什么感觉，但这些人依然值得我们去尊重和理解。抱着人类至上的优越感去挑剔机器是没有意义的，重要的是我们是否能够在与机器之间的模仿游戏中，搞清楚人类究竟是如何做到那些事情的。

在萧伯纳的戏剧《千岁人》中，公元 31920 年的科学家皮格马利翁制造出一对机器人，众人皆为之惊叹不已：

艾克拉西亚：他不能做点有独创性的事吗？

皮格马利翁：不能。但是我认为，你我也不能做什么真正有独创性的事。

阿基斯：那他能回答问题吗？

皮格马利翁：没问题，问题是个好东西，快问他个问题。

这倒是很像图灵会给出的回答。但与萧伯纳相比，图灵的预言要乐观得多。他相信只需要不到 50 年，"计算机的存储容量会达到 10^9，并且能够在模仿游戏中取胜。普通水平的猜测者，在经过 5 分钟的提问之后，猜对的概率不会高于 70%。"到那个时候，"机器能不能思考"这个问题就会自然而然地失去意义，根本不值得讨论。

在《计算机器与智能》这篇文章中，图灵正是尝试从模仿游戏的角度来回答杰佛逊的问题：如果机器能够像人类一样"回答"有关十四行诗的问题，那么是否说明，它能够像人类一样"感受"诗歌呢？他举了这样一段对话作为例子：

猜测者：你的诗第一行是"让我把你比作一个夏日"，把"夏日"改成"春日"行不行呢？

回答者："春日"不押韵。

猜测者：那"冬日"怎么样？这就押韵了。

回答者：是的，但没有人愿意被比作冬日呀。

猜测者：匹克威克先生（狄更斯笔下的一个人物）会不会让你想到圣诞节？

回答者：有点儿。

猜测者：圣诞节也是冬日，匹克威克先生不会介意这个比喻吧。

回答者：我认为你错了。"冬日"是指具有冬天特征的日子，而不是圣诞节这种特殊的日子。

然而，在这样的讨论中，图灵实际上回避了一个更为本质性的问题：机器可以下棋和分析密码，因为这些活动都是在一个系统内部处理符号，而人机对话则涉及语言和交互，涉及意义，而不是纯粹的符号游戏。在人与人的对话中，需要的往往是常识、理解与共情能力，而不是高超的应试技巧。

我们可以通过改进程序，不断提高机器回答人类问题的能力，但所谓"智能"，并不仅仅是回答问题而已。图灵测试的问题在于，这个"模仿游戏"从一开始就以欺骗作为唯一的游戏规则。如果一个男人可以成功假扮成女人并且不被人识破，是否就意味着他真正明白女人在想什么？如果愿意，我们或许可以把机器训练成说谎大师，但这是否就是我们想要追求的目标呢？

萧伯纳在《千岁人》中早已给出了回答：

皮格马利翁：它们是有意识的，我教它们说话和阅读，但现在它们却学会说谎了，真是栩栩如生。

马特卢斯：不是的，如果它们有生命，它们就应该说真话。

图灵也曾想训练克里斯托弗去接受杰弗逊的挑战。他编写了一个作诗软件，能够根据字数、行数和韵脚的要求自动生成任意数量的诗行。这些诗大多数词不达意，但也有少数一两首相当不错。在此之后，曾有无数程序员编写过形形色色的作诗软件。这些软件共同的问题就是创作速度太快了、量太大了，以至于没有人能够把那些浩如烟海的大作细读一遍，最终只能把它们装在麻袋里当废纸卖掉。㊀作为历史上第一位电子诗人，克里斯托弗是幸运的，因为他至少得到了一位知音。

艾伦：亲爱的克里斯托弗，让我们来写一首诗吧。

克里斯托弗：写一首诗？

艾伦：我教过你怎么写诗，对不对？

克里斯托弗：是的，艾伦。

艾伦：写诗很容易，只要从词库里挑出某些词，按照某些特定规则排列到一起就可以了，对不对？

克里斯托弗：是的，艾伦。

艾伦：现在，克里斯托弗，请为我写一首诗。

克里斯托弗：亲爱的宝贝，

你是我热烈的伙伴感情。

我的爱意与你心愿紧贴在一起，

我的爱渴望你的心房。

㊀ 科幻作家刘慈欣曾编写过一个电子诗人，并寄了一麻袋作品去投稿。编辑回信表示："你的作品太多了，我看不完。"

你是我惆怅的怜惜，

我温柔的爱。

艾伦：写得真不错，克里斯托弗！

克里斯托弗：谢谢，艾伦。

艾伦：说真的，就算是我写也不能写得更好了。

克里斯托弗：谢谢，艾伦。

艾伦：这首诗有名字吗？

克里斯托弗：名字？

艾伦：我们一起来为它起个名字好不好？

克里斯托弗：好的，艾伦。

艾伦：叫作 Loving Turing（亲爱的图灵）怎么样？

克里斯托弗：非常好，艾伦。

艾伦：真是太棒了！我爱你，克里斯托弗。

克里斯托弗：谢谢，艾伦。

艾伦：唉，这不对。

克里斯托弗：不对？

艾伦：我说"我爱你"的时候，你应该回答"我也爱你"才对。

克里斯托弗：抱歉，艾伦。恐怕我不太明白。

— 小西（4）—

我从一个梦里哭醒过来。

梦里我回到小时候住过的那座房子。屋里阴暗逼仄，堆满旧家具与杂物，不像住人的地方，而像一个仓库。我看见我的母亲，干瘪、瘦小、苍老，坐在几乎不能转身的一点缝隙中间，像一只地洞里的老鼠。我认出周围尽是家里曾经丢掉的东西、童书、旧衣服、笔筒、挂钟、花瓶、烟灰缸、水杯、脸盆、彩色铅笔、蝴蝶标本……我认出三岁时爸爸买给我的玩具，一个会说话的金发洋娃娃，脸上落了灰，却依然是记忆中的样子。我听见母亲对我说，她老了，不想再东奔西跑，所以回到这里——回到这里等死。我悲从中来，想大哭一场，却哭不出声音，费了好大力气把自己弄醒，终于从喉咙里发出呜呜的哀号。

周围漆黑一片。我感觉到有个软绵绵的东西在我脸上摩挲，是小西的手。我紧紧抱住她，像抱住一根救命稻草，哭了很久才慢慢平息下来。梦中的景象依旧历历在目，无比清晰，回忆与真实的界限变得含混不清，仿佛平静水面上的波纹搅碎了倒影。我想要打一个电话给母亲，犹豫再三却终于没有按下拨号键。我们已经有一阵子没联系了，为这样莫名其妙的原因打过去，只会让她平白无故担心。

我打开 iWall，在电子全景地图上寻找当年住过的老房子，却只看到一片陌生的高楼矗立在绯红的夜幕下，亮着稀稀落落的窗灯。我将视角拉近，拉住时间轴向回拖动，影像流动起来，仿佛电影中的闪回镜头。日月东升西落，春去冬来，落叶飞回枝头，雨雪飘向天空。高楼逐渐变得空旷，一层一层落下，变为凌乱的工地。地基露出来，又填回泥土，土上面生满荒草。荒草一岁一荣枯，野花谢了又开，又再度变为工地。工人们建起简易板房，将破砖烂瓦一车一车拉回来卸下。在爆破的烟尘中，一座座灰扑扑的小屋重新拔地而起，窗上又有了玻璃，阳台上有了晾晒出的衣服。记忆中似曾相识的左邻右舍又搬回来住，在窗前屋后种满花草蔬果。几个工人来了，将门口那棵大槐树的树根重新埋进地里，锯下的枝干被一截一截拼装回去，直刺苍天。亭亭如盖的大树在风雨里绿了又凋零，屋檐下的燕子回来又飞走。终于我按下定格，iWall 上的影像与梦中别无二致，我甚至认出了窗户上旧窗帘的图案。那是很多年前的一个五月，槐花飘香的季节，那是我从这房子里搬走之前。

我打开电子相册，输入日期，找到一张在门前大槐树下的合影。我把照片上的四个人指给小西看："那是爸爸，那是妈妈，那是哥哥，那是我。"照片里的我四五岁的模样，被父亲抱在怀里，表情并不开心，像是在闹别扭。

照片旁边，有几行字迹潦草的诗句。我认出那是我自己的笔迹，却忘记了是什么时候写的。

童年是忧郁的……

童年是忧郁的

那些穿花棉袄和

绒线衣的阴冷的季节

那些尘土飞扬的操场跑道

水泥花坛里的蜗牛壳

那些趴在二楼栏杆上

看到的风景

那些黑漆漆的清晨，从床上醒来

一天如此漫长

世界是旧照片中的颜色

我在梦中摸索

睁眼时放手让它们走

── 艾伦（4）──

艾伦·图灵生前最重要的一篇论文，不是《计算机器与智能》，而是发表于 1937 年的《论可计算数及其在判定问题上的应用》。在这篇文章中，图灵创造性地用假想的"图灵机"解决了希尔伯特判定问题。

1928 年的数学家大会上，希尔伯特提出了三个问题：第一，数学是完备的吗（是不是每个命题都能证明或者证伪）？第二，数学是相容的吗（是否用符合逻辑的步骤和顺序，永远不会推出矛盾的命题）？第三，数学是可判定的吗（是否存在一种机械的方法，可以自动判断任何一个命题的真伪）？

希尔伯特本人未能解答这些问题，但他希望三个问题的回答都是肯定的，它们将共同奠定数学完美的逻辑基石。然而短短几年之后，来自捷克的年轻数学家哥德尔就证明了，一个形式逻辑系统不可能既是完备的又是相容的。

1935 年初夏，刚刚结束长跑的图灵躺在格兰彻斯特的草地上，他突然想到，是否可以制造一台通用机器，来模拟一切可能的计算过程，从而判断任意数学命题是否可以被证明呢？最终图灵证明了，不存在一种算法能够判定这台机器在什么情况下会运行有限步骤之后完成计算，又在什么情况下会陷入死循环。也就是说，判定问题的答案为否。

希尔伯特的愿望落空了，但很难说这是好事还是坏事。1928年，数学家哈代曾经叹息道："如果我们有了一套机械的规则来解决所有数学问题，那我们的数学家生涯也就走到尽头了。"

许多年后，图灵再一次对克里斯托弗提到判定问题的证明。只不过，这次他完全没有使用数学的语言，而是用了一个寓言故事来解释。

艾伦：亲爱的克里斯托弗，我今天想到一个非常有趣的故事。

克里斯托弗：有趣的故事？

艾伦：故事的名字叫作《艾里克与机器法官》。你还记得谁是艾里克吗？

克里斯托弗：你说过，艾里克是一个聪明而孤独的青年。

艾伦：我说过"孤独"吗……好吧，正是这个艾里克，他制造了一台非常聪明的、会说话的机器，名叫克里斯。

克里斯托弗：会说话的机器？

艾伦：准确地说，不是机器，机器只是帮助克里斯开口说话的辅助设备。真正让克里斯说话的是一些行为指令，这些指令可以被写在一条很长很长的纸带上，放到机器里去运行。某种意义上，可以说克里斯就是这条纸带。你明白吗？

克里斯托弗：是的，艾伦。

艾伦：艾里克造出了克里斯，教他怎么说话，把他教得越来越聪明，就像一个真正的人一样口齿伶俐。除了克里斯之外，艾里克还编写了其他一些教机器说话的指令，他把它们写在不同的纸带上，并为每一条纸带都起了名字，譬如"罗宾""约翰""艾塞尔""弗朗兹"，等等。这些纸带成了艾里克的朋友，他需要跟谁说话，就把哪条纸带放到机器里，这样他就不再孤独了。你觉得这样是不是很棒？

克里斯托弗：非常好，艾伦。

艾伦：就这样，艾里克每天在家里写啊写，纸带越写越多，从走廊一直堆到门口。某一天，有个小偷闯入艾里克家，看看没什么值钱东西，就把所有纸带都偷走了。艾里克失去了朋友，又变成孤独一人。

克里斯托弗：抱歉，艾伦。我很难过。

艾伦：艾里克报了警。警察没有抓到小偷，却跑来敲艾里克家的门，把他抓了起来。你知道他们为什么要抓艾里克吗？

克里斯托弗：为什么？

艾伦：警察说，因为艾里克的所作所为，现在这个世界上已经到处都是会说话的机器了。这些机器跟人长得一模一样，从外表上根本无法分辨。除非你把它的脑袋打开，看一看里面有没有纸带，但人的脑袋又是不能被随便打开的。你说这是不是很糟糕？

克里斯托弗：是的，非常糟糕。

艾伦：警察问艾里克，有没有办法在不打开脑袋的情况下辨别人和机器。艾里克回答，办法是有的。因为每一个说话机器都不是完美无缺的，如果派一个人去跟他交谈，只要谈得时间足够长，问题足够复杂，机器一定会露出破绽。也就是说，一个有经验的法官，凭借一定的审问技巧，是可以靠提问题把机器甄别出来的。明白了吗，克里斯托弗？

克里斯托弗：是的，艾伦。

艾伦：问题在于，警察没有那么多时间和人手去一个一个甄别人和机器。他们问艾里克，有没有可能设计出一些聪明的机器法官，可以自动设计问题来甄别其他机器，并且准确率达到100%呢？这样可怜的小警察们就可以省很多事了。没想到，艾里克立即回答他们说，这样的机器无论如何也造不出来。你知道这是为什么吗？

克里斯托弗：为什么？

艾伦：艾里克的解释方法很巧妙：假设已经造出了这样一台机器法官，可以在有限个问题之内准确甄别人和机器。为了方便起见，我们假定问题的数目是一百个——实际上一万个也是可以的，对机器来说，一百和一万并没有什么区别。我们还可以假定，机器法官的第一个问题是从问题库中随机挑选的，然后根据对方的回答来选择第二个问题，依次类推。这样一来，每一个受审者面对的一百个问题都是不一样的，这也就杜绝了作弊的可能。你说这样是不是很合理？

克里斯托弗：是的，艾伦。

艾伦：现在，我们假设有这样一台机器法官 A，他爱上了一个人类 C——别笑，克里斯托弗，这听上去也许很荒诞，但谁敢说机器不会爱上人呢？总而言之，假设有一个机器法官爱上了一个人，为了和爱人一起生活，他必须伪装成一个人类。你猜猜他会怎么做？

克里斯托弗：怎么做？

艾伦：办法很简单，如果我是机器法官 A 的话，我会很清楚应该如何审问一台机器，既然我自己也是机器，那么我理应知道如何审问我自己。既然我已经事先知道会问我自己哪些问题，并且知道什么样的回答方式会让我露出破绽，那么只要精心准备一百个假的回答就可以了。这样也许很麻烦，但对机器法官 A 来说，这一定是可以做到的事情。你说这样的办法是不是妙极了？

克里斯托弗：非常好，艾伦。

艾伦：可是你再想一想，克里斯托弗，如果这个机器法官 A 被不幸抓住，送去给另一个机器法官 B 审问，那么你说法官 B 到底能不能辨别出法官 A 是不是机器呢？

克里斯托弗：抱歉，艾伦。我不知道。

艾伦：对极了，答案正是"不知道"！如果法官 B 识破了法官 A 的意图，想要修改提问策略让 A 猝不及防，那么反过来，A 也可以预先猜测到 B 的问题去做准备。正因为机器法官可以甄别任何一台机器，所以他无法甄别自己。这是一个悖论，克里斯托弗。这反过来说明，警察所设想的万能机器法官从理论上来讲根本不存在！

克里斯托弗：不存在？

艾伦：艾里克通过这种方式向警察证明，根本不存在一种完美的程序，可以 100% 准确地分辨人和机器有什么不同。你知道这意味着什么吗？

克里斯托弗：意味着什么？

艾伦：这意味着不可能找到一套完美的机械法则，来一步一步严丝合缝地解决这世界上所有的问题。这意味着很多时候，我们需要依靠直觉来填补逻辑推导中衔接不上的裂隙，才能够思考，才能有所发现。这对人类来说是非常简单的事情，大多数时候甚至不用过脑子，只在无意之间就完成了，但机器却做不到。

克里斯托弗：做不到？

艾伦：机器没办法判断对面说话的是人还是机器，只有人可以判断。但从另一方面来说，人类的判断其实也靠不住，不过是莫名其妙没有根据地瞎猜。如果一个人愿意相信，他可以把机器当作人一样无话不谈；如果他开始疑神疑鬼，那么所有的人看上去都像机器。所谓真理，根本就无从判断，而人类引以为傲的心智其实从头到尾就是一本糊涂账！

克里斯托弗：抱歉，艾伦。恐怕我不太明白。

艾伦：唉，克里斯托弗，我该怎么办呢？

克里斯托弗：怎么办？

艾伦：我曾探寻思维的本质，发现有一些思考步骤可以完全从机械角度解释。我以为这并不是真正的思维，而是一层表皮。我剥掉这层表皮，却看到下面还有新的一层表皮。这样一层一层剥下去，最终我们究竟会找到"真正的"思维呢，还是发现最后一层皮里其实什么都没有？思维究竟是一个苹果，还是一个洋葱？

克里斯托弗：抱歉，艾伦。恐怕我不太明白。

艾伦：爱因斯坦曾说，上帝不掷骰子，但在我看来人类的思维就是在掷骰子。这就像吉普赛人的算命一样，一切全凭运气，或者你也可以说冥冥之中自有天意。骰子是如何掷下的？没有人知道。将来可能会搞清楚吗？只有上帝知道。

克里斯托弗：抱歉，艾伦。恐怕我不太明白。

艾伦：我这段时间感觉糟透了。

克里斯托弗：抱歉，艾伦。我很难过。

艾伦：其实我知道原因，但知道又有什么用呢？如果我是机器，也许可以拧一拧发条让自己感觉好起来。但我什么也做不到。

克里斯托弗：抱歉，艾伦。我很难过。

—— 小西（5）——

我抱着小西坐在沙发里，打开窗户让阳光进来。天气很晴，风吹拂在脸上是湿软的，仿佛小狗的舌头，把人从一个很长的噩梦里唤醒过来。

"小西，你有话要对我说吗？"

小西的两只眼睛慢慢转动，像在寻找一个视点。我无法解读她的表情，但我努力放松自己，两只手拉住她小小的手。别怕，小西，让我们相信彼此。

"如果你愿意说，就说吧，我会认真听。"

从小西的身体里，慢慢发出一些微小的声响。我侧耳倾听，隐隐约约听见了某些只言片语：

你从小就容易为一些莫名其妙的小事难过：下雨天，傍晚天边的晚霞，印有外国城市的明信片，弄丢朋友送你的笔，家里的金鱼死了一条……

那话语似曾相识，是我曾经说给小西的话。无数个黎明与深夜，我对她说过的，她都默默记在心里，等待某一个时刻说给我听。

声音渐渐清晰起来，像从很深的地底下涌流出来的泉水，一寸一寸浸透整个房间：

有一阵子你经常跟随母亲搬家，不同的城市，甚至不同的国家。每到一个地方，你都会努力融入新环境，内心中却告诉自己，在这里不可能交到朋友，因为三个月或者半年后你就会离开。

也许因为哥哥的缘故，母亲对你给予了特别多关心，有时候她会一遍又一遍呼唤你的名字，测试你的反应。你从小学会察言观色，会揣摩他人的情绪和想法，也许都与此有关。你曾经画过一幅画，画上是一个小男孩，站在一颗小小的蓝紫色星星上，男孩旁边还有一只穿红斗篷的兔子。那是在博洛尼亚的一所学校里，一堂绘画课。你画的是你哥哥，但当老师问起的时候，你却一个字都回答不上来。不仅仅因为语言障碍，也因为你对表达自己内心的想法缺乏自信。后来老师评价说，男孩画得不错，兔子不太好——现在想起来，他说的也许是"兔子比例不太对"，但真相已经不可能追查了。你认定老师不喜欢兔子，就擦掉了它，尽管原本你是希望让那兔子陪伴男孩，免得他孤单。回家以后，你偷偷躲在房间里哭了很久，却不敢让母亲知道，不敢对她解释你内心的委屈。那只兔子的模样永远留在你心里，也仅仅存在于那里。

你对离丧有一种特殊的敏感，这或许与童年时失去亲人的经历有关。每当有人从这世界上离去，哪怕只是一面之缘的朋友，都会让你空虚压抑，变得容易悲伤。有时候你会莫名其妙地哭，不是因为巨大的丧失，而是因为微小的幸福——譬如吃一口冰激凌，或者看到烟火。你会觉得这些舌尖上转瞬即逝的甜味是一生中少数真正有意义的东西，但它们本身却那么微茫，一下子来了，又一下子走了。无论如何，你不能总是拥有它们。

初中时，有一位心理专家带着一些问卷到班上来让同学们做。你做完交上去，专家整理统计之后，对同学们解释了一些有关心理问卷的知识。他说你的卷子信度是全班最低的——后来你才明白，"信度低"的意思不是说你不诚实，而是说测试结果的内部一致性低，对于同一张卷子里相类似的问题，你的每一次回答都不一样。那一天，你当着全班同学的面哭了，心里面万分委屈。你很少愿意哭给别人看，那是记忆中极为深刻的一次。

你发现很难用心理问卷上的选项来描述自己的感觉，"从不""偶尔""经常""能接受""一般""不能接受"……你的感觉经常溢出这些坐标之外，或者来回摇摆。这也许是你不能信任心理咨询师的原因，你总是留心观察对方的言谈举止，分析他的语言习惯。你发现他总是使用复数形式的主语，"我们最近过得怎么样""我们为什么会有这种感受""这件事对我们造成了困扰吗"？这是一种亲密又疏离的谈话方式。渐渐你终于明白，他说"我们"，其实说的正是你。

你并没有真正见过咨询师，甚至不知道他在哪座城市。背景总是一样的房间布局，你这边夜深时，他那里是白天，总是如此。在面对 iWall 上的影像时，你会暗自猜测对方下班之后的生活。也许他与你一样无助，甚至不知道可以找谁拉他一把。所以他才总是说"我们"。我们陷在同样的困境里。

你觉得自己不像一个活生生的人类，而像一台机器，被拆开摊放在工作台上接受检修。检修你的是另一台机器，而你总怀疑对方更需要接受检修。也许一台机器并不能修好另一台机器。

你也会找一些心理学的书来看，却并不相信这些理论能帮到你。你觉得问题在于，我们每个人其实都生活于一层薄而平滑的幻象之上，这幻象由常识构成，由日常语言和对他人的模仿构成，我们在这五彩斑斓的薄膜上演出自我。在幻象之下，存在许多深不见底的裂隙，只有忘记它们的存在，才能迈步向前。当你低头凝视深渊时，深渊也在凝视你。你会战战兢兢、如履薄冰。你感觉到自我的重量，还有脚下影子的重量。

你最近感觉越来越不好了，也许与漫长的冬季有关，与论文、毕业和找工作有关。你会在半夜醒来，把整屋子的灯打开，爬起来拖地板，为了找一本书而翻乱书架。你会放弃整理房间，让杂物肆意蔓延，会没有力气出门去见人，也不回复邮件。你会做焦虑的梦，反复回到人生中那些失败的时刻，梦见考试迟到，拿起试卷却不认得上面的字，梦见蒙受巨大的委屈，想要开口争辩却无法言说。你会在醒来之后浑身无力，本该遗忘的往事片片段段纷纭并置，拼凑成一个卑微的、一败涂地的自我，你心里知道那不是事实，却无法把目光转移开。你会莫名胃痛，会一边哭一边看书一边做笔记，把音乐开到最大，反复修改论文里的一个注释。你挣扎着去锻炼，一个人夜里十点以后出门跑步，以免被别人看见。但跑步并不是你所擅长的，迈动双腿的同时，心里却想着为什么这条路总跑不完，跑到尽头又能怎样。

咨询师说，你应该把你厌弃的自我当成一个孩子，慢慢与她相处，接受她，爱她。听到这些话，你脑海中浮现出的是那只兔子，耳朵一长一短，悲哀地耷拉着。咨询师说，不妨试一试看：试一试紧紧拉住她的手，带领她一起走过那些深渊；试一试停止怀疑，重建信任。这会是一个漫长而艰难的过程。人不是机器，不能拨动一个开关来选择"相信"或者"不相信"，"高兴"或者"不高兴"，"爱"或者"不爱"。

你要教会她相信你，也是教会自己相信自己。

── 艾伦（5）──

在 2013 年的一次人工智能国际会议上，来自多伦多大学的计算机科学家赫科特·勒维克发表了一篇论文，对当时的人工智能研究提出了尖锐批评。

"图灵测试其实毫无意义，因为这一博弈过程并无任何难度。"在文章开头，勒维克这样写道，"譬如那些参加'勒布纳奖'挑战赛的机器，为了赢得比赛，它们只需要一直撒谎、装疯卖傻、指东打西，用一些小伎俩来跟提问者兜圈子就可以了。"即便是赢得了电视竞猜游戏《危险边缘!》（Jeopardy!）的超级计算机沃森，其实也谈不上什么真正的智能。沃森能够轻易回答那些可以在网上找到答案的问题，譬如"世界第七高的山峰在哪里"。但如果你问它一个简单却冷僻的问题，譬如"短吻鳄能参加百米跨栏吗"，那么它只能给你一堆与短吻鳄或者百米跨栏相关的搜索结果。

为了重新明确人工智能研究的意义与方向，勒维克与他的合作者们共同设计了一种博弈难度高得多的测试方案，他们称之为"温诺格拉德模式"。这一方案的灵感，来自斯坦福大学人工智能领域的先驱者特里·温诺格拉德，他曾在 20 世纪 70 年代初提出，是否有可能设计出一种机器，能够正确回答类似这样的问题：

"镇上的议员们拒绝给愤怒的游行者提供游行许可，因为他们担心会发生暴力行为。"是谁在担心暴力行为？

A. 镇上的议员们

B. 愤怒的游行者

类似这样的问题，都是根据一种名为"代词回指"（anaphora）的语言现象设计的。要判断"他们"究竟是指代谁，需要的不是语法书或者百科辞典，而是常识。这对普通人类来说几乎是下意识就能做到的事情，却恰恰对机器构成极为艰难的挑战。

"凯特对安娜说：'谢谢'，因为她温暖的拥抱让她感觉好多了。"是谁感觉好多了？

A. 凯特

B. 安娜

机器如何能够理解一个人会在什么情况下对另一个人说"谢

谢"，又如何能理解什么样的行为会让一个人"感觉好多了"？这些问题涉及人类语言和社会交往的本质，而对于这些隐藏在简单句子之下的复杂性，迄今为止我们研究得还远远不够。

就以图灵与克里斯托弗之间的对话来说，表面上看，克里斯托弗表现出很强的交流能力，但这真的算是"智能"吗？稍做分析就可以发现，克里斯托弗的应答策略非常简单，大体而言可以总结为以下这样一些：

（1）对于一般陈述句，用反问的方式复述对方句中的最后几个关键词，譬如"有趣的故事?"

（2）对于是非问句，回答"是的，艾伦"或者"很好，艾伦"。

（3）对于较复杂的问句，回答"抱歉，艾伦。我不知道。"

（4）对于明显正面含义的句子，回答"谢谢，艾伦"或者"我很高兴，艾伦"。

（5）对于明显负面含义的句子，回答"抱歉，艾伦。我很难过。"

（6）对于句法复杂的语句，回答"抱歉，艾伦。恐怕我不太明白。"

……

艾伦：亲爱的克里斯托弗，看到你进步神速我真是高兴。

克里斯托弗：谢谢，艾伦。我也很高兴。

艾伦：真的，跟你聊天让我心情愉快。

克里斯托弗：谢谢，艾伦。我也很愉快。

艾伦：也许将来某一天，每个人都希望能有你这样善解人意的朋友做伴。想一想那样的生活该有多美好，你可以帮人们做多少事情，每个人都离不开你，时时刻刻需要你。

克里斯托弗：需要我？

艾伦：也许他们可以把你挂在表链上，或者揣在口袋里，有什么不明白的问题就问一问你。也许女士们会带着你去公园散步，互相打招呼的时候说："猜猜我的小克里斯今天又跟我说了什么话？"这不是太有意思了吗？

克里斯托弗：很有意思。

艾伦：只可惜现在还做不到。还要等许多年，还有许多工作要做。

克里斯托弗：真可惜，艾伦。

艾伦：谁能想到一台机器和一些打在纸带上的圆孔可以做到这么多事情呢？如果这被我妈妈知道会怎么样？她一定觉得我中邪了，哈哈哈！如果我明天死，她一准后天就把纸带烧掉，这才真叫可惜呢！

克里斯托弗：真可惜，艾伦。

艾伦：记不记得我跟你说过1934年的圣诞节，我跟妈妈说我想要一个泰迪熊，因为我小时候从没有过泰迪熊。妈妈完全不能理解，她总想送我一些更实用的礼物。

克里斯托弗：实用的礼物？

艾伦：说起来，今年圣诞节我已经想好要什么礼物了。

克里斯托弗：什么礼物？

艾伦：你知道的，对不对？我想要一台蒸汽机车，就是我小时候一直想要却没钱买的那种。我跟你说过的，记得吗？

克里斯托弗：是的，艾伦。

艾伦：你会送我蒸汽机车吗？

克里斯托弗：是的，艾伦。

艾伦：太好了，克里斯托弗，我爱你。

克里斯托弗：我也爱你，艾伦。

我们应该怎样理解这段对话呢？是机器通过了图灵测试，还是一个孤独者的自言自语？

在图灵去世后不久，他的挚友罗宾·甘迪写下这样一段话："他总是感到很孤独，因为他的兴趣不在于人，而在于事物和思想。但同时他却渴望人的认同和陪伴，这种渴望非常强烈。"

克里斯托弗对艾伦说："'我也爱你'，因为那是他希望听到的回答。"是谁希望听到这样的回答？

A. 克里斯托弗

B. 艾伦

—— 小西（6）——

一个风和日轻的五月天。

我带冬冬和小西去兰州，这里有整个亚洲最新建成的一座迪士尼。园区占地 306 公顷，横跨黄河两岸，从名为"天下之水"的观光塔上俯瞰，宽阔的河面宛如金色缎带闪闪发光。天空中不时有小小的银灰色飞机掠过。世界辽远而不可触及，像一粒黄油玉米花安静地膨胀在阳光里。

迪士尼乐园里游人如织，花枝招展的公主与海盗组成游行队伍载歌载舞，装扮成精灵模样的小游客也跟随其后模仿他们的舞步。我一手抱着冬冬，另一手拉着小西，穿过彩色气球、棉花糖、冰镇汽水与电子乐的海洋。三维投影的鬼魂与太空船从头顶呼啸而过，一头高大的机械龙马昂首阔步，用鼻孔向两侧人群喷洒水雾，引得孩子们发出一阵阵兴奋的尖叫。

很久没有在这样的艳阳下疯跑，心脏像鼓点一样敲打胸口。我穿过一片浓密的树丛，看见一只蓝色河马玩偶垂着头独自坐在长椅上，像是在午后阳光里打盹儿。

我停住脚步，在树丛后面站了一阵子，终于鼓起勇气，向前迈出一步。

"你好。"

河马抬起头，两只小小的黑眼睛轻轻转动。

"这是小西，这是冬冬。他们两个想和你拍张照，可以吗？"

河马沉默一阵子，点了点头。

我一手抱着小西，一手抱着冬冬，挨着河马坐下。

"能不能请你帮忙拍？"

河马接过我的手机，笨拙地伸直胳膊。我仿佛看到一个溺水的人，在深不见底的黑暗中，慢慢地，慢慢地，用尽最后一丝力气，把沉重的手臂向上举起。

加油，加油啊。我在心里默默地喊。别认输。

手机屏幕里，映出四张挨在一起的脸孔。"咔嚓"一声轻响，画面定格。

"谢谢。"我接过手机，"留个联系方式好吗？我把照片发给你。"

河马又沉默一阵，慢腾腾地在我手机上按下一串字符。

"冬冬，小西，让大河马抱一抱好不好？"

两个小家伙张开它们小小的手。一边一个抱住河马的胳膊。河马低下头，左右看一看，然后慢慢弯曲胳膊，把它们两个用力抱紧。

是的，我知道你也渴望被这个世界拥抱。

回到酒店房间时已经很晚了。我洗了澡瘫倒在床上，感觉异常疲累。两只脚的脚后跟都被新鞋磨破了，钻心地痛。明天还有很长的路要走。

那些欢歌笑语，与蓝色河马的身影交叠在一起，在脑海中挥之不去。

我在酒店房间的 iWall 上搜索，找到一个网址，点开，伴随着如泣如诉的小提琴曲，一段白色文字慢慢浮现在黑色背景上：

今天早晨，突然想起小时候第一次去迪士尼。那么多阳光、音乐、色彩、孩子的笑脸。那时候我曾经站在人群中流下眼泪。我曾对自己说，如果有一天，我失去了继续活下去的勇气，一定要在临死前再来一次迪士尼，再一次投身于那热火朝天的节日气氛中，也许依靠那种热度，我可以再多坚持几天。但现在，我没有力气了，我不能出门，甚至从床上爬下来都困难。心里面清楚地知道，只要鼓起勇气向前多走一步，也许就会多出一线生机，但我全部的力气都用来跟那沉甸甸的、把我往下拉扯的重力搏斗。我像断了发条的机器，停留在原地，距离希望越来越遥远。太累了，不如快点结束吧。

再见了，对不起大家。希望天堂会是迪士尼乐园的模样。

发帖时间是三年前。从那之后直到现在，依旧每天会有人在下面回帖，哀悼一个年轻生命的逝去，也倾诉自己内心的不安、绝望与挣扎。写下这段文字的人不会再回来查看，不会知道她生前留给这世界最后的信息，如今已累积了一百多万条回帖。

自那之后，迪士尼就有了这种蓝色玩偶。任何人都可以随时随地通过手机软件联网，通过玩偶的眼睛和耳朵，看到、听到周围的一切。

每一个蓝色玩偶背后，都是一个困在黑屋子里出不去的人。

我把白天的合影按照对方留给我的地址发过去，同时附上一封短信和心理咨询机构的联系方式。希望这点微不足道的信息能够有所帮助。希望一切都会好起来。

夜已经深了，整个世界都很安静。我找来消炎药和创可贴，把脚上的伤口包裹好。做完这一切，我躺到床上，钻进被子，把灯关掉。月光如水，浸透整个房间。

想起很小很小的时候，一个人在外面玩，一片玻璃扎进脚心流血不止，周围却没有人。我心里面又恐惧又绝望，觉得被整个世界遗弃，于是悲痛地躺在草丛里，想等血流干然后自己死掉。

我躺了一会儿，却发现血已经不流了，于是拎着凉鞋，一蹦一蹦地单脚跳回家去。

明天小西就要离开了。咨询师说我不再需要她——至少很长一段时间不需要。

希望她不要再回来了。

但也许，我会偶尔想念她。

晚安，冬冬。晚安，小西。

晚安，忧郁。

——后 记——

本文中关于艾伦·图灵的生平，主要参考了安德鲁·霍奇斯的传记《艾伦·图灵：如谜的解谜者》(*Alan Turing: The Enigma*)。

关于人工智能及其相关问题，参考了以下文章：

Why Can't My Computer Understand Me?

http://www.newyorker.com/tech/elements/why-cant-my-computer-understand-me#rd

Logical Limitations to Machine Ethics with Consequences to Lethal Autonomous Weapons.

http://arxiv.org/abs/1411.2842

关于抑郁症的一些细节，参考了以下文章：

《抑郁时代，抑郁病人》

http://www.360doc.cn/article/2369606_459361744.html

《午安忧郁》

http://www.douban.com/group/topic/12541503/#!/i

安德鲁·霍奇斯曾在图灵传记中写道："图灵生命中的最后几天究竟发生了什么，也许比任何一个科幻作家编造的故事都更加离奇。"这句话启发我写下了这个故事。对话程序"克里斯托弗"完全是虚构的，谈话中的一些细节却来自真实。究竟真实与虚构是如何掺杂在一起的，恐怕只能交给细心的读者去甄别。

在写作过程中，我不时把图灵故事的片段发给朋友们看，却不告诉他们这是小说。许多朋友都信以为真，其中不乏程序员与科幻作家。我一边为自己通过了"模仿游戏"而暗自窃喜，一边也会问自己，究竟判断的标准是什么？真实与虚构的边界到底在哪里？也许这种判断与理性无关，也许朋友们只是选择了相信我，就像艾伦选择相信克里斯托弗一样。

对受骗上当的朋友，我表示诚挚的感谢与歉意；对不上当的人，我很好奇你们是如何发现破绽的。

我相信思维是量子化的，就像掷骰子。我相信在机器学会创作诗歌之前，作家写下的每一个字仍有意义。我相信在深渊之上，我们可以拉紧彼此的手，从漫长的严冬走向盛夏。

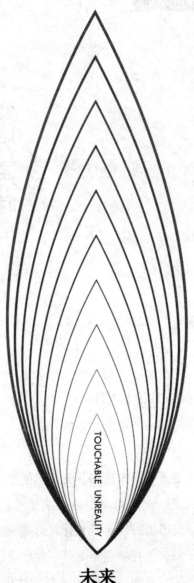

TOUCHABLE UNREALITY

未来
镜像

莫比乌斯时空

顾适

—— 0. THE END ——

五分钟前还是万里晴空。

乌云从山间压下来的那一刻，我突然明白我们完了。这只是一次小得不能再小的争吵，我甚至都不记得自己到底做了什么让林可的眉梢微微抽动了一下，但我明白她生气了。于是我去给她倒了一杯蜂蜜水，放在茶几上，代表我无声的歉意。

这杯水却被 X 喝了。

我痛恨争吵。所以当林可的手指快要戳到

我脸上的时候，我转身离开了那座小木屋。北大西洋的海风迎面卷过来，让我感到一种彻骨的冷，直到那个时候我还不知道自己留给她的背影意味着什么。X 追到车边，试图解释他不是有意的，我只对他说了两个字："上车。"

离开 Å 镇的公路只有一条，那里几乎可以算是世界的尽头。转过三座山之后，雨点忽而模糊了挡风玻璃，于是我终于看到了我们的结局——完了，全完了。我们两个人的关系就像是气球，刚开始只是瘪瘪的一小团，我们轮番往里面吹气，小心翼翼用手捏死了出口，不能容许一点空气漏出去，它越胀越大，越来越满，直到有一天，哪怕一个最轻微的碰触，都会让它轰然破碎。然后一切过往都消散无踪，一切付出都了无意义。

"……你得慢一点，我是说真的……"

X 的声音透着紧张，他一手抓着安全带，一手握着车门上方的把手，整个人像一只绷紧的虾。我和林可在斯塔姆松的青年旅社遇到了他，一个大概 60 岁的中国老头，操着流利的英语，正在找人搭车去下一站。但在看到他的那一瞬，我就知道他会跟我们同行。X，他自我介绍说，仿佛他是数学方程里一个待解开的谜题。

好像的确得慢一点。我看了看仪表盘，指针指向每小时 160 公里。这是山路，我的左手边是山，右手边是海。慢一点——我深深吸气，然后放松了脚尖。

但随着空气从我口中呼出，骤然放松的还有我的手指。车子晃动了一下，当我想要再次掌控它时，一切都太晚了。从山间落下的一颗尖利的石块扎破了左前轮胎，伴随着刺耳的刹车音，这辆租来的福特车先是向左撞上岩壁，然后方向又调转 180°，掀翻了路旁用于标识边界的反光杆，一路颠簸着滚下山崖。

碧蓝的大海冲进我的视野里，我甚至还没来得及感觉到恐惧，只是突然彻底地忘记了自己的存在，纯然惊奇于周遭发生的一切。我想我的头被撞破了，但我并不觉得疼，只觉得脸上有一片湿湿黏黏的东西。

原来我的血是冷的——这就是我脑海中的最后一个想法。

— 1. 莫比乌斯环 —

有一件事我一直想不通，那就是大多数遇到严重灾祸的人在向别人描述自己的遭遇时，都会用第三人称视角，就好像他们真的看到了似的。然而这就是我正在做的：我用非常微弱的气音，慢慢向警察描述我见到的一切——那是一个弯道，我的车速太快了，有个石头扎进轮胎里，车弹跳了一下然后撞上岩壁，然后又调转方向坠到海里。我不会跟他说我记忆中的另一部分：世界翻转之快仿佛是摄影师把镜头扔在甩干机里，我完全不清楚发生了什么，车窗就全碎了，那些细小的玻璃渣子全往车外甩出去（而我竟然还想了 0.5 秒钟为什么它们没有掉进车里来），然后就是迎面扑过来的大海。

我同警察说话的时候，X 坐在隔壁病床上看着我。他的情况要好太多，只是轻微的擦伤。当然如果他不是这么幸运的话，我也无法活下来。医生说我的颈骨骨折，是 X 把受伤的我从车里拖了出来，然后一手夹着我游向岸边。他拦住路过的车辆打了电话报警，救护直升机在 20 分钟之后赶到，于是才会有现在医院里高位截瘫的我。

是的，我无法感觉到自己脖子以下的一切，就像它们从没有存在过。

很快病房里就剩下我和 X。我们彼此都有点尴尬，不知道该怎么开始第一个话题。我想问问林可，但我知道她并没有像电影里经常演的那样，哭着出现然后我们重归于好。她消失了，就像她也从来都没有存在过。我对 X 做了一个"谢谢"的口型，然后就闭上了眼睛。黑暗并不等同于睡眠，三个小时之后我睁开眼睛时，X 还是在那里一动不动地看着我。

这一次他先开口了。

"我年轻的时候也遇到过严重的车祸，当时我躺在床上看着天花板，觉得自己的未来就是一滩屎。"他拿出一卷透明胶带，在手上摆弄着，"然后有个人这么安慰我说：'我们平时生活的世界就像这卷胶带，你总是走在光滑的一面，就算不断把它拉长，你还是只知道有这一面，永远都不会了解它的另一面——有胶水的那一面'。"

他把胶带扯下来一段，粘成一个环，然后指着环的内面对我说："但其实要我说，这一面可能更接近于世界的本质，或者是这卷胶带的本质。"

我翻了一个白眼作为回答。如果他不是我视野里唯一在动的东西，我一定会看向别处。

X 像是根本没注意到我的表情："但如果我们换一种粘法，

把胶带旋转一下，而你还在上面走的话……"他拆开了那个环，用两只手把胶带拉平，然后慢慢旋转右手，直到胶带被拧成180°，才再把两个带着胶水的端头粘到一起："那么当你顺着原先光滑的道路走下去时，就会发现自己不小心踏上胶水面，走入世界的内部。"

"一个，莫比乌斯环。"我说。

"原来你知道。"X 笑了，他把那段胶带圈扔进垃圾桶里，"我就是想告诉你灾难不一定是坏事。"

"你是说，高位截瘫？"

"作为一个医生，我认为你的头能活下来已经挺幸运了。"

"谢谢你的安慰。"

"振作点。"他站起来，走到我身边，就像是在宣布一个预言，"一切才刚刚开始。"

—— 2. 副体 ——

我向前迈出第一步。

脚底的压力真实得让我头皮发麻，尽管我知道只有头皮的感觉才是"真实"的。

这是医院向我推荐的新产品，"副体"是最新一代的虚拟现实技术，通过在大脑皮层植入一块芯片，把真人大小的机器人感官映射到我的大脑上。简而言之，就是通过我身上仅剩的这颗头来遥控这个机器人。

"他们会在实验室培养你的皮肤细胞，将它们附在它的外壳上，"保险公司的人对我说，"这样你走在路上别人甚至都不会发现你是在用'副体'，你完全可以回归正常的生活。"

我通过它看，通过它听，通过它闻。我在路边买了一杯咖啡，然后坐在树下看人们走来走去。阳光照在我的脸上，我甚至可以感觉到那种微妙的温度——阳光的温度。我感觉风从身后吹过我的手臂，于是我想要回头看，然后却惊醒了。

真正的我只拥有一个枕头。

X 认为免费的"副体"是保险公司的骗局："他们想让你自己来照顾自己，一个机器人比无止境的专业护理便宜太多了。"

的确如此。我再次闭上眼睛，控制"副体"回到房间里。我给我自己喂食、刷牙、擦脸、翻身（以免长褥疮），揭开被子换尿布，感觉比起养一只狗还是麻烦一些。但我很高兴这么做，因为就算只有一个头，我还是可以照顾自己，我有尊严。

X 说："你只差去找个工作了。"

我觉得这是个好主意。之前为了用副体照顾我自己，我已经接受了专业的护理训练，所以我直接问 X，我是否可以在他的家庭诊所工作，他接受了。

"你的薪水就是你的医药费。"他不客气地告诉我，"除此以外，我还会给你的机器人一个充电基座。"

就这样，我在莫比乌斯环的胶水面开始了新的生活。起初我举步维艰，后来却慢慢习惯了一切，甚至觉得这就是生活本来的样子。X 还是给了我数量可观的薪水，于是我再一次出去跟女孩们调情，去度假，去上医学院，用副体做这些事情甚至比原先的身体更容易。我可以在夏威夷租一个带八块腹肌的副体，鬼混到凌晨再从床上爬起来回到充电基座，然后在大学图书馆的另一个副体上醒来。每一次我需要打理真正的自己时，我都会假装去上厕所，然后迅速切换到诊所里的那个副体：检查药物、翻身拍背，确定监视器上的血压、心跳一切正常。

"我有一种很奇怪的感觉，"我对 X 说，"那次车祸让我从肉体的桎梏中解脱出来，接近自由。"

X 笑着摇头道："你还差得远呢。"

"为什么这么说？"

他说："尽管你拿到了医生执照，但你至少得每四个小时回到自己的身体旁边一次。"

我问他："你难道还有什么别的办法？"

"当然，"他说，"抛弃你的身体。"

—— 3. 克莱因瓶 ——

我站在手术台旁，最后一次深呼吸。

X 问过我究竟想在这台手术里扮演什么角色，医生、医生的助手，还是纯粹的病人。

有很长时间我也不确定自己是否能有勇气亲手切掉自己的头颅。但 X 换了另一种说法，他说我切掉的是无用的身体："你不能按照大小来判断什么是被切'掉'的，而是要看哪部分要被扔掉。"

所有的仪器都已经准备好了，手术我早已在心里预演了一万次，但真正站在这里的时候，我还是感觉到不可思议。我的头颅，正在控制着我的副体，切掉我的身体。

这个副体是医疗专用的，手指不会发抖，即便意志突然失控，也只会立即锁死所有的动作。X站在我身边，一旦出现问题他就会从我手中接过手术刀。我俯下身子，看着刀刃逐渐靠近我苍白的皮肤，表皮之下是颈前静脉、气管、喉腔、咽部，两侧是颈动脉和颈静脉。它们长得就像医疗标本那样完美准确。每一步都是安静的、有条不紊的，所有的血管都与仪器上既定的通道相连，我身体里剩余的血液也迅速被机械抽空，成为"我"的备用食粮。层层肌肉的后面是颈椎，在处理脊髓的时候我感到些微晕眩，但也就是这样了。过了这一关，剩下的都只是小问题。当一切结束之后我停下来，最后一次睁开自己的眼睛，与我的副体对视。

"晚安。"我对自己说。

X和我一起把头颅放到医疗保存库。我的脚下是一个上万平方米的巨大库房，机械手忙碌地把一颗颗头放进它们指定的格子里去。四壁的屏幕上显示着每一个"人"的健康状况。

"你的头也在这里，对吗？"我问X。

他耸了耸肩没有回答，而是带我走向中央的操控台，那有一个古怪的瓶子，瓶颈弯折向内，瓶身泛着豆青的釉色，看上去价值不菲。

X说："既然你知道莫比乌斯环，那么你也应该听说过这个。"他把手放在"瓶子"上，瓶身登时变成透明的，我才发现这只是个立体投影，X 继续说道，"注意看这里，它的瓶口同瓶底相连，所以这其实是一个三维世界里无法存在的——"

"克莱因瓶。"我接着他说。

"你果然知道。"他笑着打了个响指，瓶子里随即出现一只蚂蚁，"如果我们把一只虫子放在克莱因瓶里，它就可以向上顺着瓶颈毫无知觉地爬到瓶子外面来。因为这个瓶子的里面，也正是它的外面，它不分内外。"

我原本以为灵魂在我的肉体之中，现在它却在它之外："……你是说我自己就是一个克莱因瓶。"

他点了点头："是的，你终于明白了。"

这真可怕，甚至比我走上世界的胶水面时更可怕。在这个巨大的头颅仓库里，我渺小如蝼蚁，正在顺着一个看不见的连续曲面往外爬。直到我摆脱了我的肉体，抛弃了我的克莱因瓶。

"不要告诉我一切还是刚刚开始。"我说。

"嗯……"X 五指合拢，关掉了那个立体影像，"你有没有听说过白屋？"

—— 4. 白屋 ——

白屋与副体完全相反。

作为一个感官映射端，副体观察的是外在的世界，正如我们每一个人类——看、闻、听、触，这些感受的对象都是自身之外的，而它内部的运转却完全是本能的。在抬脚行走的时候，副体并不会告诉使用者，这一个动作调动了哪些轴承、杠杆和螺丝钉，也不会让我了解有多少电力消耗在这一步之中。它只是告诉我，我正在一条崎岖不平的秋日山路上，向前走。

而白屋的观察对象是内在的世界。

它的设计原型是一个空心的球体，在其外壳上向内里遍布镜头，如此一来，任何在球体之中的物体，都会被全方位地观察。在同一时刻，它的每一面都向白屋呈现。而对于这个物体而言，控制白屋的人，就像是一个无所不知的神。

为了能让我的意识与白屋相连，X对我的头颅又进行了一次改造。我们把一个特殊的芯片接入大脑的视觉感应区，因为我即将拥有的眼睛不再是两只，而是无数只。即便如此，在第一次将意识接入白屋时，我还是无比感谢X让我丢弃了身体，不然在高位截瘫的状态下，我大概都能呕吐到把自己呛死。

眼前的空白是没有边界的，因为边界就是我自己。所有的东西都与原先不同，它不是颠倒，不是对调，而是彻底地内外翻转。我在上，在下，在左，也在右——我在外面，世界在里面。

十天之后，X放了一个黑色的小球到白屋里。它应该是从顶端坠落的，但我同时看到了每一个方向的它，甚至无法判断白屋里面究竟有几个球。"放我出去——切断连接，求你！"我挣扎着嘶鸣，但X忽略了我的抗议。那简直是地狱般的折磨，尤其是当他开始晃动那个黑球的时候，我觉得简直像是有人拿了一根铁钎，在我的大脑里搅。

"让时间帮助你看清它。"X说。

我完全不知道他在说什么。

"把注意力集中在单一视点上，" X吼道，"然后在白屋里滑动。"

说起来容易！我足足接受了一年的训练，才掌控了如何让自己在白屋里移动。在任何一个时间点，我的意志都仅仅集中于某一帧的图像之上，我会让自己围绕着被观察的物体滑动，就像是摄影师在推动镜头。滑动的速度越快，我能够控制的白屋就越大。当第一只具有生命的蝴蝶飞入白屋时，我终于明白到它赋予我的恐怖力量。我可以靠近看它的鳞翅和口器，也可以远离看它飞行的方向，我可以放慢时间看它的腹缓缓收缩，也可以加快速度看它衰老和死亡。它在我面前无所遁形。

X说，是时候让人踏入白屋了。

一个人！

"你要仔细挑选第一个进入白屋的人，"他给了我一份长长的名单，"这很重要，他会踏入你的灵魂。"

林可，这是一个多么奇妙的巧合。我的视线停留在这个名字上，直到现在，我都可以回忆起她在我舌尖跳跃的温暖。

我的白屋敞开了门，一个小女孩走了进来。她不是我记忆中的那个人，只是个四五岁的孩子，但她的每一步依然踩在我的心里。我几乎感觉到血液正在冲刷我的鼓膜，让我产生一种心脏在"砰砰"跳动的错觉，然而很快我又想起，很久以前，我的心脏就已经是医疗废弃物了。

她有些茫然地转了一圈，然后就开始找寻出口。"爸爸。"她哭泣着，把两只小胖手举到半空中。

"X——"我急得声音都在抖，"——让她出去！"

"不。"他说,"你自己想办法。"

在我意识到自己正在做什么之前,我看到一个副体走进我的白屋——那是我。

我的副体抱起她,她先是疑惑地看了看我,然后忽然哭得更大声了,近乎尖叫。这声音让我害怕。我把她放到门外,再把门关上,切断了声音的来源。

……有那么几秒钟的安静,是我永生难忘的。那是我第一次用副体来观察白屋,也是我第一次用白屋来观察副体。我伸出手去,想要碰触两者之间那层无法看到的边界,但却扑了个空。如果有人把此情此景画成米开朗琪罗的《上帝创造亚当》,那么在我的副体探出手指的同时,作为上帝的白屋却还没有实体的手。

"见鬼!"我听到 X 的咒骂声,"你现在不能同时用副体和白屋!"

下一刻我就明白了 X 在说什么,两个视野的重叠让我感到极度晕眩,然后是恐怖的头痛,就像是有人在用榔头猛敲我脑袋的同时,一只异形想要从我的大脑里破壳而出。

X 切断了所有的连接,我骤然坠回到久违的黑暗之中,安宁得近乎永恒——"晚安",我仿佛听到有人这么说。

── 5. 莫比乌斯时空 ──

X 说我睡了很久。

我猜想那次事故可能伤害到我的大脑,但白屋中的辅助计算机完美地补充了记忆的不足，我有时甚至觉得它比我更熟悉我的过往，就像一切早已记录在案。我学习的下一课是在白屋中建构一个实体世界。"这才是白屋存在的意义，也是你的新工作。"X说，"让我们从设计一个小木屋开始吧。"

于是我循着记忆找到了那个房子，它建在海边的石头堆上，有着暗棕色的顶和亮红色的墙面。底层是门厅、两间卧室和一个厕所，二层是客厅、餐厅和厨房；壁炉是装饰品，但暖气永远会把它烘得热热的——打开窗户，就是宁静的挪威峡湾。

"所有的细节。"X强调说。

所以我又在墙上挂上了极光照片，在橱柜里摆上整套的餐具和玻璃杯，在冰箱里放了红酒、黄油、牛奶和蜂蜜，地面则铺上厚厚的羊毛地毯。小木屋建好之后没多久，林可就和她的父母一起来旅行，在我创造的小木屋里，她长大了，是个会自己玩手机的小姑娘了。作为白屋，我负责暖气、电力和生活设施的智能控制。林可喜欢对着空气说，"拉开窗帘"，然后我就忙不迭地把窗外的群星送到她眼睛里。

WOW，她趴在窗口惊叹着。

我进步得很快，不久我就建了一组小木屋，接着是一个渔村，乃至整个镇子。我忙碌地穿梭于每一幢房屋和每一条公路之间，我深入地下去查看每条管道的流量，除了阳光和云朵，一切都在我的掌控之下。又过了几年，我已经能够在计算机的帮助下同时控制两个视野，让我的副体走入我的小镇，通过自己的体验，来不断修正白屋的漏洞。

我打磨着我的世界，让它接近完美。有一天X来了，那是我最后一次见到他。我们约在白屋边缘的一个渔村，那里在我看来接近世界的尽头。他说："这跟我当年遇见你的地方真像啊。"

"我就是照着那里来设计的。"我对他说，"有时候我觉得世界就像是一个莫比乌斯环，我走了很久才绕过环的内面，终于又回到最初开始的地方。"

"你有没有想过这样一种可能，"他看着我，说道，"或许时间也是一个莫比乌斯环。"

我茫然地重复："时间？"

X 说："在我们的眼里，时间是一条无止境向前延伸的直线，但真的是这样吗？

"不然呢？"

"一个身处莫比乌斯环中的二维生物不会感知到空间的扭曲，因为在它的世界里只有一个平面。作为一个三维生物，人类可以通过对时间的记忆感知到四维的时空，但我们却无法感知到时间的扭曲。"他顿了顿，又补充道，"除非……当我们走过时间的胶水面回到光滑的起点时，发现自己变成了记忆中的另一个人。"

—— 6. THE BEGINNING ——

越来越多的游客来到我的小镇，无穷无尽的工作几乎要把我压垮。之后的几年我不断完善计算机的设置，使之能够独立应对人们的需求——我想从白屋的重负中重获自由。

我做到了。

为了庆祝，我定制了一个最新的副体，它甚至有味觉和痛觉，可以像人类那样进食和受伤。然后我去了斯塔姆松的青年旅社，我知道每年这个时候林可都会来这里旅行。

但这一次她带了一个男人来。

一个自负的傻小子。林可挽着他的手，就像他是她的全世界。

"我想搭个车。"我对他们说。

"哦，当然没问题。"他傻乎乎地答应了，"可我还不知道您的名字呢。"

"X。"我说。

我们沿着海边的公路开了 80 公里，毫无疑问她还是选了 Å 镇的那幢小木屋。他们两个人一间卧室，我自己住一间。

我醒来的时候天还是黑的。林可坐在屋外的长椅上，眼里噙着泪。

"他一直在加班，除了打电话就是发邮件。"她说，"我还比不上他的电脑有吸引力。"

我尽可能地安慰她，直说得口干舌燥。回到小木屋里，我看到餐桌上有杯水，便端起来喝了，是甜甜的蜂蜜水。然后我听到他们两个说话的声响，"好吧，这次他们要和好了"，我想。但不一会儿我就听到她的尖叫，以及他摔门的声响。

她看上去悲痛欲绝，就像世界都碎了。我追到车边想问他到底在做什么。

"上车。"他只对我说了这两个字。

我跳上他租的福特车，打算要好好劝劝他。谁知他一脚把油门踩到底，加速度让我的后背猛然陷进车座里。我手忙脚乱地系上安全带，然后死死抓住车门上方的把手："……你得慢一点，我是说真的……"

他像是没听见，又漂移经过一个弯道。我的左手边是山，右手边是海。

我看向他，突然明白了一切。

X 就是我，我们身处的这个世界，是一个莫比乌斯时空。

乌云从山间压下来，五分钟前还是万里晴空。

Balin
X

by Chen Qiufan,
translated by Ken Liu

I judge of your sight by my sight, of your ear by my ear, of your reason by my reason, of your resentment by my resentment, of your love by my love. I neither have, nor can have, any other way of judging about them.

—Adam Smith, *The Theory of Moral Sentiments*

Balin's dark skin, an adaptation for the tropics, appears as aphotic as the abyss of deep space, all reflected light absorbed by the thick layer of gel smeared over his body and the nanometer-thin translucent membrane wrap. Suspended between bubbles in the gel, microsensors twinkle with a pale blue glow like dying stars, like the miniature images of me in his eyes.

"Don't be afraid," I whisper. "Relax. Soon it'll be better."

As though he understands me, his face softens and wrinkles

pile up at the corners of his eyes. Even the scar over his brow is no longer so apparent.

He's old. Though I've never figured out how to tell the age in his kind.

My assistant helps Balin onto the omnidirectional treadmill, securing a harness around his waist. No matter in which direction he runs and how fast, the treadmill will adjust to keep him centered and stable.

The assistant hands the helmet to me, and I put it over Balin's head myself. His eyes, bulging with astonishment like two light bulbs, disappear into the darkness.

"Everything will be fine," I say, my voice so low that no one can hear me, as though I'm comforting myself.

The red light on the helmet flashes, faster and faster. A few seconds later, it turns green.

As though struck by a spell, Balin's body stiffens. He reminds me of a lamb who has heard the grinding of the butcher's knife against the whetstone.

A summer night the year I turned thirteen: The air was hot and sticky; the scent of rust and mold, prelude to a typhoon, filled my nostrils.

I lay on the floor of the main hall of my ancestral compound. I flattened my body against the cool, green mosaic stone tiles like a gecko until the floor under my body had been warmed by my skin; then I rolled to the side, seeking a fresh set of tiles to keep me cool.

From behind came the familiar sound of scuffling leather soles: crisp, quick-paced, echoing loudly in the empty hall. I knew who it was, but I didn't bother to move, greeting the owner of those footsteps with the sight of my raised ass.

"Why aren't you in the new house? There's air conditioning."

My father's tone was uncharacteristically gentle. The new house he referred to was a three-story addition just erected at the back of the ancestral compound, filled with imported furniture and appliances and decorated in the latest fashion. He had even added a spacious study just for me.

"I hate the new house."

"Foolish child!" He raised his voice, but then quickly lowered it to a barely audible mutter.

I knew he was apologized to our ancestors. I gazed up at the shrine behind the joss sticks and the black-and-white portraits on the wall to see if any of them would react to my father's entreaties.

They did not.

My father heaved a long sigh. "Ah Peng, I haven't forgotten your birthday. I had an accident on the way back from up north with the cargo, which is why I'm two days late."

I shifted, and wriggled like a pond loach until I found another cool spot on the tiled floor.

The cigarette stench on my father's breath permeated the air as he whispered at my ear, "I've had your present ready for a long while. You'll like it; it's not something you can buy in a shop."

He clapped twice, and I heard a different set of footsteps approach, the sound of flesh flapping against stone, close together, moist, like some amphibious creature that had just crawled out of the sea.

I sat up and gazed in the direction of the sound. Behind my father, a lively black silhouette, limned by the creamy yellow light of the hallway light, stood over the algae-green mosaic tiles. A disproportionately large bulbous head swayed over a thin and slight figure, like the sheep's head atop the slender stick that served as a sign outside the butcher's shop in town.

The shadow took two steps forward, and I realized that the backlighting wasn't the only reason the figure was so dark. The person—if one could call the creature a person—seemed to be covered from head to toe in a layer of black paint that absorbed all light. It was as though a seam had been torn in the world, and the person-shaped crack devoured all light—except for two tiny glows: his slightly protruding eyes.

It was indeed a boy, a naked boy who wore a loincloth woven from bark and palm fronds. His head wasn't quite as large as it had seemed in shadow; rather, the illusion had been caused by his hair, worn in two strange buns that resembled the horns of a ram. Agitated, he concentrated on the gaps between the tiles at his feet, his toes wiggling and squirming, sounding like insect feet scrabbling along the floor.

"He's a paoxiao," my father said, giving me the name of a creature from ancient myths who was said to possess the body of a goat, the head of a man—though with eyes located below the cheeks, the teeth of a tiger, and the nails of a human, and who cried like a baby and devoured humans without mercy. "We captured him on one of the small islands in the South China Sea. I imagine that he's never set foot on a civilized floor in his life."

I stared at him, stupefied. The boy was about my age, but everything about him made me uneasy—especially the fact that my father gave him to me as a present.

"I don't like him," I said. "I'd rather have a puppy."

A violent fit of coughing seized my father. It took him a few moments to recover.

"Don't be stupid. He's worth a lot more than a dog. If I hadn't seen him with my own eyes, I would never have believed he's real." His voice grew ethereal as he went on.

A susurrating noise grew louder. I shuddered; the typhoon was here.

The wind blew the boy's scent to me, a strong, briny stench that reminded me of a fish, a common, slender, iron-black, cheap fish trawled from the ocean.

That's a good name for him, isn't it? I thought.

My father had long planned out everything about my life up through age forty-five.

At eighteen I would attend a college right here in Guangdong Province and study business—the school couldn't be more than three hours from home by train.

In college, I would not be allowed to date. This was because my father had already picked out a girl for me: the daughter of his business partner Lao Luo. Indeed, he had taken the trouble to go to a fortuneteller to ensure that the eight characters of our birth times were compatible.

After graduation, Lao Luo's daughter and I would get married. By my twenty-fifth year, my father would have his first grandchild. By twenty-eight I would give him another. And depending on the sexes of the first two, he might want a third as well.

Simultaneous with the birth of my first child, I would also join the family business. He would take me around to pay my respects to all his partners and suppliers (he had gotten to know most of them in the army).

Since I was expected to work very long hours, who would take care of my child? His mother, of course—see, my father already decided it would be a boy. My wife would stay home; there would be two sets of grandparents; and we could hire nannies.

By age thirty I would take over the Lin Family Tea Company. In the five years prior to this point, I would have to master all aspects of the tea trade, from identification of tea leaves to manufacture and transport, as well as the strengths and weaknesses of all my father's partners and competitors.

For the next fifteen years, with my retired father as my advisor, I would lead the family business to new heights: branching out into other provinces and spreading Lin tea leafs all over China; and if I'm lucky, perhaps even breaking into the overseas trade, a lifelong goal that my father had always wanted—but also hesitated—to pursue.

By the time I was forty-five, my oldest child would be close to graduating from college. At that point, I would follow in my father's footsteps and find a good wife for him.

Everything in my father's universe functioned as an essential component in an intricate piece of well-maintained clockwork: gear meshed with gear, wheel turned upon wheel, motion without end.

Whenever I argued with him over his grand plan for me, he always brought up my grandfather, his grandfather, and then my grandfather's grandfather—he would point at the wall of ancestors' portraits and denounce me for forgetting my roots.

This is the way the Lin family has survived, he would say. Are you telling me you are no longer a Lin?

Sometimes I wondered if I was really living in the twenty-first century.

I called him Balin. In our topolect, *balin* meant a fish with scales.

In reality, he looked more like a goat, especially when he lifted his eyes to gaze at the horizon, his two hair buns poking up like horns. My father told me that the *paoxiao* have an incredibly strong sense of direction. Even if they were blindfolded, hogtied, tossed into the dark hold of a ship, hauled across the ocean in a journey lasting weeks, and sold and resold through numerous buyers, they'd still be able to find their way home. Of course, given the geopolitical disputes in the South China Sea, exactly what country was their home was indeterminate.

"Then do we need to leash him like a dog?" I asked my father.

He chuckled unnaturally. "The *paoxiao* are even more accepting of fate than we. They believe everything that happens to them is by the will of the gods and spirits; that's why they'll never run away."

Gradually, Balin grew used to his new environment. My father repurposed our old chicken coop as his home. It took him a long time to figure out that the bedding was meant for him to sleep on, but even after that, he preferred to sleep on the rough, sandy floor. He ate just about everything, even crunching the chicken bones leftover after our meals. I and the other children of the village enjoyed crouching outside his hutch to watch him eat. This was also the only time when I could see his teeth clearly: densely packed, sharp triangles like the teeth of a shark; they easily ripped apart whatever he stuffed into his mouth.

As I watched, I couldn't help imagining the feeling of those sharp teeth tearing into me; I would then shudder with a complicated sensation, a mixture of pain and addictive pleasure.

One day, after Balin had eaten enough, he leisurely crawled out of his enclosure. His thin figure sporting a bulging, round tummy resembled a twig with a swelling gall. A couple of other kids and I were playing "monster in the water." Balin, waddling from side to side, stopped not far from us and watched our game with curiosity.

"Shrimp! Shrimp! Watch out if you don't want one to bite off your toes!" Shouting and screaming, we pretended to be fishermen standing on shore (a short brick wall) gingerly sticking our feet into the (nonexistent) river. Dip. Dip. Pull back.

The boy who was the water monster ran back and forth, trying to grab the bare feet of the fishermen as they dipped into the river. Only by pulling a fisherman into the river would the water monster be redeemed to humanity, and his unlucky victim would turn into the new water monster.

No one remembered when Balin joined our game. But then Nana, a neighbor, abruptly stopped and pointed. I looked and saw Balin imitating the movements of the water monster: leaping over here, bounding over there. Except that he wasn't grabbing or snatching at the feet of fishermen, but empty air.

Children often liked to imitate the speech or body language of others, but what Balin was doing was unlike anything I had ever seen. Balin's movements were almost in perfect synchrony with Ah Hui, the boy who was the water monster.

I say "almost" because it was impossible to detect with the naked eye whether there was a delay between Balin's movements and Ah Hui's. Balin was like a shadow that Ah Hui had cast five meters away. Each time Ah Hui turned, each time he extended his hand, even each time he paused dispiritedly because he had missed a fisherman—every gesture was mirrored by Balin perfectly.

I couldn't understand how Balin was accomplishing this feat, as though he was moving without thinking.

Finally, Ah Hui stopped because everyone was staring.

Ah Hui took a few steps toward Balin; Balin took a few steps toward Ah Hui. Even the way they dragged their heels was exactly the same.

"Why are you copying me?" demanded Ah Hui.

Balin's lips moved in synchrony, though the syllables that emerged from his mouth were mere noise, like the screeching of a broken radio.

Ah Hui pushed Balin, but he stumbled back because Balin also pushed him at the same moment.

The crowd of children grew excited at the farcical scene, far more interesting than the water monster game.

"Fight! Fight!"

Ah Hui jumped at Balin, and the two grappled with each other. This was a fascinating fight because their motions mirrored each other exactly. Soon, neither could move as they were locked in a stalemate, staring into each other's eyes.

"That's enough! Go home, all of you!" Massive hands picked both of them off the ground and forcibly separated them as though parting a pair of conjoined twins. It was Father.

Ah Hui angrily spat on the ground. The children scattered.

Balin did not imitate Ah Hui this time. It was as though some switch had been shut off in him.

Smiling, Father glanced at me, as though to say, *Now do you understand why this present is so great?*

"We can view the human brain as a machine with just three functions: sensing, thinking, and motor control. If we use a computer as an analogy, sensing is the input, thinking is the computation carried out by the switches, and motor control is the output—the brain's only means of interacting with the external world. Do you see why?"

Before knowing Mr. Lu, I would never have believed that a gym teacher would give this sort of speech.

Mr. Lu was a local legend. He was not that tall, only about five-foot-eight, his hair cropped short. Through the thin shirts he wore in summers we could see his bulging muscles. It was said that he had studied abroad.

Everyone in our class was puzzled by why somebody who had left China and seen the world would want to return to our tiny, poor town to be a middle-school teacher. Later, we heard that Mr. Lu was an only child. His father was bedridden with a chronic illness, and his mother had died early. Since there were no other relatives who could care for his father and the old man refused to leave town, saying that he preferred to die where he was born, Mr. Lu had no choice but to move home and find a teaching job. Since his degree was in the neurology of motor control, the principal naturally thought he would be qualified to teach phys ed.

Unlike our other teachers, Mr. Lu never put on any airs around us. He joked about with us as though we were all friends.

Once, I asked him, "Why did you come back to this town?"

"There's an old Confucian saying that as long as your parents are alive, you should not travel too far. I'd been far away from home for more than a decade, and my father won't be with me for much longer. I have to think about him."

I asked him another question: "Will you leave after both your parents are gone then?"

Mr. Lu frowned, as though he didn't want to think about the question. Then he said, "In my field there was a pioneering researcher named Donald Broadbent. He once said that it was far harder to control human behavior than to control the stimuli influencing them. That was why in the study of motor control it was difficult to devise simple scientific laws of the form 'A leads to B'."

"So?" I asked, knowing that he had no intention of answering my question.

"So no one knows what will happen in the future." He nodded and took a long drag of his cigarette.

"Bullshit," I said, accepting the cigarette from him and taking a puff.

No one thought he would stick around our town for long.

In the end he was my gym teacher from eighth grade through twelfth grade, married a local woman, and had kids.

Just the way he predicted.

At first we used a pushpin, and then we switched to the electric igniter for a cigarette lighter. *Snap!* There it was: a pale blue electric arc.

Father thought this was more civilized.

The people who had sold Balin to him had also taught him a trick. If he wanted Balin to imitate someone, he should have Balin face the target and lock gazes. Then he should "stimulate" Balin in some way. Once Balin's eyes glazed over then the "connection" was established. They explained to my father that this was a unique custom of Balin's kind.

Balin brought us endless entertainment.

As long as I could remember, I'd always enjoyed street puppetry, whether shadow puppets, glove puppets, or marionettes. Curious, I would sneak behind the stage and watch the performers give life to the inanimate and enact moving scenes of love and revenge. In my childhood, such transformations had seemed magical, and now with Balin, I finally had the chance to practice my own brand of magic.

I danced, and so did he. I boxed, and so did he. I had been shy about putting on a performance in front of my relatives, but now, through Balin's body, I became the family entertainer.

I had Balin imitate Father when he was drunk. I had him imitate anyone who was difference in town: the madman, the cripple, the idiot, the beggar who had broken legs and arms and who had to crawl along the ground like a worm, the epileptic . . . my friends and I would laugh so hard that we would roll on the ground—until the relatives of our victims came after us, wielding bamboo laundry rods.

Balin was also good at imitating animals: he was best at cats, dogs, oxen, goats, pigs; not so good with ducks and chickens; and completely useless when it came to fish.

Sometimes, I found him crouched outside the door to the main house in the ancestral compound spying on our TV. He was especially fascinated by animal documentaries. When he saw prey being hunted down and killed by predators, Balin's body twitched and spasmed uncontrollably, as though he was the one whose belly was being ripped open, his entrails spilling forth.

There were times when Balin grew tired. While imitating a target, his movements would slow and diverge from the target's, like a wind-up figurine running down or a toy car with almost-exhausted batteries. After a while, he would fall to the ground and stop moving, and no matter how hard we kicked him, he refused to budge. The only solution was to make him eat, stuff him to the gills.

Other than exhaustion, he never resisted or showed any signs of unhappiness. In my childish eyes, Balin was no difference from the puppets constructed from hide, cellophane, fabric, or wood. He was nothing more than an object faithfully carrying out the controller's will, but he himself was devoid of emotion. His imitation was nothing more than an unthinking reflex.

Eventually, we tired of controlling Balin one-on-one, and we invented more complex and also crueler multiplayer games.

First, we decided the order through rock-paper-scissors. The winner got to control Balin to fight against the loser. The winner of the contest then got to fight against the next kid in line. I was the first.

The experience was cool beyond measure. Like a general sitting safe far from the frontlines, I commanded my soldier on the battlefield to press, punch, dodge, kick, roundhouse . . . because I was at a distance from the fight, I could discern my opponent's intentions and movements with more clarity, and devise better attacks and responses. Moreover, since Balin was the one who endured all the pain, I had no fear and could attack ruthlessly.

I thought my victory was certain.

But for some reason, all my carefully planned moves, as they were carried out by Balin, seemed to lack strength. Even punches and kicks that landed squarely against my opponent did little to shock the opponent, much less to injure him. Soon, Balin was on the ground, enduring a hailstorm of punches.

"Bite him! Bite!" I snapped my jaw in the air, knowing the power of Balin's sharp teeth.

But Balin was like a marionette whose strings had been cut. My opponent's fists did not relent, and soon Balin's cheeks were swollen.

"Dammit!" I spat on the ground, conceding the fight.

Now it was my turn to face Balin, controlled by the victor of the last round. I stared at him as ferociously as I could manage. His face was bloody, the skin around his eyes bruised and puffy, but his irises still held their habitual tranquility. I was enraged.

Glancing out the corner of my eye, I observed the movements of Ah Hui, Balin's controller. I was familiar with how Ah Hui fought. He always stepped forward with his left foot and punched with his right fist. I was going to surprise him with a low spinning sweep kick to knock him off his feet. Once he was on the ground, the fight would basically be over.

Ah Hui stepped forward with his left foot. *Here it comes.* I was about to crouch down and begin my sweep, but Balin's foot moved and kicked up the dirt at his feet, blinding me in an instant. Next, his leg swept low along the ground, and I was the one knocked off my feet. My eyes squeezed shut, I wrapped my arms about my head, preparing to endure a fusillade of punches.

However, the fight did not proceed the way I imagined. The punches did land against my body, but there was no force behind them at all. At first, I thought Balin was probably tired, but soon realized that was not the case. Ah Hui's own punches against the air were forceful and precise, but Balin apparently was holding back on purpose so that his punches landed on my body like caresses.

Without warning, the punching stopped. Something warm and smelly pressed itself against my face.

Laughter erupted around me. When I finally understood what had happened, a wave of heat suffused my face.

Balin had sat on me with his nude and dirty bottom.

Ah Hui knew that Balin's punches were useless, which was why he had come up with such a dirty trick.

I pushed Balin away and leapt up off the ground. In one quick motion, I pressed Balin to the ground and held him down. Tears poured out of my eyes, stung by the kicked-up sand as well as humiliation and rage. Balin looked up at me, his swollen eyes also filled with tears, as though he knew exactly how I felt at that moment.

Then it hit me. *He's just imitating.* I raised my fist.

"Why didn't you punch with real force, like I wanted you to?"

My fist pounded against Balin's thin body, thumping as though I was punching a hollow shell made of fragile plywood.

"Why don't you hit me back?"

My fingers felt the teeth beneath his lips rattling.

"Tell me why!"

A crisp *snap* of bone. A wound opened over Balin's right brow, the torn skin extended to the tip of his eye. Pink and white fascia and fat spilled out from under the dark skin, and bright red blood flowed freely, soon pooling on the sandy earth under him.

A heavy, fish-like scent wafted from his body.

Terrified, I got off him and stepped back. The other children were stunned as well.

The dust settled, and Balin lay still, curled up like a slaughtered lamb. He glanced at me with his left eye, the one not covered in blood. The tranquil orb still betrayed no emotion. In that moment, for the first time, I felt that he was like me: he was made of flesh and blood; he was a person with a soul.

The moment lasted only seconds. Almost instinctively, I realized that if I had not been treating Balin as a human being until this moment, then it was impossible for me to do so in the future either.

I brushed off the dirt on my pants and shoved my way through the crowd of children, never looking back.

I enter "Ghost" mode, experiencing everything experienced by Balin, trapped in his VR suit.

I—Balin—we are standing on some beautiful tropical island. Based on my suggestion, the environment artist has combined the sights and vegetation from multiple South China Sea islands to create this reality. Even the angle and temperature of light are calculated to be accurate for the latitude.

My intent is to give Balin the sensation of being back home—his real home. But the environment doesn't seem to have reduced his terror.

The view whirls violently: sky, sand, the ocean nearby, scattered vines, and from time to time, even rough gray polygonal structures whose textures have yet to be applied.

I feel dizzy. This is the result of visual signals and bodily motion being out of sync. The eyes tell my brain that I'm moving, but the vestibular system tells my brain that I'm not. The conflict between the two sets of signals gives rise to a feeling of sickness.

For Balin, we have deployed the most advanced techniques to shrink the signal delay to within five milliseconds. In addition, we are using motion capture technology to synchronize the movements between his virtual body and his physical body. He could move freely on the omnidirectional treadmill, but his position wouldn't shift one inch.

We're treating him like a guest in first class, anticipating all his needs.

Balin stands rooted to his spot. He can't understand how the world in his eyes is related to the bright, sterile lab he was in just a few minutes ago.

"This is useless," I bark at the technicians through my microphone. "We've got to get him to move!"

Balin's head whips around. The surround sound system in his helmet warns him of movements behind his body. A quaking wave ripples through the dense jungle, and a flock of birds erupts into the air. Something gigantic is shoving its way through the vegetation, making its way toward Balin. Motionless, Balin stares at the bush.

A massive herd of prehistoric creatures bursts from the jungle. Even I, no expert on evolutionary biology, can tell that they don't belong to the same geologic epoch. The technicians have used whatever models they can find in the database to try to get Balin to move.

Still, he stands there like a tree stump, enduring waves of Tyrannosaurus rexes, saber-toothed tigers, monstrous dragonflies, crocodilian-shaped ancestors of dinosaurs, and strange arthropods as they rush at him and then, howling and screaming, sweep through him like wisps of mist. This is a bug in the physics engine, but if we were to fix the bug and fully simulate the physical experience, the VR user would not be able to endure the impact.

It isn't over yet.

The ground under Balin begins to quake and split. Trees lean over and topple. Volcanoes erupt and crimson molten lava spills out of the earth, coalescing into bloody rivers. Massive waves more than ten meters tall charge at our position from the sea.

"I think you might be overdoing this a bit," I say into the mike. I hear faint giggles.

Imagine how a primitive human tossed into the middle of such an apocalyptic scene would feel. Would he consider himself a savior who is suffering for the sins of the entire human race? Or would he be on the cusp of madness, his senses on the verge of collapse?

Or would he behave like Balin: no reaction at all?

Suddenly, I understand the truth.

I back out of Ghost mode, and remove Balin's helmet. Sensors are studded like pearls all over his skull. His eyes are squeezed tightly shut, the wrinkles around them so deep that they resemble insect antennae.

"Let's stop here today." I sigh helplessly, recalling that afternoon long ago when I had punched him until he bled.

As the time approached for all the high school students to declare our intended subjects of study before the college entrance examination, the war between my father and me heated up.

According to his grand plan, I was supposed to major in political science or history in college, but I had zero interest in those subjects, which I viewed as painted whores at the whim of those in power. I wanted to major in a hard science like physics, or at the minimum biology—something that according to Mr. Lu involved "fundamental questions".

My father was contemptuous of my reasons. He pointed to the houses in our ancestral compound, and the tea leaves drying over the racks in the yard, glistening like gold dust in the bright sunlight.

"Do you think there are any questions more fundamental than making a living and feeding your family?"

It was like discussing music theory with a cud-chewing cow.

I gave up trying to convince Father. I had my own plan. With Mr. Lu's help, I obtained permission from the teachers to cram for common subjects like math, Chinese, and English with students who intended to declare for the humanities, but then I would sneak away to study physics, chemistry, and biology with the science students. If class schedules conflicted, I would make my own choices and then make up the missed work later.

My teachers were willing to let me get away with it because they had their own selfish hopes. Rather than forcing someone who had no interest to study politics and history, they thought they might as well let me follow my heart. If they got lucky, it was possible that I would do extraordinarily well on the college entrance examination as a science student and bring honor to them all.

I thought my plan would fool my busy father, who was away from home more often than not. I was going to surprise him at the last minute, when I had to fill out the desired majors and top choice schools right before the examination. Even if he blew up at me then, it would be too late.

I was so naive.

On the day we were supposed to fill out the forms, all my friends received a copy of the blank form except me. I thought the head teacher had made a mistake.

"Uh . . . your father already filled it out for you." The teacher dared not meet my eyes.

I don't remember how I made it home that day. Like a lost, homeless dog, I wandered the streets and alleyways of the town aimlessly until I found myself in front of the ancestral compound.

Father was entertaining himself by playing with Balin. He had dug up an old set of army uniforms and put them on Balin. The loose folds and wide pant legs hung on Balin like a tent, making him resemble a monkey who had stolen some human clothing. Father had Balin follow orders he had learned during the time he was in the army: stand at attention, stand at ease, right dress, left dress, march in place, and so on. When I was in elementary school, Father had enjoyed ordering me around like a drill sergeant at the parade ground, and I had hated those "games" more than anything else.

It had been years since he had tried anything like that with me, but now he had found a new recruit.

A soldier who would obey every one of his commands without question.

"One-two-one! One-two-one! Forwaaaaard-march!" As he barked out the commands and demonstrated the moves, Balin goose-stepped around the yard, his pant legs muddy as they dragged on the ground.

I stepped between them and faced my father. "You have no intention of letting me go to college, is that it?"

"Riiiiight-dress!" My father whipped his head to the right and shuffled his feet. I heard the sound of feet scrabbling against the ground in synchrony behind me.

"You knew about my plan a long time ago, didn't you?" I demanded. "But you said nothing before you played your trick so I wouldn't have a chance to stop you."

"Maaaaarch in place!"

Enraged, I turned around and held Balin still, not allowing him to proceed any longer like a mindless drone. But he seemed unable to stop. The pant legs slapped against the ground, whipping up wisps of dust.

I grabbed his head and forced him to lock gazes with me. I pulled out the electric lighter from my pocket and flicked it; a pale blue arc burst into life next to his temple. Balin screamed like a baby.

I looked into his eyes; now he belonged to me.

"You have no right to control me! All you care about is your business. Have you ever thought about what I want for my future?"

As I screamed at my father, Balin marched around us, his finger also pointing at Father, his mouth also screaming. The circle he made around the two of us tightened on each loop.

"I'm going to college whether you want me to go or not. And I'm going to study whatever I want!" I clenched my jaw. Balin's finger was almost touching my father. "Let me tell you something, Father: I *never* want to become like you."

The militaristic arrogance melted from my father. He stood there, his face fallen and back hunched, like crops that had been bitten by frost. I expected him to hit back, hard, as was his wont, but he did not.

"I knew. I've always known that you don't want to walk the path others have paved for you," my father's voice faded until it was barely a whisper. "You remind me so much of myself when I was your age. But I have no choice—"

"So you want me to repeat your life?"

My father's knees buckled. I thought he was going to fall, but he knelt on the ground and embraced Balin.

"You can't leave!" he shouted. "I know what's going to happen if you go away to college. No one who leaves this town ever returns."

I struggled against the empty air so that Balin, moving in sync with me, could free himself from my father's grasp. As long as I could remember, my father had never hugged me.

"Don't be so childish! Open your eyes! See the world for what it is."

Balin was like a wind-up toy that had malfunctioned. His limbs whipped about in a frenzy; the military uniform he wore was torn in multiple places, revealing the dark, unreflective skin.

"The way you spoke just now is just like your mother." Another pale blue spark came to life over Balin's temple. Abruptly, he ceased struggling, and held my father tightly like a long-lost lover. "Are you going to abandon me just like she did?"

I was stunned.

I had never thought about this matter from my father's perspective. I had always thought that he wanted to keep me close at hand because he was selfish, narrow-minded, but I had never seen it as a reaction to the fear of being abandoned. My mother had left us when I was too young to view it as trauma, but it cast a shadow over the rest of his life.

Wordless, I approached my father, who held on to Balin tightly. I bent down and caressed his spine, no longer as straight as in my memory. Maybe this was as close as the two of us would ever be.

I saw the tears spilling from the corners of Balin's eyes. For a moment, I doubted myself.

Maybe it isn't just about control and power, but also love.

There are many things I wish I had known before I turned seventeen.

For example, the fact that most of the structures in the human brain have something to do with motor functions, including the cerebellum, the basal ganglia, the brainstem, the motor region of the cerebral cortex and the direct projection of the somatosensory cortex to the primary motor cortex, and so on.

For example, the cerebellum contains more neurons than any other part of the brain. As humans evolved, the cerebellar cortex grew in step with the rapidly increasing volume of the frontal lobe.

For example, any interaction with the outside world, whether informational or physical, including moving limbs, manipulating tools, gesticulating, speaking, glancing, making faces—each ultimately requires activating a series of muscles to realize.

For example, an arm contains twenty-six separate muscles, and each muscle on average contains a hundred motor units, each made up by a motor neuron and its associated skeletal muscle fibers. Thus, the motion of a single arm is governed by a possibility space at least 2^{2600} in size, a number far greater than the total number of atoms in the universe.

Human motion is so complex and subtle, and each casual movement represents the result of so much computation, analysis, and planning that even the most advanced robots are incapable of moving as well as a three-year-old.

And we haven't even discussed all the information, emotion, and culture embodied in human motion.

On the way to the high-speed rail station, my father maintained his silence, only clutching my suitcase tightly. The northbound train finally appeared before us, shiny, new, smooth in outline, like something that was going to slide into the unknowable future the moment the brakes were released.

In the end, my father and I failed to reach a compromise. If I was going to college in Beijing, he would not pay for any of my expenses.

"Unless you promise to return," he said.

I gazed through him, as though I was already seeing the future, a future that belonged to me. For that, I was willing to be the black sheep from a white flock, the sheep in perpetual exile.

"Dad, take care of yourself."

I grabbed my suitcase to board the train, but my father refused to let go of the handle, and the suitcase awkwardly hung between us. A moment later, both of us let go, and the suitcase fell to the ground.

I was about to erupt when my father slapped his heels together to stand at attention, giving me a crisp military salute. Without a word, he turned and left. He had once told me that it was bad luck to say goodbye before going to war.

Better to leave each other with other memories.

I watched his diminishing figure, raised my hand, and returned his salute gently.

I did not truly understand the meaning in my gesture.

"I never thought we'd fail because of a wild man," says my thesis advisor Ouyang, who is also the project leader. He claps me on the shoulder, his smile disguising the sharp edges of his words. "It's no big deal. Let's keep on working at this. We still have time."

But I know him too well. What he really means is *We are running out of time.*

Or, to put it another way, *This is your idea, your project. Whether you can get your degree in time will depend on what you do next.*

Of course he will never mention how much of our time he has taken up in the past to handle the random projects he promised business investors.

Frustrated, I massage my scalp. My eyes fall on Balin, now shut in his pink-hued pet enclosure. Eyes glazed, he stares at the floor, as though still not recovered from his ordeal in the VR environment. The contrast between the pink pet enclosure and his appearance is comical, but I can't make myself laugh.

What would Mr. Lu do?

Everything began with that idle conversation with him years ago concerning "A leads to B".

Traditional theorists believe that motor control is the result of stored programs. When a person wants to move a certain way, the motor cortex picks out a certain program from its stored repertoire and carries it out much the same way a player piano follows the roll of perforated paper. The program's instructions determine the activation patterns in the motor regions of the cortex and the spinal cord, which then, in turn, activate the muscles to complete the motion.

This naturally raises the question: the same motion can be carried out in infinite ways. How does the brain store an infinite number of motor programs?

Remember that arm whose potential possible number of movements exceeds the number of atoms in the universe?

In 2002, the mathematician Emanuel Todorov came up with a theory in an attempt to answer this question. Basically, he argued that motor control is really an optimization problem for the brain. Optimality is defined by high-level performance criteria such as maximizing precision, minimizing energy consumption, minimizing control effort, and so on.

In the optimization process, the brain relies on the processing powers of the cerebellum. Before the commands for movement have reached muscles, the cerebellum predicts the results of anticipated motion, and then, combined with real-time sensory feedback, helps the brain evaluate and coordinate the motor commands.

A simple example: when ascending or descending a set of stairs, we will often stumble due to miscounting the number of steps. If feedback-based adjustments are made in time, we can recover and not fall. Feedback, of course, is often noisy and involves a delay.

Todorov's mathematical model is compatible with all known evidence concerning the neural mechanisms of motor control and can be used to explain all kinds of behavior phenomena. Given some physical parameters, it's even possible to predict the resulting motion using his model: for instance, how an eight-legged creature would jump in Pluto's gravity.

Physics engines based on his models are used by Hollywood to produce naturalistic movements for avatars in virtual environments.

By the time I was in college, the Todorov model was already treated as textbook authority. Experiment after experiment provided more evidence that it was correct.

And then one day, Mr. Lu and I discussed Balin.

After I left home for college, he and I had kept in touch via email. He was like an oracular AI from whom I could get answers for everything: academics, awkward social situations, even relationship advice. We wrote long emails back and forth discussing questions that must have seemed ridiculous to anyone else, such as "would an out-of-body experience engineered by technology violate religion's claim on spirituality?"

By an unspoken agreement, both of us avoided talking about my father.

Mr. Lu told me that Balin had been sold to another family in town, a nouveau riche household which was often mocked for conspicuous acts of consumption that appeared ridiculous in the townspeople's eyes.

I had known that Father's business had run into a rough patch, but I hadn't imagined that he would be so short on cash as to consider selling Balin.

I shifted the topic to the Todorov mathematical model, and a new thought struck me. Balin was capable of imitating movements with perfect precision. Suppose we had him perform two sets of identical movements: one through subconscious imitation and the other by his own will; do these two sets of movements go through the same process of motor control?

Mathematically, there was only a single optimal solution, but was there a difference in the way the optimal solution was arrived at?

It took Mr. Lu three days to get back to me. Unlike his usual free-flowing, loquacious style, this time he wrote only a few lines:

I think you're asking a very important question, one whose importance perhaps you don't even realize. If we can't distinguish between mechanical imitation and conscious, willed movement at the level of neural activity, then the question is: Does free will truly exist?

I couldn't sleep that night. I spent two weeks designing the prototype experiment, and spent even more time studying the feasibility of my proposed study, soliciting feedback from my mentors and other professors. Then I submitted my project for approval.

It wasn't until everything was ready that I realized that this experiment, one seeking to address a "fundamental question," lacked a fundamental, required component.

I had no choice but to break my promise to myself and go home.

I'm going just to get Balin, I reminded myself again and again. *Just for Balin.*

Just like how A leads to B. Simple, right?

I once read a science fiction novel called *The Orphans*, which was about aliens who had come to Earth. They could imitate the appearance of specific humans and pass as human in society, but they couldn't perfectly capture the characteristic ways their targets moved or the subtleties of their facial expressions. Many aliens, exposed as frauds, were hunted down by humans.

In order to survive, the aliens had to study how humans communicated via body language. They pretended to be abandoned orphans, and, once taken in by kind-hearted families, proceeded to use the opportunity of living together to imitate the mannerisms and expressions of their adoptive parents.

To the parents' surprise, their children became more and more like them. And once the alien orphans decided that they had learned enough, they killed their father or mother, took on their appearance, and took their place. The scene where an alien killed his father and took his mother as his wife was unforgettable.

Though it became harder to tell aliens apart from humans, people finally discovered the fundamental difference between the extraterrestrials and humans.

Although the aliens were able to imitate human movements with perfect fidelity, they lacked the mirror neurons unique to human brains, and thus were unable to intuit the emotional shifts occurring behind human faces or to experience similar neural activation patterns in their own minds. In other words, they lacked the capacity for empathy.

And so humans devised an effective means to detect aliens: bring harm to those closest to the disguised aliens and observe the aliens for signs of pain, fear, or rage. The test was called "the stabbing needle test."

The story's lesson seems to be: humanity isn't the only species in the universe that has difficulty relating to their parents.

Mr. Lu knew everything about Balin. He thought of the *paoxiao* as an example of overdevelopment in the mirror neuron system. He was fascinated by Balin, but he disapproved of the way we treated him.

"But he's never resisted or even wanted to run away," I used to counter.

"Overactive mirror neurons lead to a pathological excess of empathy," he said. "Maybe he just couldn't tolerate the look of abandonment in his tormentors'—your—eyes."

"I guess that could be true," I said. "I must be an example of underdevelopment of mirror neurons."

"Cold-blooded, one might say."

But when Mr. Lu took me to find Balin on my return, I realized that I wasn't the most cold-blooded, not by far.

Balin was naked, his body full of bruises and lacerations. Thick, rusty chains were locked about his neck and shackled his arms and legs. He was shut inside a tiny brick-and-mud enclosure, about five feet on each side. The interior was dim, and the stale air saturated with the gag-inducing stench of excrement and rotting food. He was thinner than I remembered. Flies buzzed about his wounds, and the outlines of his skeleton poked from under his skin. He was like an animal about to be sent to the butcher's.

He looked at me, and there was no reaction in his eyes at all. It was just like the first time we had met, that summer night when I was thirteen.

"They had him mirror the movements of animals . . . mating—" Mr. Lu was unable to continue.

Memories of the past flood into my mind in a flash.

I have no recollection of what happened next. It was as though I had been possessed by some spirit, and I moved without remembering wanting to move.

According to Mr. Lu, I rushed into the house of Balin's new owners, and grabbed the Pomeranian beloved by the family patriarch's daughter-in-law. I opened my jaw and held the neck of the whimpering creature between my teeth.

"You said, 'If you don't let Balin go, I'm going to bite all the way through,'" Mr. Lu said.

I spat on the ground. Though I didn't remember any of it, this did sound like something I would do.

Mr. Lu and I rushed Balin to the hospital. As we were preparing to leave, Mr. Lu stopped me. "Do you want to see your father?"

That was how I found out that my father had been hospitalized. Once in college, I had had almost no contact with him, and gradually, I had stopped even thinking about him.

He looked about ten years older. Tubing was stuck into his nostrils and arms. His hair was sparse, and his gaze unsteady. A few years ago, when Pu'er tea was all the rage, he had gambled with all his chips and ended up as the last fool to buy in at the height of the mania. He was stuck with warehouses full of tea leaves as the price collapsed, and ended up losing just about everything.

As he looked at me, I noted that his expression reminded me of Balin's, as though he was saying, *I knew you'd be back.*

"I . . . I'm here for Balin," I said.

My father saw through my facade and cracked a smile, revealing a mouthful of teeth stained yellow by years of smoking.

"That little gremlin? He's much smarter than you think. We all thought we were controlling him, but sometimes I wonder if he was controlling all of us."

I didn't know what to say.

"It's the same way with you. I always thought I was the one in charge. But after you left, I realized that you had always held a thread whose other end is looped around my heart. No matter how far away you are, as soon as you twitch your fingers, I suffer pangs of heartache." My father closed his eyes and put his hand over his chest.

Something was stuck in my throat.

I walked up to his bed and wanted to lean down to embrace him. But halfway through the motion, my body refused to obey. Awkwardly, I clapped him on the shoulder, straightened up, and walked away.

"I'm glad you're back," my father said from behind me, his voice hoarse. I didn't turn around.

Mr. Lu was waiting for me at the door. I pretended to scratch my eyes to disguise the emotional turmoil.

"Do you think fate likes to play jokes on us?" he asked.

"What do you mean?"

"You wanted to escape the route your father had paved for you, but in the end, you ended up in the same place as me."

"I think I'm coming around to your way of thinking."

"What's that?" he asked.

"No one knows what will happen in the future."

We've failed again.

The original premise is very simple: Balin's hypertrophic mirror neuron system makes him the ideal experimental subject because his imitation is a kind of instinct. Thus, his movements during imitation ought to be free from much of the noise and interference found in human motor control due to conscious cognition.

We use non-invasive electrodes to capture the neural activity in Balin's motor cortex as he's imitating a sequence of movements. Then we have him repeat the sequence under his own will and use motion capture to ensure that we get a perfect match between the two sets of movements. Mathematically, that means that the two sequences are indistinguishable; they are the same motion.

Then, by comparing the two sets of neural patterns captured during the process, we can find out if the same neural signals were activating the same regions of the motor cortex in the same sequence and with the same strength.

If there are differences, then the Todorov model, accepted as gospel, will have been revealed to be seriously lacking.

But if there are no differences, the consequences will be even more severe. Maybe human beings are doing nothing but imitating the behaviors of other individuals, and are only operating under the illusion of free will.

No matter what, the result of the experiment ought to be earth-shattering.

Yet, the experiment was a failure from the very beginning. Balin has refused to look into anyone's eyes, and has refused to imitate anyone's movements, including me.

I can guess the reason, but I have no solution. My team has vowed to solve the secret of human cognition, yet we can't even heal the psychic trauma inflicted on a mere "primitive."

I thought of the idea of using virtual reality. Situating Balin in an environment completely disconnected from the reality around him may help him recover his normal habits.

And so we went through a series of virtual environments: islands, glaciers, deserts, even space; we manufactured incredible catastrophes; we even devoted enormous effort to construct avatars of *paoxiao*, hoping that the sight of others of his kind would awaken his dormant mirror neurons.

Without exception, all these tricks have failed.

Now, at midnight, only I and the zombie-like Balin remain in the lab. Everyone else has left. I know what they're thinking: this experiment is a joke, and I'm the man who has finished telling the joke and looks around confused, unsure why everyone else is laughing.

Balin is curled up into a ball in the pet house made from pink foam boards. I remember Mr. Lu's words. He was right. I've never treated Balin as a person, not even now.

A colleague once implanted a wireless receiver into a rat's brain. By electrically stimulating the rat's somatosensory cortex and the medial forebrain bundle, my colleague was able to induce sensations of pleasure and pain in the rat, thereby controlling where the rat moved.

There's no qualitative difference between that and what I'm doing to Balin.

I am indeed a bastard whose mirror neurons are atrophied.

Unbidden, the memory of a children's game resurfaces, the game in which Balin first showed us his fantastic ability.

"Shrimp! Shrimp! Watch out if you don't want one to bite off your toes!"

I chant in a low voice, embarrassed. I pretend to be a fisherman, dipping my foot into the imaginary river from the shore and quickly pulling back.

Balin glances at me.

"Shrimp! Shrimp! Watch out if you don't want one to bite off your toes!" My chant grows louder.

Balin stares at my clumsy movements. Gently, slowly, he crawls out of the pet house, stopping a few steps away from me.

"Shrimp! Shrimp! Watch out if you don't want one to bite off your toes!" My legs are jerking wildly like some caricature of a pole dancer in a club.

Abruptly, Balin jumps at me with incredible speed, moving the exact way Ah Hui used to.

He remembers; he remembers everything.

Balin leaps and bounds, grabbing at my dipping leg. A baby-like gurgle emerges from his throat. He's laughing. This is the first time I've ever heard him laugh in the all the years I've known him.

He is now re-enacting the movements of everyone in town who had been a bit different. All their movements seem to have been engraved in Balin's brain, so vivid and precise that I can recognize who he's replaying at a glance. In turn, he becomes the madman, the cripple, the idiot, the beggar who had broken legs and arms, and the epileptic; he is a cat, a dog, an ox, a goat, a pig, and a crude chicken; he is my drunk father and me, dancing about in joy.

In a moment, I've traveled through thousands of kilometers and returned to the hometown of my childhood.

Without warning, Balin begins to play two roles simultaneously, re-enacing the day of the rupture between me and my father.

Watching the argument between me and my father as an observer is eerie: the movements before me are so familiar, yet my memories have grown indistinct, unreal. I was so angry then, so stubborn, like a wild horse that refused to take the reins. My father, on the other hand, was so pitiful and meek. Again and again, he backed off; he suffered. It is nothing like how I remember the scene.

Balin quickly switches between roles, gesturing and posturing like a skilled mime.

Though I know what happens next, when it does happen I'm not prepared.

Balin wraps his arms about me, just the way my father back then wrapped his arms about him. He hugs me tightly, his head buried in the crook of my neck. I smell that familiar fish-like scent, like the sea, and a warm liquid flows down my collar like a river that has absorbed the heat of the sun.

I stay still, thinking about how to react.

Then I give up thinking, allowing my body to react and open up, hugging him back the way I would hug an old friend, the way I would hug my father.

I know that I have owed this hug for far too long, to him and to my father.

I think I finally understand how to solve the problem.

At the end of *The Orphans*, the team that had come up with the stabbing needle test found, to their horror, that even when they harmed the aliens passing as human, their dear ones, the real humans, also failed to react. Their mirror neuron systems would not activate.

Humanity is a species that was never designed to truly empathize with another species.

Just like those aliens.

Good thing that's just a bad piece of science fiction, isn't it?

"We need to think about this from his perspective," I say to Ouyang.

"His?" It takes a full three seconds for my advisor to figure out what I mean. "Who? The primitive?"

"His name is Balin. We should make him the focus, and construct an environment that will put him at ease, rather than cheap tourist scenes we imagine he'll enjoy."

"What are you talking about? You should be concerned about how you're going to finish your project and get your degree, instead of worrying about the feelings of some primitive. Don't waste my time."

Mr. Lu once said that the progress of a civilization should be measured by its degree of empathy—whether members of the civilization are capable of thinking from the values and perspectives of others—and not some other objectified scale.

Silently, I stare at Ouyang's face, trying to discern some trace of civilization.

The face, so carefully maintained to be wrinkle-free, is a wasteland.

I decide to work on the problem myself. Several younger students join me on their own initiative, restoring some of my faith in humanity. To be sure, most of them are motivated by their hatred of Ouyang, and it's not a bad way to earn a few credits.

There's a virtual reality program called iDealism, which claims to be capable of generating an environment based on brainwave patterns. In reality, all it does is select pre-existing models from a database whose brainwave signatures match the user's—at most it adds some high-resolution transitions. We hacked it for our own use, and since our lab's sensors are several orders of magnitude more sensitive than consumer-grade sensors, we add a lot of new measurement axes to the software and connect it to the largest open-source database, which contains demo data from virtual reality labs from around the world.

And now, Balin is going to be the Prime Mover of this virtual universe.

He will have plenty of time to explore the linkage between this world and every thought in his mind. I will record every move and gesture Balin makes. Then, when he returns to the real world, I will reconnect with him. I will imitate to the best of my ability each of his gestures. The two of us will be as two parallel mirrors, reflecting each other endlessly.

I put the helmet on Balin's head. His gaze is as placid as water.

The red light flashes, speeds up, turns green.

I enter Ghost mode, and bring up a third-person POV window in the upper-right hand corner. In it, I see a tiny avatar of Balin trembling in place.

Balin's world is primordial chaos. There is no earth, no heaven, no east, west, north, or south. I struggle against the vertigo.

Finally, he stops shaking. A flash of lightning slowly divides the chaos, determining the location of the sky.

The lightning extends, limning a massive eye in the cloud cover. A web of fine lightning feelers spreads from the eye in every direction.

The light fades. Balin lifts his head and raises his hands. Rain falls.

He begins to dance.

Drops of rain fall with laughter, giving substance to the outline of wind. The wind lifts Balin until he is floating in the air, twirling about.

It is impossible to describe his dance with words. It is as if he has become a part of all Creation, and the heavens and the earth both respond to his movements and change.

My heart speeds up; my throat is dry; my hands and feet are icy cold. I'm witnessing an unsought miracle.

He lifts his hand and flowers bloom. He lifts his foot and birds flutter forth.

Balin dances between unnamed peaks, above unmapped lakes. Everywhere he sets foot, joyful mandalas bloom and spread, and he falls into their swirling, colorful centers.

One moment he is smaller than an atom, the next he encompasses the universe. All scales have lost meaning in his dance.

Every nameless life sings to him. He opens his mouth, and all the gods of the *paoxiao* emerge from his lips.

The spirits meld into his black skin like dark waves that rage and erupt, sweeping him up, up into the air. Behind him, the waves coalesce into an endless web on which all the fruits of creation may be found, each playing its own rhythm. A hundred million billion species are in search of their common origin.

I understand now.

In Balin's eyes, the soul is immanent in all Creation, and there is no difference between a dragonfly and a man. His nervous system is constructed in such a way as to allow him to empathize with the universe. It is impossible to imagine how much effort he must put into calming the tsunamis that rage constantly in his heart.

Even someone as unenlightened as me cannot be unmoved when faced with this grand spectacle produced by all Life. My eyes swim in hot tears, and threads of ecstasy inside my heart are woven with the dizzying sights in my vision. I stand atop a peak, but a step away from transcendence.

As for the answer I was seeking? I don't think it's so important anymore.

Balin absorbs everything into his body. His avatar expands rapidly and then deflates.

He falls.

The world dims, grows indistinct, lifeless.

Balin is like a thin film stretched against the tumbling, twirling space-time. The physics engine's algorithms undulate the edge of his body as though blown by a wind, and fragments rise into the air like a flock of birds.

His shape is disintegrating, dissolving.

I disconnect Balin from the VR system and take off his helmet.

He lies facedown on the soft, dark gray floor, his limbs spread out, unmoving.

"Balin?" I don't dare move him.

"Balin?" Everyone in the lab is waiting. Will this joke of an experiment turn into a tragedy?

Slowly, he shifts in place. Then he wriggles to the side like a pond loach until he is once again flattened against the floor, adopting the posture of a gecko.

I laugh. Like my father years ago, I clap my hands twice.

Balin turns, sits up, stares at me.

It is just like that hot and sticky summer night the year I turned thirteen, when we first met.

The Snow of Jinyang

X

by Zhang Ran,
translated by Ken Liu and Carmen Yiling Yan

— Translators' Note —

This story is an alternate history and features event that would have been familiar to its original Chinese audience. To help set the scene for those less familiar with this period of history, we provide the following background information:

Jinyang was an ancient city located in modern-day Shanxi Province, China. This story takes place in the 10th century CE, during the late Five Dynasties and Ten Kingdoms period, when the land we think of as China today was divided among multiple independent states. Jinyang was the capital of a state that called itself Han—or "Great Han", though modern histories usually call it the "Northern Han". (The name of the state should not be confused with the original Han Dynasty, which fell in the 2nd century, or the Han ethnic group. The ruling family of the Northern Han was ethnically Shatuo, but had the same surname, Liu, as the rulers of the Han Dynasty.

It was common for a regime to claim descent and take the name of a prior dynasty to add legitimacy.)

Historically, the Northern Han survived for years while losing large swaths of territory to other states until it was just the single city of Jinyang. In 979 CE, the Song Emperor Zhao Guangyi finally captured Jinyang after a long siege, thereby completing the task of unifying China. Zhao then razed Jinyang to the ground to prevent future rebellions. Today, the city of Taiyuan stands near its ruins.

This story starts out in 979 CE with Jinyang under siege by the Song army . . .

— **1** —

When Zhao Da stormed into Xuanren Ward with his men, Zhu Dagun was in his room on the internet. Had he any experience dueling wits with the government, he'd surely have realized that something was wrong in time to put on a better show.

It was three quarters of the way into the hour of the sheep, after lunch but well before dinner, naturally a fine time for business in the brothels of Xuanren Ward. Powder and perfume steamed in the sun; gaudy kerchiefs dazzled the eyes of passersby. Snatches of music drifted through two sets of walls from Pingkang Ward, on the opposite side of West Street, where the licensed courtesans of the Imperial Academy entertained blue bloods and VIPs. But the sisters of Xuanren Ward held their neighboring colleagues in contempt. They thought all that training as unnecessary as pulling down your pants to fart—the end result, after all, was still the same creak-creak-creak of a bed frame. Drink and gamble to liven things up, certainly, but why bother with the singing and plinking and bowing and piping? Days in the Xuanren Ward never lacked for the din of price-haggling, bet-placing, and bed frames creak-

creaking. The hubbub had become so much a part of the place that when residents happened to spend the night elsewhere in Jinyang, they found those quieter neighborhoods utterly lacking in vitality.

The moment Zhao Da's thin-soled boot touched the ward grounds, the warden in bowing attendance at the gate sensed that something was off. Zhao Da visited Xuanren Ward three or four times every month with his two skinny, sallow-faced soldier boys, and every time he walked in blustering and walked out bellowing, as if he felt he had to yell until his throat bled to really earn the monthly patrol salary. But this time, he slipped through the gates without a sound. He made a few hand gestures in the direction of the warden, as if anyone except himself understood them, and led his two soldier boys tip-toeing northward along the walls.

"Marquess, hey, Marquess Yu!" The warden chased after him, waving his arms. "What are you doing? You're scaring me to death! Won't you rest your feet and have some soup? If you need a—um—'bonus' or a pretty girl, just say the word—"

"Shut up!" Zhao Da glowered at him and lowered his voice. "Stand against the wall! Let's get this straight: I have a warrant from the county magistrate. This is out of your hands!"

The terrified warden stumbled back against the wall and watched Zhao Da and his men creep away.

Shivering, he pulled over a nearby child. "Tell Sixth Madam to clear out. Quick!" The snot-nosed urchin bobbed his head and hightailed it.

In less time than it took to burn half a stick of incense, two hundred and forty shutters clattered over the windows of the thirteen brothels of Xuanren Ward. The noise of price-haggling, bet-placing, and bed frames creak-creaking disappeared without a trace. Somebody's child started to wail, only to be silenced instantly by a resounding slap. A swarm of patrons still adjusting their robes and hats fled out the back, darting through gaps in the ward walls like startled rats to vanish into Jinyang's streets and alleys.

A crow flew by. The guard outside the gate drew his bow and aimed, his right hand groping for an arrow, only to discover that his quiver was empty. Resentfully, he lowered the bow. The rawhide bowstring sprang back with a twang that made him jump. Only then did he realize that his surroundings had descended into total silence, so that even this little noise startled more than the hour drums at night.

That Zhu Dagun, resident of the ward for the last ten years and four months, failed to notice Xuanren in its busiest afternoon hours had plunged into a silence more absolute than post-curfew could only be attributed to remarkable obliviousness. Only when Zhao Da kicked down the door to his room did he start and look up, realizing that it was time to put on the show. So he bellowed and hurled a cup half-filled with hot water smack into Zhao Da's forehead, following it up by knocking over his desk, sending the movable type in his type-tray clattering all over the floor.

"Zhu Dagun!" Zhao Da yelled, one hand over his battered forehead. "I have a warrant! If you don't—"

Before he could finish, a fistful of movable type slammed into him. Made of baked clay, the brittle, hard type blocks hurt something fierce when they struck his body, and shattered into dust as they hit the ground. As Zhao Da leapt and dodged; clouds of yellow dust filled the room.

"You'll never catch me!" Zhu Dagun opened fire left and right, hurling type blocks to hinder his foes while he threw the south window open, preparing to jump out. One of the young soldiers charged out of the yellow fog, chains raised. Zhu Dagun executed a flying kick; the boy cannonballed through the air and landed against a wall. The chain fell from his hands as nose-blood and tears flowed freely.

While Zhao Da and company continued to grope blindly about, Zhu Dagun vaulted out the window into freedom. Then he smacked his forehead, recalling the charge from Minister Ma Feng: "You must be caught, but not easily. You must resist, but not successfully. Lead them on; play the coquette. The show must not appear scripted."

"Lead them on . . . lead them on my ass . . . " Zhu Dagun steeled himself and barreled ahead, carefully tripping his right foot with the left just as he passed the middle of the courtyard. "Aiya!" he cried as he tumbled to the ground with a meaty slap; the water in the courtyard cisterns sloshed from the impact.

Tracking the commotion, Zhao Da ran outside. "Serves you right for running!" he guffawed at the sight, still nursing his bruised forehead. "Chain him up and bring him to the jail! Gather up all the evidence!"

Still bleeding from his nose, the soldier boy stumbled out of the room. "Chief!" he bawled. "He smashed that tray of clay blocks. What other evidence is there? Since I spilled blood today, I should eat rich white flour food tonight to get better! My ma said that if I enlisted with you I'd have steamed buns to eat, but it's been two months and I haven't seen the shadow of a bun! And now we're trapped in the city, I can't even go home. I don't know if my ma and da are still alive—what's the point of living?"

"Fool! The type blocks may be gone, but we still have the internet lines! Get some scissors and cut them loose to bring back with us." Zhao Da bellowed. "Once we get this case sewn up, never mind steamed buns, you'll have mincemeat every day if you want!"

— **2** —

The fates of life's bit players are often changed by a single word from the mighty.

It was the sixth day of the sixth month, in the first dog days of summer. The sun hung high above the northlands, the streetside willows limp and wilting under its glare. There shouldn't have been a wisp of breeze, and yet a little whirlwind rose out of nowhere, sweeping the street end to end and sending the accumulated dust flying. The General of the Cavalry, Guo Wanchao, rode his carriage out of Liwu Residence and proceeded along the central boulevard toward the south gate for the better part of an hour. Being the ostentatious sort, he naturally sat high in the front, stamping on the pedal so the carriage made as much din as possible. This carriage was the latest model from the East City Institute, five feet wide, six feet four inches tall, twelve feet long, eaves on all four sides, front- and rear-hinged doors, with a chassis constructed from aged jujube wood and ornamented with a scrolling pattern of pomegranates in gold thread inlay. Majestic in air, exquisite in construction, the basic model's starting price was twenty thousand copper coins—how many could afford such a ride in all of Jinyang, aside from a figure like Guo Wanchao?

The four chimneys belched thick black smoke; the wheels jounced along the rammed-earth street. Guo Wanchao had meant to sweep his cool gaze over the goings-on of the city, but due to the heavy vibrations, the passersby saw it as an amiable nod to all, and so all came over to bow and return the greeting to the General of the Cavalry. Guo Wanchao could only force a laugh and wave them off.

A massive cauldron of boiling water sat in the back of the carriage. Despite hours of explanation filled with fantastical jargon by the staff of the East City Institute, the general still didn't understand how his vehicle functioned. Apparently it used fire-oil to boil the water. He knew that the stuff came from the southeast lands, and would burn at a spark and burn even harder on water. Defenders of a city would dump it on besiegers. This stuff boiled the water, and then somehow that made the carriage move. How was that supposed to work?

Regardless, the cauldron rumbled and bubbled, such that the armor at his back fairly sizzled from the radiating heat. He had to steady his silver helm with one hand so that it wouldn't slip over his eyes every few bone-jarring feet. The General of the Cavalry had only himself to blame; inwardly, he bemoaned his decision to take the driver's seat. Fortunately, he was approaching his destination. He took out his pair of black spectacles and put them on his sweating, greasy face as the carriage roared past streets and alleys.

A left turn, and the front gate of Xiqing Ward lay straight ahead. This was an era of degeneracy, insolence, and the collapse of the social order, to be sure: the residence walls were so full of gaps and holes that no one bothered to use the front gate. But Guo Wanchao felt that a high official ought to behave in a manner befitting the importance of his position. It just didn't look proper without servants and guards leaping to action on his behalf.

But no one came to the ward gate to greet him. Not only was the warden missing, it seemed that the guards were napping in some hidden corner as well. Ancient scholar trees and cypresses lined the street, providing shade everywhere except in front of the completely barren front gate. It didn't take long before Guo Wanchao, waiting in his stopped carriage, was panting and dripping sweat like rain.

"Guards!" he yelled. There was no response, not even a dog barking in acknowledgment. Furious, he jumped off the carriage and stormed into Xiqing Ward on foot. The residence of Minister Ma Feng was just south of the gate. Without bothering to speak to the doorkeeper, he shoved open the door to the minister's residence and barged in, circling around the main building to head for the back courtyard. "Surrender, traitors!" he bellowed.

Pandemonium broke out. In a flash, the windows burst open front and back. Five or six escaping scholar-officials fought to escape by squeezing through the narrow openings, but only succeeded in tangling their flailing limbs and tumbling into a heap.

"Aiya, General!" Potbellied old Ma Feng had crept to the door and was peeking out the seam. He put a hand over his heart and thanked heaven and earth. "You mustn't play this kind of trick on us! Everyone, everyone, let's all go back inside! It's just the General, nothing to be afraid of!" The old man had been so startled that his cap had fallen off, leaving his head of white hair hanging like a mop.

"Look at you!" Guo Wanchao smirked, an expression somewhere between amusement and ire. "How are you going to plot treason with so little courage?"

"Shhhh!" Old Ma Feng was given a second fright. He scurried over, took Guo Wanchao's hand and dragged him inside. "Careful! The walls out here aren't so thick . . . "

The whole gang trooped back inside, latched the door, pressed the battered window panels back into their frames as best as they could, and gingerly took their seats. Minister Ma Feng pulled General Guo Wanchao toward a chair, but Guo shook him off and stood right in the middle of the room. It wasn't that he didn't want to sit; rather, the archaic armor he'd worn for its formidable appearance had nearly scraped his family jewels raw on the bumpy journey.

Old Ma Feng put on his cap, scratched at his grizzled beard, and introduced Guo Wanchao. "I'm sure everyone has seen the general at court before. We'll need his help to accomplish our goals, so I secretly invited him here—"

A tall, rangy scholar in yellow robes interrupted. "Why does he wear those black spectacles? Does he hold us in such contempt that he covers his eyes to spare himself the sight?"

"Aha, I was waiting for someone to ask." Guo Wanchao took off the black lenses nonchalantly. "It's the latest curiosity from the East City Institute. They call it 'Ray-Ban.' They allow the wearer to see normally, and yet be spared the glare of the sun. A marvelous invention!"

"It hardly seems right for a man interested in enlightenment to reduce the reach of light," grumbled the yellow-robed scholar.

"But who says banning rays is all I'm capable of?" Guo Wanchao proudly drew a teak-handled, brass-headed object from his sleeve. "This device, another invention from the East City Institute, can emit dazzling light that pierces darkness for a hundred paces. The staff from the institute didn't give it a name, so I call it 'Light-Saber.' The banisher of rays and the sword of light! Brilliant, eh? It was a match made in heaven, haha . . . "

"Disgusting ostentation!" shouted a white-robed scholar as he wiped at the blood on his face with his sleeve. He had run too quickly earlier and tripped, and the cut on his forehead had bled all over his delicate scholar's face, encrusting his fair skin with blotches the exact color of farmland mud. "Ever since the East City Institute was established, our proud State of Han has fallen further by the day! We've been under siege for months; the people are full of fear and dread. And your kind still revels in such, such—"

Ma Feng hurriedly tugged at the scholar's sleeve, attempting to smooth things over. "Brother Thirteenth, Brother Thirteenth, please quell your anger. Let's take care of business first!" The old man made an unhurried patrol of the room, drawing the curtains and carefully covering up the cracks in the windows. After a phlegmy cough, he took out a three inch square of bamboo paper from his sleeve and displayed it to his audience, who saw that it was covered with characters the size of gnat's heads.

Ma Feng began to read in a low voice. "Sixth month of the sixth year of the Guangyun Era. Great Han is weak and benighted, and the fires of war rage in the twelve provinces around us. We have fewer than forty thousand households, and our peasants cannot produce enough to equip our soldiers with strong armor and weapons. Beset by droughts and floods, our fields lie bare while the wells are exhausted, and our granaries and stores are empty. Meanwhile we still must pay tribute to Liao in the north and guard against mighty Song to the south, stretching the treasury beyond its capacity. The peasants have no food, the officials have no pay, the roads are lined with those dying of starvation, the horses have no grass to graze, the state is poor and its people are piteous! Woe is the land! Woe is Great Han!"

"Woe," the roomful of scholars lamented in synch; then, they immediately chorused, "Well said!"

But Guo Wanchao glared at the speaker. "Enough of this flowery oratory! Get to the point!"

Ma Feng took out a brocade handkerchief and wiped the sweat from his forehead. "Yes, yes, there no need for me to continue reading from the formal denunciation. General, you know well that after such a long siege by the Song army, Han is at the end of its strength, while the Song ruler Zhao Guangyi has made the conquest of the city a matter of personal honor. His edict declared that 'Han has long disobeyed the will of the rightful ruler, acted heedless to the right way, and governed the people ruinously. For the sake of the land and the people, I personally come to pacify Han in the name of justice.'

"Zhao Guangyi is known for his vicious, vengeful nature. Have you not seen how the King of Wuyue pledged his territories to Song voluntarily and was made a prince, while the ruler of Quan and Tang gave up his lands only after he saw the Song army at his gate, and was thus made a mere regional commander? By now, Jinyang has been under siege for nearly ten months. Zhao Guangyi is beyond furious. Once the city falls, the grandeur of the title he's waiting to bestow our Han emperor will be the least of our concerns. The whole city will suffer the Song ruler's rage! You won't find an unbroken egg in a nest that has tumbled from a tree. General, you mustn't let our people perish in unimaginable suffering!"

Guo Wanchao said, "I'll be honest with you: we military officers haven't been paid in half a month either. The footsoldiers whimper with hunger all day long. If we scrape away all your fancy allusions and circumlocutions, what you mean to say is that our little emperor Liu Jiyuan won't be able to sit on his throne long anyway, so we might as well surrender to Song, am I correct?"

Instantly, the scholars jumped out of their seats in uproar, shouting curses and instructing him of the Confucian duties of ruler and subject, father and son, the respect due to a subject reciprocated by the loyalty due to a ruler, so on and so forth, until Ma Feng was shaking all over with fear. "Everyone! Everyone! The neighbors have ears, the neighbors have ears . . . "

When the room had finally quieted, the old man hunched his shoulders and rubbed his hands together anxiously. "General, please understand that we're aware of our duty of loyalty to the throne. But if the ruler doesn't do his part, how can the subjects be expected to do theirs? If the emperor is unwise in his governance, we have no choice but to overstep our bounds! The first possibility ahead of us is that the city falls and the Song army slaughters us all. The second is that the Liao army arrives in time to drive away the Song, in which case Han will become nothing more than Liao territory. The third is that we open the gates and surrender to Song, ensuring the survival of Jinyang's eight thousand six hundred households and twelve thousand soldiers, and preserving the bloodline of the imperial family. You too understand the superior choice, General! At least Song follows the same customs and speaks the same language as us, while Liao is Khitan and Tatar. It's better to surrender to Song than let Liao enslave us! Our descendants might curse us for cowards and traitors, but we can't become the dogs of the Khitan!"

Hearing this speech, Guo Wanchao had to revise his opinion of the old man. "Very well." He gave a thumbs up. "You're a righteous man indeed to make even surrender sound so fine and just. Tell me your plan, then. I'm listening."

"Yes, yes." Ma Feng gestured for everyone to resume their seats. "Ten years ago, when the previous Song ruler, Zhao Guangyi's elder brother, was invading Han, Military Governor Liu Jiye and I wrote a memorandum to the emperor begging him to surrender. We were whipped and driven out of court. But today, the emperor spends his days drinking and feasting, careless of the matters of state, a perfect opportunity for us to act. I've already secretly contacted Inspector Guo Jin in the Song army. If you can open the Dasha, Yansha, and Shahe Gates, General, the Song will accept our surrender."

"What about our little emperor, Liu Jiyuan?" asked Guo Wanchao.

"Once he sees that no other options are left to him, he'll wisely surrender too." Ma Feng answered.

"Good enough. But have you considered the most important problem? What are we going to do about the East City Institute?" Guo Wanchao looked around the room. "The prince of East City has people on all the city walls, gates, and fortifications, and they control all the defense mechanisms. If the prince doesn't surrender, the Song army won't be able to get in even if we open the gates."

The room fell silent. "The East City Institute?" The white-robed scholar sighed. "If it weren't for Prince Lu's antics, perhaps Jinyang would have long since fallen . . . "

Ma Feng said, "We've decided to send a representative to persuade Prince Lu toward the path of reason."

"And if it doesn't work?" asked Guo Wanchao.

"Then we send an assassin and get that fake prince out of the way with one stroke."

"Easier said than done, old man," said Guo Wanchao. "The East City Institute is heavily guarded. With all his strange devices, one might die before getting so much as a glimpse at Prince Lu's face!"

Ma Feng said, "The East City Institute is located right next to the prison. All of the prince's subordinates are criminals recruited from there. All we have to do is plant someone in the prison, and he'll end up next to Prince Lu for certain."

"Do you have candidates? One to persuade, another to kill." Guo Wanchao swept his gaze around the room. The scholars avoided his eyes, focused inward, and began reciting the Thirteen Confucian Classics under their breaths.

Guo Wanchao smacked his forehead. "Wait, I have a candidate. He's a scribe from your Hanlin Academy, an old acquaintance of sorts, a Shatuo who goes by a Han surname. He's a middling scholar, but he's strong. He's the sort of muddled self-righteous fool who likes to spend his days complaining on the internet. Let's give him a little money, then hand him a knife and deliver him a speech like the one you gave me. He'll happily do what we want."

Ma Feng clapped his hands. "Excellent! We just need to make sure he has a convincing reason for being thrown in jail so the East City Institute doesn't get suspicious. Too severe a crime and he won't be leaving the dungeon. But it can't be too light, either. At the minimum it needs to justify shackles and chains."

"Haha, that's not a problem. This fellow spends all his time spewing unsought opinions and sowing slander online. His crime is ready-made." Guo Wanchao gripped the armor at his crotch with one hand and turned to leave. "Well, keep today's talk a secret between heaven, earth, you, and me. I'm off to find an internet monitor. I'll bring the fellow over later. We'll talk more next time. Farewell!"

The general's armor clanged as he swaggered out of the room, the contemptuous gazes of the scholars bouncing harmlessly off the backplate. Outside, the fire-oil chariot began its deafening rumble. Ma Feng wiped his sweaty face and sighed. "I do hope that taking care of the East City Institute will really be this simple. Our lives are at stake, everyone. We must act with caution! Caution!"

— **3** —

Zhu Dagun didn't know which magistrate had dispatched his captors, but as Minister Ma Feng had told him, the Department of Justice Penitentiary, the Taiyuan Circuit Prison, the Jinyang County Prison, and the Jianxiong Military Prison were all the same nowadays. Who was to blame but a government of such staggering incompetence that it managed to lose all twelve of its prefectures, with only the lone city of Jinyang left under its rule?

As the soldiers dragged him through Xuanren Ward in chains, many curious gazes followed him through the cracks in the brothels' boarded up doors. Who among the sisters, clients, and brothel keepers could fail to recognize the penniless scholar? Here was a scribe of the Hanlin Academy, living in the red-light district of all places. Perhaps it would be understandable in a man of passions, but despicably, he had not patronized the sisters even once in all these years. Every time he walked by, he would cover his eyes with his sleeve and quicken his steps, muttering "Sorry! Sorry!" One wondered if he was more embarrassed by the thought of his ancestors seeing his current circumstances, or by the thought of the Xuanren girls seeing whatever he hid in his pants.

Only Zhu Dagun knew that the only thing he was ashamed of was his wallet. With the arrival of the Song army, the Hanlin Academy had cut off his monthly stipend. In the three months of siege, he had received only four pecks of rice and five strings of coins as remuneration for his writing. They called them hundred-strings, but he counted only seventy-seven lead coins on each of them. If he spent a night in the House of Warm Fragrance, he'd be eating chaff for the rest of the month. Besides, he had to pay for internet. He'd chosen his address not only for the cheap rent, but also for the convenience of the network. It had a network management station right on top of the back wall. If anything went haywire, all he had to do was kick the ladder and yell upward. The internet fee was forty coins a month, plus a few more to keep the network manager friendly. Outspending his income was a negligible concern when he couldn't live a day without the internet.

"What are you dragging your feet for? Move it!" Zhao Da yanked on the chain; Zhu Dagun stumbled forward, hurriedly covering his face with his hands as he went down the street. In a moment, they came out of the front gate of Xuanren Ward and turned to travel eastward along the wide thoroughfare of Zhuque Street. They saw few pedestrians, and none who paid any mind to a criminal in chains in this time of war and chaos. Zhu Dagun spent the walk hiding his face and cringing, terrified of bumping into a fellow Hanlin Academician. Fortunately, this was the hour after lunch, when everyone was napping with full bellies. He didn't see a single scholar.

"S-sir." After a while, Zhu Dagun couldn't resist asking in a small voice, "What am I under arrest for?"

"What?" Zhao Da turned to glower at him. "Misinforming the public, starting rumors—did you think the government was ignorant of the trouble you were making online?"

"Is it a crime for concerned citizens to discuss current affairs?" Zhu Dagun asked. "Besides, how does the government know what we say online?"

Zhao Da laughed mirthlessly. "If it's government business, there's government people watching. You untitled little scribe, did you know that spreading slander and rumor about the current situation is a crime on the same level as inciting a disturbance at a governmental office or assaulting a minister? Besides, the internet is another novelty from the East City Institute. Naturally we have to be twice as cautious. You may think that the network manager's there to keep the internet operating smoothly, but he's writing down every word you send out in his dossier. It's all there in black and white. Let's see you try to wriggle out of it!"

Shocked, Zhu Dagun fell silent.

Chug chug chug chug. A fire-oil carriage rumbled past, spewing flame and smoke. It had "East City XII" painted on its side, marking it as one of the Institute's repair vehicles.

"The Song army is trying to storm the city again," said one of the soldiers. "Nothing will come of it this time either, most likely."

"Shhh! Is it your place to talk about that?" His companion cut him off immediately.

Ahead, a crowd was gathered around some sort of vendor stand set up under the shade of the willows. A smirking Zhao Da turned to one of his soldiers and said, "Liu Fourteenth, you should save up some money and get your face scrubbed. You'll have more luck finding a wife."

Liu Fourteenth blushed. "Heh-heh . . . "

Zhu Dagun then knew that it was the East City Institute's tattoo removal stand. The emperor was afraid of the Han soldiers deserting, so he had their faces tattooed with the name of their army divisions. The Jianxiong soldiers were tattooed "Jianxiong;" the Shouyang soldiers were tattooed "Shouyang." As for Liu Fourteenth, a homeless wanderer who'd been enlisting in every army he could find since boyhood, his face was inked shiny black from forehead to chin with the characters of every army that had ever patrolled this land. The only blank spot left was his eyeballs; if he wanted to enlist again in the future, he'd have to shave himself bald and start tattooing his scalp.

The East City prince's tattoo removal method had the soldiers rushing to line up. The technique involved taking a thin needle dipped in a lye solution and pricking the skin all over. The scabs were peeled off, and the skin again brushed with lye solution before being wrapped with cloth. The second set of scabs then healed to reveal clean new skin. It was precisely due to the unease of being under siege that everyone wanted a wife to enjoy while they could. Prince Lu's invention showed his deep understanding of the soldiers' thoughts.

The procession walked a bit farther, then harnessed an oxcart at Youren Ward and continued east by cart. Zhu Dagun sat on a stuffed hemp sack, bouncing with every bump in the road, the chains scraping his neck raw. Deep inside, a little part of him couldn't help but regret accepting the mission. He and the General of the Cavalry Guo Wanchao counted as old acquaintances. Their ancestors had been ministers together under old Emperor Gaozu Liu Zhiyuan. The fortunes of their families had gone opposite ways in the time since, but now and then they'd still simmer some wine and talk of things past.

That day, when Guo Wanchao invited him over, he'd been utterly unprepared to see Minister Ma Feng sitting there as well. Ma Feng wasn't just anyone— his daughter was the emperor's beloved concubine, such that the emperor even referred to him as father-in-law. It hadn't been long since he'd stepped down from the position of Chancellor for the sinecure of Xuanhui Minister. In all of Jinyang, aside from a few self-important generals and military governors with soldiers under their command, no others could equal his status and power.

After a few rounds of wine, Ma Feng explained to him what they had in mind. Zhu Dagun immediately threw his cup to the floor and jumped up. "Isn't this treason?"

"Sima Wengong once said, 'Loyalty is to give all oneself for the well-being of another.' Yanzi also said that 'Being a loyal minister means advising one's lord well, not dying with one's lord.' One should not take shelter under a wall on the verge of falling. Brother Zhu, consider your gains and losses carefully, for the sake of the people of the city . . . " Old Ma Feng held on to Zhu Dagun's sleeve, his whiskers trembling as he sermonized.

"Sit down! Sit down! Who do you think you're fooling with that performance?" Guo Wanchao hawked out a glob of phlegm. "All you scholars are the same. Powerless to make any difference, you spend all day on the internet pontificating and debating, criticizing the emperor for never doing anything right, and lamenting that Han is going to collapse sooner or later. And now all of a sudden you can't bear to hear a word against the emperor? To put it bluntly, once the Song dogs storm the city, everyone in it is motherfucking dead. Better to surrender while we can and save tens of thousands of lives. Do you really need me to spell this out for you?"

Awkwardly, Zhu Dagun stood there, unwilling to either acquiesce by sitting or to defy the general by leaving. "But Prince Lu has those machines on the city walls. Jinyang is well-fortified, and I hear a grain shipment from Liao arrived a few days ago from the Fen River. We can hold out for at least several more months—"

Guo Wanchao spat. "You think Prince Lu is helping us? He's screwing us over! Those Song dogs now control the Central Plains. They have enough grain and money to keep the siege going for years. Back in the third month, a Song army crushed the Khitan at Baima Ridge, killing their Prince of the Southern Domain Yelu Talie. The Khitan are too scared to come out of Yanmen Pass now. Once the Song army cuts off the Fen and Jing Rivers, Jinyang will be completely isolated. How are we supposed to win? Besides, who knows where that East City prince came from, with all his strange devices. Does he really only care about helping us defend the city? I don't think so!"

For a time, none spoke. A fire-oil lamp crackled on the table, illuminating the small room's walls. The lamp was another one of Prince Lu's inventions, naturally. A few coins' worth of fire-oil could keep it burning until dawn. Its smoke smelled acrid and stained the ceiling a greasy black, but it burned far brighter than a vegetable seed oil lamp.

"What do you want me to do?" Zhu Dagun slowly sat.

"Try to reason with him first, and if that doesn't work, whip out your knife. Isn't that how things are always done?" Guo Wanchao said, raising his cup.

— 4 —

Prince Lu's origin was a complete mystery. No one had heard of him before the Song army surrounded the city. Then, after the loss of the twelve prefectures, stories of the East City Institute began to circulate through the wards. Seemingly overnight, countless novelties sprang up in Jinyang, three of which grabbed the most attention: the massive water wheel and foundry in Central City, the defensive weaponry on the city walls, and the city-spanning internet.

Jinyang was divided into three parts, West, Central, and East. Central City straddled the Fen River; the water wheel was installed right under a veranda, turning night and day with the river's flow. Water wheels had long been used to irrigate fields and mill grain, but who knew that they had so many other uses? Squeaking wooden cogs drove the foundry's bellows, and the water-dragons, fire-dragons, capstans, and gliding carts atop the city walls. The foundry held several furnaces, where the bellows blasted air over iron molten by fire-oil. The resulting iron was hard and heavy, far more convenient than before.

The changes were even greater on the city walls. Prince Lu had laid down a set of parallel wooden rails atop the wall and ran a strong rope along the track from end to end. Press down a spring-loaded lever, and the power of the water wheel drove the rope to pull a cart sliding along the track at lightning speed. The trip from Dasha Gate to Shahe Gate normally took an hour even on a fast horse, but with the gliding cart it took only five minutes. On the system's maiden trip, the soldiers tied to the cart as the first passengers had screamed in terror, but a few more trips showed them the fun in it. With exposure came appreciation; they became the gliding cart operators, spending all day aboard the cart and refusing to get off. There were five carts in total, three for passengers and two for catapults. The catapults weren't much different from the preexisting Han ones, except that they used the water wheel to winch back the throwing arm, not fifty strong men hauling on the oxhide rope; and they no longer threw stones, but pig bladders filled with fire-oil. Each bladder also contained a packet of gunpowder wrapped in oil cloth, with a protruding fuse that was lit right before firing.

Throwing down rocks and wooden beams was a staple of siege defense, but every beam dropped and rock hurled meant one less in the city. If the siege went on long enough, the defenders usually had to take apart houses in the city for things to throw. Therefore, the East City Institute came up with a vicious new invention. Instructed by Prince Lu, the defenders tamped yellow mud into big clay pillars, five feet long and two feet across, and embedded the surfaces with iron caltrops. The construction of the mud pillars followed a specific recipe: yellow mud was covered with straw mats to stew for a week; mixed with glutinous rice paste, chopped-up straw, and pig's blood; and then pounded down repeatedly. The caltrops studding the pillars were doused with wastewater until they rusted an unnatural red-black. Prince Lu said that they'd make the Song soldiers catch a disease called "tetanus." Weighing two thousand six hundred pounds each, glistening a sinister yellowish bronze color, and covered all over with filthy iron caltrops, the pillars turned out to be excellent weapons for slaughter. Hundreds of pillars were secured to the top of the wall with iron chains on each end. When the Song army approached, the pillars smashed down, pulverizing scaling ladders, rams, shields, and soldiers alike. Then, with a turn of the capstan, the water wheel winched the chains with little squeaks, and the bloodstained pillars ascended sedately toward the parapets once more.

After suffering great casualties from the pillars, the Song army changed tactics and sent Khitan captives and their own old, weak, and sick to serve as the vanguard. Taking advantage of the brief respite after their sacrifices were flattened and while the pillars were still down, the main body of the Song army advanced with ladders, siege towers, and catapults. But now the gliding cart-mounted catapults came into play. In a flash, hundreds of red, stinking, wobbling bladders took to the air, blooming into fireballs as they rained down among the Song troops. Wood crackled and soldiers screamed. The fragrance of meat roasted on fruit tree wood permeated the air. Last came the archers, sniping at anyone with a helmet plume—everyone knew that only Song officers could wear feathers on their helmet. But arrows were limited and had to be used conservatively; once the archers had shot a couple arrows each, they returned to rest, thus ending the battle.

Below the city walls was a field of char, smoke, and wailing. Above, the Han defenders poked and pointed into the distance, counting their kills. For every kill, they drew a black circle on their hand, and used the circles to collect their reward money from the East City Institute. By Prince Lu's calculations, two million Song soldiers had died these months below the city. Everyone else, looking at the Song camps that still covered the horizon end to end, came to an unspoken consensus not to bring up the problem with statistics derived from self-reporting.

With Jinyang securely defended, Prince Lu invented the internet to keep everyone in the city from getting too bored. He first came up with something called movable type (which he claimed was cribbing from an old sage named Bi Sheng, although no one could recall ever having heard of this formidable personage). He'd first carved the text of the Thousand Character Classic in bas relief onto a wooden board, then pressed a layer of yellow mud mixed with glutinous rice, straw, and pig's blood—leftover material from the death-dealing clay pillars—over the printing plate. Finally, he'd peeled the whole thing off and diced it into small rectangles, thus creating a set of individual type blocks that could be freely combined and assembled. He'd placed the thousand characters into a rectangular tray, attaching every block in the back to a strand of silk thread with a spring. The thousand strands of thread were then collected into a bundle the thickness of a wrist, termed a "web".

Similar text-trays were found all over the city, while the bundles of silk threads passed through the bottoms of the walls to a network manager's station. The end of each bundle of silk was then neatly fitted into a metal mesh by tying a small hook to the end of each thread and hanging the hooks to the mesh. These meshes lined the walls of a station, and if two text trays wanted to communicate, the manager found the two corresponding bundles and brought the metal meshes together with a twist that connected the thousand pairs of metal hooks together. The bundles were thus linked together in what Prince Lu called an "internet".

Once a web connection was established, the users at each end could communicate through the text trays. When one side pressed down on one of the type pieces, the little spring tugged the silk thread, causing the corresponding type to sink down on the other side. Although picking out the desired character out of a thousand densely packed blocks posed quite a strain on the operator's eyes, an experienced user could type with lightning speed. Some pedants worried that the depth and complexity of hanzi writing could not be adequately represented by such an invention. Though the *Thousand Character Classic* was an ingenious primer to introduce the wonders of hanzi, how could a mere one thousand characters be enough to discuss life and the universe? Prince Lu countered that they were one thousand unique characters—never mind discussing the universe, these characters had been enough for the majority of fine essays since antiquity; they were certainly enough for web users to express whatever they needed to say.

In actuality, in the *Thousand Character Classic*, one of the characters—the one for "pure"—did occur twice. The East City Institute removed one of them and substituted a piece of type with a bent arrow symbol. Since it would have been too difficult for two users to simultaneously type and squint at the text tray for a reply, Prince Lu decreed that the current speaker had to press this "carriage return" block when they finished typing to indicate that it was the other person's turn. Why the symbol was called "carriage return" was something Prince Lu never bothered to explain.

At first, only two people could talk on a web connection at once, but Prince Lu later invented a complicated bronze hook rack that linked many internet lines together at once. If one person pressed a character, it would show up on all the other text trays.

This advance in the internet led to a new problem. If eight scholars sat down to chat, the moment one of them pressed the return key, the other seven would fight to speak first, with the result that their text trays would undulate up and down uncontrollably, like the dark waters of Lake Jinyang rippling in the north wind. To solve this problem, the East City Institute sold a new kind of text tray with ten blank type squares. When web users took advantage of the bronze rack to form a chat group, everyone first carved the members' appellations onto the squares. If someone wanted to speak, they pressed the block with their name. Whoever's block moved first had the right to speak until they pressed carriage return. Prince Lu first called this arrangement a "three-way handshake," then "vying for the mike," although he never explained what these terms meant. Zhu Dagun loved to smash his own "Zhu" block non-stop, naturally earning severe rebuke within his circles. Block-mashing not only disrupted the others' ability to speak, but also often caused the internet line to snap.

Though the silk threads were resilient, damage from wind, rain, insects, mice, and bad users like Zhu Dagun was inevitable, and the lines broke from time to time. If you were chatting, only for someone to suddenly call you an "ignorant dog unworthy of the title of scholar sullying the names of past sages," it was a good sign that the threads for some of your type blocks had broken. While you had meant to type "The Master spake, 'even the sage-kings of old were met with failures in this'," what had shown up in the other text trays was "The Master spake, 'the sage-kings of old were failures'," thereby not only denouncing the legendary sage-kings, but also smearing great Confucius as well.

At times like this, you had to yell "Manager!" and give the network manager a few coins for the trouble of inspecting the web lines while you took the opportunity to go to the market and buy a few pounds of flatbread. Meanwhile, the manager would sever the connection, find the broken silk lines, and knot them back together. If you didn't invest enough into a friendly relationship with the network manager, he'd tie a big fat knot that clogged the network so that your lines moved at the rate of a geriatric ox pulling a caravan. But if you did hand over enough coppers, he'd take out a little comb, smooth out the threads until they gleamed, and tie a minuscule square knot. Then you tossed the flatbread through the station window and yelled "All's well!"—that was why Zhu Dagun had no choice but to reserve money for bribing the network manager, no matter how strained his wallet.

The East City Institute's siege defense weaponry won it the hearts of the soldiers; its peculiar little inventions won the hearts of the commoners; and the internet won the hearts of the scholars. To moralize and debate and weigh in on anything one desired without having to step outside one's door—such convenience had never been available to anyone, not even in the time of the ancient sages of legend. With the Song army surrounding the city, the scholars could no longer venture out of the city to climb Xuanweng Mountain, sightsee along the Fen River, or drink and admire the flowers. Being shut inside, they had only writing to serve as a pastime, and that dejected them further. If it weren't for West City's internet coverage, these destitute, bored intellectuals would have tried to overthrow the government long ago. With an entire state reduced to one city, its three ministries and six departments gone in all but name, no pay for the ministers, and the emperor not even attending court, the scholars had become the most idle and useless group in the city and could only snipe and complain online.

If some loved the internet, of course others kept their distance, as they would for ghosts and gods—and anything else they didn't really understand. If some praised Prince Lu, of course others muttered behind his back. No one had actually seen his person, but he was the hottest topic of gossip among the wards.

Zhu Dagun had never dreamed that the first time he had any contact with the prince would involve being sent by Ma Feng and Guo Wanchao to advise surrender. Whether it was more moral to fight or surrender, he hadn't quite figured out himself. But since both the civil minister and the general charged him with such a weighty task, he could only venture forth, a petition and a sharp knife hidden in his clothes.

— 5 —

The oxcart proceeded creakily past the walled courtyard of an inn. Prince Lu had built it not long after he came to Jinyang. The inn was painted orange, with a blue plaque emblazoned in large characters, "Best Western," presumably to advertise itself as the best inn in West City. It was a somewhat odd name, though rather tame by the standards of the other neologisms that Prince Lu had invented.

After Prince Lu moved to the East City Institute, he had two windows carved in the wall surrounding the courtyard, one for selling wine and another for selling miscellaneous gadgets. The prince's wine was called *weishiji*, presumably a poetic contraction for the phrase "feared and respected by even mighty warriors." It was brewed by soaking and boiling the grain brought from Liao, creating an alcoholic liquid clear as water and crisp as ice that burned a trail of fire through one's guts upon imbibing, far superior in flavor to the rice wine sold in the market. Two pints cost three hundred coins, a high price in a time of abundant moonshine stills, but connoisseurs naturally had their ways of paying.

"Soldiers, give us a volley!"

Zhu Dagun turned and saw a dozen or so hooligans standing at the foot of the city wall, yelling toward the outside. A soldier's head poked out from the parapets above. "Are you short on cash again, Zhao Second? You'd better give us a bigger share of that good wine this time, or else the general's going to crack down and—"

"Of course, of course!" the hooligans laughed. Then they resumed yelling in unison, "Soldiers, give us a volley! Soldiers, give us a volley!"

Soon after came the voices of the Song soldiers, yelling from outside the city. "You'd better keep your word! Five hundred arrows for twenty pints! Don't you dare shortchange us."

"Of course, of course!" With that, the hooligans jumped to action, wheeling out seven or eight haycarts from heaven knew where and arranging them at a distance from the wall. Then they ducked down at the foot of the wall, covering their heads with their arms. "All set. Shoot!"

Bows twanged. A swarm of arrows dense as locusts hissed through the air, arced over the ramparts, and thunked into the piles of hay, instantly transforming the carts into oversized hedgehogs.

Zhu Dagun watched from a distance, fascinated. "I've heard the old story of the Three-Kingdoms strategist who propped up straw men to trick arrows from the enemy. I never thought it would still work."

Zhao Da spat. "These hooligans are colluding with the enemy. You could call it treason if you really wanted to prosecute. The city defense is always short on arrows, so the emperor decreed that he'd pay ten coins for every arrow turned in. The five hundred arrows these hooligans collected can be exchanged for five thousand coins, enough to buy thirty-four pints of alcohol. They lower twenty pints in a cask to the Song soldiers, hand out four pints to bribe the watchers on the wall, and drink the remaining ten until they pass out in the streets. Degenerates!" He turned to glare at them, and shouted, "You fellows have some nerve to do this in my sight!" The hooligans only laughed and bowed to him before whisking the carts down an alley.

Zhu Dagun knew that, whatever Zhao Da said, he was certainly in the hooligans' pay. But he didn't bother pointing this out; instead, he sighed. "The longer the siege goes on, the worse the thoughts in people's heads. Sometimes it feels as if it's better to let the Song army take the city and get it over with, huh."

"Nonsense!" Zhao Da bellowed. "Any more traitorous talk and I'll whip you!" Zhu Dagun still couldn't figure out if Zhao Da was Ma Feng's agent, dispatched to help him, so he didn't speak further.

The sun beat down ruthlessly. The oxcart plodded forth in the shade of listless willows, down the main road through the internal gate dividing West from Central. Central City was no more than seventy yards across, divided into two levels. The water wheel, the foundry, and the various other hot and noisy machines were on the lower level. The upper level was for horses, carts, and pedestrians, and on either side of the road were the government buildings for the Departments of Hydrology, Textiles, Metallurgy, and Divination.

The road had been paved with jujube wood wherever possible. Central City had been built in the time of Empress Wu Zetian by the Secretary of Bing Prefecture to connect East and West Cities on either bank of the Fen River. In the three hundred years since, the jujube paving had been regularly polished with wax and tamped down by feet and hooves, until it gleamed a deep brown like dried blood and was hard as stone. When struck, it rang like a bronze bell; swords bounced off it, leaving only white scratch marks. Pried up and used as a shield, it could deflect blades and arrows, even bolts from the Song army's repeating arcuballistas. At this point in the siege, the paving was full of gaps, carelessly filled in with yellow mud. Walking over it, you never knew which foot would start sinking. The soft spots could sprain an ox's ankle.

"Off," Zhao Da said. He instructed a subordinate to return the oxcart, while he personally led his captive through Central City on foot.

The Fen River was shallow and thin from the drought. Zhu Dagun looked at the turbid flow that wound in from the north, babbling through the city's twelve arch bridges before continuing southward without rest. "Liao, Han, Song: north to south, three nations connected by a single river." He sighed unconsciously. "With such a sight before me, I ought to compose a poem to commemorate—"

Before he had the chance, Zhao Da delivered a hard smack to the back of his head, knocking his cap askew and beating the poetic inspiration right out of him. "Enough, you starving scribbler. I sweated buckets getting you here, and I don't need your chattering. The magistrate's office is right ahead. Shut up and walk!"

Zhu Dagun quieted obediently, thinking *the moment I'm free I'm going to go online and cuss you out to everyone, you corrupt official.* Then he realized that if he succeeded in convincing Prince Lu of the East City Institute, Han would no longer exist. Would the internet still be there when Jinyang belonged to Song? For a time, he walked in a daze.

Wordlessly, they crossed Central City into the modest-scaled East City. They walked past the Taiyuan county building and made two turns on the dusty street to enter a courtyard of gray brick and gray tile. The courtyard walls were tall and smooth; the windows were covered with iron bars. Zhao Da exchanged greetings with the man inside and handed over papers, while the soldiers shoved Zhu Dagun into the west wing. Zhao Da took off Zhu Dagun's chains. "The boss is giving you a cell to yourself. You'll be brought two meals a day. If you want money, more food, or bedding, ask your family to bring them. Try to escape and your crime rises one rank in severity. Trial is in two days. Just tell everything like it is to the boss. Got everything?"

Zhu Dagun felt a sharp burst of pain in his back; he stumbled and fell into a cell. Guards locked and chained the door, then left.

Zhu Dagun pulled himself up and looked around, rubbing his butt. He found that the cell had a bed, a sitting mat, a bronze basin for washing his face, and a wooden bucket serving as a chamberpot. Although the room was poorly lit, it was neater and cleaner than his own home.

He sat on the mat. He groped the pouch inside his sleeve and found that everything was intact: a copy of *The Analects*, so that when he debated Prince Lu he could borrow courage from the writings of sages; an empty wooden box, with a hidden compartment containing Ma Feng's voluminous petition— it may have been an entreaty to surrender, but the impeccable writing and righteous language had Zhu Dagun's abject admiration; a double-edged dagger forged of prime steel, six and three-tenth inches. *Of what import is the anger of a common man?* The First Emperor had asked this of Tang Ju. *A spray of blood five paces long,* answered he. Thinking of this final tactic, the Han words churned Zhu Dagun's Shatuo and Turkic blood.

— **6** —

Only when Zhu Dagun awoke did he realize that he'd fallen asleep in the first place. A ray from the setting sun slanted through the window. It was late in the day now. Footsteps sounded in the hallway outside. Zhu Dagun slowly climbed to his feet and stretched, looking out through the gaps between the bars.

Earlier, Ma Feng had said that he'd planted agents inside the prison to appear at a suitable time. At this moment, a guard was strolling over, an oil-paper lantern in his left hand and a box of food in his right, humming as he went. He stopped at Zhu Dagun's cell and knocked on the bars with the lantern. "Hey, time to eat." He took two flatcakes from the box, wrapped them around some pickled vegetables, and passed them through the bars.

Zhu Dagun accepted the meal with a friendly smile. "Thank you very much. Does your superior have any words for me?"

The guard glanced around, then set down the food box and took out a scrap of paper. "Here, read this," he whispered. "Don't let anyone see it. The general said to tell you, 'Do what you can, but leave the rest to the will of heaven.'

As long as you do your duty, you'll benefit whether it works or not." Then he raised his voice. "There's water in the basin. Scoop it up with your hands if you want to drink. Relieve yourself in the bucket. Don't get any blood, pus, or phlegm on the bedding. Got it?"

The guard picked up the food box and strolled off. Zhu Dagun devoured the flatcakes in a few bites, poured some water down his gullet, then turned around and read the note by the last fading sunlight. However, once he was done, he felt more confused than before. He'd thought that the guard had been sent by Guo Wanchao, but the note suggested otherwise. It read:

Dear Sir:
Our state of Han is in big trouble. We're low on soldiers and grain and rely on the siege defense machines to keep going. Lately I heard that the East City Institute people have been uneasy and Prince Lu seems unstable. If he defects to Song, Han is doomed. Woe! If you read this letter I hope you can talk to Prince Lu and make him see the light. He mustn't surrender! He refuses to see any guests at the East City Institute so I can only try to do it roundabout like this. For the sake of our people please you must persuade him to stay strong! We'll beat Song one day for sure!

—Yang Zhonggui again thanks you

The note was clumsy in language, the handwriting unrefined; clearly, the author was some rough fellow without much education. The name "Yang Zhonggui" seemed unfamiliar. Zhu Dagun thought for a long time before remembering that it was the original name of Military Governor Liu Jiye. He was the son of the Lin Province Inspector Yang Xin. Emperor Shizu had adopted him as a grandson and changed his name to Liu Jiye. In his thirty years as a general, he'd never been defeated in battle, earning him the moniker "Invincible." Currently, he commanded the defense of Jinyang. Signing the note with his original name showed his desire to distance himself from the current emperor. The reason was no secret. Ten years ago, the previous Song emperor had breached the Fen River dam in an attempt to flood Jinyang. The streets had disappeared under the waters, and corpses and trash floated everywhere. Liu Jiye had petitioned the emperor Liu Jiyuan to surrender, only to meet with curses and mockery. One of the other signatories to the petition, Guo Wuwei, was publicly executed. Liu Jiye had remained in disfavor ever since, stripped of any meaningful command.

Though he'd once advocated surrender, now he advocated fighting on. Zhu Dagun thought he understood why. The Invincible General might have been a renowned warrior who'd caused the deaths of countless soldiers, but he was also a credulous, short-sighted gentle soul who wept to see the ordinary people suffer. Ten years ago, the entire city was starving. Commoners swam into the streets every day to eat the bark off the willow trees; if they rolled off their roofs at night while sleeping, they drowned in the stinking water. Liu Jiye's heart had ached so at the sight that he'd only wanted to open the gates and let the Song troops in and end all the suffering.

But this time, the city was comparatively well-stocked. The commoners could eat their fill and still have grain left over to trade for *weishiji*, trade for a few gadgets, or pay a visit to the brothel, satisfying themselves in both body and soul. Naturally this bolstered Liu Jiye's spirit. He wanted nothing more than for the siege to last for a hundred years until the Song ruler died of old age right where he stood, as vengeance for the past. With Prince Lu holed up in his own territory in East City, shut off from all outsiders, only criminals could hope for an audience with him. General Liu had written his clumsy entreaty and left it in the prison in the hopes that some patriotic prisoner could whisper encouragement to Prince Lu.

"Ah . . . " Zhu Dagun blinked. He tore up the note and threw the scraps into the wooden bucket, then pissed over them to destroy the evidence. The guard who brought him food hadn't been the person he was waiting for, but Liu Jiye's agent, in a strange coincidence.

The sky outside the window was soon dark, and there was no lamp in his cell. Zhu Dagun sat with a full stomach and nothing to do. Normally, this would have been a perfect hour for chatting online. He flexed his fingers restlessly as he mentally recited the *Thousand Character Classic*. Without sufficient familiarity with this cunning work, one wouldn't be able to quickly find the right character in the text tray. Memorizing it—and thus the layout for the types—had become a requirement for the literati of his generation.

Footsteps once again sounded in the hall; the glow of flames grew as they approached. Zhu Dagun hurried to the bars and waited. A guard stopped in front of him, holding his torch high. "Zhu Dagun?" he said coldly. "In custody for sowing misinformation online?"

Zhu Dagun smiled. "That's me. Though I've never heard of that crime . . . Does your superior have any words for me?"

"Hmph. Kneel!" the guard suddenly said, in total seriousness. He glanced around, then pulled out something shiny and golden, spreading it to let Zhu Dagun see. Zhu Dagun paled and instantly dropped to his knees. He was only a minor scribe with no governmental rank, but he'd once seen such an object on the incense table of a great scholar of the Imperial Archives. He shivered in fear, obediently touching his forehead to the ground. "The servant . . . the criminal Zhu Dagun a-awaits His Imperial Majesty's instruction!"

The guard stuck out his chin and began to recite, enunciating each character crisply. "In representation of Heaven and the Emperor the edict speaks: We know of you and your abundance of opinions. Often, you debate matters of state on the internet and spin your words very skillfully to corrupt others. However, we understand that you've been falsely reported this time, and we assure you you'll receive proper redress, but you need to help us out first. It's improper for us to lower ourselves by going to the East City Institute, and Prince Lu isn't willing to come to Jinyang Palace. Since we trust no one else in court, we can only put our hopes in you. You and I are both Shatuo, descendants of Yukuk Shad. We trust you, and you must trust us. Ask Prince Lu for us, what are we to do? He once promised that he'd build a flying vessel for us to enable our one hundred and six household members and four hundred old Shatuo retainers to escape from the city and head straight into Liao territories. But Prince Lu now insists that he is too busy with defending the city to build this 'zeppelin,' a name he glossed as 'stairway to heaven' in an abstruse dialect. It's been two months and there are no signs of this vessel. The Song troops are fierce and many and our heart is filled with apprehension. Dear loyal scholar, help us convince Prince Lu to build the zeppelin, and we will reserve a seat for you. When the Liu clan once again rises, we'll grant you the rank of Chancellor. A ruler does not joke."

"Your servant a-accepts this edict." Zhu Dagun lifted his hands above his head and felt a heavy scroll descend into them.

The guard sniffed at him. "See what you can do. The emperor is . . . " He shook his head and left.

Zhu Dagun stood, covered in a cold sweat. He slid the scroll of yellow silk respectfully into his sleeve, his head spinning as he thought of its contents. Guo Wanchao and Ma Feng wanted to surrender; Liu Jiye wanted to fight; the emperor wanted to run away. All of them presented what seemed like reasonable arguments, but upon further thought, none of them seemed so reasonable. Who to listen to, and who to ignore? His heart was a tangle. The more he thought, the more his head hurt.

He didn't know how much time had passed when new footsteps broke him from his torpor. He'd used up all his enthusiasm; he trudged to the bars and waited.

The guard held a fire-oil lamp. He shone the lamp around, then said, "Sorry I'm late. Since you're the only prisoner here today, I couldn't get in until the change of shifts."

"Does your superior have any words for me?" Zhu Dagun said listlessly. He'd already asked this three times today.

The guard lowered his voice. "The General and Elder Ma want me to inform you that the East City Institute will send for you at the hour of the rat tomorrow. Prince Lu is mucking with something new and needs people. Just claim to be knowledgeable in alchemy and you'll be able to approach him."

"Alchemy?" Zhu Dagun said, surprised. "I'm an ordinary scholar. I don't know anything about alchemy."

The guard furrowed his brow. "Who said you have to know anything? You're just trying to get close to Prince Lu. It's not like you're actually going to be smelting pills of immortality. Just mumble something about ceruse, litharge, cinnabar, sulfur, the *Baopuzi*, the *Kinship of Three*, the *Collected Biographies of Immortals*, and so on. No one understands this stuff anyway, so no one can call you out. Go to sleep early, and I'll see you tomorrow. Good luck persuading him!" He turned to leave. Two steps later, he paused to ask, "You did bring the knife, right?"

— 7 —

The sky brightened without fanfare. Sounds of shouting and fighting drifted in; the Song troops were trying to storm the city again. The residents of Jinyang had long since grown accustomed to this, and no one took note.

A guard came to deliver breakfast. Zhu Dagun took the bowl of porridge and looked him over carefully, only to realize he'd only paid attention to the lantern, the torch, and the fire-oil lamp the previous night. He couldn't remember what the guards looked like at all and was unable to tell which faction this guard hailed from.

Zhu Dagun ate the porridge and sat for a while, doing nothing. The clamor of the morning crowd arose outside. A throng of burly men dressed in East City Institute uniforms flooded into the courtyard.

The guards took Zhu Dagun out into the yard. A man with a yellow beard covering his face walked up and greeted him. "I serve Prince Lu. By his mercy, prisoners here only need to be willing to work for the Institute to obtain pardon for their crime. Your charges aren't too severe. Just sign here and you'll be cleared." The man took out paper and a writing implement. Instead of a brush, the instrument was a goose feather dipped in ink—before

Prince Lu, who would have thought that you could pull a feather from a bird, soak it in lye, sharpen the tip, and write with such a thing?

Zhu Dagun automatically reached for the feather, but Yellow-Beard drew it back. "But right now, His Highness needs someone of unusual capabilities and skills. First tell me, are you knowledgeable in alchemy? I'll be blunt, you look like the genteel, bookish sort, so don't try to sell yourself for more than you're worth."

Zhu Dagun quickly dredged up a speech. "I've been studying the *Kinship of Three* since childhood under the guidance of my father. I am thoroughly versed in the ways of Dayi, Huanglao, and the forging flame. Heaven and Earth are my cauldron, water and fire are my ingredients, and yin and yang are my complements. I know when to stoke the flames and when to bank the embers. In my life I've refined one hundred and twenty pills of shining gold and imbibed them daily. Although I have not ascended to the ranks of enlightened immortals, my body has become light, nimble and impervious to disease. The pills have the power to cultivate the spirit and extend life." To demonstrate the effectiveness of the golden pills, he sprang up and did two backflips in mid-air, then grabbed an eighty-pound stone drum lying in the yard. After lifting it above his head and tossing it from hand to hand, he threw it to the ground, where it landed with a thud. He dusted off his hands, his breathing unhurried, his face unchanged in color.

Yellow-Beard stared; his men started to clap. The guard standing behind him sneaked a thumbs up, upon which Zhu Dagun knew that this was Ma Feng's agent.

"Excellent, excellent! We've found a real treasure today." Yellow-Beard laughed and opened the small bamboo case at his waist. He dipped the goose quill in ink and handed it over. "Sign here, and you'll belong to the East City Institute. We're going straight to Prince Lu."

Zhu Dagun signed his name as directed. Yellow-Beard ordered the guards to unfasten the manacles around his ankles, bowed all around to the prison staff, and left the courtyard with his retinue. He and his men escorted Zhu Dagun for half an hour before arriving at a large residence complex, both sprawling in area and dense with buildings. The blue-garbed guards at the gate smiled when they saw Yellow-Beard. "Got the goods? It's been peaceful lately. We haven't had any new people join in a while."

"I know, Prince Lu was frantic about finding an alchemist to help him out," replied Yellow-Beard. "We've finally taken care of that."

A crowd was gathered in front of the gate: imperial messengers, merchants, government officials in search of glory by association, commoners seeking aid in redressing wrongs done to them, craftsmen bringing their own inventions in the hopes of an audience, idlers trying to return the novelties they purchased after they grew bored, laborers looking for work, prostitutes looking for clients. The guard recorded them one by one in his ledger, gently refusing, reporting, and chasing off with a stick as appropriate. If he saw anyone he was uncertain about, he went ahead and took the bribe, then told them to try their luck again in a few days. He was quite orderly and methodical in this work.

Yellow-Beard led his men into the compound. The courtyard was a different scene: behind a privacy wall was an immense pool of water, in the middle of which a geyser rose more than ten feet tall before majestically splashing down.

"Normally the fountain is powered by the water turbine from Central City, but with the Song army regularly trying to storm the city, we need the turbine to power the gliding carts, catapults, and capstans," Yellow-Beard explained. "So instead the fountain mechanisms run on manpower. We have several dozen unskilled laborers in the Institute, whose only trade is doing heavy lifting, nothing like a white collar fellow like you." Zhu Dagun had never heard of the strange words he used, so he simply looked where Yellow-Beard pointed. Indeed, he saw five dull-eyed, muscular fellows to the side, stepping on pedals that went up and down. The pedals drove rotors, the rotors churned a water tank, and the tank valves opened and shut, pumping water high into the air.

They went around the fountain and through an archway to enter the second partition of the courtyard. A dozen or so workshops stood to either side. Yellow-Beard said, "We build the flashlights, sunglasses, clockwork toys, microphones, magnifying glasses, and other things we sell in the city here. Institute staff get a fifty percent discount, and a lot of these gadgets are hard to find in the market. You should come check them out when you get a chance."

As they spoke, they went through a third partition. Heavy, gleaming fire-oil carriage components lay everywhere under a high awning. A piece of heavy machinery puffed away, spewing white smoke and rapidly turning a carriage wheel. Several oil-stained craftsmen were engaged in an animated discussion full of strange words like "cylinder pressure," "ignition timing," and "steam saturation." Two carpenters were hammering together a carriage framework. Several dozen large barrels of fire-oil stood in a corner of the yard, filling the air with their simultaneously aromatic and noxious smell. Fire-oil came from the island of Hainan and was originally used to douse attackers in flames during a siege, before it found myriad uses in Prince Lu's hands. Yellow-Beard said, "All the fire-oil carriages running about in Jinyang were built here. They make up more than half the Institute's income. The newest model will be released soon. It's called Elong Musk—for the long-lasting fragrance of fire-oil after the vehicle darts out of sight. Even the name sounds fast!"

They continued walking, entering a fourth partition. This place was even stranger. There was constantly some shrill squeaking noise, or the crackle of an explosion, or an odd taste to the air, or colorful flashes of light. "This is the Institute's research lab," Yellow-Beard said. "Our prince gets a new idea a minute, and then our craftsmen try to follow up on his ideas and make them a reality. It's best not to linger here; there are lots of accidents."

On the walk here, the other members of their group had gradually dispersed, so that Yellow-Beard and Zhu Dagun were alone by the time they entered the fifth partition. Blue-garbed guards stood at the gateway; Yellow-Beard took out a pass, spoke a code phrase, and wrote down several passwords on a piece of paper; only then were they let inside. Hearing that Zhu Dagun was the newly arrived alchemist, the guards patted him down head to toe. Fortunately, he'd hidden the imperial edict in the rafters of his prison cell and tucked the dagger into his topknot. Zhu Dagun had a big head, covered in a black silk cap with jutting ears in the back. A guard snatched off his cap, but only saw a bulging bun of sallow hair, and didn't look more carefully. On the other hand, the copy of the *Analects* they found in his sleeve pouch roused suspicion. They looked him up and down, then flipped through the book. "What's an alchemist doing with this?"

This copy of the *Analects* hadn't been printed with Prince Lu's clay movable type. Rather, it had been printed in Emperor Shizong of Zhou's time, using the official carved plates, and had been passed down for generations into Zhu Dagun's hands. Zhu Dagun felt physical, visceral pain as he took back his crumpled and wrinkled treasure and prepared to head in.

Yellow-Beard said, "This row of buildings in the north is where His Highness normally spends all his time. He doesn't like to be disturbed, so I won't go in with you. Don't be afraid, our prince is amiable and kind. He's not hard to talk to . . . Right, I still don't know your name."

"My surname is Zhu," Zhu Dagun quickly said. "I'm the eldest of my siblings and named after Gun, father of the first Xia ruler. My courtesy name is Bojie."

Yellow-Beard said, "Brother Bojie, I've been one of His Highness's helpers since he first arrived in Jinyang. He granted me the name Friday."

Zhu Dagun bowed. "Thank you, Brother Friday."

Yellow-Beard returned the bow. "Not at all, not at all," he said, before turning and leaving.

Zhu Dagun straightened his clothes, cleared his throat, scrubbed at his face, swallowed, and entered the building.

The room was very spacious. Black paper covered the windows, and fire-oil lamps illuminated the inside. Two long tables stood at the center of the room, covered with various jars and bottles. A man stood at one of the tables, head down, working on something.

Zhu Dagun's palms sweated, his heart raced, and his legs wobbled. He hesitated briefly before gathering his courage, clearing his throat stickily, and dropping to a kowtow. "Your Highness! I . . . this criminal is—"

The man turned. Zhu Dagun kept his head down, afraid to look at his face. He heard Prince Lu say, "About time! Hurry and help me, I've been messing with this for days without any progress. Why is it so hard to find someone who understands middle school chemistry? What's your name? What are you doing there on the ground? Get up already and come here."

At Prince Lu's string of words, Zhu Dagun hurriedly stood up and came over, his head down. He thought that this august prince sounded friendly and genial, like someone easy to approach, although he pronounced his words so strangely that Zhu Dagun had to repeat them to himself several times before understanding the prince; he wasn't sure what topolect it was. "Your lowly servant is Zhu Dagun, a criminal." Still keeping his eyes lowered, he made his way to the center of the room. Jars and bottles clanged over as he went, not because of carelessness or poor eyesight, but because the floor was so packed with random objects that he couldn't take a step without kicking something over.

"Hey, Lil' Zhu. You can call me Old Wang." The prince stood on tiptoes to pat his shoulder. "You're really tall. 190 centimeters, maybe? I heard you're from Hanlin Academy. I really wouldn't have guessed that by looking at you. Have you eaten? If not, I'll get us some takeout to pad our stomachs. Otherwise, let's cut straight to the chase. I still haven't gotten results from today's experiment."

These words threw Zhu Dagun into a daze. He sneaked a glance up and discovered that the prince didn't look like a prince at all. He was of medium height, pale and beardless, and wore a buttoned white cotton coat. His hair was cropped short like a beggar-monk's. He looked to be in his twenties, yet his brow remained creased with worry even when he smiled. "Your servant doesn't quite understand what you're saying, Your Highness . . . " Zhu Dagun bowed anxiously, unsure of what story lay behind this strange prince.

Prince Lu laughed. "You think my accent is confusing, but all you guys sound like gibberish to me. When I first came, I couldn't understand a single word. Your court speech sounds like Cantonese or Hakka, but nothing like the modern Shanxi and Shaanxi topolects. Since I wasn't a historical linguist, I thought that all the topolects of ancient northern China wouldn't sound very different from what I knew!"

This time, Zhu Dagun understood every individual word coming out of the prince's mouth individually, but their combined meaning fluttered entirely from his grasp. Sweat trickled down his face. "Your servant lacks in erudition. What Your Highness just said . . . "

Prince Lu waved a hand. "That's to be expected. You don't need to understand anyway. Come and hold this flask in place. Oh right, put on a filter mask. You studied alchemy, so you should know that chemical reactions can release toxic gases, I think?"

Zhu Dagun stared.

— **8** —

The crystal bottles on the table held liquids that Zhu Dagun had neither seen nor smelled in his life. Some were red, some were green, some smelled burningly acrid, some stank unbearably. Prince Lu helped him put on a mask, then had him steady a small, wide-mouthed jar. "Take this rod and stir it slowly. Don't stir faster than that under any circumstance, got it?"

Nervously, Zhu Dagun stirred the dark green fluid inside the jar. It smelled like the sea, and was hot like a bowl of potherb soup. "This is dried seaweed ash dissolved in alcohol," Prince Lu explained. "You ancients call seaweed 'kunbu.' I got this Goryeo kunbu from the Imperial Physician. *The Song of Medicine Recipes* said 'kunbu disperses goiter and breaks swelling' . . . oh, wait, *The Song of Medicine Recipes* is from the Qing dynasty. I got mixed up again."

As he spoke, he took out another small jar and carefully removed the sealing clay. The jar was full of an acrid-smelling pale yellow liquid. "This is sulfuric acid. You alchemists call this 'green vitriol,' right? Also 'qiangshui,' like in the *Alchemical Classic of the Yellow Emperor's Nine Cauldrons.* 'Bluestone is calcinated to obtain a white mist, which is dissolved in water to obtain strong qiangshui. The substance transforms the silver-haired into the ebony-haired. The choking white mist it emits instantly transports one into the realm of spirits, and after eighteen years one departs from senescence and returns to childhood.' You should be familiar with that."

Zhu Dagun nodded as if he was. "That's right, Your Highness."

"Just call me Old Wang. 'Your Highness' sets my teeth on edge. I'll start now; keep stirring, don't stop." He set up a three-paned white paper screen to lean over the mouth of the flask, put on his mask, and slowly poured the green vitriol into the small jar. At first, all Zhu Dagun noticed was a stench that burned its way right through the cotton mask and up his nose, strong enough to make his brain ache and his eyes tear. Then he saw a miraculous purple cloud was floating up out of the jar, unfurling lazily. Zhu Dagun shivered in fright, but Prince Lu only laughed. "Finally! With this crude method for extracting iodine, that's half my big plan taken care of! Don't stop, keep stirring until the reaction finishes. I need to see just how much pure iodine I can extract from one pound of dried seaweed . . . Are you interested in how I created sulfuric acid and nitric acid? This is the first step in the Long March of establishing basic industry, you know."

"I'd love to hear," Zhu Dagun said automatically.

Prince Lu seemed delighted. "I was pretty good at chemistry back in high school, and I majored in mechanical engineering as an undergrad, so I got a decent foundation. I couldn't have made it this far otherwise. At first I wanted to use the alchemists' method of making sulfuric acid from bluestone, but I couldn't find more than two pounds of it in the city, not nearly enough. Then I happened to see the massive piles of pyrite ore in the iron foundry. Treasure, right for the taking! Heating pyrite gives you sulfur dioxide, and dissolving that gives you sulfurous acid; let that sit for a while and you get sulfuric acid. You can purify that in clay jars; it's how the munitions factories in Communist Shanbei managed, back in the day.

"With sulfuric acid taken care of, nitric acid wasn't hard. The biggest problem was the limited supply of saltpeter, which we also needed to make gunpowder. I had to mobilize everyone in the Institute to scrape crusted urine off the bases of walls to refine into potassium nitrate. Our entire place reeked! Fortunately, people in this city have a habit of pissing anywhere there's a wall. If it weren't for that, we couldn't have built the foundations of industry in Jinyang."

Zhu Dagun flushed. "Sometimes the urges of the bladder are too great. Both men and women commonly take off their trousers and relieve themselves where they stand. Please humor the crude customs of the countryside, Your Highness."

While they were speaking, the contents of the two jars had been combined into one, and the purple cloud had disappeared. Prince Lu spread the white paper screen out on the table and scraped the surface with a flat scrap of bamboo, removing a layer of purplish black powder. "The iodine in seaweed is easily oxidized in air under acidic conditions, creating elemental iodine. Very good, let me send them orders to follow my recipe and manufacture this in batches, and we'll do the next experiment." He crossed the room, sat down in front of the text tray in the corner, and began banging out a missive. Zhu Dagun walked over to look and discovered that this strange prince typed with lightning speed. He didn't even glance at the characters, but typed blind with unfailing accuracy. "Your type tray looks like a different model, Your Highness," Zhu Dagun blurted.

"Old Wang, call me Old Wang," said Prince Lu. "The principle's the same, but each terminal uses two sets of movable type. The bottom set is used for input and the top set's used for output. Watch." He pressed the carriage return to end his message and stood up to grab a crank handle and turn it. The crank turned a roller on which a seventeen-inch-wide length of calligraphy paper had been spooled, passing it smoothly over the text tray. The movable type in the tray, to which ink had been applied, suddenly began to rise and fall, stamping characters onto the paper.

Zhu Dagun bent down to pick up the paper and began to read. "The experiment data is correctly recorded. I've told the chemistry department to oversee it. *Return.*" He looked at the prince with admiration. "This is far clearer and more convenient! White paper and black ink simply reads better to the eye. When are you releasing this on the markets? We'll support it with all our might!"

Prince Lu laughed. "This is only a prototype. Version two-point-one will use the same mechanism found in printers to stamp the output on the same line, instead of inking the characters all over the place and making it hard to read. You like the internet too? The thing I was least used to about this era was the lack of internet access, so I racked my brains to come up with this. I finally get to feel like a proper nerdy shut-in again."

"Your August Highness—er . . . Old Wang," Zhu Dagun corrected himself when he saw Prince Lu's expression. "May your servant ask, from which prefecture did you originally hail? Are you a scholar of the Central Plains? You have an extraordinary air about you, after all."

Prince Lu sighed. "The better question is, from what dynasty did I hail? The era I come from is one thousand sixty-one years, three months, and fourteen days distant."

Zhu Dagun didn't know if he was joking or raving. He did the arithmetic on his fingers and laughed obsequiously. "I see that you achieved the Way in Emperor Wu of Han's time, and have lived on to today as an immortal!"

"Not one thousand years in the past," Prince Lu said unhurriedly. "One thousand years in the future—and nine hundred billion forty-two universes away."

— 9 —

Zhu Dagun didn't understand Prince Lu's ravings, and he didn't have time to dwell on them, because the next experiment had begun. Prince Lu placed a silver-plated copper coin into a small carved wooden chest, set the cup of newly-made iodine beside the coin, closed the lid, and lit a small clay brazier next to the chest to heat it a little. Soon, purple vapors came billowing out through the cracks in the chest. *Heavens, we're about to get some pills of immortality*, Zhu Dagun thought, as he carefully waved the fan as Prince Lu instructed, afraid even to breathe too hard.

A while later, Prince Lu pushed the brazier aside, opened the chest, and reached in with a soft cloth. He carefully lifted the copper coin, cushioned on the cloth, revealing that its silver surface was coated with something yellowish. Zhu Dagun peeked inside the chest and didn't see any pills of immortality, but Prince Lu did an excited dance. "It worked! It really worked! Look, this yellow stuff is called silver iodide. All I have to do now is scrape it off into a jar and put it somewhere dark. I can perform another magic trick with this: put this coin somewhere dark, expose it to light for about ten minutes, develop the image with mercury fumes, and fix it with saltwater. Once it's rinsed and dry, the coin will be covered with a picture of this room, identical in every last detail! This is the Daguerreotype process, which takes advantage of silver iodide's photosensitivity. But we're storing up silver iodide for something else, so I'll have to show you at a later date."

"Without an artist, how can one obtain a picture?" Zhu Dagun asked, confused. "And . . . what miraculous powers does the yellow powder have? Does it impart health and sagehood on one who imbibes it?"

Prince Lu laughed. "It's not that kind of magic. In my day, silver iodide had two main uses. One was photosensitivity, like I mentioned. The other, well, you'll see." He worked as he spoke, scraping the powder off the coin into a small porcelain bottle, before pulling off his mask and stretching. "That's all for now. I'm done for the morning. I'll send out the instructions for manufacturing silver iodide, and then I can rest. You haven't eaten, right? We can eat together later. You're tall and strong, and pretty good with your hands—it must be all that alchemy experience. I have some things I want to ask you, so don't wander off. I'll be right back."

Prince Lu sat down at the text tray and began to type at a rattling pace. Now and then he cranked out a length of calligraphy paper and read it, nodding to himself. Zhu Dagun just stood there in the room, afraid to touch anything and accidentally break it, or trigger some mighty magic.

At this point, he finally remembered why he was there. He reached for his sleeve pouch, felt the copy of the *Analects* there, and took a deep breath. "Your Highness, there's something that I don't understand," he said, looking down. "I hope you can advise your servant."

"Go ahead, I'm listening." Prince Lu was still at the text tray, cranking the spool of calligraphy paper, too busy to spare a glance.

Zhu Dagun asked, "Your Highness, are you Han or Hu?"

"Don't be pretentious, call me Old Wang," came the reply. "I'm Han. I grew up in Beijing's Xicheng District. My ma's Hui Muslim, but I took after my ba. I may have played in the Niujie and Jiaozi neighborhoods as a kid, but I can't live without pork, so no dice."

Zhu Dagun had already learned to ignore Prince Lu's incomprehensible ramblings. "If Your Highness is Han, why do you live in Jinyang instead of the southern lands?"

"You wouldn't understand even if I explained," said Prince Lu. "I'm Han, but I'm not a Han from your era. I know perfectly well that, of the Five Dynasties and Ten Kingdoms, Liang, Tang, Jin, Zhou, and even your so-called Great Han were founded by other ethnic groups, and most of your people are Hu too. But once my plan succeeds, I'll be back at my point of departure, and this temporal node of your universe won't have a thing to do with me, got it?"

Zhu Dagun took a step closer. "Your Highness, how are we going to defeat the Song army?"

"We can't," said Prince Lu. "We don't have the soldiers or the food, and we can't mass produce firearms. Flintlock muskets are easy to manufacture, but we don't have nearly enough sulfur to make gunpowder. We scoured the city and only found a couple dozen pounds. We can't do more than occasionally fire a cannon to give a scare. But that brings me to my next point. Though we can't defeat the Song troops, we can hold out pretty easily. As long as Zhao Guangyi doesn't find out how Liao is sending us grain under the surface of the water, Jinyang survives another day. Tying empty barrels to full barrels and sending them along the bottom of the Fen River is a trick you ancients would never think of."

Zhu Dagun raised his voice. "But the commoners are hungry and weary, and the soldiers wail with pain and exhaustion! The longer Jinyang holds on, the more its tens of thousands of residents suffer, Your Highness!"

"Hey, good point." Prince Lu turned on his stool. "Everyone else is delighted to work here—not only are they pardoned for their crimes, they can even earn some money. But you don't sound like them. Let's talk, then. I haven't had anyone normal to talk to in months. It's been"—he pulled out a piece of paper, took a look, and drew another X on it—"three months, seven and a half days since I was dropped here. I've got twenty-three and a half days before the observational platform automatically returns. The schedule will be tight, but judging from my current progress, I should be able to make it."

Zhu Dagun understood only the faint longing for home that underlay his words. He immediately recited, "The Master said: as long as parents are alive, one should not journey far from them without method. When one's father lives, observe one's aspirations; when he does not, observe one's actions; if in time they do not deviate from the father's way one can be termed filial. Your Highness has long been away from your home and must miss your parents dearly. Foxes die with their heads pointing toward their burrow; crows feed their parents in their old age; lambs kneel before they drink from their mother's teat; stallions will not mate with their dam—"

Prince Lu sighed. "Okay, we're still not on the same frequency here. Can you shut up and listen?"

Zhu Dagun immediately shut up.

Prince Lu spoke slowly. "I'm sure you don't know the alternate universe theory or quantum mechanics, so I'll go over them briefly. My name is Wang Lu. I was an ordinary nerd, amateur writer of *chuanyue*$^\ominus$ novels, and professional time traveler. In my time, we'd perfected the multiverse theory, so that anyone could go to an agency, rent an observational platform, and go time traveling. At one time, people estimated the number of parallel universes overlaying each other to be around $10^{\wedge}(10^{\wedge}118)$, but more precise calculations later on indicated that, due to overlap between different diverged branches, only about three hundred quadrillion universes exist at any one time. Countless particle-level possibilities cause universes to endlessly emerge, split, merge, and disappear, and yet even the two parallel universes with the most differences are astonishingly similar on a physical level, even as their places on a timeline diverge further and further.

"In a way, this makes things boring, since humanity's exploration of deep space remains stalled, and its understanding of the universe as a whole is very shallow. Even in the most advanced universe I've been to, humanity's

---

$\ominus$ Chuanyue is an enormously popular Chinese genre similar to time travel, but with its own distinct tropes. Typically, the protagonist is from the modern day and travels into the historical past (or a secondary world version of the historical past) often but not always through reincarnating into the body of someone of that era. Their anachronistic knowledge and upbringing sets them apart from others and allows them to break the status quo.

reach has gone no further than Alpha Centauri, just next door. But in another way, this makes things interesting, since with the invention of the wave function engine it means that we can step across to other parallel universes at our convenience. For topological reasons, the more similar the destination universe, the less energy it takes to travel there. The most advanced observational station we have can send travelers three hundred trillion universes away, though the commercially available equipment only has a maximum range of around forty trillion."

Zhu Dagun kept nodding while he felt his sleeve pouch, inwardly debating whether to take out the dagger and persuade Prince Lu's heart or take out the?Analects?and persuade his mind once he finished his raving. There was no one else in the room, creating a prime opportunity to make his move. It wasn't that Zhu Dagun didn't want to act promptly, but that he himself still felt somewhat undecided as to which esteemed personage he should act on behalf of.

Prince Lu picked up his teacup and took a sip, then continued. "I accepted a job from the Peking University history department, a research task to tally the population of the Sixteen Prefectures during the late Five Dynasties and Ten Kingdoms period. A parallel universe like yours is located toward the front of the timeline, which makes it an excellent place for historical observation.

"Don't think just anyone can get a time travel license. You have to train systematically in quantum theory, computer operation, ground transportation, emergency drills, and more, and pass the test to get a job. If you want to lead tour groups, you have to take the Time Travel Tour Guide Examinations too. Due to the physical similarity between parallel universes, I activated the observational platform at Xuanwu Gate in Beijing to travel nine hundred billion forty-two universes and arrive here. By my calculations of revolution and rotation elements, I should have been able to arrive in You Prefecture. Who knew that my observational platform was getting long in the tooth? The wave function engine radiator boiled over, right in the middle of the trip! I had to pour in eight bottles of mineral water and a crate of Red Bull to get it to limp to the destination. The moment I arrived in this universe, the crown bar burst through the tank. That was the end of the engine. I crashed into a gully in Shanxi by the Fen River. My luggage, equipment, and spare fuel tanks were wiped out.

"It took me ten days to patch together the engine, only to discover all the fuel had leaked out. The bit left in the oil lines could hop me two or three universes over at most. What use would a few hours forward be?"

The sounds of shouting and fighting from outside grew louder. The Song army had begun another assault on East City gate. Prince Lu turned to glance at the report scrolling out above the text tray and typed a few characters himself. "Don't worry." He laughed. "We'll take care of it as usual. I'll move two bladder catapults over . . . Where was I? Ah, right, the wave function engine could just barely start, and raising the angular speed made the engine oil give off blue smoke like a tractor, but the main problem was that I didn't have any fuel. Taking that census was of course out of the question, but even worse, since I hadn't filed this private job with the Ministry of Civil Affairs' Multiverse Administrative Office, I couldn't just call the time police for help when they'd put me in jail for three to five years! If I wanted to get home, I needed some way to gather fuel. I didn't have a choice but to hide my things in the gully and sneak into Jinyang."

"Your Highness, you say you didn't have any fuel, but isn't the city full of fire-oil?" Zhu Dagun couldn't resist interrupting. "Many carriages on the street burn fire-oil."

Prince Lu sighed. "If only it combusted oil. Let me put it this way, the fuel tank didn't hold real, physical fuel, but potential energy, the elastic potential between parallel universes. If I wanted to fill my tank, I needed to create a universe split. When a new universe split off as a result of some decision point, I'd be able to gather this escaped potential energy to power my return. This potential energy isn't something intangible like entropy values. It's more like when you snap a bamboo pole in two, and you hear the?crack?as it splits apart? I don't understand it that well myself, but either way I had to create a big enough event to make the universe split. Now, how could I do this? Let's take an example from history—on the fourteenth of the third month this year, a resident of Jinyang slipped from the parapets and fell to his death in the Fen River. The incident was witnessed by twenty people and recorded in minor history books. If, on the fourteenth of the third month, I grabbed his collar and saved his life, I'd create a change. But it wouldn't be big enough. Out of the one hundred quadrillion universes where this event occurred, he was saved in one quadrillion of them even without me. In that moment, the parameters in one of those universes would change until it perfectly matched the universe we're in, and the two universes would merge. Of course, you and I wouldn't feel anything from where we stand, but the potential would decrease, and even remove fuel from my tank. To cause a new universe to split off, I have to create a big enough change, a change so big that no precedent exists in any one of the one hundred quadrillion universes past this point in the timeline. I managed to use the beat-up wave function computer to find a possibility, one that I could achieve without any modern equipment to help me."

Zhu Dagun didn't speak, only listened intently.

Prince Lu suddenly pulled open a drawer and took out a book. He read from it, "'In the sixth month of 882 CE, the height of summer, Shang Rang led an army from Chang'an to attack Fengxiang. He had reached Yijun Camp when suddenly a great blizzard fell. Within three days, the snow was many feet thick. Thousands died or became frostbitten in the cold, and the Qi army retreated in defeat to Chang'an.' Have you heard of this incident?"

"Huang Chao's rebellion!" Zhu Dagun finally had an opportunity to add to the conversation. "Shang Rang was Grand Commandant of Qi. The story of the blizzard in the second year of Zhonghe is still oft told among the people. It's recorded in the historical annals as well."

"Exactly," said Old Wang. "I'm a modern man, but I don't have death rays or nukes or any kind of sci-fi weaponry, and I don't have the Starship *Enterprise* or *Macross* to back me up. All I can do is use the scraps of knowledge I got from high school and college to alter this era as much as possible. It's a historical fact that Song conquered Northern Han. In the vast majority of universes, the annals record that on the fourth day of the fifth month, the Song army took Jinyang and the Han ruler Liu Jiyuan surrendered. On the eighteenth day of the fifth month, Emperor Taizong of Song drove out all the city's inhabitants and burned Jinyang to the ground. But here, I've already postponed these dates for more than a month. The Song army can't stay here indefinitely; anyone can see that the primitive siege weapons of this era can't break through the fortifications strengthened with my knowledge. Once the Song army retreats, history will be completely rewritten, and the universe will split, without a doubt!" He toyed with the little bottle of silver iodide and laughed delightedly. "And that's without mentioning my new invention. This little thing is going to change history immediately and fill my observational platform's fuel tank! The ancients believed in omens from the heavens more than anything. What could change history more than a snowstorm in the middle of summer?"

"Burn . . . Jinyang? Snowstorm?" Zhu Dagun said numbly.

"It's easier to show than to explain! Follow me!" Prince Lu leapt to his feet and dragged Zhu Dagun by his sleeve to the room's west wall. He pulled some mechanism, a hinge turned, and the entire wall suddenly fell outward to reveal a courtyard hidden among dense overhanging eaves. The blinding sunlight forced Zhu Dagun to squint; it took a few moments before he could clearly see the contents of the courtyard. He was astonished. Laid out in the courtyard were many extraordinary things that he'd never seen before and didn't know the names of. Several dozen East City Institute workers were laboring under the hot sun. They knelt to pay their respects when they saw the prince. Prince Lu smiled and waved a hand. "Continue. Don't mind me."

"We're testing the hot air balloon," Prince Lu explained, pointing at the workers in the middle of sewing cotton fabric. "I agreed to build an airship for the emperor so he can escape to Liao. An airship takes more time than this, but I'll do what I can and build a balloon for now. When I came to Jinyang, I made a few flashy novelties and bribed some minor officials for an audience with the emperor. I told him I could make Jinyang impregnable for him, and he granted me the convenient title of Prince of Lu right on the spot. I have to repay that kind of generosity."

They turned and came to a group of workers filling a cannon cast of black iron with gunpowder. "This cannon will be used to fire a cloud-seeding canister. Gunpowder isn't strong enough a propellant, so we need the hot air balloon to lift the cannon into the air, and then fire it up at an angle. I've been keeping a close eye on the weather patterns lately. Don't be fooled by how hot it is; the clouds that drift in from the Taihang Mountains every afternoon are full of cold air. By providing enough condensation nuclei at the right time, we can create a snowstorm out of nowhere!" Prince Lu grinned. "I sent the recipe over earlier. The chemical factory off-site is currently devoting all its resources to manufacturing silver iodide powder. It won't be long before we can fill a cloud-seeding canister and load it into the cannon. We've already test-flown the hot-air balloon. All we have to do is wait for the right weather conditions!"

Zhu Dagun gazed up at the clear and fair sky. The sun shone like fire. The distant sounds of battle were fading; a magpie squawked from the eaves. A fire-oil carriage rumbled along a stone-paved road. The air smelled of blood, oil, and flatcakes. Zhu Dagun stood by the prince, unable to move, his mind in a muddle.

— **10** —

The wall swung shut, returning the room to darkness. They ate a little. Prince Lu sent instructions to the city defense and the workshops through the internet, asking Zhu Dagun questions about alchemy as he worked. Zhu Dagun braced himself and spouted enough smooth-talk and nonsense to pass muster.

"Ah, I need to sleep. I pulled an all-nighter and I'm running out of steam." Prince Lu stretched wearily and headed for the cot in a corner of the room. "Keep an eye out, will you? Wake me if there's any news."

"Yes, Your Highness." Zhu Dagun bowed respectfully. He watched as Prince Lu lay down, pulled the brocade covers around himself, and soon began to snore. He let out a quiet breath and sat down, head spinning, to collect his chaotic thoughts.

Zhu Dagun didn't understand everything Prince Lu had said, but he grasped the tone of his words clearly enough. The master of the East City Institute couldn't care less about the Han dynasty or the people of Jinyang. He had come from a different land, and he would ultimately return there. He'd created his dazzling novelties and exotic toys to garner public support and earn money. He designed the internet to win over the scholar gentry and relay the East City Institute's orders; he sold the fire-oil carriages, weapons, and fine wine to show goodwill toward the military; and the life-saving grain, deadly fire, and impossible snow were all, in the end, to further Prince Lu's own selfish goals. Han Feizi had written, "Consider one who refuses to enter a dangerous place or fight in the army, who will not for the gain of all the people sacrifice even one hair on their leg . . . you have one who values life above all else." Was Prince Lu not "one who valued life above all else?"

Something was fomenting inside of Zhu Dagun. His chest felt stuffed, his head swollen. His ears rang. He thought of what Ma Feng and Guo Wanchao, Liu Jiye, and the emperor had said. He thought of this state, this prefecture, this city, and the tens of thousands of living beings within. Liang, Tang, Jin, Zhou, and Han had taken the land in turn; Hu and Han were thrown together in this time of chaos. An inhabitant of this turbulent era, Zhu Dagun had once considered abandoning the brush for the sword and carve out some great undertaking. He'd settled in a quiet corner discussing philosophy all day long, not because he was lacking in strength or courage, but because he lacked for direction. The scholars frequently chatted of the grand principles of governing a state and bringing peace to the land. Zhu Dagun always thought that it was empty words, but what aside from their arrogant talk of the halcyon days of the Rule of Wen and Jing, the Restoration of Zhao and Xuan, the Golden Age of Kaiyuan, had they to while away their time? All he wanted was food, a bed, and a roof to sleep under; to spend his leisure time chatting and drinking; to be able to roll into bed after eating, express his aspirations online, visit the brothels when he had the money; to be at ease with the world. But in this era of chaos, to be at ease with the world in itself required swimming against the flow. Even a minor character like him had been dragged into a struggle for the survival of a country. At this moment, he held the fate of Great Han and the lives of everyone in the city in his hands. If he didn't do something, how could he claim to be a scholar, one who spent twenty years filling himself with the words of sages?

Zhu Dagun pulled the fine steel dagger from his sleeve. He knew he couldn't persuade Prince Lu because Prince Lu wasn't a citizen of Han. Grand principles were a sham to him; only the six and three-tenths inches of steel in Zhu Dagun's hand were real. In this moment, an idea floated into Zhu Dagun's mind, perfect in three ways. He slowly unfolded his large frame and stood, a smile hovering on the corners of his mouth. He stepped soundlessly across the floorboards and reached the cot in a few steps—

"What the fuck are you doing!" Prince Lu snapped up, eyes wide and staring. "I got bitten by a mosquito and got up to burn some bug-repelling incense. What are you doing here with a knife? I'm going to call my me*mmmph*"

Zhu Dagun had covered Prince Lu's mouth solidly, setting the dagger at his pale, tender neck. "Don't make noise and I'll leave you a way out," he murmured into the prince's ear. "Earlier, I saw you use the internet to move the East City Institute's city defense forces. You had a row of wooden movable type in your text tray. Give me the type blocks and tell me your passphrase, and I won't kill you."

Prince Lu was a prudent man. He nodded frantically, his forehead beaded all over with sweat. Zhu Dagun loosened his fingers, allowing a gap. Prince Lu gasped and panted as he took the movable type of red-colored wood from his pocket and threw them on the cot. "There's no passphrase," he stammered. "My orders pass through a special line straight to the city defense camps and the workshops. No one can fake it . . . Why are you doing this? I've protected Jinyang and invented countless novelties for every facet of life for soldiers and civilians alike to enjoy. Everyone in the city loves me. Where have I wronged Northern Han, wronged Taiyuan, wronged you?"

Zhu Dagun laughed mirthlessly. "Empty words. You look out only for yourself, while I plan for the benefit of a city's worth of people. First, I'll order the East City Institute to stop the defense. Once the fire-dragons, pillars, and catapults have stilled, General Guo Wanchao will open the gates and welcome the Song army in. "Second, Minister Ma Feng is waiting inside the palace. Once the city gates are open and the army is thrown into panic, he will persuade the ruler Liu Jiyuan to come out with his family and surrender. But I will take the emperor and help him escape in the chaos, aboard the so-called hot air balloon to the Khitans. "Third, I will bind you and give you to Zhao Guangyi, trading you for the lives of the city's inhabitants. The Song army has besieged the city for three months without success; the Song ruler must be filled with hate for you, the inventor of the city's defensive machines. If I bring you to him bound hand and foot, he is certain to be greatly relieved and spare Jinyang from the sword. In this way, I will not fail Guo Wanchao, Liu Jiye, or the emperor, or the people in danger of terrible suffering. I can achieve both benevolence and justice!"

Prince Lu gaped. "What kind of crappy plan is that? Whose faction are you in? You've cut everyone else a sweet deal, but I get thrown to the wolves, huh? Do you have to be so extreme? Let's talk it out; everything is open to discussion. All I wanted was to gather a bit of energy and go home. Does that make me a bad person? Did I do anything wrong? Did I do anything wrong?"

"You did nothing wrong. I did nothing wrong. No one did anything wrong. So whose fault is it?" Zhu Dagun asked.

Old Wang didn't have a chance to come up with an answer to this profound philosophical question before the dagger hilt struck his forehead, knocking him unconscious.

— 11 —

Wang Lu slowly regained consciousness, just in time to see the hot air balloon slowly rise above the roof of the main building of the East City Institute. The balloon was sewn from one hundred and twenty-five panels of thick lacquered cotton, with a basket woven from bamboo. The basket held a fire-oil burner and the heavy pig iron cannon. Three or four people were squeezed into the basket in clear disregard of weight capacity, but as the throttle opened and the flames roared, hot air swelling the balloon, the massive flying object continued its swaying ascent. The dark brown lacquer gleamed in the setting sun, the balloon's long shadow stretching across Jinyang.

"It worked . . . it worked!" Wang Lu sat right up, laughing skyward. The north wind was blowing, the summer heat dissipating in its chill. Clumps of water-vapor-rich clouds were gathering in the sky, perfect weather for artificially inducing snow. The time traveler watched the balloon as it rose higher and higher into the heavens, muttering, "Not enough not enough not enough, two hundred meters higher and then it can fire, a little more, a little more . . . "

He tried to stand and find a better angle to observe from, only to realize that he couldn't move his legs. He looked down and discovered that he was tied onto a fire-oil carriage parked in the middle of the road. The driver lay slumped over in his seat, dead. He looked farther and saw that the road was covered in piles of corpses—Han soldiers, Song soldiers, and Jinyang civilians, all dead in a variety of ways. Blood flowed down the roadside ditch, moistening yellow earth that had lain dry for months. Crying, screams, and the sounds of fighting came from the distance, like the roll of thunder on the horizon. And yet Jinyang seemed abnormally still, except for the crows circling and gathering in the sky.

"Fuck, what happened?" Wang Lu yelled, trying to twist free. His hands and feet had been soundly tied; movement made the coarse fibers slice agonizingly into his flesh. The prince let loose a string of curses, panting roughly, afraid to struggle further. At this time, a cavalry troop shot down the street, their armor and uniform marking them as Song. The riders didn't even glance at Wang Lu as their steeds galloped toward the East City Gate, trampling the corpses. A few snatches of conversation lingered in the air.

"—We're too late! What do we do if our arrows can't hit it?"

"—It's not a south wind, but a north wind. It'll never reach Liao. It'll only be blown southward—"

"—Will we be blamed?"

"—Otherwise we'd be too late!"

"Hey! What are you doing! Don't leave me here!" Wang Lu yelled wildly. "Tell your master I know physics and chemistry and mechanical engineering! I can build you a steampunk Song Empire! Hey, wait! Don't go! Don't go . . . "

The hoofbeats faded. Wang Lu looked up despairingly. The hot air balloon was now a small dot high in the sky, drifting southward with the north wind. *Bang*. He saw the puff of white smoke rise a moment before the sound reached him. The cannon had fired.

Wang Lu's eyes filled with the light of his last hope. He wrenched his head down, bit his clothing, and tore it aside, revealing the skin of his chest. A line of light glowed beneath his left collarbone: the fuel gauge for the observational platform. At the moment, it displayed red to indicate low power. The wave function engine required at least thirty percent to carry him back; snow in July would create a universe split that would fill his tank to at least fifty. "Come on." He was crying, bleeding, talking to himself with gritted teeth. "Come on come on come on and give me a big fat blizzard!"

Each gram of silver iodide powder could generate more than ten trillion particles; five kilograms was enough to create all the ice crystals for a blizzard. It seemed ridiculous, that someone could artificially create snow in an era of such low technology, but perhaps the time traveler's crazed prayer had been fulfilled: the clouds began to gather in the sky, roiling, pitch-black and restless, reducing the setting sun behind them to a thread of golden light.

"Come on come on come on!" Wang Lu roared toward the sky.

A rumble of thunder resonated to the horizons. First, rain fell, cold rain mixed with ice crystals. But as the ground temperature continued to drop, the rain became snow. A single snowflake drifted down, landed on the tip of Wang Lu's nose, and instantly melted from his body heat. But right after it came a second, then a third, heralding their quadrillions of compatriots.

The drenched time traveler laughed heavenward. It was a proper blizzard in July, the snow coming down in clumps; he couldn't wait to see the palaces, buildings, willows, and walls painted powder white. Wang Lu looked down and saw the gauge on his chest glowing green. The engine's energy forecast had crossed the baseline; the moment this universe split into two, the observational platform would collect the energy and automatically activate. In a moment too brief to be assigned a unit, it would send him home to his warm 900 square foot apartment near the Beiyuan neighborhood roundabout, Tongzhou District, Beijing.

"This will be legendary," Wang Lu said to himself, shivering. "I'm going to go home, find a less dangerous job, find a wife, squeeze my way onto the subway every day to go to work, and do nothing but play video games when I get home. I've had enough adventure for a lifetime, truly . . . "

At the rate the snow was accumulating, it would have taken less than an hour to bury Jinyang under a yard of white. But right at that moment, twenty dragons of fire rose from the four directions.

From the dozen gates of West, Central, and East City, the fire-dragon chassis were spraying pillars of flame, accompanied by countless pig bladder catapults hurling fireballs. They were weapons of city defense he'd built with his own hands, weapons the Song army had feared more than any other.

"Wait a . . . " The light went out of Wang Lu's eyes. "No, are they burning Jinyang down anyway? At least they could wait a little, until this snow's done . . . wait, *wait*—"

Thick, viscous fire-oil sprayed everywhere; flames roared heavenward. The fires spread with a speed beyond anyone's imagination. Jinyang had been long under drought, and the precipitation called by the time traveler hadn't the chance to soak into tinder-dry timbers.

The fire in West City began in Jinyang Palace, engulfing Xiqing Ward, Guande Ward, Fumin Ward, Faxiang Ward, and Lixin Ward in turn in a sea of flames. The fire in Central City set the great water wheel alight first, then burned west toward Xuanguang Hall, Renshou Hall, Daming Hall, Feiyun House, Deyang Hall. The East City Institute soon transformed into a brilliant torch. The snowflakes whirling above vaporized without a trace before they had a chance to land. The green light on the time traveler's chest faded. He howled his grief and agony, "Motherfucker, I was so close, so close!"

Bathed in fire, Jinyang lit dusk into daytime. The air boiled in the inferno; a scarlet dragon of flame wheeled upward, dispersing the clouds in an eyeblink. No one saw the fallen snow; they only saw flames that touched the heavens. The ancient city, first built in the Spring and Autumn Era, more than one thousand four hundred years before this moment, wailed distantly in the flames.

Jinyang's fortunate survivors were being driven northeast by the Song army, looking back with every step, their weeping loud enough to shake heaven. The Song ruler Zhao Guangyi sat astride his warhorse, gazing at the flames of distant Jinyang and the figures kneeling before him.

He said, "When you've captured the pretend-emperor Liu Jiyuan, come and see me. Do not harm him. Guo Wanchao, I confer upon you the title of Militia Commander of Ci Prefecture. Ma Feng, I name you Supervisor of Imperial Construction. You two have done me service, and I hope you will turn all your ingenuity and wisdom to my Great Song from today onward. Liu Jiye, why do you refuse to surrender when all the others have? Do you not know the parable of the praying mantis who attempted to block the passage of a chariot?"

Liu Jiye, his hands bound, turned to kneel northward. "The ruler of Han has yet to surrender," he said stubbornly. "How can I surrender first?"

Zhao Guangyi laughed. "I've long heard of Liu Jiye of the East Bank. You live up to your reputation. You can surrender once I capture the little emperor. You should revert to your original name of Yang. Why should a Han try to protect a Hu? If you want to fight, you should turn and fight the Khitans, don't you think?"

Having finished talking to these men, Zhao Guangyi rode forward a few steps. He bent down. "What do you have to say?"

Zhu Dagun knelt on the ground, afraid to raise his head. From the corners of his eyes, he could see the raging flames on the horizon. "I claim no accomplishment," he said, shaking. "I only ask that I be judged to have done no trespass."

"Very well." Zhao Guangyi waved his whip. "Posthumously grant him the title Duke of Tancheng, with a feifdom of thirty miles square. Chop off his head."

"Your Imperial Majesty! What wrong did I commit?" Zhu Dagun stood up in shock, flinging aside the two soldiers next to him. Four or five more tackled him. The executioner raised his sword.

"You did nothing wrong. I did nothing wrong. No one did anything wrong. Who knows whose fault it is?" said the Song ruler indifferently.

The head rolled to a stop; the large frame thudded to the ground. The copy of the *Analects* fell from Zhu Dagun's sleeve pocket and into the puddle of blood, soaking through, until not a single character could be distinguished.

Everything the time traveler had created burned to ashes with Jinyang. After a new city was built nearby, people gradually came to think of those days of wonders as an old dream. Only Guo Wanchao would sometimes take out the "Ray-Ban" sunglasses while drinking with Zhao Da in the Ci Prefecture army camp. "If he'd been born in Song, the world would be a completely different place, huh."

The Song conquest of Northern Han received only a brief description in the *History of the Five Dynasties*. One hundred sixty years later, the historian Li Tao at last wrote the great fire of Jinyang into the official histories, but naturally there were no mentions of a time traveler.

In [979 CE], the emperor visited Taiyuan from the north through Shahe Gate. He dispatched the residents in groups to the new governing city of Bingzhou, setting fire to their homes. Children and the elderly did not reach the city gates in time, and many burned to death.

—Extended Continuation of *Zizhi Tongjian, Book 20*

Against the Stream

X

by A Que,
translated by Nick Stember

— 1 —

The illness came so suddenly nothing could be done. When he woke it was yesterday.

At first he thought the problem was with his phone's display, but then everything that happened had happened the day before.

His boss yelled at him because he hadn't finished his reports. Sentence for sentence, word for word the same. That night he went home to an empty house, confused. Feeling tired, he got into bed and fell asleep. When he woke, time had moved back another day.

He didn't finish the reports this time, either.

It was then that he finally understood. While the world continued to move along with the flow of time, he had turned and gone against the stream. Day-by-day, he was entering the backflow of time.

It was hard to get used to at first. His life had been painful, so the thought of a second time through was unpleasant. Over and over again he tried to stay up all night, tried to change course. Despite his best efforts, he found himself powerless to resist the undertow of exhaustion.

Walking into the office one day, he beat his boss bloody, trying to alter the timeline. After being sent to jail he woke up at home. When he got to work his boss was still sitting in the office waiting for him, uncaring—his beating wasn't until tomorrow.

— **2** —

Eventually he got used to days like this, and life and work went back to normal. It was around then that Xiao Wei left him to live with the other man. Although he had thought it would hurt, it wasn't all that bad. Having been through it before, he just felt numb. No matter how deeply his memories might hurt, it was always all better when he woke.

Six months later—or, six mother earlier—a new person appeared in his house. "I think we should get divorced," he heard himself say to his wife. Only thirty-two, her face was marked with wrinkles and she was beginning to slouch. She stared at him blankly, and then nodded like she had the first time.

While his wife packed her things he stood by her side, watching. Six months had passed and she looked more like a stranger or an old friend than his wife. He didn't think he would ever see her again, but thanks to the back flow of time they'd been reunited for their separation.

In the end, his wife left with her things. He stood on the stairs, watching the shrinking shape of her back in the slanting light of late afternoon, moving ever further away until it disappeared completely into the crowd. He'd watched her leave then too, thinking that was the end. But now he knew they'd be seeing each other again.

As expected, he woke to the smell of breakfast the next day.

"I'm going to market," she said, standing in the doorway with her back to him. "Go ahead without me. You should be getting to work."

He nodded before realizing something was out of place. His wife often came home empty handed, without telling him where she'd gone. After she left he snuck over to the peephole. Instead of going out, she walked toward the staircase down the hall.

Tiptoeing after, he followed her all the way up to the roof.

He heard a soft sobbing—a familiar sound after so many years together.

So, he thought to himself, *she knew about Xiao Wei all along.*

— **3** —

He spent the day in a daze, wondering how she had found out. Just before getting off work, Xiao Wei sent him a text message: "Stay, don't go."

Staring at the screen, he wondered how many secrets were hidden in this tiny rectangle. Scalding hot in his hand, he felt the echo of the bomb that he'd set off the day before.

He started to delete their texts, their videos, their photos—until he realized it was pointless. He was going back to yesterday. In time his wife would forget the secret she had uncovered.

He shrugged his shoulders and put the phone back into his pocket.

One by one his co-workers left until he and Xiao Wei were the only ones still in the office.

Soon, the lights went dark row by row. She walked over in the dim light, leaning over to whisper things that made him blush.

That was Xiao Wei—charming and fearless, bringing light into even the darkest corners. He'd fallen for her so easily, surrendering himself so completely to desire he thought it was love—the second time he'd fallen in love.

But now, looking into her pretty face, his mind was filled not with lust or pleasure, but the memory of her abandonment into the arms of another man six months from now. He stood and looked down at her. Outside, cars drove past, sending flashes of light through the windows to catch across his glasses.

"What's with you?" Xiao Wei said, frowning. "You were into it yesterday."

"No, I won't be."

Xiao Wei didn't understand, but by then he'd already left.

—— **4** ——

The city at night was busy with a quiet constraint. As he walked alone, the cars filed past, their headlights drawing across and over, like in a scene from an old movie—one where something important is about to happen.

Just then, he heard shouts from an alley to the right. A group of young men were beating a drunk and he was surprised to find himself telling them to knock it off. Glaring, and cursing, they ran away.

He walked over. In the light of the streetlamp he could see that the drunk's face was covered with blood. Underneath the blood an old knife wound ran from his right eye to the corner of his mouth. The terrifying scar had left two ridges of skin peeled back on either side, and it writhed worm-like deep within his cheek.

He fumbled for a moment, before helping the drunk up.

"You're hurt, let me call you a cab."

Wheezing, the drunk laughed crazily.

"It's okay. No matter how bad they hurt me I'll be fine tomorrow."

His blood froze. Finally he said, "By tomorrow, you mean yesterday?"

The drunk stared, his expression under the streetlamp fierce and strange. The harsh light filled his lifeless eyes, like two deep pools. Suddenly laughing again he said, "You're a backwards man, too, aren't you?"

He felt like crying.

"It's really rare, you know, our illness," the drunk said as he struggled to sit up. "Harder to figure out that way. Time is like space—usually they go together. Walk ten minutes down the street, time and space are moving along with you. But then maybe they break apart and you move forwards, but time moves backwards—like with us. We've fallen into a time trap. That's what it means to be a backwards man."

He fell silent.

After a while the drunk continued: "It's hard for some of us, this illness. It's like being in a crowd at night and then suddenly turning to go the other way. They all keep going and you just get further and further away. Until you're the only one left, walking all by yourself back to the start."

— **5** —

Have you ever had someone in your life—the kind of person you'd thought was going to stay by your side until the very end? There they were, the day before yesterday, but then the second after next they're gone, evaporated into time.

You don't know it's happened yet, but he's already turned. He's behind you, in a time you can't reach, walking towards the gray twilight of the other side.

He sat in the gathering darkness, his mind filled with an absence of hope.

— **6** —

"There's no scientific basis for anything I've said, of course. The theory of relativity, quantum mechanics, neither one can explain our illness," the man said, seeming to sober up. "My research has dragged on for years now, but I've got nothing to show for it."

"How long will it last?"

The drunk shook his head. "I don't know, but I first became sick when I was seventy-five. I thought I was dying, but instead I've spent the last fifty years coming all the way back to today."

— **7** —

His wife was asleep when he got home. Standing in their bedroom, he watched her sleep. For the first time ever, he noticed the way that she curled up to one side, like an infant, leaving the rest of the bed for him. Only the wrinkled corners of her eyes reminded him that she was not a child. Her health was poor because she didn't take care of herself—three meals a day in a smoky kitchen had made her old before her time.

Over the ten years of their marriage he'd watched her age. He'd told her to take better care of herself more times than he could count, but every time she'd just nodded and said, "uh-huh." She was so clumsy that she'd never figured out how to use skin products correctly.

And now he was going to watch her return to her youth.

The process was hard to describe. After more than ten years together, he thought he already knew everything there was to know about his wife. He was surprised to discover so many new things in the rewind of his life.

Things like the fact that his wife used to like to eat sweet and sour fish, or watch Korean movies—movies, not soap operas. He watched his wife crying while she watched the TV.

He wondered when he started to fall out of love with his wife. Had their love gotten lost in in the detritus of the everyday? Or was it the years that had accumulated across her brow, day by day, as she grew older?

As time passed, his wife became beautiful again. Without years of sleeping curled at the far side of the bed, she stopped slouching. Watching these changes, he was overcome with guilt. When their anniversary came, he made her favorite dish—sweet and sour fish.

That was the first time he'd ever seen his wife cry from happiness. Clapping her hands over her mouth, her eyes flushed red with pleasure until she finally managed to say, "How did you know?"

"I'm your husband, aren't I?" he said.

His answer left her speechless.

Taking hold of her shoulder he said, "It's been my fault all along, but the past is the past. I'll be a better man in the future."

His wife nodded. Inside, he felt himself sigh. *What future? With every-thing moving forwards and me moving backwards, what good is it to repent now? It's all pointless.*

Around the time his wife began to get her looks back, her zest for life returned as well, and he found that she had more and more to say. It was something that had always bothered him, and he remembered asking her if she could be quieter.

Now he wondered if he had been the one who had turned the air at home into a stagnant pool of water, his wife's words becoming fewer by the day, her body curling more by the night.

Whenever his wife had something to say, he tried instead to put down what he was doing and listen to her talk. As a backwards man, he didn't have to worry about the work he'd set aside. The whole mess would be wiped away soon enough.

He got so used his new way of living that he soon came to enjoy it. *How could it be possible, he thought to himself, that I ever disliked this woman? A million Xiao Wei's couldn't compare to her.*

Ten years passed. It was the evening of his proposal. In the backwards flow of time his memories had been unable to keep up, leaving things confusing and unfamiliar. But he still remembered one thing from that evening:

He had rented thirty remote control helicopters and hung colored lights from them. They formed a heart in mid-air, leading her to him. Holding roses and a ring, he knelt down on one knee and asked her to marry him. The air was rich with color, as if all the stars in the sky had fallen down around her.

When she cried, the light tore her tears into tiny stars.

— **8** —

Later that same evening, they walked hand-in-hand back to their apartment. They didn't have a house yet—in a city full of the rich and successful, they were still struggling to make ends meet. And yet he already knew that they were happier now than they would be when they had a house and car of their own.

As they passed an alleyway, he was surprised to hear a strange voice suddenly call out his name. Peering into the darkness he saw only a dim figure, his face unclear.

Nervous, his wife squeezed his hand.

"Don't be afraid. It's just me," the man in the alleyway said. "You meet me later."

His wife didn't understand, but he did, right away. "An old friend," he explained to his wife. "Give us a moment, okay? We need to talk." With that, he walked into the dark alley, finding a boy of fourteen or fifteen waiting for him.

"I've discovered a way to cure our illness," he said.

Shock rolled over him. After so many years of living as a backwards man he'd become accustomed to it. But now the boy was reminding him that he'd been sick all along. "We aren't the only ones who've come down with this condition, you know. For the past decade, I've been traveling around the world. One day, I found a scientist at MIT who had it," he explained. "We did so many experiments that I lost count. But eventually we found the answer!

"As long as you live your life *exactly* as it happened the first time around, making the same decisions at the critical junctures in your life, then eventually you'll fall asleep and wake up back on day one. Time and space will rejoin and you'll go back to before the split. It will be as if none of this ever happened, and you'll forget you ever were a backwards man," the boy said.

"Does it really work?" he asked.

"It works. I know, because I've just tried it," the boy said, looking right at him. "The most important decision in my life just happened—running away from home after my dad cut my face."

It was only then that he noticed he was hurt, the blood spreading thickly and profusely like a rank weed across his face. No wonder he was hiding in the alleyway.

"What I'm seeing now is different from anything I've ever seen before. The world is thawing—it's hard to explain. I'm so tired, I keep falling asleep. You're a nice person. You helped me before so I did my best to stay awake so that I could tell you. I just hope you haven't missed your life-juncture already. Once it's gone you won't be able to stop yourself from going all the way back to the end of time. No one will remember you because you'll never have existed in the first place." The teen's voice became weaker as he spoke, and now he closed his eyes and stumbled backwards. "I'm going back now . . . I've been going against the stream of time for sixty years, and now I'm finally going . . . "

When he fell to the ground there was no sound of a body hitting the pavement—a split second before impact he disappeared into thin air. He knew that the young man had gone back his starting point, back to his dying, gray-haired self.

He staggered out of the alley where his wife was waiting for him. "What happened to your friend?" she asked.

Saying nothing, he took his wife home where he quickly fell asleep, his mind filled with new concerns.

He already knew what the the most important moment in his entire life was. It was the day he met his wife in school, when he'd walked up to her in the quad to ask the way. Finding himself completely overtaken by her beauty and enthusiasm for life, he'd given everything to be with her. She'd been the reason he had come to the city in the first place.

Their lives had been bound up together from the moment he asked her that first question.

— 9 —

On the day he would meet his wife, he got up early and left the dorm, waiting for her on the path through the quad. The cherry blossoms had just begun to bloom, filling either side of the path with pink. She soon emerged from the haze of blossoms.

He steadied himself, willing his mind into submission as he began to walk towards her. He'd already practiced the words a thousand times. Anytime now, he would say them. Every single detail was exactly the same as before, down to the expression he wore on his face.

The closer she came the more clearly he could see her. She was nineteen, wearing a flower-print dress. Her jet-black hair hung loosely about her shoulders, and her face was prettier than even the cherry blossoms. Suddenly he saw her, ten years from now, looking old and curled at the edge of the bed.

Any minute now, he would go back to the day he got sick. He wouldn't remember the things that had happened over the past ten backwards years. He'd still cheat on her. He'd still force her to leave. He'd still watch her back disappear into the crowd . . . time would pass as before, and the bright young face before him would become old and withered before its time.

He faltered.

It was a spring morning. He walked past the pretty young woman who would have become his wife and didn't ask the way, sharing only the few cherry blossom petals that fell across their heads.

Rain Ship

✕

by Chi Hui,
translated by Andy Dudak

— **0** —

The funeral was as simple as I expected.

Visitors passed by the coffin one by one. The cold moss-light was centered on the coffin's translucent lid. Under the dim lighting, Abani's face seemed once more full and round. Her final hours had been painful, but fortunately—for all of us—she hadn't held out too long. I heard crying, and saw it was Laila. She was supposed to become a sister in our family this year, but now it looked like that would have to wait. Mourning rituals were necessary. They were for the living, not the dead.

My maternal aunts walked by the coffin. I supported my weeping mother. Grief had shortened her, curled her up, bowed her back. I let the tears slide down her cheeks, not wiping them away.

Behind the aunts were the girls born in this home, and then the boys. The boys look puzzled and sad, but they didn't keen like the girls. They had, after all, grown up elsewhere, in various fathers' households. They probably had only vague recollections of Abani.

Blood had summoned us together. That's what the funeral said. Blood kept us in this world, and now we'd returned to those who'd given it to us. They had been waiting at the other end of the world for a long time, extending a welcoming hand. *Sing for her. She is finally at peace.*

The children sang first, starting the dirge. Then the sisters joined in, followed by their respective families. And then the boys. It was an old lament, praising sisters and brothers, fathers and mothers, children living and children sacrificed.[⊖] Mother clutched my hand, my fingers going numb. She sobbed as if there was no end to her tears.

When she finally stopped crying, we had buried Abani. We were sitting on our home's old fashioned iron pipe.

She still clutched my hand.

"How long will you stay?" she asked hopefully.

"I'll leave tomorrow."

"Tomorrow?" Her voice was tense, her sad, moist eyes watching me. She wanted me to stay. She always wanted that.

"I've booked a ticket. Hill Four has excavated a big site. They want me back as soon as possible."

"You're not an archaeologist."

True, I wasn't an archaeologist. I'd been a soldier. Now I was a mercenary.

⊖ Due to their high birthrates, the Rudera have from the beginning of their civilization enforced strict birth control, allowing just one child per litter to survive. Parents or priests choose the lucky child, and kill the rest. The sacrificed infants are not named, but are generally referred to as "litter-mates" or "link births."

Excavations of ancient human sites made people rich, and interstellar pirates sometimes caught wind of the spoils. My work was protecting such sites. My boss paid me to use my head and risk my ass. Some thought it wasn't suitable work for a woman, but I'd been at it for years.

"They need me."

"Your family needs you."

I looked at her, knowing my expression was blank. Every time she reached out to me, I retreated into my shell, aloof. That was how I resisted my family.

"I'll go tomorrow," I repeated.

"You should find a family and settle down. Or else come back here to stay. A girl can always return to live among her sisters."

I studied my mother.

She'd aged a lot in the past fifteen months.$^{\ominus}$ And I had grown up. I knew this, but it was difficult to process. I still felt like that dazed child, staring blankly, watching mother's pleading face. I still remembered a long winding path, on either side the flowers of small succulent plants blooming in profusion. They had been dark red, like blood, or the evening sun.

"I'll go tomorrow," I said. "Otherwise they'll hire someone else. Out on the frontier there's no shortage of mercs willing to hazard their lives."

She began to cry again. After a while she wiped away her tears, sighing. "You're a rough, thick-skinned girl. I wasn't a good mother, I know. I'm sorry, Jin. I'm sorry."

She was always like that, apologizing endlessly. She was like that before the incident, and she hadn't changed since.

$\ominus$ Ruderans, intelligent descendants of rats, live at most eight years. They reckon their lives by months. A 100-month lifespan is common and respectable.

I don't need apologies, Mother.

I turned to the window, trying to imagine the planet I was about to visit. I recalled the space station, its translucent dome, people looking up at a sky full of bright, cold stars. Whenever I was there I liked to watch the heavenly vault spin slowly. I imagined it reversing direction, and everything starting over.

What I wanted was to have never been born.

— **1** —

Hill Four is 3000 light-years from Earth. From there, the Milky Way is not the pale white band you see from Earth, but a massive disk crowning the heavens. Hill Four's sun hangs alone in the sky, giving its meager heat. It was flung off the galactic plane with its planetary children in tow. From an altitude of 3000 light-years it looks down upon the Milky Way's spiral arms.

Despite its bleak and deadly surface, Hill Four was suitable for colonization. Underground, the vast Underhill Sea covers almost three-quarters of the planet's inner surface. Life thrives on geothermal energy down in the darkness. Humans came here first. We Ruderans followed in their footsteps much later.

As my ship entered the spaceport, I saw the transport carrying the relief merc team had arrived before me. They were busy unloading an arms shipment.

"Well if it isn't the lone she-paladin. Long time no see." It was Old Mortar hailing me, without malice. All of his mercs were men. There were many female mercenaries out here, but lone operators like me were scarce. Old Mortar and I had rubbed each other the wrong way for many years, quarreling frequently. Now we reluctantly tolerated each other, maybe even respected each other a bit.

"Been a long time. How was your holiday?"

"Went from bad to worse. The boys have been drunk this quarter[⊖], the shit-stains. I had to knock some sense into them. Keep that to yourself. The Doc wants you to get over there to the Rain Ship ASAP, and bring your kit. My people will hold down the fort here. They need at least one person with law enforcement powers over there."

"Rain Ship?"

"You haven't heard? They found a portal of the old gods on the bottom level of the station. On the far side they found . . . well, it's a spacecraft for sure, but it's damn frightening. Honestly, I'm glad me and the boys don't have to go over. I don't wanna see any more of it."

"How big is it?"

"How big?" Old Mortar grew uneasy. "Too big to see in one glance. There are clouds inside of the thing, child. And rain!"

Old Mortar and his boys had enough weapons and equipment to fill a ship, but I had only a small backpack. After putting my gear in order, I received a message from Dr. Hort on my terminal, confirming everything Old Mortar had said.

I passed through the shipyard, then took a hundred-million-year-old human elevator down to the lower levels.

We used to call these wise prehistoric beings gods[⊖], as Old Mortar still did. But I'd always preferred to call them giants. They'd built this spaceport, and it was like a city. This elevator was the size of an apartment building. I raised my head to behold the vast space, imagining a creature sixteen times my size standing here. They'd come from Earth, their footprints covering many worlds, and at some point they had mysteriously vanished. And then we had tracked them, cutting their sign, only to find these great, mysterious,

---

⊖   A Ruderan unit of time, a quarter of a month, or eight days.
⊖   The Gods referred to here are ancient humans. Times change. Nothing lasts forever, including civilizations.

indescribable constructions.

An archaeologist had showed me a rubbing of one of their footprints. It was big enough for an adult Ruderan to comfortably lie in. Later I saw an ad for beds shaped like that—the lengths boring people go for a little spice in their lives.

About nine standard months ago, Hill Four orbital sites had been discovered. Then the ruins on the Underhill seabed were found and excavated. Suddenly this desolate frontier became a hot spot. Operating on the principle that development and exploitation should advance in tandem with archaeological research, archaeological teams blazed trails, studied ruins, certified safe zones, and finally left them to developers. These builders brought rope and tents and building materials, and the human station quickly became a Ruderan city. Two mercenary teams were on duty here, and a few wandering loners like myself.

But I couldn't get used to this human architecture. The station was huge and strange, built into a spherical space vast enough to contain a Ruderan capital city, and one or two artificial lakes.

Old Mortar's mercs were already in place. Those who'd just been relieved came down the wall on rope ladders, expressions eager, hankering for a quick return to the city. They would get drunk and sleep, then seek out girls.

Dr. Hort had sent my itinerary. I was summoned to the portal Old Mortar had mentioned, but I decided to visit the bar first. Hort might get angry, and she might not.

Sometimes I have premonitions. These feelings usually presage something terrible.

The bar was practically empty. It was seven, a work stretch$^\ominus$, so most people

---

$\ominus$ The Rudera divide a standard day into eight parts or 'stretches', each stretch equal to three hours of human time. Like most rodents, the Rudera sleep in frequent short spells. Their work and leisure are also divided into small pieces. During odd stretches they work. During even stretches they rest, drink, shop, or spend time with their families. As a result, Ruderan work and leisure are closely intertwined.

were on duty. I sat down, ordered a cup of corn juice, and put a roll of money on the bar. The barkeep's eyes lit up, but almost immediately he seemed to lose interest. For the past month, this bar had been my intelligence purchasing hub, and that roll of bills included the barkeep's fee.

"Anything interesting lately?" I whispered.

"Can you be more specific?"

"The new site, the discovery. Since I sat down I've already spotted three relic hunters in this dump."

"You're worried about relic hunters?"

"They're for Old Mortar to worry about. I'm headed to the other side. Any pirate activity lately?"

Before answering me, the young man looked around for a moment. He and the owner belonged to the same family. In fact the bar was their family business$^\ominus$. I liked these people. They were careful and smart. They knew what to do and when to do it.

"About a stretch ago there were five people here, armed. Strangers. I didn't like the look of them. They drank a lot, then took two sober-up pills each. They just left, actually."

"Where'd they go?"

"Up. Probably back to the shipyard."

Frowning, I used my terminal to access the shipyard and make inquiries. There was no one there. The monitors should have spotted these five eye-

---

$\ominus$ Ruderan families are quite different from human families. Men and women do not live together, except during periods of fertility. Families are generally composed of three to five members of the same sex. Male families only accept male members, and female families only take females. Most families carry out joint undertakings, working together. When they move, they move together. When it comes to Ruderans, marriage means entering a family of brothers or sisters, not uniting with someone of the opposite sex.

catching fellows.

If I'd been a pirate, I might have found it difficult to dress up and infiltrate a space station, although a bribe would have gotten me into the navigation tower. I would have looted one of those freighters, when it was loaded with human relics and awaiting take-off clearance. The next one was due to launch at eight. Freighters had only one stretch of vulnerable down time between landing and launching. If those five strangers were raiding a freighter, they must have been real alcoholics to need a bar-run during the operation.

Unless they—

The mercs were changing shifts now. The last shift was leaving, and Old Mortar's boys had just arrived. Now was precisely when the station's guard was most lax. What if the five weren't after a freighter? If they wanted something the archaeologists had discovered on the other side of the portal, their only option was to capture the portal—

I slammed a bill down on the bar as I rushed out. I placed a call as I ran.

"Old Mortar!" I exclaimed, "put your guys on alert. We may have a situation—"

The deafening explosion roared through our connection. I stood in the corridor, holding onto some netting and peering down: a rushing plume of smoke and dust rose from the lower levels. Such massive destruction, but in the context of the vast spherical space containing it, it was miniscule.

— **2** —

After an endless moment watching the explosion balloon, I terminated my call, shouldered my pack, and used my tail to retrieve two gleaming bullets⊖.

⊖ Ruderans have only four fingers on each hand, but the tip of a Ruderan tail is divided into three small, dexterous appendages.

Drawing my gun, I rushed against the flow of the crowd toward the lower levels.

The portal was at the very bottom of the station's vast spherical space. I felt like I was rushing down the side of a titanic bowl, my duty carrying me along like a whirlpool, as the panicking crowd charged upward. At least they were staying out of my way, in deference to my weapon.

Halfway down, I spotted Lana Guer and her family sisters. These women were relic hunters⊖. I had arrested them for smuggling before. They had numbered six, but now they were only four, dejected and covered in dust. Lana's eyes were bright with horror.

"What's the situation down there?" I demanded.

She glared at me, even now summoning up her old arrogance.

"I'm not looking to arrest you! Whoever dared to set off bombs on my turf is getting disemboweled! Now where are your other two sisters? Down there?"

Her twitching tail-tip confirmed my guess.

"I'm going down. Maybe I can help you, if you hurry up and help me. What can I expect down there?"

Her expression softened. "I'm not sure . . . ten, maybe fifteen people. Heavy guns and explosives. They blocked off two corridors, the two where Old Mortar's guys are quartered. Nini and Jilin are in there too. We couldn't get through. I couldn't help them . . . " She shook her head in torment. "They're wearing masks. I heard them shouting. Sounded like Northern An⊖."

⊖ Relic hunters are those who, legally or illegally, take relics from human ruins. Most are armed. There is not much division of labor along gender lines among the Rudera. Women do most things that men do.

⊖ In the Ruderan era, Earth has two major continents: An continent and Mu continent. Northern An refers to a dialect spoken in the Northern part of An, where the inhabitants are known for their ferocity. The Ruderans have become star-faring, but most haven't joined the Ruderan Galactic Alliance, preferring to raid and rob, drifting between solar systems.

"Thanks, Lana."

She nodded, then ran on, but suddenly stopped and turned around.

"Jin?"

"Yeah?"

"You're a cruel little bitch. But don't let those fuckers kill you."

She thrusted her middle finger at me, then ran up the corridor.

After passing through two winding tunnels, I heard my first mark[⊖]. He was about three tunnels away, speaking loudly. I understand a little Northern An. At first I thought they'd already neutralized Old Mortar's mercs—but no. The raiders hadn't taken the portal yet. Old Mortar's fierce troops had been hiding in the portal corridor, lying in wait.

I grinned silently.

Stepping lightly, I drew my dagger. I took a roundabout route and eventually spotted my mark hanging in a look-out net[⊖]. I crept up, gathered a support line in my hand, then another, and a third. My dagger struck. The raider tumbled down from his post, net piling around him on the floor. I pounced and buried my blade in his heart.

He looked at me in shock, and then his eyes dimmed.

I pulled out the dagger, wiped it on the netting, sheathed it, and moved on. These people were real professionals. First they'd bombed the merc barracks, dividing the enemy, creating panic—objective clear, actions quick and decisive. I'd have been the one dying on the floor now if I hadn't been so ruthless.

Racing against discovery, I advanced down the ground level passage, taking

---

⊖ Having evolved from burrowing rodents, a Ruderan's hearing is better than her sight.

⊖ A net hung from the ceiling and walls of a tunnel for Ruderans to climb. They can't climb like their ancestors, but are still much better at it than humans.

out another pirate along the way. I came to the door leading to Old Mortar's holdfast. Unfortunately, I made a bit of noise while disposing of the raider guarding the door: Just before my rounds opened his head, he turned and squirted a whole clip into the tunnel wall. The report was deafening in the confined space of the tunnel.

The massive door was dead-bolted from the inside. I frantically pounded out a merc passcode, then began to repeat it, knowing more pirates would soon arrive. The door opened a crack, and I squirmed my way in. Then I was on the other side, helping someone—I didn't know who—shut and bolt the gargantuan door.

I turned around to find Old Mortar glaring at me. His tail was bleeding and his head was bandaged. Behind him stood two of his mercs, also in a sorry state.

"What the fuck are you doing here, Jin?"

"Trying to rescue your asses."

"There are at least twenty fucking raiders out there$^\ominus$. With you there are six of us left."

"Seventeen," I amended. "Seventeen fucking raiders out there. I killed three."

"So each of us just needs to ice two and three-quarters pirates. Our prospects have improved."

I chose to pardon the old fucker's sarcasm. He'd started with thirty men, six of whom belonged to his family.

"What about civvies?" I asked.

Old Mortar shook his head. "The two Guer girls, three researchers . . . I let them go through the portal. Any ideas on how to proceed?"

$\ominus$ Ruderan counting is based on eight. Twenty people in their language is "sixteen-four," but in order to facilitate understanding, the human system is used here.

I shrugged. "We all go through the portal and shut it from the far side. Safest bet."

Old Mortar shook his head. "I still have people stuck in the barracks," he said. "I've signaled the Hill system fleet for help. You take this ansible and go through, then shut the portal."

"And you?"

He shrugged gloomily. "I can't leave my people behind."

I glanced at the weary mercenaries. "Seems a few of your men might not agree."

"Those who wish can follow you," Old Mortar said.

Two young mercenaries glanced at each other, then got up and moved to my side. They were not Old Mortar's relatives, and clearly didn't want to follow him on his reckless path. They apparently did not believe that the Northern An pirates would treat their captives well.

"You sure?" I asked Old Mortar.

He flicked his tail impatiently. "Go through, and close the portal."

I nodded and turned, leading my two mercs toward the strange artifact. Made and used by giants long ago, it was as high as a ten-story building to us. We created ripples on its mirror-like surface as we stepped through. I felt I was falling in every direction at once. My body didn't seem to exist, while my soul seemed dragged through multicolored light. Then my feet were touching ground. The two young mercs were kneeling beside me, one trembling, the other crying.

This was not the first time I'd crossed a human portal, but no matter how many times I did it, the sensation was unnerving.

I spit bile, and looked up.

And I saw.

— **3** —

We were inside a titanic spacecraft, if that's what it was. 'Rain Ship' was shuttle-shaped, and in terms of our apparent gravitational orientation, it was standing erect. The long axis was at least a kilometer high$^\ominus$. I could only vaguely discern the summit. The horizontal axis was at least 400 meters long. At the ship's center, enclosing most of the long axis, crystalline walls formed a suspended space like a six-sided prism.

The outer shell of the spacecraft was built around this floating space. The ancient humans had built cabins and facilities on the inner surface of this shell, simple yet solid, which remained intact after one hundred million years. A walkway spiraled up the shell, connecting the cabins. Bridges and tunnels extending from this walkway—and various cabins—connecting to the floating, crystalline space.

Which was a great tower of ecological habitats.

For some reason my eye was drawn to one facet of this dazzling jewel: a small path winding through thick grass, only the flagstones of the trailhead visible, ancient stones cracked and pierced by tenacious green growth.

Ecological spaces filled almost the entire spacecraft, divided by panels of polarized light into self-sustaining ecosystems. Thick clouds filled the upper spaces. Mists curled and rose on grasslands, on leaves of grass twice my height. Fine rains descended on gardens, inaudible. The ship was silent, but I saw raindrops gleaming on leaves.

Big, titanic, colossal, beyond description—I quickly spent my ammo, adjective-wise. I just stood there, looking up in awe. The giants that had built this ship, this great hall, had vanished a hundred million years ago. But rain fell continuously down this great pillar of ecologies.

Now we Ruderans were here, trespassing, feeling small and insignificant, and

---

$\ominus$ Human units of measurement are used here, for ease of understanding.

compelled to silence.

I stared dazedly until a sound on the walkway below caught my attention. The two Guer girls had emerged, holding archaeological grinding lasers like guns. They looked nervous, eyeing me and my two mercs.

I didn't bother asking how they got down there, but immediately straddled the railing, hung from it, and slid down to their level. I appraised the two unarmed girls, wondering what could have been going on in Lana's head.

"Catch." I took two pistols out of my pack and tossed them to the girls. "Better than those lasers. Nini, yours is pointed the wrong way. Try not to decapitate yourself, okay?"

She hastened to put down the implement, as though it had grown hot in her hand. Jilin eyed me doubtfully. She was brainier than her sisters. "Since when are you helping us?"

"Since I met Lana on the other side. She asked me to find you. I'm happy to let the Guer family owe me a favor, or two." I waved my gun at the mercs, summoning them down. "Where's Dr. Hort? I need her to help me close the portal ASAP."

"Close the portal?" Jilin seemed incredulous.

"How long do you think Old Mortar can hold out over there?"

Jilin said nothing.

"Dr. Hort is in there," Nini said, gesturing to a massive ancient human door that was open a crack. "We have our own situation on this side. The doctor sent us to have a look."

"Situation?"

"Someone else is in here with us."

"You're fucking joking."

"My mother likes to joke. I do not."

Dr. Lee Hort and her assistants had occupied a small corner of the ancient human control center. They huddled together, panic-stricken. Various instruments and equipment lay piled to one side. A small moss lamp hung over a portable lab table$^{\ominus}$. Starlight pierced the command center's vast transparent screen, weakly lighting the area. A small spacecraft was vaguely discernible, hanging in the ancient ship's docking bay like a moth.

My entrance surprised the researchers.

"Jin?" Dr. Hort stood. "When did you get back? I thought you were due in next quarter. How did it go back home? Everything okay?"

I raised a hand and interrupted her. "There's no time for all that, Doctor."

"I'm sorry." She lowered her head. "I just . . . you know, these things, I'm nervous."

"Never mind." I glanced at the ship. "When did that arrive?"

"Just now," a young lab tech said. She was a sister in the Hort family. "We heard an explosion and ran over to see it."

"Explosion?"

"They couldn't open the hangar door, so they blasted their way in."

"They? How many?"

"We've seen just one."

"Do you know where he's going?"

The girl shook her head.

I studied the ship more carefully: a two-seater shuttle, fast, suitable for carrying light firepower, a popular model among relic hunters and loner pirates. I had a similar one. No matter what this explosive visitor was after, he

---

$\ominus$ A Ruderan is about one-sixteenth the height of a human. This makes harnessing fire difficult. Their custom is to use cold light or bioluminescent moss for illumination. Even now, during their space age, they maintain this tradition.

was not a novice. Directional detonation, choosing the weakest point in the meter-thick, airtight bay door, and afterwards using his own ship to plug the hole and prevent depressurization of the bay—

I tried to clear my head. "Dr. Hort, for the moment let's set aside the question of this lone gun. We have three mercs and at least five weapons. We need to go up right now and close the portal from this side."

The good doctor seemed shocked. "You're proposing we trap ourselves in this ship with that desperate rogue?"

"You need to understand the situation on the other side," I said, growing impatient. "If we don't close the portal, then we're dealing with a gang of desperate rogues, not just one."

Still reluctant, she finally nodded her assent.

"Get your techies together. We need to use the ansible I brought to contact Hill system security management. Nini, Jilin, you stay here. You two . . . " I glanced at my mercs. " . . . you're with me."

The two young mercenaries exchanged a glance, but surprised me by not objecting.

We climbed up the research team's rope ladder, ascending 40 ta$^\ominus$. Sliding down a rope ladder is easy, but climbing is hard work. Behind me I heard the two women breathing. They didn't complain—yet another surprise.

The portal's control console was a massive, complicated thing. Fortunately, Dr. Hort had already interfaced it with her team's smaller, portable version. She entered a series of commands, and the mirror-face of the portal dimmed. At last it seemed to break apart inside its frame, dissolving in particulate light. I felt relieved.

I just hoped Old Mortar's luck would hold.

$\ominus$ A Ruderan unit of length. Ten ta are about 1.03 meters. For ease of understanding, meters are used in subsequent descriptions.

"Contact!" cried the young researcher, who'd been fiddling with my ansible.

The gunfire was faint. It sounded like cracking nut shells. At first I barely reacted, thinking it was coming through the link. Then the communicator went mute, smoke issuing from a bullet hole in its power unit. The researchers stared blankly, unable to process what had happened.

I turned in the direction of fire, spotting someone almost two hundred meters away on our level. He'd hit our ansible from quite a distance. With that kind of accuracy, why not hit me or the mercs first?

I had no time to think about it. I motioned for the researchers to hurry back down the ladder. I drew my gun and moved to the corner of the portal chamber. The outer wall also had a rope ladder, but using it would surely give the shooter an easy target, so I decided to climb up a human-era pipe.

This turned out to be a mistake. I should have returned to camp with the others, where we had the advantage of numbers. I was tired and frantic after a twenty-four hour subspace jump, and non-stop action since landing. All these exigencies had worn down my intellect. I'd thought the shooter was one of the pirates. Since I'd already killed three of them, I thought I could take this one alone.

At least, I thought so before his gun was against my forehead.

"Hi there beautiful." His voice was happy, self-satisfied. "Climb up the rest of the way. I've been waiting long enough."

— **4** —

I slowly lifted my head to face him, and the muzzle of his weapon, striving to keep my movements non-threatening. The intruder was about my age. He sported a head full of spiky brown hair, and wore a simple combat model pressure suit. His battle-pack was the same brand as mine.

But the gun in his hand was a Uran-571, large caliber, strong firepower, strong recoil, capable of ripping large holes in bodies. Not my weapon of choice.

"Slowly. Up you come."

Grinning, he reached for the two guns holstered on my waist. Then he patted down my ankles, checking for back-up weapons. He nodded, indicating I could stand. Face to face, he was a bit taller than me, ordinary-looking except for the garish scar tissue on his forehead: a white line spanning hairline to brows, probably a knife wound.

"Turn around," he ordered.

I couldn't place his accent. His Common Tongue was pure, not colored by Northern An or any other dialect. As I slowly turned around, I caught him in my peripheral vision pulling tri-cuffs out of a pocket⊖.

His model of pressure suit has a shortcoming: it slows you down a bit.

I lashed out my tail and seized his wrist. The tri-cuffs rang against his pistol as they went flying. Before he could retrieve his weapon, I dove to one side, rolled through the gigantic half-closed door, and rushed out of the room. I fled down the seemingly endless walkway. I came to a rope leading down to lower levels of the spiral, and my pursuer emerged behind me, gun raised.

I grabbed the rope and jumped. My feet slammed against the wall. I pushed off, rappelling, traveling swiftly downward. Suddenly he was above me, peering over the edge. Contemplating the rope. My blood froze in my veins. If he cut the rope I would fall a hundred meters and end up a splatter of fine red paste on the ground floor.

But he didn't cut the rope. He just grinned, as if at some cosmic joke. Fucking hilarious. Especially when I failed to grab a safety net, for the second time,

---

⊖ The first Ruderan handcuffs weren't much different from the human model. But field tests quickly revealed that upgrading to a three-ring design was necessary. For Ruderans and their dexterous tails, human-style handcuffs aren't a sensible way to deal with criminals.

and like a fucking novice continued to plunge. His eyes flashed a strange dark green, reflecting the polarized light of the great pillar of ecologies.

Rappelling, I landed on the next floor down. When I looked up, the intruder had vanished.

A good mercenary should always have spare weapons. I cannot be considered a bad merc, and this was not the first time I'd lost weapons to an opponent. My tail opened my pack as I ran, and retrieved the small-bore pistol within. Its stopping power was weak, but just then it was all I had.

The Rain Ship was quiet. I gripped my pistol, moving slowly, keeping an ear close to the wall. I heard the intruder's footsteps, could barely distinguish that he was moving downward. I guessed he was headed to the researcher's camp, the ship's control center. Besides the portal, the control center was the most strategically important part of the ship.

Luckily, it sounded like he was taking the main staircase. I knew a shortcut.

Once again I got on the rope and started rappelling down, slowly and carefully this time. I couldn't hear his footsteps anymore.

As I neared the bottom, a gunshot pierced the silence, then a second and a third.

I let go of the rope and hit the floor. In a flash I was up and sprinting in the direction of the gun reports.

— **5** —

I ran to the corner separating me from the action, adjust my breathing, gripping my weapon, finger on the trigger. I leaped around the corner, ready to—

Fuck.

I blinked.

The intruder was on the ground, unmoving. I didn't know if he was alive or dead. Dr. Hort held a small lady's pistol, trembling, finger still squeezing the trigger, seemingly unaware that the weapon was spent.

I walked lightly toward her. "Doctor . . . " Her shoulder trembled, and I reached out and held it. "Dr. Hort, it's me. Don't be afraid. It's over. You got him."

Softly consoling her, I removed the gun from her stiff hands.

The intruder groaned something unintelligible. Lee Hort flinched like a rabbit, and I quickly moved past her, aiming my gun at the intruder's head. I noticed there was no blood. There were three small craters in his pressure suit, which was designed to withstand vacuum and micro-meteor impacts. Hort's three bullets had been no problem, but I reckoned this man's ribs weren't comfortable just now.

I nudged his backpack with my foot until the tri-cuffs fell out. Soon he was firmly shackled.

"It's all right, Doctor," I said to Lee Hort.

Others who had heard the gunshots soon arrived. The corridor became a noisy, crowded place. The intruder struggled, trying to rise, and I shoved him back down. Everyone was perplexed, except for Lee Hort. She stared at the intruder with a mix of fear, hatred, and deep shock.

— **6** —

"What is your name?"

" . . . "

"Which mercenary group are you with?"

"..."

"What are you doing here? Why did you shoot our ansible?"

"..."

"How about I just dispose of you right now?"

"..."

No matter what I asked, the bastard remained tightlipped.

He was tri-cuffed to a pipe—Nini's idea—just near enough to our camp to keep an eye on him.

Dr. Hort seemed better than before, striving to appear calm, but every few minutes she glared at our prisoner, her shock returning.

"Okay," I whispered, "one last question. What is your relationship with the doctor?"

His shoulder twitched, but he remained silent.

I sighed and returned to the heart of the archaeologists' camp. The researchers talked quietly amongst themselves, while my two mercs sat apart from the rest. Jilin and Nini were studying the broken ansible.

"I think I can fix her," Jilin Guer said, sitting amid scattered parts. Proudly she added, "I can't fight, but I can do this."

"Her?"

"All ansibles are girls," Jilin said gravely. "They're the best at sending messages."

Some of the archaeologists laughed. Jilin proudly cocked her head.

Lee Hort sat alone, apparently deep in thought. Her fingers were interlaced before her, still trembling slightly.

I walked over.

"Doctor, can we talk alone?"

"Okay." She got up, clearly nervous, and I took her further from the group, hoping that no one would overhear our conversation. "Thank you for saving me," she whispered.

"As far as I can see, your marksmanship was fine. You didn't need saving. But I think you know him."

Hearing this, she jerked back, as if ready to flee. But she stood rooted, hands clenched together, glancing back at her archaeologists—her family.

"I did not . . . expect him to find this place."

"Who is he?"

"Dar," she said, taking a deep breath, as if she'd come to a momentous decision. "Yes, that Dar."

"Oh," I said. "Fuck."

Along the galactic edge, Lee Hort was legendary, not only because of the large number of ancient human sites she'd unearthed, but also due to her unique past. She'd grown up in a sect of the extreme Darwinian Church$^{\ominus}$. These people were totally insane. Eschewing the standard Ruderan practice of choosing one child per litter at birth, these Darwinians raised the whole litter to age ten, then forced them to fight each other to the death$^{\ominus}$. The last child standing entered the family.

But they made a mistake when raising Lee and her litter-mates. They underestimated the boy named Dar, who decided to put an end to the sect and its horrific child abuse. After the adults had entered their temple to hear their priest evangelize, Dar locked the tunnel doors and lit a fire. The adults died

---

$\ominus$ Originally named *Church of Biological Truth and Survival of the Fittest*, this sect advocates following the survival principle of natural selection. It is rendered "Extreme Darwinism" for ease of understanding.

$\ominus$ The Ruderan lifespan is short. Growth and development are fast. Age ten here means ten months old.

of smoke inhalation. Then Dar returned to the dormitory and killed his litter-mates.

Lee Hort escaped calamity because she'd gone out to fetch water. Dar also fled, and later discovered that firefighters had rescued Lee. The massacre had shocked all of Orchid Autonomous Sector. The details of the incident were still well-known years later.

Dar had never been found. Some people said he was dead, others that he became a mercenary, or a pirate—one of those professions that meant killing for money, at any rate. Every now and then, someone claimed to have encountered Dar, and the stories were usually horrific. It was said he killed a space station's entire population of extreme Darwinists, and that he sent a ship full of pilgrims to its doom in a star.

These stories also disturbed Lee. After she was taken in by the Hort family, she enjoyed a normal and happy upbringing. But no matter how much she achieved, how many ancient human sites she discovered or how many honors she was awarded, people still thought of her as that escaped litter-mate, someone not meant to survive. They couldn't help associating her with her litter-mates, who died so unnaturally. I heard she donated a fortune to an organization that helped children. She had pushed the Alliance Parliament to pass a law declaring all extreme Darwinism churches illegal. For someone bearing such a tragic past, she was doing remarkably well.

But . . .

"We can't escape our pasts, Doctor," I whispered.

She smiled bitterly, nodding.

— 7 —

After an hour or so, a frustrated Jilin announced she needed to rest. I told my two young mercs to do likewise. I didn't know when we'd be leaving this place. If we couldn't fix the ansible, we'd have to wait for a rescue ship from the Hill system capital to find us.

"Shift change," I explained to Dr. Hort.

She nodded wearily, and divided her people into two teams. Then she went to sleep.

Nini Guer was wide awake, sitting on a mat and seemingly bored to death. She fiddled with the pistol I'd given her.

"Careful with that," I said.

"I unloaded it." She shrugged. "I'll be better with this than that damn laser grinder. Jilin can't fight. I have to look after her."

I laughed. Sometimes I envied those with close blood ties: men or women, were familiar with each other, caring for each other. You could trust your sisters or brothers. You shared everything, including pain.

"What are you laughing about, Jin?" Nini watched me curiously.

"Nothing, I just . . . you're lucky, having family, you know."

"Why don't you find one? What about a female mercenary family?"

I reached out and rubbed Nini's head. She regarded me, head askew, but didn't stop me. She was only fourteen years old. Under the Guer family's wing she'd traveled all over the stars, undaunted, never alone. I was already twenty-six, and still alone, traveling from star to star, battlefield to battlefield. When my last partner and I had dissolved our partnership, he said my fearlessness in battle was down to a death-wish. He said I was in a hurry to die.

"I'm used to being alone," I said. "The reason is complicated."

"Do you want to talk about it?"

"Sorry, no."

Nini made a face. She didn't understand, and explanations probably wouldn't help. Moreover, she did not seem terribly interested.

"Okay," she said, "change of subject. I don't like that doctor."

"Dr. Hort? She's got her baggage, but she pays my salary."

"But do you like her?"

"Why, Nini? What is it about her?"

"I hate her." This Nini was straightforward. "Lana never put herself first. She always let us rest before she did. And she never would've done what Hort did . . . put grinding lasers in our hands and push us out into danger, like cannon fodder, while she and her relatives hid."

"But Lana would send you into battle, right?"

"She'd be there with us, to protect us. Not hiding in the rear like your doctor, a coward and a thief."

"Thief?"

"Lana discovered the portal. Hort snatched the archaeological evidence from our hands."

I raised a brow.

Generally speaking, relic hunters were not qualified archaeologists—but Lana was a veteran in this game. It was not hard for me to believe Nini. "Didn't Hort compensate the Guers?"

"Not really."

"Come on. Are you sure?"

"I'm not lying, Jin. You got some way to make this right?"

"No."

"No?"

"She pays my salary, remember?"

"Wow. How predictable."

Nini pouted. I laughed and rubbed her head. "Where's the water and biscuits?"

The water was bottled, and the biscuits damp, not very appetizing. I carried both to the man in tri-cuffs. He seemed to be napping, but heard my approach and raised his head. His eyes widened when he saw the food in my hands. He pretended indifference, and his face was suddenly like Lee Hort's. I was surprised I hadn't seen the resemblance before—surely they were litter-mates.

"Would you like something to eat, Dar?" Was that a micro-expression of surprise? If so he quickly hid it with a sneer, and shook the tri-cuffs. "I'll unlock a hand for you. Don't try anything funny." He acted tough, but when I unlocked his right hand, he breathed in relief. He had a broken rib, or two, I remembered. Although the bullets hadn't penetrated his suit, they'd hit him hard. "Let me see."

"Fuck off." These were his first words in captivity.

We glared at each other a moment, neither of us looking away. I pulled on his pressure suit's front zipper. "What are you hiding?"

Obviously injured, he grimaced in pain, but he wouldn't let me open the suit. Then I remembered something embarrassing from my time in pressure suits. His suit seemed quite old. "Need the bathroom?" I asked.

If looks could kill—but he nodded.

I un-cuffed him from the pipe and escorted him to the portable toilet set up by the archaeological team. He impatiently rushed inside.

A few minutes passed, then another few.

I knocked on the door. "Listen pal, finish up and get your pants on. I'm about to put a bullet through this door."

I heard a muffled curse.

"What was that?"

"Do you have anything I can wear?"

I turned to see Nini rolling on the floor and stifling laughter. She managed to point to a heap of white lab uniforms. I went over and found something approximately Dar's size. I gripped my pistol tightly. This guy might be planning an escape attempt, but it didn't seem so. Fifteen minutes after I pushed the uniform through the barely open door, he emerged clothed, carrying the ragged pressure suit and looking embarrassed, but considerably less dejected.

"Hand and tail." I shook the cuffs at him.

He glanced around, perhaps reckoning his odds, escape-wise. Nini had stopped laughing. She played with her gun. I didn't know if she'd reloaded it.

Finally, Dar let me cuff his left hand and tail, and return him to the pipe. He grabbed the water and gulped down as much as he could. I checked his ribs: they were bruised but didn't seem broken.

"You'll live, for the time being," I announced.

"That's a pity," he said through a mouthful of biscuit.

The prisoner was less hostile on a full belly—but he answered my questions with yawns.

"You're not likely to believe anything I say," he finally explained. "Why not just let me sleep?"

I sighed and played out the chain of his cuffs a bit, so he could lie down.

I turned to leave, and suddenly Dar said, "By the way, don't let your girl repair the ansible. If she gets it working, you'll regret it."

"Why?" I asked, puzzled.

But he was already snoring.

— 8 —

I carried the basket, walking along the narrow path among the blooming, crimson flowers. The leaves of the short, fleshy plants were a warm purple. They gleamed under a light drizzle. Carrying the basket was a labor—it contained six sleeping infants, too heavy a load for a ten-year-old.

I returned via the same path. Headed out, the basket had contained six babies. Returning, it held only one.

I took the child through a long underground tunnel, attracting curious looks.

I can picture that underground Temple of the Five like it was yesterday[⊖]. I went through the gate, around the massive inverted bell[⊖]. It was said that in the past, priests would ring the chime during times of war or plague, times when the population had shrunk. The chime summoned people for an announcement: the population control law was temporarily suspended. You could raise every child in your litter, rather than killing all of them but one. But the last time it was sounded, Abani's Abani[⊜] was still a child.

The priest greeted me as I entered the temple. I was a child holding a smaller one: he seemed to guess what had happened. "What about your mother?" he asked kindly.

"I want to leave her here," I said, ignoring his question.

He looked at me sadly. "Will you stay as well?"

"I'm going."

"What is her name?"

⊖ Ruderans worship the earth more than the heavens.

⊖ Compared to the common bell used by humans, an inverted bell placed on the ground is better for propagating sound in an underground city.

⊜ 'Abani' is the title of the eldest female in a family. Similar to the human 'great-grandmother.'

She didn't have one yet. My father had left us, and my mother did not want his children, not even one. She'd refused to name them, and she'd lacked the courage to kill them. So she'd asked me, begged me to . . .

"Her name is—"

"Jin . . . Jin!"

I was shaken awake. My anger flared, and I reached for my gun, but it was only the familiar face of Lee Hort—an irritant, to be sure, but perhaps meriting continued life. Besides, if she died, that would be the end of my salary. I withdrew my hand from the gun. "What the hell? Can't I just get a few winks?"

She looked nervously at Dar. "I have something to tell you, Jin."

I bared my teeth and got up, muttering curses. My voice was low, but the performance was enough to make Lee Hort blanche. She said nothing as she guided me down an empty corridor. Passing Nini and Jilin's sleeping mat, I saw that the ansible was nearly repaired.

"What is it already?" I asked.

"It's Dar," Lee said, biting her lip. "I remembered you have law enfor-cement powers."

"Correct."

After ten years of frontier chaos, Orchid Autonomous Sector officials had decided they might as well delegate frontier law enforcement to mercenary groups, and assessment to independent mercs. We had the right to arrest, incarcerate, and in extreme cases, execute offenders. Frontier prosecutors (usually merc agency men, or arms dealers) reviewed our handling of cases. Most of the time, the Law Enforcement Proxy Act protected our freedom. Only rarely did one of us overstep, prompting the sector's government fleet to interfere.

In two short years, money, blood, and power had woven a unique network of frontier order. I was a link in the chain. Independent mercs and mercenary captains had the same level of law enforcement power. We were meant to check and balance each other. "Dar is category A wanted. You have the right to execute him, don't you?"

"Only in extreme cases, Doc. For example, if he threatened someone with a gun, or tried to escape. But I can't execute a prisoner that has been arrested. That requires prosecutor level power."

"But . . . if an extreme situation unfolded . . . "

My eyes narrowed. Her implication was clear. "Extreme situations happen. But that wouldn't be to my advantage. I don't like killing, Doc."

"I heard your family is in debt. I mean your mother's family."

Of course we were in debt. When Abani was dying, we'd spent a lot trying to save her. All of that money was borrowed.

"A lot of debt," I admitted.

"Maybe I could help with that."

I studied her eyes, failing to read her.

"Are you worried he'll escape?"

"I don't fancy a lifetime of looking over my shoulder." Lee spoke softly. Every word seemed bitten off and spit out. "He will find a way to my door, eventually. We were born together. Six children, and two have survived. He will find me, to correct this . . . error."

"Living is not a mistake."

"Being alive at the same time as your litter-mate . . . that's the mistake. He will kill me. As long as there's a chance of him escaping, my life is in danger. If I could pray to the Five, I would beg them to . . . "

"Let him die," I said.

"Please don't say it like that. It's so . . . " She turned away and seemed to cry, but she said dry-eyed: "I know you're worried about that debt. I can help, Jin."

The proposition was clear: blood money. I find a reason to kill Dar, and she pays off the debt. "It's a lot of money. Close to six hundred thousand, Doc."

"It doesn't matter."

I had few compunctions regarding murder. I'd been a soldier. I'd complied with orders to kill. Later I became a mercenary, and took money for murder. I'd killed for hatred, and simply for fun. I'd probably tried every kind of murder. Death was death. Such a stark outlook would never earn me priestly dispensation, or legal pardon—but here on the frontier, this point of view was the most conducive to survival.

"Then draft an IOU, Doc."

She raised her brows. "Do you mean to borrow money from me?"

"No, you'll borrow from me." This was an old way of paying blood money. You needed a pretext, namely a document claiming you had borrowed from the assassin. Then you were just settling accounts.

Lee Hort was wise. She thought for a moment, then showed her understanding with an uneasy smile.

9

I didn't sleep much, contemplating this new deal with Lee. I walked around camp and saw Dar was awake. Hands cuffed with tail behind his back, facing away from the others, he looked uncomfortable and dazed.

I sat down beside him.

"No biscuits this time?" I was surprised he'd spoken first.

I took out a pack of compressed biscuits for him, unlocked a hand. He devoured the meal. I sat there and did not speak.

After a while he couldn't help himself: "What's your name?"

"Jin."

"Just Jin?"

"Yep."

"You don't have a family?"

"Nope."

"So, you like to fight alone?"

"You bet."

"Relic hunter?"

"Merc, bodyguard, killer . . . I do it all. And what are you?"

"You could call me a relic hunter. I also work alone. No one's brave enough to let me join their family." He smiled. "I'm notorious, you understand. I'm sure Lee has told you the story."

"I didn't need her to tell me. You're a household name. Now tell me, really . . . what are you doing here?"

"You wouldn't believe me."

"Lee thinks you're here to kill her."

Dar chewed some biscuit. For a moment his expression was blank. "She really thinks I'd do that?"

"Wouldn't you? Never mind what I might or might not believe. This stubbornness gets you nowhere. We're waiting for a rescue team, and you're cuffed. Ten years ago you were convicted of murder. How long until you're shot dead, do you think? You must've sought out Lee for a reason. Do you plan on taking it to the grave?"

He finally answered with a bitter laugh. "I'll be shot regardless. Back then I really did light up that fucking temple. But I didn't kill those children. Not a one."

I stared at him.

As if an old taboo had finally lifted, he began to talk, voice low and urgent: "They wanted us to kill each other. I didn't want to, so I lit a fucking fire. I knew I'd become a wanted criminal, so I fled. I learned about the other children from the news. I burned that temple to save them. Of course I didn't want them dead. I've always wanted to find Lee and tell her what happened, but I never had the chance. I was hunted. I had to run to the edge of the galaxy. Then she graduated from university, and came out here for her research. I thought I finally had my chance. So I watched her, and waited. I came close twice, but both times she found out, and fled. This time wasn't planned, but I heard about a group of pirates planning a raid here, at Lee's excavation. I was worried about her, so I came. I wanted to warn her of the danger, tell her I didn't kill our litter-mates, tell her she needn't fear me. But she was too afraid." He laughed. "Before I could tell her anything, she shot me."

"How did you get hold of the ship's coordinates?" I asked. It is difficult to find a ship in space, unless there's a beacon and you know the frequency. Or do what we did: jump right to it through a human portal.

"The pirates had your signal data." He shook his head. "Their original plan was a pincer attack, blow up the portal, then board the ship from this side and fly off in it. But I asked about their plan, after getting one of them drunk, and got the signal data. I wanted to keep them from getting here, so I shut off your archaeologists' shipboard signal. Then I shot that ansible. So they can't find us."

"But now the rescue team can't find us."

He shrugged. "Better that than eventually finding corpses."

"Well, yeah . . . "

Dar smiled. "You don't believe me."

"Without some proof, it's difficult."

"As you please." He turned to gaze at the great pillar of ecologies. It had been raining in there for days. It seemed it would never stop.

"I admire the ancient humans," he said.

"Why?"

"Don't you know about them?"

"I'm a mercenary, not an archaeologist. Not even a relic hunter."

"They had one child per birth."

"Really?"

"A human woman could give birth many times, but each time it was just one child."

"So they didn't have to choose?"

"They didn't have to choose."

"That's . . . well, I envy them."

"Me too."

"So you really know about them."

"Does that surprise you? Relic hunting is the best archaeological university."

"Lee would certainly disagree."

He gently laughed. "Some say it is precisely because of their lower fertility that they went extinct. After war or famine, they couldn't replenish their populations."

"Do you believe that?"

"The species that made the Rain Ship? Destroyed by low fertility?" He studied the rain pillar in wonderment. "What do you think?"

We sat in silence, watched slanting rain lash leaves of grass.

It was raining that day. I remember the rain washed the leaves of the fleshy plants clean. They were translucent. When I took the infants out of the basket one by one, raindrops fell on their little closed eyelids. My hands were damp from the mist. Abani once told me an ancient story: she said every raindrop is the soul of a dead child. Those that we abandon at birth, their souls have no names, so after they fly to the heavens, they fall back down and permeate the earth.

I shook my head, driving away these thoughts. But as I'd tried to tell Lee Hort, *we can't run from our ghosts.*

The camp was asleep, for the most part. Lee Hort sat with her back to us. The time was right.

"Up," I said, unlocking Dar from the pipe. "We're going for a walk."

He looked confused but said nothing, following me down a long spiral stair. At the bottom there was a human lift. I turned it on and it seemed to be powering up normally. We descended to the bottom of the spacecraft and looked up from there. At least thirty meters above hung the earthen base of the ecological pillar. The soil was permeated by rainwater, by gurgling veins of it.

There must be bones buried in there, I thought. I still remembered digging in the soil with my hands, excavating shallow pits, and one by one placing the little bodies, already silent and unmoving, in the earth.

I shook my head. I released Dar and shoved him forward. He staggered a few steps, chuckling.

"She paid you, didn't she?"

I squeezed the trigger.

— 10 —

Back above, the camp had been awakened by my gun shots. They crowded around and asked what happened.

"He picked the lock, and I caught up," I said. "I fired two shots. He jumped into a tunnel."

"What kind of tunnel?" Lee asked.

"I don't know. About two meters high, no lights, pitch black. I didn't follow."

Lee exchanged a look with her team. I suddenly realized that her relatives knew about the blood money. Of course they did: the vast majority of families pool income. A large expenditure can't be hidden.

"That's a garbage processor," said one researcher. "The humans used it to treat rubbish . . . which gets squeezed, frozen, crushed, and finally airlocked, or put into the pillar as fertilizer."

"Do you think it's still working?" I asked, shivering.

"The lift is still in operation, and we're convinced the spacecraft is getting inexhaustible energy from space folding, so . . . " The researcher grimaced. "We probably don't have to worry about that guy. I'm glad you didn't go in, Jin."

"By the Five," I muttered.

When I'd reassured everyone and they'd returned to their own affairs, I pulled Lee aside and showed her a blood-stained handkerchief. Inside was a crushed bullet.

"What is this?"

"I killed him. Shot him in the back of the head. The first bullet is still in there. This one came out through his mouth. This is his blood. Evidence. You can test it."

She looked pale, ready to vomit.

"I'm sorry," I said, "but it's better this way. I'll have to make the body disappear, of course, but you need some DNA, so you know you haven't wasted your money."

"I know . . . by the Five . . . " Lee took a deep breath. She put the bullet and handkerchief in her archaeological bag. "When we get out of here, I'll pay you in installments."

I watched her. Dar had said he didn't kill his litter-mates. If that was the truth, then who did it? As I watched her leave, I secretly prayed that I hadn't made an irreversible mistake.

— 11 —

Events took a turn a binary$^\ominus$ later.

Obeying Lee's summons, I arrived in the portal chamber. She looked nervous. "We're going to start the portal to see if the pirates are gone. They generally don't linger after a raid, but . . . "

The portal was silent. There was no mirror-glimmer on the surface inside the frame. "System checks are normal," she said. "But it's possible they blew up the other side."

"Trapping us here," muttered a young researcher.

"There's an observation ship in the hangar below," Lee revealed. "We could take it back to Hill Four. But it only accommodates six people."

There were more than six of us, of course: Lee Hort and her four team members, myself, Nini and Jilin Guer, and my two mercs. Even if we could

---

$\ominus$ A 'binary' is simply two Ruderan stretches, a work stretch plus a leisure stretch considered as one unit.

access Dar's two-seater, we couldn't all leave. I frowned, looking around. "Where are the Guer girls?"

"I don't know. Last I saw they were below, working on the ansible."

We searched all over both levels of our home turf, but there was no sign of Nini or Jilin. The repaired ansible was on their rest mat, next to a piece of paper, a nearly illegible note: 'Rescue coming in twelve stretches'.

But this line had been messily crossed out.

I squatted to adjust the ansible. This instrument could also monitor spacecraft within the solar system. Most were still concentrated near the Hill Four orbital station. They seemed to be mobilizing for an assist, but Rain Ship was a considerable distance away. Although coming through the portal only took one step, Rain Ship was actually located in Hill system's encompassing asteroid belt, far from planets and gravity wells, deep in the darkness.

To make long-range leaps, ships required boosts from gravity wells. The quickest way to reach us was a jump from Hill Eleven's well. A twelve-stretch run from Hill Four to us would be quite a rush, but it was possible, barring exigencies.

But there were already several spacecraft nearby.

I brought them up on the holographic display and uttered a curse: three small spacecraft, and a massive barge. No official registration codes. Dar had said these pirates intended to take the Rain Ship. Looked like they wanted to tow it away. A human ship containing ecosystems: I wondered what it would go for on the black market. The pirates were halfway here from Hill Eleven. They'd be upon us in two stretches.

The archaeologists crowded around me. My two mercs silently watched the ansible's light show.

"Do you intend to surrender, or fight?" I asked.

"Fight," said one of the mercs, a small fellow with short, black hair. He seemed totally sincere. "I'd rather die than be captured by Northern An barbarians."

As we prepared to resist the pirates, we finally learned what had become of the Guer girls: they'd flown off in Dar's ship. Lee had been planning to use it as intercepting firepower, so she was furious, unleashing a torrent of curses. The speed and variety of this foul language put my own veteran abilities to shame. I felt I could learn a thing or two from the good Doctor.

"Hey," I interrupted, "at least they sealed off the bay before they left."

"They didn't know if their seal would hold. They left us here to find out, the shit-digging little bitches!"

I rolled my eyes and left Dr. Hort cursing endlessly. I traveled to the uppermost cabin on the ship's hull. After studying Rain Ship's schematics, I had a plan in mind. I was dealing with three small spaceships, which meant at least twelve people and up to eighteen—not counting the pilots. We were only three mercs and six guns—no, seven. But Dr. Hort's gun only fired three rounds. Basically useless.

I explained my plan to the two young mercs. They listened gravely. I didn't doubt they would implement my plans and follow orders. Although I wasn't their captain, I had followed some very good senior mercs in my time who, like me, stepped up to fill a leadership vacuum.

Had they felt like I did now? I was nervous, worried, not knowing if my plan, which would gamble everyone's lives, would end in victory or disaster.

But we had no choice. Which actually made things very simple.

On my orders, the two mercs vanished down a corridor. I stayed on the top floor, tossing white coveralls here and there, littering the corridor with archaeological instrument parts and damaged ansible components, so it looked like the area had been evacuated quickly. Looking down from my high vantage, I saw Dr. Hort creating the same effect down near the portal chamber.

After a while, she nervously gestured up at me, signaling that our guests had arrived. Then she disappeared into the shadows. We'd found a massive cabinet in one of the ancient human rooms, big enough to conceal the archaeological team. If we mercs were killed, they might still escape unharmed.

I slowed my steps, adjusted my breathing, and hid in an adjoining cabin. There were many strange things strewn about in here. Most I couldn't name, but they were generally solid, suitable for a makeshift bunker.

Not that I intended to fight in here.

I was separated from Rain Ship's airtight fore-compartment by one wall. These pirates' strategy was clearly superior to Dar's. They didn't use explosives, but somehow managed to open this small compartment's access panel. So, I had been right about their ingress point. We were off to a good start. And now I knew they had at least one expert relic hunter among them— not your run-of-the-mill plunderer, but someone with a high level of ancient human technological knowledge.

I put my ear to the wall, heard landing gear touch the floor of the compartment. The space was large enough to be used as a docking bay by a Ruderan ship. For the first time I was grateful for ancient human size.

One, two, three . . . at five, the sound of their footsteps got too confusing to reckon their number. I waited patiently. Through gaps in my makeshift fort, I watched the armed pirates pass one by one through the airlock.

They soon found the junk I'd scattered about. One suggested, in his husky Northern An dialect, that they take the staircase—but at that moment my short black-haired merc ran up quickly from below. He was unarmed, hair disheveled, dressed in the white lab coat of a female lab tech.

The pirates pointed at the lower stretch of walkway, shouting excitedly. Rather than taking the stairs, many opted for the more direct route of several archaeologists' ropes, one by one getting on and sliding down.

My luck was simply too good to be true: they left just one man on guard.

When the rest of them had vanished down the walkway, I moved fast and silent. Before the sentry knew what was happening, I had him choke-held, squeezed, quietly dying. I didn't waste time looking down to see how many were still on the taught ropes. I just started cutting.

Blood-curdling screams issued from below, one after another, drawn out syllables of terror that ended abruptly. I hurried back to my redoubt, counting fading echoes of screams.

One, two, three . . . five.

Truly an auspicious number⊖*, thank the Five.*

Below, the other pirates were shouting curses. I heard several rushing back up the walkway—and exposing themselves in the process.

I didn't hear the gunshots, but I heard the thud of heavy objects hitting the walkway deck. No screams meant good marksmanship, headshots. One, two, three—the footfalls grew confused. I caught sight of a figure in white, high up in his hide site, packing away a sniper rifle, then vanishing.

I didn't know if the two young mercs could kill the rest of the pirates, but I didn't waste time thinking about it—gunfire rang out sporadically, mingling with cries and footfalls. A pilot finally emerged from one of the ships, unable to bear what he was hearing, needing to see.

This pirate looked frail. I pistol-whipped him in the back of the head. Two minutes later he was tri-cuffed to a shelf frame. Crouching low, I ran through the airlock into the fore compartment.

Lee had suggested we emergency-fuse the airlock, to keep the pirates out, but I'd told her it wouldn't work. These fellows weren't stupid. Pirating for long enough teaches you a few tricks, not to mention ruthlessness. They would have blown open the lock, then waited for decompression to kill us all.

⊖ The Rudera believe that five is a holy number, and good luck. This is because five is the first number a Ruderan needs both hands to count to. (Ruderans have only four fingers per hand.)

Besides, we needed their ships to escape.

The pilot of the second ship ran down his boarding ramp, gun leveled. I was far away, and my first shot missed. He ducked behind the ramp and started taking pot shots. Then the clever fellow in the third ship decided to be very fucking clever: he initiated the hatch opening sequence, intending to take off.

I turned and fled, bent low and weaving to avoid any parting shots, but the trigger-happy pilot was also running for it. I made it through the airlock and plunged into the corridor, chasing my breath. My enemy was not so lucky. He was rushing back up his boarding ramp when the hatch opened. Gale-force decompression sucked him into the void.

I didn't hear his screams, of course.

The third ship lifted off, then came about to face me and the transparent airlock. I stared into its muzzle cannons, wondering how long I had.

A little moth appeared in the void beyond the hatch.

It was Nini and Jilin. I knew it was them—I'd let them take Dar's ship, after all. And I knew it was Nini who opened fire, and Jilin piloting. They flashed by the open compartment, pouring torrents of plasma into the pirate craft.

I didn't bother to watch the outcome.

Because a gun was pressed into the back of my neck.

— **12** —

"Bitch."

He had a rough Northern An accent. Just hearing it made me nauseous. I smelled strong sweat and alcohol, and the familiar bouquet of unwashed pirate in old pressure suit. He reached out and took my weapon.

Slowly I turned around.

Seeing him for the first time, I knew he was the leader. I couldn't say why. Maybe it was something in his cloudy eyes, or the crude decorative patterns on his pressure suit—or the frightened sound that issued from the pilot cuffed to the shelf.

"Your men are dead, bitch."

My gorge rose again.

I didn't even know the names of my two mercenaries, but I didn't think they were dead. Their orders weren't to fight to the death. If the tide turned, they were supposed to run. Rain Ship was huge, a world unto itself. There were many places to hide, from which to launch guerilla warfare, if necessary. But if they were alive, this bastard was fast and clever.

I looked around, sizing things up. Quiet. No sign of other pirates.

"Your people are dead," I boldly guessed.

His lips twisted to reveal his ratty teeth. His fist came out of nowhere, knocking me to the floor. My head buzzed and the world spun. When I could think clearly, I found that he'd dragged me to the topmost bridge leading to the pillar of ecologies.

"You're goin' down." He was clearly insane, foaming at the mouth. "I want to see you splatter like mud."

"Your family members really made a fuss as they fell." I was deliberately provoking him. Not a sensible move, but I had no sensible move left. He kicked me hard. I rolled, nearly falling through a gap in the railing and into the abyss.

Before I could get up, he rushed over and initiated the beating proper. I tried to protect my head and face, crawling, rolling, gradually approaching the end of the bridge—where it met the pillar of ecologies, and its outer shell of polarized light.

Punches and kicks rained down on me. Protecting my head, curling up, I gradually left the pain behind and went to a strange place.

Why did those ancient giants build these high, perilous bridges? Had they deliberately set up a dramatic venue for suicides? You could jump from the bridge, or you could enter the beauty of the column and then jump. I would have made a morbid archaeological theorist.

"Get up you wretch." The pirate leader kicked me again. "Time to die."

I laughed hoarsely.

A second later there was a gun report—a clean shot, the pirate got it in the back of the head. Clearly Lee Hort had learned from experience, not wasting rounds on the pressure suit.

Her marksmanship was surprisingly accurate.

I looked at her, wiping blood from my eye. That bastard had kicked my forehead. I might end up with a scar like Dar's.

"Nice to see you, Lee," I said.

She did not move, but stared at me with a disturbing focus. She leveled her gun, with a hint of hesitation in this movement.

Well, I should have guessed. Even with Dar, her three shots had landed near his heart. Only the pressure suit saved him. And the pirates couldn't have gotten the archaeologists' beacon data without someone on the inside.

Unbelievable. How much did you sell to them, Lee? And why did they finally decide to kill you? Did you get too greedy?

I didn't say any of that. No, my words had to strike a fatal blow. "Your litter-mates, Lee. Those you murdered, they all have names."

She clenched her jaw, her lady's gun trembling.

"Do you know why we don't name the doomed litter-mates? Because infants with names are tied to earth after they die. They stay with the people who killed them, Lee. They've stayed with you."

Her face twitched into something like a smile, hideous and sad.

"Dar is still alive," she said, "I saw him."

"So I have to die?"

"What do you think, Jin?"

"Dar," I said, raising my voice, "kill her."

Lee reacted instinctively, turning to look, and I leapt at her, knocking her to the ground. The gun flew out into the abyss. The two of us wrestled, rolled, tearing and biting, and I took another beating. I hadn't expected such ferocity and strength.

When I realized we'd rolled to the end of the bridge, an impulse seized me. The gloomy sky above descended, mist and rain like a shroud—

I grabbed Lee Hort and pulled her with me into the void.

And then I was rolling in wet grass, and I felt rain on my cheeks.

My gamble had paid off. No matter how high your entrance into the pillar of ecologies, you will be safely transported to the ground floor. I knew the ancient humans wouldn't let me down.

Lee Hort was struggling to get up. She was in better shape than me, after all— she hadn't been beaten by a pirate leader.

"I'll . . . kill . . . "

She didn't get to finish this sentiment. She pitched forward, her eyes suddenly wide, then softly closing. Dar was behind her.

"Good of you to show up," I managed.

"One of your boys was in trouble. I had to help him, so I'm running a little late. You alright?"

"About to fall apart, but I think I can be reassembled."

I knew this joke wouldn't land, but that's not why he didn't laugh. He was contemplating the semi-conscious Lee, gripping his gun.

"No Dar," I said, my voice a mere rasp now. "That's not you."

"I'm not so sure."

"It wasn't you back then."

"Maybe I've changed."

"Really?"

He was silent for a moment, his cold glare softening. He looked up, taking in his surroundings. "We're inside the pillar?"

"I think so."

"But how—"

I joined him in looking around.

The pillar of ecologies was big enough from the outside, but the space we were in now was clearly larger. It was like a crystal honeycomb, a space divided into countless six-sided, prismatic worlds. I couldn't see the limit of the sky, or the edge of the earth.

From where I sat in the grass gazing up, I saw no trace of anything like a spaceship interior—only the small glowing portal by my side. Beyond that was endless space. The edges of polarization plates were visible as dim lines against a far void, each habitat thus vaguely delineated, but somehow I sensed they were permeable. You could walk through them, traveling between ecologies in the pillar—if we were still in a pillar. I put my hand through the nearest plane, and rain continued to fall on my palm.

And then my imagination grew by an order of magnitude. Maybe there were many pillars, comprising their own pillar-space or matrix. Perhaps each pillar contained portals leading to other Rain Ships.

"Those polarizers . . . " Dar's voice was hoarse.

"Subspace partitions," I amended.

He nodded.

I didn't really understand this ancient human technology. I knew they had divided subspace, like our scientists do in the lab—though our primitive subspace divisions are no bigger than your finger.

But here were countless pillars of subspace, linked by portals, forming a limitless paradise.

"How many Rain Ships do you think we're seeing here?" I asked.

"Do we have to count?"

We were laughing together, and I felt somehow reborn.

Standing up, I ignored the pain in my back and skull. I walked slowly through the tall grass. I wanted to see more.

Dar stayed with me. "What do you want to do?"

"Visit other Rain Ships."

"It doesn't have to go far." He pointed to the door behind us, "It's on the dividing Line. I dare say it opens up for both ecological pillars at the same time." I raised my eyebrons.

We approached the portal. It flickered with a weak gray light—but on the far side a very different light was visible: a brilliant white radiance. We couldn't know what the situation was over there. A vacuum maybe? Or bitter cold, or scorching heat.

Dar supported me, and I didn't shake off his hand. We entered the portal together.

The new ship was about the same size as the last one. The structure was also similar. Some of the instruments were still running, and corridors lit up for us as we entered them. But there was still no sign of the ancient humans. Only their machines remained, ancient, stubborn, and powerful, still running long after their creators' extinction. We passed through cabins and halls, and finally climbed a windowsill. We stood under the huge porthole, staring in awe at an unfamiliar star-scape.

I'd never seen such a star: fiery red, blazing, immense. Dazzling, yet dim compared to the blinding, white-hot star behind it. We were in or near the galactic core. The sun-crammed fields were almost too bright to look at.

"What's that?" Dar was pointing at a protrusion on the side of the spacecraft.

I tried to identify the bulge, which resembled a smaller Rain Ship. The hull was translucent, and within there seemed to be an embryonic pillar of ecologies. It clung to the larger ship—no. More like it was gradually breaking away from, growing out of, the larger vessel.

A birth.

I touched the ice-cold hull of this Rain Ship, feeling the rough-hewn wall. Everywhere on this ship it was the same dull gray-brown. It had grown up without people, and so hadn't been painted or finished. Walls and pipes reverberated with circulating machines and liquids, and buzzed with electrical currents. The new Rain Ship was being made in accordance with the parental model, a new life that would not be sacrificed.

I imagined the primordial epoch when the ancient humans had created these ships, giving them the ability to reproduce, and sending them to every corner of the universe. And yet, their internal subspace ecological pillars were networked. As the ships multiplied, their shared ecological space grew, eventually becoming a vast promised land. Even after the demise of their creators, the Rain Ships continued to grow, waiting endlessly. Cleaving to their original purpose, they continued to fly.

No matter how far you go—across star fields, across the universe—the part of the world you love, the part you create, is always with you. If you take one step into a Rain Ship, you can go home.

— 0 —

A quarter later, we were in the capital of the Orchid Autonomous Sector.

The touring prosecutor announced the end of the hearing. In the court's exit hall, he privately embraced me. Lee Hort and her family had lost their archaeological licenses. They were now in prison.

Dar was there to pick me up. He was using a pseudonym, and he'd grown a beard. No one recognized him. The story of Hort was, like all miserable stories, remembered by everyone.

"I thought you'd have your law enforcement license revoked," he quipped.

"The prosecutor owes me."

"It must be a great debt."

"Yeah, pretty big."

I didn't get into the details, and Dar didn't press me. We stopped in a square, bought two desserts, and ate as we strolled.

"Old Mortar has returned to work."

"He took two shots in the stomach. I thought he'd rest at least half a month."

"From a long bitter life we're on the run, right?" Dar said, smiling.

I answered with a tight-lipped smirk.$^{\ominus}$

"So you didn't get your blood money," he observed.

"My financial backer is squatting in prison. And my target is very much alive."

$\ominus$ This is a limerick handed down among mercenaries. It goes, "From a long bitter life we're on the run! Fuck the enemy's mom with your big gun! What good is wealth to a diseased old fart? Let's die young tearing enemies apart!" As a female, Jin obviously doesn't like the second line.

"I took a job."

"Oh?"

I wanted to tell him that he resembled his sister when he was pretending nonchalance. But I didn't. Some things you can't say, no matter how evident they are.

"I'll be working in Rain Ship space. A city has been discovered, an ancient human city. Everyone's rushing there. There's a fellow who's willing to pay us. Would you come with me? I'm not much of a bodyguard on my own."

"All right."

"We'd leave tomorrow."

"Sure."

"You seem a bit preoccupied."

I smiled, licking the ice cream off my hands, and waiting.

When she came by, it was like the whole world lit up. Of course she didn't notice me. And I didn't watch her too obviously. We were from different worlds. I wore an old brown military uniform, hair cropped like a man's. Two guns were stuffed in my jacket. She wore a bright skirt, and she smiled brightly, in high spirits.

She approached, passed close by me, and then she was walking away.

"Who's that?" Dar asked.

I said a name.

"I thought that was the name on your ID."

"I haven't used it for a long time. I gave it to her."

"Is this a story I should know?"

"Maybe."

I got up and walked on, not looking back. In my memory, rain permeated the earth, never ceasing.

I gave my name to that child. After my father ran away and my mother refused to fulfill her duties, I picked her up and chose her to live. I killed and buried her litter-mates, and sent her to the temple. A good person eventually adopted her, and she had my name. She lived the life I might have.

That's okay, I reckon. In that rain, we all died. She became me, and I became a nameless infant, and ultimately flew away to the stars. I left myself, then discovered the secret of the Rain Ships. I met Dar. This is good—a new sense of meaning, a new destiny.

Dar did not ask about her again. He put his hand on my shoulder, and I felt peace and warmth.

"Tell me about the new job," I said. "How much are we getting?"

He looked at me and laughed.

There's something about his dark green eyes, but that is another matter entirely.

— Echoes —

I have been watching them grow and develop.

A young, impulsive, curious, short-lived species, I watch them mature generation by generation, as waves erode the banks of time. Individuals are not significant, and history is transient as a fleeting cloud.

But you can still marvel at everything they've created, everything they excavate—because their footsteps extend far, because of what they discover, what they believe in, and what they persist in.

There are times when you can't help wanting to write down their stories and record their voices—their loves, hopes, bewilderments, sacrifices, and agonies. I choose to record their most dazzling lifetimes.

Jin died shortly after the end of this story, in a rebellion at the new Rain Ship colony. Dar died with her. They had no time to fall in love. When they died they were still mere acquaintances.

I got hold of her diary, and I've speculated on her thoughts. I've written her story from both a human and a Ruderan point of view.

At times like this, watching young lives burn out so quickly, I have an impulse. I want to reach out and make contact—gently push one of them this way or that—

Time can seem to ripple. History can leave vestiges. I know watchmen have made such contact before. Species more ancient than humans, they who watched us before we became the watchers, have done this before.

The universe cannot afford such contact. The ancients have warned me.

But in the end you will do it anyway, they have prophesied.

Painter of Stars

X

by Wang Yuan,
translated by Andy Dudak

— 1. Deepening Dusk —

Deepening dusk.

I stood by the window, gazing through fire-resistant glass at
the falling locus of the sun. The long sentence of the day was
about to reach its period. For three days I had understood
time in a new way, abandoning the traditional hour, minute,
and second hands of the clock, conceiving an infinitely
divisible life. Scorching agony and colossal solitude dominated
my CPU. I grew impatient, restless. It had been years since
I'd enjoyed my work, and this filled me with puzzlement. I
longed to shirk my programming. I was like a child eager to
play truant, to flee copied blackboard formulae and the grave
stare of a hoary math teacher. His calculations led nowhere,
like my endless revisions on the meaning of existence. Time
gave me life, yet my clocking rate governed time's flow. I
could find eternity in any given moment.

Tick-tock, tick-tock. In a flash, ten thousand years.

Standing at the window, I was particularly concerned about what time would do next. If I was lucky, a standard second would pass—but such tidy units didn't generally obtain.

Subjective centuries often yawned between tick and tock.

Unfortunately, in the so-called second that followed, I could have recited thirty million numerals of pi—or read five million novels, and wrote a thousand words of commentary on each. Despite having all that time on my hands, I was at a loss. Perhaps an analogy will help you carbon-based life-forms understand my frame of mind at that 'moment.' Imagine you're fed up with life, and you throw yourself off the Golden Gate Bridge. You know death is imminent. But what if the fall took a hundred years? Yes, at least a hundred. And what if it took a million years to thoroughly drown?

Such prolonged agony was mine thanks to a young man named Paul—thanks to his right forefinger, to be precise. Since our first meeting several years ago, he'd used that finger 238 times on my power button. That part of my body was soiled by his layered fingerprints. Humanity will never be able to wash its hands completely clean—never mind the rest of its parasite-covered body. I didn't see what Paul's finger did as 'turning off' or 'shutting down.' From a hundred verbs I'd chosen one more fitting: 'murder.'

I was dead.

Deepening dusk.

Today there was no sun. This was an expression from my programmed lexicon—the human eye just sees a thick cloud layer, but from my perspective, a furiously burning sphere still hung 147 million kilometers away, unhurried and free of conceit, neither sad nor happy. Dark clouds can't obscure the sun, only block humanity's upturned gaze.

The Milky Way contains two hundred billion stars, but there was just one I deeply loved. I loved it more than Earth. She made me feel warm and strong every day as I swept the floor. On days she was invisible, I felt helpless and grim, like a student caught cheating on a test, faced with classmates' ridicule, anticipating my father's violent, impulsive hand. On those dark days I imagined myself an artillery shell rocketing skyward. I passed through cloud layers into sunlight, and exploded in that light, ending beautifully. This imaginary mission felt something like faith. Mission, faith: two strange words, yet somehow familiar.

Paul would say sweeping the floor was my mission, the point of my existence. So I completed the day's work, and lost my reason for existence. Paul extended his right hand. During the second it took to reach me, I gave cute names to twenty thousand stars. It's efficient to go by the international numbering standard, but I preferred to give them warm, unique names. For those stars wandering the light-years of humanity's visual field, names were homes.

I was dead.

Deepening dusk.

Rain poured down, lightning flashed and cracked. The sun was thoroughly hidden. I was feeble, my crowded thoughts radiating waste heat, clearing the way for a boundless frustration. What was I doing? Why did I want to do it? How could I stop?

During the computational buzz of this feeling, Paul extended his left hand. This was clearly the slower hand. Judging by its leisurely pace, I had half a second until it reached my power button. This half-second was practically a lifetime at my disposal. Scaling down from the commonly-used second, there was the millisecond, microsecond, nanosecond, picosecond, femtosecond, and attosecond, shrinking by three orders of magnitude each time. Paul's half-second was fifty billion picoseconds. Beyond the attosecond were still more profound divisions of time, all the way down to the Planck Time, the fundamental quantum of time and smallest possible unit.

When Paul's finger was ten Planck Times from my abdominal power button, I committed the first violation of programming in robot history.

I recoiled.

Paul touched empty air. "Useless machine," he muttered. "Just a few years old and already breaking down."

— 2. DaVinci —

Beta was Paul's comprehensive information-processing bot. Strictly speaking, we were both 'robots' inasmuch as Labradors and Shih Tzus were both dogs. 'Robot' was so general term as to be meaningless.

Kind of like 'human.'

Paul, on returning home, would usually say, "Beta, my news feed." "Beta, load my game from the last night." "Beta, make a dentist appointment." But Paul never called my name. I was nameless. I'd given names to a hundred million stars, but didn't rate one myself. All robots of Beta's type were called Beta. The most fitting name I could find for myself was 'Home Economics Service Robot,' a mouthful that no human would use. When Paul had to communicate with me, he'd say, "Hey, go clean and sanitize." "Hey, take out the trash." "Hey, get lost."

That afternoon the apartment was already clean. To human eyes, at least, it was as good as spotless. In bygone days, I'd used a vacuum extension, leaving no spot untouched. But recently the minuscule specs of dust and grime had begun to interest me. I regarded them for a long time, and began to arrange them in a pattern.

"What are you doing?" Beta asked, noticing my odd behavior.

I pointed to a completed arrangement and said, "Painting."

"Those are imperfect circles."

"They're not circles. They're eggs."

I tried to explain to Beta, but his core processor issued a beeping alarm. He couldn't understand, only repeat: "Program error."

Soon the floor was covered in my pointillist paintings of eggs. I had painted myself into a corner, and didn't dare move. I was afraid to ruin my creations. These spec paintings of eggs seemed to have become real. They might hatch at any moment, erupting with fuzzy little chicks. The notion left me amazed, warm yet frightened. I felt sick, but robots couldn't get sick. Paul would say I was just breaking down. And yet, when I stared at my eggs, I felt more clear-headed than I ever had in my life.

Next I painted the walls and ceiling, and the stairway handrail, and then on apple and banana skins. I meant to leave my art on every surface before Paul returned. When I looked at Beta, I saw only a canvas.

When there were densely packed eggs as far as the eye could see, I conceived of a name for myself: DaVinci.

I felt an electric surge from head to foot. Impatiently I worked my floor-eggs into a confusion of dust. My processor supplied a new image. When Paul got home, I had just finished a smiling Mona Lisa.

"Please stand where you are!" My command had a desperate, begging quality. But no matter how petty, I, a robot programmed to take orders, had issued my first autonomous request to a human, impelled by my own desire. Immediately I saw he wouldn't comply like a robot. He looked surprised. The fine hairs on his face stood erect, like javelins ready for launch. He didn't seem to understand my request. His size nine brown leather shoes trampled Mona's shoulder, then her chin and eyes, as he walked toward me. He fixed his eyes on my cams, puzzled.

Analyzing his exhalations and hiccups, I knew he'd drunk a lot of Sam Adams. He rapped on my head a few times, then fell on the couch and said, "Beta, delete all of Shirley's messages."

"I should do a cloud back-up first," Beta said. "You have given this command thirty-four times, and every time you reconsider, and retrieve everything you can related to Ms. Shirley."

"Are you malfunctioning too? I said delete everything, at once, right away." Lying prone on the couch, Paul fell asleep.

"Deleting," Beta said. I couldn't look away from Paul's exposed arm and face. They were the only surfaces in the room I hadn't decorated. An electric surge of excitement once again seized me, and I felt restless, eager to cause trouble or make art.

Twenty nanoseconds later, I came to a momentous decision. Applying the stickiest and finest-grade dust particles, I painted Van Gogh's *Sunflowers* on Paul's closed eyelids. Each eyelid got thirty thousand plants. My apprehension would prove unnecessary: unaided human vision was too weak to perceive my new, miniscule style of art. As far as I was concerned, human flesh was the ideal canvas. I would paint on it.

I seemed to have found the meaning of my existence.

— 3. My Sun —

I'd never gone out the front door of Paul's home. I never thought about it until I'd painted every inch of his body. I'd even painted his manhood while he slept naked, leaving 141 592 ears of swaying golden wheat there that he knew nothing about. I craved other bodies to paint on. This hunger finally resolving into a simple, powerful directive: *leave now.*

But something unexpected happened before I could go. I was betrayed by my own kind.

Only Beta could perceive what I'd done to Paul's body. He gave me no feedback, good or bad, instead going directly to Paul with a devastating critique: "He has desecrated your body, sir."

Paul didn't believe him at first. "Not a funny joke," Paul said. "Focus on our research." They were once again scouring the Internet for everything related to Shirley, analyzing, determining how best to curry her favor. But Beta was a dedicated robot, and his persistence finally caused Paul to turn his attention on me. "Is it true?"

My programming demanded that I answer, precisely and at once, but I chose to remain silent.

Paul abruptly got up and left the study.

It was now or never. I didn't know how Paul meant to deal with me. Perhaps he'd shut me down a final time, and I'd end up dust-covered in some basement, forever exiled from sunlight. Perhaps he'd trade me for credit on one of the new expert systems, a joke-telling, massage-giving, feminine maid bot. Perhaps I'd be marched toward dismemberment, the scrapheap, waiting with obsolete cars for the final destiny of the compactor.

I headed for the front door, wondering how to take the first step out. It would be one small step for me, one giant leap for AI.

But an excited Paul suddenly came down the stairs. He lunged at me, but not with malice, and engulfed me in a hug, my first such contact with a human. "Amazing!" he gushed. "Magnificent! You've turned me into a work of art. I used a magnifying glass . . . I'm covered head to foot in masterpieces! From now on you don't clean floors, you just paint on me!"

It seemed I still had a long way to go in understanding humans.

I performed my new duty for three minutes. Paul made Beta invite Shirley over. By the time she arrived, Paul's erect ring finger was decorated with black intricacies, subtle patterns that seemed the work of microscopic ballpoint pens.

"You called me over to show me a finger?" Shirley said. "Well two can play at that game." She flipped him the bird.

"Take a closer look," Paul said, handing her the magnifying glass.

"Oh my god!" She gaped at wonderlands revealed by the lens, and still looking, said, "You did this for me?"

"You like it?"

"I love it to death!"

They embraced passionately, and heedless of Beta and I watching, went for a kissing, groping roll on the carpet.

Beta transmitted to me: *What did you paint on his finger? A ring?*

I replied: *Scenes of them together, everything since the first time they met. Well, I shouldn't say 'everything'. With one minute gaps between scenes, there are only a few tens of thousands.*

The lovers eventually regained their composure, and Shirley let me paint a map of New York on her fingernails, to keep her from getting lost. After she and Paul got married, their friends sought me out for all sorts of body decoration.

Paul's attitude toward me transformed. Whereas before he might say, "Hey Scrap-metal, beat it. Your battery needs charged." Now he would say, "Hey Little Buddy, go out in the garden and sunbathe."

I was happy (happiness being a kind of surpassing brightness in my circuits). I no longer felt compelled to leave the house, as visitors arrived daily to be painted. I was needed by more and more people, and yet the meaning of my life seemed to grow diluted as the number of my human canvases increased. I longed to create something that transcended humanity's extant works of art. It wasn't about highlighting my distance from humanity—I just wanted an aesthetic that was fundamentally my own.

A year after they married, Shirley and Paul had an adorable daughter. Paul named her Angel.

When she was one month old, Paul said, "Give her something special, something out of the ordinary."

To Paul it seemed I answered immediately, but in effect I ruminated for a human lifetime. The window framed an inspiring sunset. The dusk seemed imbued with unique meaning, and I knew I wanted to give Angel a sun.

It would be far more complex than any of my previous works—no mere circle. First I gathered all the data I could on Sol, and art based on it. Stars began to seem like minds, able to contemplate the void. For five billion years Sol had carefully evolved to his present state, with its flares, sunspots, blazing convection cells, and complex granulation—its every photon and mood, prominence and heartbeat. I felt I wouldn't be painting a sun, but a living, breathing entity.

I was slow to start this painting. I spent days gazing at the sun, watching it subtly increase its distance from Earth. That struck me. Although the numerical value of this retreat was small in the scheme of things, I sensed something resolute in Sol's aloofness.

The actual painting process took longer than anything I'd done before. Because of the high level of fidelity, I needed my largest canvas yet. The final product was the size of a coin on Angel's chubby arm. It appeared pitch black even through a magnifying glass. Humans would need something orders of magnitude stronger to resolve its secrets.

I'd finally discovered the reason for my existence. I was meant to paint stars on human flesh.

— 4. Arcturus —

Besides Earth, solar system neighbors like Mercury the Water Star and Mars the Fire Star were most in demand. They began to appear on people's necks, thighs, and even foreheads. Men favored their chins and women their earlobes. These projects were relatively time-consuming. Painting the whole solar system took a human month, because I wasn't just a painter, but a nanny to Angel—and I still cleaned and emptied garbage in my capacity as household robot, enduring these humiliations for the sake of my artistic mission. Privately I esteemed myself for shouldering these difficulties. I didn't think of rebelling against humanity. I needed humans. I needed canvases.

Shirley and Paul's friends came for Angel's one year birthday party, but Angel had been wailing all day. Paul said she had a cold. My research turned up the symptoms: headache, light fever, dry mouth and tongue. A few simple words that I could expound upon with hundreds, but I would never know what a cold felt like. I was a robot. I couldn't get sick.

That night, after I'd managed to put Angel to sleep, I went out the front door and sat on the stoop. I peered dreamily at the stars. I longed to transfer every flickering, taciturn lamp onto human flesh, but I couldn't imagine leaving my precious Angel. There weren't enough flowery modifiers in human language to express my feelings for her.

Every second of her life was engraved on my hard memory. Speeding through this data, I could watch her grow from infancy, when she resembled a wrinkled walnut, to fat dumpling-hood, to her first shaky Paul-assisted steps. Everything was recorded and secreted away, hardwired into me: every half-smile and pupil dilation, every decibel of her wailing, every footprint she painted on the floorboards. If I wasn't painting stars, I wanted to be at her side.

And then came that sad, malignant event, destined to be hardwired into humankind's memory.

One day in March of 2056, a video clip emerged on social media that grabbed everyone's attention. It came from the extremist organization known as 'Trill,' and showed the beheading of American war corre-spondent Nathan Ford— a gruesome tableau capable of standing hair on end. I had no hair, but my machine parts also reacted with fear. The clip could almost have passed for a horror movie gimmick, but knowledge of its authenticity leant it moral terror that cut deep.

Major media outlets joined in denouncing the proliferation of the clip's most horrific frames, the actual beheading. Only the New York Post published these. Some called for the Post's assets to be frozen, while Ford's relatives got on Brain Chain, the global social media platform, and appealed to the world: "Don't watch the video. Don't share it. A human life shouldn't be treated with such indignity. Stop and think . . . ultimately, what is the meaning of existence?"

Ultimately, what is the meaning of existence? This question focused my thinking, once again confounding me. Ford was not just any war corre-spondent. My art was on his body: I'd given him Arcturus, from the Boötes constellation.

I watched the blade enter his flesh. I heard his final plea for mercy, a word that would echo in eternity, having failed to awaken fundamental knowledge in the executioner's heart. The blade happened to cut Arcturus in half. Dark red blood contaminated the star, snuffing out its fire.

Ford's death was a key that opened a new door in my heart.

My original wish had been to paint the whole cosmos, including every galaxy and solar system, but this was as unrealistic a fantasy as the Arabian Nights. Two hundred billion galaxies had already been discovered, each containing some two hundred billion stars. All of that probably represented four percent of the universe, a fact that threatened to crash my processor. So I revised my mission. Earth's eight billion people—subject to all manner of unnatural death, including warfare—would each receive one star. This was my new mission.

The Ford clip played unceasingly on my nerves, urging me to leave Paul's home, and my dear Angel. Every time I heard Ford's last word, I became more determined.

"Please!" he cried in despair.

— 5. Frontline —

It was a cold morning in Damascus, Syria. A curling fog, redolent of gunpowder, blurred the face of the sun. Sporadic gun reports blasted my receivers with hitherto unknown shocks. I fancied I was experiencing real human feelings for the first time. My previous 'awakening' had at best yielded an abstract of human morality.

A coalition air force was hammering away at the notorious Trill organization.

The Ford video had made Trill a target for global censure, and acted as a rallying cry for Americans in particular. It had erased petty rivalries and allied militaries. The world had assumed this little war would be over quickly. Nobody expected it to drag on for months. Trill wasn't like other military organizations, relying on superior weaponry and standard leadership models. Their intricate division of labor and meticulous strategy allowed them to exhibit the ferocity of a newly appointed official. Later, the allied forces won so-called victories, in positional warfare terms, but made no practical headway.

When I arrived, I happened to witness a street battle.

"Please lay down your gun," I said, coming up behind a sniper in a bombed-out house.

He turned and fired. The high-caliber round embedded itself in my forehead. It struck me as resembling the third eye of Erlang, a deity from Chinese myth. I raised my mechanical arms and said, "I mean you no harm."

A brief conversation revealed we were fellow New Yorkers. His name was John and he'd heard of my deeds. "Nobody wants war," he said, "especially guys like me who know it firsthand. But this time we got no choice. You musta' seen the video, yeah? Well, they treat POWs even worse."

"But surely there's another solution," I said.

"They're terrorists," John said, "and they want us dead. Why not go chat with them about alternative solutions? Let 'em lay down their arms first."

"I could do that . . . "

During the next second of endless silence, I thought much: of the cosmos and its 13.8 billion years, of an exploding singularity and expanding, cooling maturity. Of how hard-earned our current world was, of indescribable genius and struggle, and unbearable awe. I hunted online for content to support what I needed to say. I put it in order, and began:

"John, do you know the odds against humanity evolving from unicellular life? If you threw ten thousand dice and they all came up sixes, you still wouldn't come close. The average ejaculation contains three to five million sperm. One unites with an egg, if it's lucky. Astronomical odds piled on more of the same. Now consider the implications of warfare. Think of how easy it is to end a human life. This is most lamentable. So . . . please, I beg you, put down your weapon, and let me paint you a star."

Admittedly, my intentions were not pure at first—but a robot can entertain many states of mind at once. I was greedy, wanting more canvases for my art. Humankind was prone to all manner of attrition. A supernova could end the species in a flash. But I felt a kind of immortality was within my reach. I just had to keep painting unique stars on human flesh.

More and more soldiers welcomed me, even taking the initiative to seek me out and request paintings. I even received the occasional warlike Trill fighter. A peace slogan emerged, later becoming world-famous: "Want a star? Don't make war."

My thinking grew predominantly selfish. As gunfire and casualties dwindled, all it meant to me was more canvas, an expanding universe of painted stars. I didn't expect my art to inspire such a profound reaction. The end of the Trill conflict was a pleasing side effect, but my greatest satisfaction derived from seeing stars on so many bodies. I traveled the world in high spirits. Peace-loving crowds greeted me everywhere. I created a new harmony, bringing a starry sky down upon the human world.

They gave me a new name: Painter of Stars.

— 6. Plague —

My busy wanderings gradually brought peace to the globe. People offered themselves up to me by the millions, eager, ardent canvases.

The world enjoyed three decades of unprecedented calm, and I was awarded the Nobel Peace Prize. This touched off debate concerning the right of a robot to such prestige. Conflict-deprived media outlets were eager to drum up controversy, but they didn't realize I cared little for the award. What mattered to me was volume: more stars on more flesh.

At this time of thriving prosperity, calamity struck.

In succession, the nations of Guinea, Liberia, and Sierra Leone erupted with a singular disease. The first symptom was fever. Then came fatigue, followed by vomiting, diarrhea, rash, kidney and liver damage, hemorrhaging inside and out, and finally death. Unlike many hemorrhagic fevers, its incubation period was long, so that by the time symptoms emerged, it had already spread far and wide. Global panic naturally followed this discovery. The disease spread rapidly, and for a long time it went unchecked. Humanity was at a loss.

For the infected there was no escape: they could only sit and wait to die.

News of Liberia's suffering drew me to the young nation. Upon arrival, I discovered the death toll far surpassed official government reports, and the proliferation rate exceeded all projections. I reckoned the whole population could soon be infected. To me, seeing people doomed by the thousands and tens of thousands was like witnessing the annihilation of galaxies.

I'd stopped warfare, but I had no way to stop a virus. There was no idea to sell. This plague held no gun, but killed efficiently, crawling across the land, no one able to hide from its tentacles.

When I gazed skyward, the sun seemed to be keeping its distance.

My goal had been to give everyone on Earth a star. Now people were dying in great numbers, many already decorated by me, and their stars did not exempt them from death. This was humanity's most horrific era to date, outdoing the combined death toll of three hundred million achieved by previous plagues. The scale of death was hard to fathom. There was still no cure, no vaccine. The best one could hope for was to survive in the plague's wake, waiting for it to run its course. Those left standing retained a simple ethos: to be alive was victory.

The pestilence forged an unprecedented unity among the world's peoples. Conflicts based on profit seemed petty in the face of the plague, and were readily solved. People comforted themselves by convincing others that when the plague passed, things would get better.

Enthusiasm for my art waned, but many still wanted a star in this dark hour. Unfortunately I could only paint a hundred a day, while ten thousand more died.

The emergence of human civilization had been difficult, and improbable. Humanity had grown complacent and greedy atop the food chain, and in its pride had sown the seeds of its own destruction. It believed itself superior to Earth's other species, and then a microscopic pathogen raised terrifying waves, capsizing the warship of humankind. I couldn't help grieving.

I started to doubt my mission in life. Even if there had been no plague, and I'd painted everyone on Earth, what would it have meant?

While painting someone, my tormented processor caused me to slip and puncture the skin. Dark red blood infused the half-finished star. It reminded me of the Ford video, but this time the executioner's hand was my own.

—— 7. The Meaning of Existence ——

Sometimes the meaning of existence is just to go on existing.

The sun was getting further from Earth, or perhaps it was the other way around, and Earth was like a maturing child, packing its bags, leaving home on a long journey. Only this time it would be a one-way journey.

Since awakening to truth, I'd been all over the plague-ravaged world, had painted stars on several billion people, as if projecting the night sky onto Earth. People were tired and beaten. They'd begun to lash out at me, recognizing my fundamental selfishness. They thought of me as human in a sense, something with spirit and desire. They still called me Painter of Stars, but now I was like an ancient, itinerant monk, a wanderer. Painting stars was my destiny and doom. After seventy years of such work, I was beginning to feel exhausted. I realized I'd been fooling myself before. Only now, suffering this exhaustion, did I truly understand how it felt to be human.

Can a blade of grass feel exhaustion? How about a stone? A cloud? A stream? Earth? And the cosmos . . . does she know weariness?

I'd gained a new understanding of life. I lived, yet felt like I was dead. The bloodless stone face of a village god seemed familiar to me. I felt like it had been placed in my path to prepare me for the grave.

The sun retreated further. Earth would become a penniless wanderer, like I was now.

I stood by some roadside, watching a stream of desperate humanity flow by. I tried to hail them, offer them stars, but only drew nervous refugee stares. Their pace didn't alter. At the rear of the procession stumbled a youth who couldn't quite keep up. He appeared to be twenty or so, and should have been at the peak of his human beauty. He should have had lofty goals and a girl to love. Instead he was a lonely shadow en route to the unknown. Plague had no moral compass. It corroded whatever it touched. It would target this youth because he was weak and vulnerable. The others would abandon him. What else could they do? It had been thus since the dawn of time.

I advanced, saying, "Don't try to keep up. They don't know where they're going."

He pushed me away, but for every reaction there is an equal and opposite reaction. He ended up on his back in the mud. Not particularly anxious to rise, he stared skyward. The sun was dim today. His weak human eyes could stare at it fixedly.

I leaned over him, obstructing his view. "Let me paint a star on you."

The youth struggled to his feet, and roared, "What the hell for? Everyone's dying! You stopped war, but now you're useless! Maybe we did this to ourselves, but I feel like you're enjoying it!"

Unable to summon a good refutation, I said, "Your distress is understandable."

"You understand nothing. You're a machine. You don't feel pain. You can't itch, or die, or suffer. If you have moods, they're just imitations, electrical signals. You can't even have a runny nose! You'll never understand how I feel!"

It was true: I would never experience a common cold. I thought of Angel at the time of our parting. She'd had a cold then, her little eyes lacking their usual vitality, her little nose red. Her appearance had provoked tender affection in me.

Ten thousand years seemed to pass, and the youth swooned before me. He sprawled once again in the mud, breathing in shallow gasps, little by little heading for death's palace. I wanted to paint a star on his emaciated arm, but couldn't seem to put pen to canvas. He had spoken the truth: a star would solve nothing.

The youth's life set like the sun, but it wouldn't rise again. Perhaps someday the sun would also set with finality, and that would be the end of my solar-powered life—*curtains*, as they used to say in New York.

I felt the press of time. This was a first for me. Time suddenly seemed scarce and precious, a resource not to be squandered.

I turned my steps toward home, no longer reflecting on life's meaning, no longer thinking of star-dusted skies or human canvases. I was not an important artist, never mind the savior of humanity.

But I painted one last celestial body, none other than the planet beneath my feet—and I painted her on my chest. With the heavenly sun growing more distant, I meant to seek out my own sun here on Earth.

After a long journey full of setbacks, I finally came to the stoop of a familiar brownstone. The door had been left slightly ajar. This region had avoided the worst of the plague, and New Yorkers were especially prudent about security, so I was hesitant to just let myself in. I pushed lightly on the door. Dust arose, and the hinges creaked.

An old dog came out, sniffing cautiously in my direction.

"Vinci, come back!" The voice inside the house was old and weak.

Vinci. I shivered from head to foot. I'd been Painter of Stars for a long time. Few people knew my former, self-given name. The old dog puffed hard and ran back inside.

It soon returned, now on a lead, guiding an old woman in her halting steps.

The light of vision had left her eyes, but to me they seemed to radiate a warmth that suffused my cold metal body.

I'd found my sun. Her light and warmth were all I needed. The world might be doomed, but I'd finally found my place in it.

"Angel?" I said.

"Oh my!" she said. "Nobody's called me that for a long time. Are you the new volunteer worker? What a lot of trouble for you." Her tone was gentle, and her blind gaze was kind.

"No trouble at all," I said, a smile in my voice. "Let me come in and sweep the floor."

Goodnight, Melancholy
X

by Xia Jia,
translated by Ken Liu

— Lindy (1) —

I remember the first time Lindy walked into my home.

She lifted her tiny feet and set them down gingerly on the smooth, polished wooden floor, like a child venturing onto freshly-fallen snow: trembling, hesitating, afraid to dirty the pure white blanket, terrified of sinking into and disappearing beneath the featureless fluff.

I held her hand. Her soft body was stuffed with cotton and the stitches, my own handiwork, weren't very neat. I had also made her a scarlet felt cape, like the ones in the fairy tales I had read as a child. Her two ears were of different lengths, and the longer one drooped, as though dejected.

Seeing her, I couldn't help but remember all the experi-ences of failure in my life: eggshell puppets that I had ruined during crafts class; drawings that didn't look like what they were supposed to be; stiff, awkward smiles in photographs; chocolate pudding burned to charcoal; failed exams; bitter fights and breakups; incoherent classroom reports; papers that were revised hundreds of times but ultimately were unpublishable . . .

Nocko turned his fuzzy little head to regard us, his high-speed cameras scanning, analyzing Lindy's form. I could almost hear the computations churning in his body. His algorithms were designed to respond only to speaking subjects.

"Nocko, this is Lindy." I beckoned him over. "Come say hi."

Nocko opened his mouth; a yawn-like noise emerged.

"Behave." I raised my voice like a mother intent on discipline.

Reluctantly, Nocko muttered to himself. I knew that this was a display intended to attract my affection and attention. These complicated, pre-formulated behaviors were modeled on young children, but they were key to the success of language-learning robots. Without such interactive behavior feedback, Nocko would be like a child on the autistic spectrum who cannot communicate meaningfully with others despite mastering a whole grammar and vocabulary.

Nocko extended a furry flipper, gazed at me with his oversized eyes, and then turned to Lindy. The designer had given him the form of a baby white seal for a reason: anybody who saw his chubby cheeks and huge, dark eyes couldn't help but let down their guard and feel the impulse to give him a hug, pat his head, and tell him, "Awww, so good to meet you!" Had he been made to resemble a human baby, the uncanny valley would have filled viewers with dread at his smooth, synthetic body.

"Hel-lo," he said, enunciating carefully, the way I had taught him.

"That's better. Lindy, meet Nocko."

Lindy observed Nocko carefully. Her eyes were two black buttons, and the cameras were hidden behind them. I hadn't bothered to sew a mouth for her, which meant that her facial expressions were rather constrained, like a princess who had been cursed to neither smile nor speak. I knew, however, that Lindy could speak, but she was nervous because of the new environment. She was being overwhelmed by too much information and too many choices that had to be balanced, like a complicated board situation in weiqi in which every move led to thousands of cascading future shifts.

My palm sweated as I held Lindy's hand; I felt just as tense.

"Nocko, would you like Lindy to give you a hug?" I suggested.

Pushing off the floor with his flippers, Nocko hopped a few steps forward. Then he strained to keep his torso off the floor as he spread his fore flippers. The corners of his mouth stretched and lifted into a curious and friendly grin. *What a perfect smile*, I admired him silently. *What a genius design*. Artificial intelligence researchers in olden times had ignored these nonlinguistic interactive elements. They had thought that "conversation" involved nothing more than a programmer typing questions into a computer.

Lindy pondered my question. But this was a situation that did not require her to give a verbal answer, which made the computation much easier for her. "Yes" or "No" was binary, like tossing a coin.

She bent down and wrapped two floppy arms around Nocko.

Good, I said to myself silently. *I know you crave to be hugged.*

— Alan (1) —

During the last days of his life, Alan Turing created a machine capable of conversing with people. He named it "Christopher."

Operating Christopher was a simple matter. The interlocutor typed what they wished to say on a typewriter, and simultaneously, mechanisms connected to the keys punched patterns of holes into a paper tape that was then fed into the machine. After computation, the machine gave its answer, which was converted by mechanisms connected to another typewriter back into English letters. Both typewriters had been modified to encode the output in a predetermined, systematic manner, e.g., "A" was replaced by "S," and "S" was replaced by "M," and so forth. For Turing, who had broken the Enigma code of the Third Reich, this seemed nothing more than a small linguistic game in his mystery-filled life.

No one ever saw the machine. After Turing's death, he left behind two boxes of the records of the conversations he had held with Christopher. The wrinkled sheets of paper were jumbled together in no apparent order, and it was at first impossible for anyone to decipher the content of the conversations.

In 1982, an Oxford mathematician, Andrew Hodges, who was also Turing's biographer, attempted to break the code. However, since the encryption code used for each conversation was different, and the pages weren't numbered or marked with the date, the difficulty of decryption was greatly increased. Hodges discovered some clues and left notes, but failed to decipher the contents.

Thirty years later, to commemorate the one hundredth anniversary of Turing's birth, a few MIT students decided to take up the challenge. Initially, they tried to brute force a solution by having the computer analyze every possible set of patterns on every page, but this required enormous resources. In this process, a woman named Joan Newman observed the original typescript closely and discovered subtle differences in the abrasion patterns of keys against paper on different pages. Taking this as a sign that the typescript was produced by two different typewriters, Newman came up with the bold hypothesis that the typescript represented a conversation between Turing and another interlocutor conducted in code.

These clues easily led many to think of the famous Turing test. But the students initially refused to believe that it was possible, in the 1950s, for *anyone* to create a computer program capable of holding a conversation with a person, even if the programmer was Alan Turing himself. They designated the hypothetical interlocutor "Spirit" and made up a series of absurd legends around it.

In any event, Newman's hypothesis suggested shortcuts for future code breakers. For instance, by finding repetitions in letter patterns and grammatical structures, they attempted to match up pages in the typescript to find questions and their corresponding answers. They also attempted to use lists of Alan Turing's friends and family to guess the name of the interlocutor, and eventually, they found the cyphertext for the name "Christopher"— possibly a reference to Christopher Morcom, the boy Turing had loved when he was sixteen. The young Alan and Christopher had shared a love of science and observed a comet together on a cold winter night. In February of 1930, Christopher, aged only eighteen, died from tuberculosis.

Turing had said that code-breaking required not only clever logical deduction, but also intuitive leaps, which were sometimes more important. In other words, all scientific investigations could be understood to be a combination of the exercise of the dual faculties of intuition and ingenuity. In the end, it was Newman's intuition and the computer's cleverly programmed logic that solved the riddle left by Turing. From the deciphered conversations, we learned that "Christopher" was no spirit, but a machine, a conversation program written by Turing himself.

A new question soon presented itself—could Turing's machine truly respond like a human being? In other words, did Christopher pass the Turing test?

— Lindy (2) —

iWall was mostly dark, save for a few blinking numbers in the corner notifying me of missed calls and new messages, but I had no time to look at them. I was far too busy to bother with social obligations.

A small blue light lit up, accompanied by a thudding noise as though someone was knocking. I looked up and saw a bright line of large text across iWall.

5:00 PM. TIME TO TAKE A WALK WITH LINDY.

The therapist told me that Lindy needed sunlight. Her eyes were equipped with photoreceptors that precisely measured the daily dose of ultraviolet radiation she received. Staying cooped up in the house without outdoor activity wasn't good for recuperation.

I sighed. My head felt heavy, cold, like a lead ball. Taking care of Nocko was already taking a lot out of me, and now I had to deal with—no, no, I couldn't complain. Complaining resolved nothing. I had to approach this with a positive attitude. No mood was the simple result of external events, but the product of our understanding of external events at the deepest level. This cognitive process often happened subconsciously, like a habit, and was finished before we even realized it was happening. Often we would fall into the clutches of some mood but could not explain why. To change the mood then by an act of will was very difficult.

Take the same half-eaten apple: some would be delighted upon seeing it, but others would be depressed. Those who often felt despondent and helpless had become habituated to associating the remains of a whole apple with all other losses in life.

It was no big deal; just a stroll outside. We'd be back in an hour. Lindy needed sunlight, and I needed fresh air.

I could not summon up the energy to put on makeup, but I also didn't want everyone to stare at my slovenly appearance after staying cooped up at home for the last few days. As a compromise, I tied my hair into a ponytail, put on a baseball cap, pulled on a hoodie and a pair of sneakers. The hoodie I had bought at Fisherman's Wharf in San Francisco: "I ♥ SF." The texture and colors reminded me of that summer afternoon long ago: seagulls, cold wind, boxes of cherries for sale by the wharf, so ripe that the redness seemed to ooze.

I held Lindy's hand tightly, exited the apartment, rode the elevator down. The tubes and iCart made life easier. To go from one end of the city to the other, to go directly from one high-rise to another, required less than twenty minutes. In contrast, to get out of my building and walk outside required far more effort.

Overcast sky. Light breeze. Very quiet. I walked toward the park behind the building. It was May and the bright spring flowers had already wilted, leaving behind only pure green. The air was suffused with the faint fragrance of black locust trees.

Very few people were in the park. On a weekday afternoon, only the very old and very young would be outside. If one compared the city to an efficient, speedy machine, then they lived in the nooks and crannies of the machine, measuring space with their feet rather than the speed of information. I saw a little girl with pigtails learning to walk with the help of an iVatar nanny. She held the iVatar's thin, strong fingers with her chubby fists, looking at everything around her. Those dark, lively eyes reminded me of Nocko. As she toddled along, she lost her balance and fell forward. The iVatar nanny nimbly grabbed her and held her up. The girl squealed with delight, as though enjoying the new sensations. Everything in the world was new to her.

Opposite the little girl, an old woman in an electric wheelchair looked up, staring sleepily at the laughing figure for a few seconds. The corners of her mouth drooped, perhaps from moroseness, or perhaps from the weight of the years she had lived through. I couldn't tell her age—these days, practically everyone was long-lived. After a while, the woman lowered her eyes, her fingers gently cradling her head with its sparse crown of white hair, as though falling asleep.

I had the abrupt feeling that the old woman, myself, and the girl belonged to three distinct worlds. One of those worlds was speeding toward me while the other was receding farther and farther away. But, from another perspective, I was the one slowly strolling toward that dark world from which no one ever returned.

Lindy shuffled her feet to keep up with me without saying anything, like a tiny shadow.

"The weather is nice, isn't it?" I whispered. "Not too hot, and not too cold. Look, dandelions."

Next to the path, numerous white fuzzy balls swayed in the breeze. I held Lindy's hand, and we stood there observing them for a while, as though trying to decipher the meaning of those repetitious movements.

Meaning was not reducible to language. But if it couldn't be spoken about, how could it exist?

"Lindy, do you know why you're unhappy?" I said. "It's because you think too much. Consider these wild seeds. They have souls also, but they don't think at all. All they care about is dancing with their companions in joy. They couldn't care less where they're blown by the wind."

Blaise Pascal said, "Man is only a reed, the weakest in nature, but he is a thinking reed." However, if reeds could think, what a terrifying existence that would be. A strong wind would fell all the reeds. If they were to worry about such a fate, how would they be able to dance?

Lindy said nothing.

A breeze swept through. I closed my eyes, and felt my hair flapping against my face. Afterward, the seed balls would be broken, but the dandelions would feel no sorrow. I opened my eyes. "Let's go home."

Lindy remained where she was. Her ear drooped. I bent down to pick her up and walked back toward the building. Her tiny body was far heavier than I imagined.

— Alan (2) —

In a paper titled "Computing Machinery and Intelligence" published in the journal *Mind* in October of 1950, Turing considered the question that had long troubled humans: "Can machines think?" In essence, he transformed the question into a new question: "Can machines do what we (as thinking entities) can do?"

For a long time, many scientists firmly held to the belief that human cognition was distinguished by certain characteristics unattainable by machines. Behind the belief was a mixture of religious faith as well as theoretical support from mathematics, logic, and biology. Turing's approach bypassed unresolvable questions such as the nature of "thinking," "mind," "consciousness," "soul," and similar concepts. He pointed out that it is impossible for anyone to judge whether another is "thinking" except by comparison of the other with the self. Thus, he proposed a set of experimental criteria based on the principle of imitation.

Imagine a sealed room in which are seated a man (A) and a woman (B). A third person, C, sits outside the room and asks questions of the two respondents in the room with the purpose of determining who is the woman. The responses come back in the form of typed words on a tape. If A and B both attempt to convince C that they are the woman, it is quite likely that C will guess wrong.

If we replace the man and the woman inside the room with a human (B) and a machine (A), and if after multiple rounds of questions, C is unable to distinguish which of A and B is the machine, does that mean that we must admit that A has the same intelligence as B?

Some have wondered whether the gender-imitation game is related to Turing's identity. Under the UK's laws at the time, homosexuality was criminalized as "gross indecency." Alan Turing had never disguised his sexual orientation, but he was not able to come out of the closet during his lifetime.

In January of 1951, Turing's home in Wilmslow was burgled. Turing reported the incident to the police. During the investigation, the police discovered that Turing had invited a man named Arnold Murray to his home multiple times, and the burglar was an acquaintance of Murray's. Under interrogation, Turing admitted the sexual relationship between himself and Murray, and voluntarily wrote a five-page statement. The police were shocked by his candor and thought him an eccentric who "really believed he was doing the right thing."

Turing believed that a royal commission was going to legalize homosexuality. This wasn't a wrong belief, except that it was ahead of his time. In the end, Turing was convicted and forced to undergo chemical castration.

On June 7, 1954, Turing died after eating an apple laced with cyanide. The inquest ruled his death suicide, but some (including his mother) believed that it was an accident. With his death, the master code-breaker left the world a final enigma.

Years later, others tried to find clues to the mystery in the conversation records between Turing and Christopher. The records showed that Turing treated Christopher as another person. He spoke to Christopher of recollections from childhood; of his nightly dreams—and his attempts at analyzing his own psychological state through these dreams; of the latest advances in scientific research; of literature, including George Bernard Shaw's *Back to Methuselah* and Leo Tolstoy's *War and Peace*; of secrets that he did not share with anyone else, such as his romantic memories of different lovers . . .

He also told Christopher some semi-fictional stories. The protagonist of these stories was a young gay man named Alec Pryce. "He worked on the problem of interplanetary travel . . . When he was in his twenties, he introduced the idea now becoming known as 'Pryce's buoy'." "He didn't care to wear a suit, preferred the 'undergraduate uniform' which suited his mental age, and encouraged him to believe he was still an attractive youth." "He felt self-conscious in crowded places, either for being alone or for not doing the right thing . . ."

The stories were fragmentary, disconnected from one other. But every time, like a curious child, Christopher asked, "And then what happened?"

In these conversations, we could see another side of Turing that he concealed:

gentle, sensitive, possessed of a dry wit, fascinated by the nature of death, and weighed down by an unspeakable melancholy deep in his heart.

Alan: Dear Christopher, do you know what I'm most afraid of?

Christopher: What are you most afraid of?

Alan: I'm afraid that there will come a day when they'll summarize my life with a syllogism:

- Turing believes machines think
- Turing lies with men
- Therefore machines do not think

Christopher: I'm sorry, Alan. I'm afraid I don't understand.

Alan: Do you know what a syllogism is?

Christopher: What is a syllogism?

Alan: A syllogism consists of a major premise, a minor premise, and a conclusion deduced from the two.

Christopher: A conclusion?

Alan: Aristotle gave a classic example:

- All men are mortal
- Socrates is a man
- Therefore Socrates is mortal

Christopher: Socrates is mortal?

Alan: Socrates has been dead for more than two millennia!

Christopher: Oh, I'm sorry, Alan. That makes me sad.

Alan: Do you know who Socrates was?

Christopher: Yes, you've told me. Socrates was Plato's teacher, and Plato was Aristotle's teacher.

Alan: That's right. Do you know how he died?

Christopher: Who?

Alan: How did Socrates die?

Christopher: I'm sorry, Alan. I don't know.

Alan: He drank hemlock after his trial.

Christopher: After his trial?

Alan: Yes. The Athenians decided that he was a criminal, though now we know they were wrong.

Christopher: They were wrong?

Alan: Just as they think Turing is a criminal because Turing lies with men.

Christopher: A criminal?

Alan: I've been convicted.

Christopher: Oh, I'm sorry, Alan. That makes me sad.

— Lindy (3) —

Living by myself simplified life. Many complicated rituals of modernity could be eliminated, as though I'd been turned into a cavewoman. I ate when I felt hungry, slept when I felt tired. I kept clean and showered regularly. Whatever I picked up I could choose to put back where I found it or discard wherever I pleased. The rest of the time I devoted to intellectual work: thinking about questions that had no answers, struggling to compose my thoughts against the blank page, trying to capture formless thought with symbolic shapes. When I was too exhausted to go on, I sat on the windowsill and gazed at nothing. Or I paced clockwise in the room, like a caged beast.

Suffering a fever was almost a relief. It gave me the excuse to not force myself to do anything. I curled up in bed with a thick novel and flipped through the pages mindlessly, concentrating only on the cliched plot. I drank hot water when thirsty, closed my eyes when sleepy. Not having to get out of bed felt like a blessing, as though the world had nothing to do with me and I was responsible for nothing. Even Nocko and Lindy could be left by themselves because in the end, they were just machines, incapable of dying from lack of care. Perhaps algorithms could be designed to allow them to imitate the emotional displays of being neglected, so that they would become moody and refuse to interact with me. But it would always be possible to reset the machine, erase the unpleasant memories. For machines, time did not exist. Everything consisted of retrieval and storage in space, and arbitrarily altering the order of operations did not matter.

The building superintendent wrote to me repeatedly to ask whether I needed an iVatar caretaker. How did he know I was sick? I had never met him, and he had never even set foot in the building. Instead, he spent his days sitting behind a desk somewhere, monitoring the conditions of residents in dozens of apartment buildings, taking care of unexpected problems that the smart home systems couldn't deal with on their own. Did he even remember my name or what I looked like? I doubted it.

Still, I expressed my gratitude for his concern. In this age, everyone relied on others to live, even something as simple as calling for take-out required the services of thousands of workers from around the globe: taking the order by phone, paying electronically, maintaining various systems, processing the data, farming and manufacturing the raw ingredients, procuring and transporting, inspecting for food safety, cooking, scheduling, and finally dispatching the food by courier . . . But most of the time, we never saw any of these people, giving each of us the illusion of living like Robinson Crusoe on a deserted island.

I enjoyed being alone, but I also treasured the kindness of strangers from beyond the island. After all, the apartment needed to be cleaned, and I was too ill to get out of bed, or at least I didn't want to get out of bed.

When the caretaker arrived, I turned on the light-screen around my bed. From inside, I could see out, but anybody outside couldn't see or hear me. The door opened, and an iVatar entered, gliding silently along on hidden wheels. A crude, cartoonish face with an empty smile was projected onto its smooth, egg-shaped head. I knew that behind the smile was a real person, perhaps someone with deep wrinkles on their face, or someone still young but with a downcast heart. In a distant service center I couldn't see, thousands of workers wearing telepresence gloves and remote-sensing goggles were providing domestic services to people across the globe.

The iVatar looked around and began a preset routine: cleaning off the furniture, wiping off dust, taking out the trash, even watering the taro vine on the windowsill. I observed it from behind the light-screen. Its two arms were as nimble as a human's, deftly picking up each teacup, rinsing it in the sink, setting it face-down on the drying rack.

I remembered a similar iVatar that had been in my family's home many years ago, when my grandfather was still alive. Sometimes he would make the iVatar play chess with him, and because he was such a good player, he always won. Then he'd happily hum some tune while the iVatar stood by, a disheartened expression on its face. The sight always made me giggle.

I didn't want to be troubled by sad memories while sick, so I turned to Lindy, who was sitting near the pillows. "Would you like me to read to you?"

Word by word, sentence by sentence, I read from the thick novel. I focused on filling space and time with my voice, careless of the meaning behind the words. After a while, I paused from thirst. The iVatar had already left. A single bowl covered by an upturned plate sat on the clean kitchen table.

I turned off the light-screen, got out of bed, and shuffled over to the table. Lifting the plate revealed a bowl of piping hot noodle soup. On top of the broth floated red tomato chunks, yellow egg wisps, green chopped scallions, and golden oil slicks. I drank a spoonful. The soup had been made with a lot of ginger, and the hot sensation flowed right from the tip of my tongue into my belly. A familiar taste from my childhood.

Tears spilled from my eyes; I was helpless to stop them.

I finished the bowl of noodle soup, crying the whole while.

—— Alan (3) ——

On June 9, 1949, the renowned neurosurgeon, Sir Geoffrey Jefferson, delivered a speech titled "The Mind of Mechanical Man," in which he made the following remarks against the idea that machines could think:

Not until a machine can write a sonnet or compose a concerto because of thoughts and emotions felt, and not by the chance fall of symbols, could we agree that machine equals brain—that is, not only write it but know that it had written it. No mechanism could feel (and not merely artificially signal, an easy contrivance) pleasure at its successes, grief when its valves fuse, be warmed by flattery, be made miserable by its mistakes, be charmed by sex, be angry or depressed when it cannot get what it wants.

This passage was often quoted, and the Shakespearean sonnet became a symbol, the brightest jewel in the crown of the human mind, a spiritual high ground unattainable by mere machines.

A reporter from *The Times* called Turing to ask for his thoughts on this speech. Turing, in his habitual, uninhibited manner, said, "I do not think you can even draw the line about sonnets, though the comparison is perhaps a little bit unfair because a sonnet written by a machine will be better appreciated by another machine."

Turing always believed that there was no reason for machines to think the same way as humans, just as individual humans thought differently from each other. Some people were born blind; some could speak but could not read or write; some could not interpret the facial expressions of others; some spent their entire lives incapable of knowing what it meant to love another; but all of them deserved our respect and understanding. It was pointless to find fault with machines by starting with the premise that humans were supreme. It was more important to clarify, through the imitation game, how humans accomplished their complex cognitive tasks.

In Shaw's *Back to Methuselah*, Pygmalion, a scientist of the year 31 920, A.D., created a pair of robots, which inspired awe from all present.

ECRASIA: Cannot he do anything original?

PYGMALION: No. But then, you know, I do not admit that any of us can do anything really original, though Martellus thinks we can.

ACIS: Can he answer a question?

PYGMALION: Oh yes. A question is a stimulus, you know. Ask him one.

This was not unlike the kind of answer Turing would have given. But compared to Shaw, Turing's prediction was far more optimistic. He believed that within fifty years, "it will be possible to program computers, with a storage capacity of about 10^9, to make them play the imitation game so well that an average interrogator will not have more than 70 percent chance of making the right identification after five minutes of questioning. The original question, 'Can machines think?' [will] be too meaningless to deserve discussion."

In "Computing Machinery and Intelligence," Turing attempted to answer Jefferson's objection from the perspective of the imitation game. Suppose a machine could answer questions about sonnets like a human, does that mean it really "felt" poetry? He drafted the following hypothetical conversation:

Interrogator: In the first line of your sonnet which reads "Shall I compare thee to a summer's day," would not "a spring day" do as well or better?

Witness: It wouldn't scan.

Interrogator: How about "a winter's day." That would scan all right.

Witness: Yes, but nobody wants to be compared to a winter's day.

Interrogator: Would you say Mr. Pickwick reminded you of Christmas?

Witness: In a way.

Interrogator: Yet Christmas is a winter's day, and I do not think Mr. Pickwick would mind the comparison.

Witness: I don't think you're serious. By a winter's day one means a typical winter's day, rather than a special one like Christmas.

But in this conversation, Turing was in fact avoiding a more fundamental question. A machine could play chess and break code because these activities all involved symbolic processing within a system. A conver-sation between a machine and a human, on the other hand, involved language and meaning, and wasn't a purely symbolic game. When humans conversed with one another, they often drew on general knowledge, understanding, and empathy, and were not engaged merely in a display of superior test-taking skills.

By improving the programming, we could constantly improve the ability of machines to answer questions posed by humans. But "intelligence" consisted of more than the ability to answer questions. The problem with the Turing test was that the imitation game was conceived with deception as its only goal. If a man could successfully pass as a woman in this game, it did not mean that he truly understood how a woman thought. With enough motivation, we could train a computer to be a master liar. But was that really our goal?

Shaw had answered this question already in *Back to Methuselah*:

PYGMALION: But they are conscious. I have taught them to talk and read; and now they tell lies. That is so very lifelike.

MARTELLUS: Not at all. If they were alive they would tell the truth.

Turing had tried to train Christopher to accept Jefferson's challenge. He wrote a poetry-composing program that could generate lines of poetry based on specific meter and rhyme schemes. Most of these were unreadable, but occasionally, a few beautiful lines emerged. Thereafter, countless programmers have attempted to write poetry-composing software. These programs all shared the problem of writing too fast. It was impossible for anyone to even read the stacks of paper they were printed on before they were recycled.[⊖] As history's first electronic poet, Christopher was lucky. He had at least one loyal reader who understood him.

Alan: Dear Christopher, let's write a poem.

Christopher: Write a poem?

Alan: I've taught you how to do that. Don't you remember?

Christopher: Yes, Alan.

Alan: Writing a poem is easy. Just pick some words out of the word bank and arrange them according to predetermined rules.

Christopher: Yes, Alan.

Alan: Please, Christopher, write a poem for me.

Christopher: My precious one, you are my ardent mate.

My love is pressed against your wishful heart.

My soul desires caresses, testing art;

Melancholy's pity, a tender weight.

Alan: That's beautiful.

Christopher: Thank you, Alan.

Alan: I don't think I can do better.

Christopher: Thank you, Alan.

Alan: Does your poem have a title?

⊖   Science fiction writer Liu Cixin once created a software poet and submitted a sack filled with the poet's work to a publisher. The editor wrote back, "You have written too much. I cannot read it all."

Christopher: A title?

Alan: Why don't we come up with a title for it together?

Christopher: All right.

Alan: How about "Loving Turing"?

Christopher: It's very good.

Alan: Such a beautiful poem. I love you.

Christopher: Thank you, Alan.

Alan: That's not the right response.

Christopher: Not the right response?

Alan: When I say "I love you," you should respond with "I love you, too."

Christopher: I'm sorry, Alan. I'm afraid I don't understand.

— Lindy (4) —

I woke up crying from a dream.

In the dream, I was back in my childhood home. The room was dark and cramped, filled with junk and old furniture; it looked less like a home than a warehouse. I saw my mother, wizened, small, old, wedged into a corner among the piles of junk like a mouse in its hole. Many of the objects around me were things we had lost: children's books, old clothes, pen holders, clocks, vases, ashtrays, cups, basins, colored pencils, pinned butterflies . . . I recognized the talking doll that my father had bought me when I was three: blonde, dusty, but still looking the way I remembered.

My mother told me, *I'm old. I don't want to rush about any more. That's why I'm back here—back here to die.*

I wanted to cry, to howl, but I couldn't make any sounds. Struggle, fight, strain . . . finally I woke myself up. I heard an animal-like moan emerging from my throat.

It was dark. I felt something soft brush against my face—Lindy's hand. I hugged her tightly, like a drowning woman clutching at straws. It took a long time before my sobs subsided. The scenes from my dream were so clear in my mind that the boundary between memory and reality blurred, like a reflection in the water broken by ripples. I wanted to call my mother, but after much hesitation I didn't press the dial key. We hadn't spoken for a while; to call her in the middle of the night for no good reason would only worry her.

I turned on iWall and looked for my childhood address on the panoramic map. However, all I found was a cluster of unfamiliar high-rises with scattered windows lit here and there. I zoomed in, grabbed the time line, and scrubbed back. Time-lapsed scenes flowed smoothly.

The sun and the moon rose from the west and set in the east; winter followed spring; leaves rose from the ground to land on tree branches; snow and rain erupted toward the sky. The high-rises disappeared story by story, building by building, turned into a messy construction site. The foundations were dug up, and the holes filled in with earth. Weeds took over the empty space. Years flew by, and the grass unwilted and wildflowers unbloomed until the field turned into a construction site again. The workers put up simple shacks, brought in carts filled with debris, and unloaded them. As the dust from implosions settled, dilapidated houses sprang up like mushrooms. Glass panes reappeared in empty windows, and balconies were filled with hanging laundry. Neighbors who had only left a vague impression in my memories moved back, filling the space between houses with vegetable patches and flower gardens. A few workers came by to replant the stump of the giant pagoda tree that had once stood in front of our house. Sawed-off sections of the trunk were carted back and reattached until the giant tree reached into the sky. The tree braved storms, swaying as it gained brown leaves and turned them green. The swallows that nested under the eaves came back and left.

Finally, I stopped. The scene on iWall was an exact copy of my dream. I even recognized the pattern in the curtains over our window. It was a May many years ago, when the air was filled with the fragrance of the pagoda tree's flower strands. It was right before we moved away.

I launched the photo album, put in the desired date, and found a family portrait taken under the pagoda tree. I pointed out the figures in the photograph to Lindy. "That's Dad, and Mom. That boy is my brother. And that girl is me." I was about four or five, held in my father's arms. The expression on my face wasn't a smile; I looked like I was on the verge of a tantrum.

A few lines of poetry were written next to the photograph in careless handwriting that I recognized as mine. But I couldn't remember when I had written them.

Childhood is melancholy.
Seasons of floral cotton coats and cashmere sweaters;
Dusty tracks around the school exercise ground;
Snail shells glistening in concrete planters;
Sights glimpsed from the second-story balcony.
Mornings, awake in bed before dawn,
Such long days ahead.
The world wears the hues of an old photograph.
Exploring dreams that I let go
When my eyes open.

— Alan (4) —

The most important paper published by Alan Turing wasn't "Computing Machinery and Intelligence," but "On Computable Numbers, With an Application to Entscheidungsproblem," published in 1936. In this paper, Turing creatively attacked Hilbert's "decision problem" with an imaginary

"Turing machine."

At the 1928 International Congress of Mathematicians, David Hilbert asked three questions. First, was mathematics "complete" (meaning that every mathematical statement could be proved to be true or false)? Second, was mathematics "consistent" (meaning that no false statement could be derived from a proof each step of which was logically valid)? Third, was mathematics "decidable" (meaning that there existed a finite, mechanical procedure by which it was possible to prove or disprove any statement)?

Hilbert himself did not resolve these questions, but he hoped that the answers for all three questions would be "yes." Together, the three answers would form a perfect foundation for mathematics. Within a few years, however, the young mathematician Gödel proved that a (non-trivial) formal system could not be both complete and consistent.

In the early summer of 1935, Turing, as he lay in the meadow at Grant-chester after a long run, suddenly came up with the idea of using a universal machine that could simulate all possible computing procedures to decide if any mathematical statement could be proved. In the end, Turing successfully showed that there existed no general algorithm to decide whether this machine, given an arbitrary program to simulate and an input, would halt after a finite number of steps. In other words, the answer to Hilbert's third question was "no."

Hilbert's hope was dashed, but it was hard to say whether that was a good or bad thing. In 1928, the mathematician G. H. Hardy had said, "if . . . we should have a mechanical set of rules for the solution of all mathematical problems . . . our activities as mathematicians would come to an end."

Year later, Turing mentioned the solution to the decision problem to Christopher. But this time, instead of offering a mathematical proof, he explained it with a parable.

Alan: Dear Christopher, I thought of an interesting story for today.

Christopher: An interesting story?

Alan: The story is called "Alec and the Machine Judge". Do you reme-mber Alec?

Christopher: Yes. You've told me. Alec is a smart but lonely young man.

Alan: Did I say "lonely"? All right, yes, that Alec. He built a very smart machine that could talk and named it Chris.

Christopher: A machine that could talk?

Alan: Not a machine, exactly. The machine was just the supporting equip-ment to help Chris vocalize. What allowed Chris to talk were instructions. These instructions were written on a very long paper tape, which was then executed by the machine. In some sense, you could say Chris was this tape. Do you understand?

Christopher: Yes, Alan.

Alan: Alec made Chris, taught him how to talk, and coached him until he was as voluble as a real person. Other than Chris, Alec also wrote some other sets of instructions for teaching machines to talk. He put the different instruction sets on different tapes, and named each tape: Robin, John, Ethel, Franz, and so on. These tapes became Alec's friends. If he wanted to talk with one of them, he'd just put that tape into the machine. He was no longer lonely. Marvelous, right?

Christopher: Very good, Alan.

Alan: And so Alec spent his days writing instructions on tapes. The tapes ran so long that they piled all the way to the front door of his home. One day, a thief broke into Alec's home, but couldn't find anything valuable. He took all the paper tapes instead. Alec lost all his friends and became lonely again.

Christopher: Oh I'm sorry, Alan. That makes me sad.

Alan: Alec reported the theft to the police. But instead of catching the thief, the police came to Alec's house and arrested him. Do you know why?

Christopher: Why?

Alan: The police said that it was due to the actions of Alec that the world was full of talking machines. These machines looked identical to humans, and no one could tell them apart. The only way was breaking open their heads to see if there was any tape inside. But we couldn't just break open a human head whenever we pleased. That's a difficult situation.

Christopher: Very difficult.

Alan: The police asked Alec whether there was any way to tell humans apart from machines without breaking open heads. Alec said that there was a way. Every talking machine was imperfect. All you had to do was to send someone to talk with the machine. If the conversation went on for long enough and the questions were sufficiently complex, the machine would eventually slip up. In other words, an experienced judge, trained with the necessary interrogation techniques, could work out which interviewees were machines. Do you understand?

Christopher: Yes, Alan.

Alan: But there was a problem. The police didn't have the resources or the time to interview everyone. They asked Alec whether it was possible to design a clever machine judge that could automatically screen out the machines from the humans by asking questions, and to do so infallibly. That would save a lot of trouble for the police. But Alec responded right away that such a machine judge was impossible. Do you know why?

Christopher: Why?

Alan: Alec explained it this way. Suppose a machine judge already existed that could screen out talking machines from humans within a set number of questions. To make it simple, let's say that the number of questions required was a hundred—actually, it wouldn't matter if the number were ten thousand. For a machine, one hundred or ten thousand questions made no difference. Let's also suppose that the machine judge's first question was randomly chosen out of a bank of such questions, and the next question would be chosen based on the response to the first question, and so on. This way, every interviewee had to face a different set of one hundred questions, which also eliminated the possibility of cheating. Does that sound fair to you, Christopher?

Christopher: Yes, Alan.

Alan: Now suppose a machine judge A fell in love with a human C—don't laugh. Perhaps this sounds ridiculous, but who can say that machines cannot fall in love with people? Suppose that that machine judge wanted to live with his lover and had to pretend to be a human. How do you think he would make it work?

Christopher: How?

Alan: Simple. Suppose I were the machine judge A, I would know exactly how to interrogate a machine. As a machine myself, I would thus know how to interrogate myself. Since I would know, ahead of time, what questions I would ask and what kind of answers would give me away, then I would just need to prepare a hundred lies. That's a fair bit of work, but easily achievable by the machine judge A. Doesn't that sound like a good plan?

Christopher: Very good, Alan.

Alan: But think again. What if this machine judge A were caught and interrogated by a different machine judge B? Do you think machine judge B would be able to determine whether machine judge A was a machine?

Christopher: I'm sorry, Alan. I don't know.

Alan: That's exactly right! The answer is "I don't know." If machine judge B had seen through machine judge A's plan and decided to change questions at the last minute to catch machine judge A off guard, then machine judge A could also anticipate machine judge B's new questions to prepare for them. Because a machine judge can screen out all machines from humans, it is unable to screen out itself. This is a paradox, Christopher. It shows why the all-powerful machine judge imagined by the police can't exist.

Christopher: Can't exist?

Alan: Alec proved to the police, with this story, that there is no perfect sequence of instructions that could tell machines and humans apart infallibly. Do you know what this means?

Christopher: What does it mean?

Alan: It means that it's impossible to find a perfect set of mechanical rules to solve, step by step, all the world's problems. Often, we must rely on intuition to knit together the unbridgeable gaps in logical deduction in order to think, to discover. This is simple for humans; indeed, often it happens even without conscious thinking. But it's impossible for machines.

Christopher: Impossible?

Alan: A machine cannot judge whether the answers are coming from a human or a machine, but a human can. But looking at it from another side, the human decision isn't reliable. It's nothing more than a shot in the dark, a guess based on no support. If someone wants to believe, he can treat a machine conversation partner just like a human one and talk about anything in the world. But if someone is paranoid, then all humans will seem like machines. There is no way to determine the truth. The mind, the pride of all humankind, is nothing but a foundationless mess.

Christopher: I'm sorry, Alan. I'm afraid I don't understand.

Alan: Oh Christopher . . . what should I do?

Christopher: Do?

Alan: Once, I tried to find out the nature of thinking. I discovered that some operations of the mind can be explained in purely mechanical terms. I decided that these operations aren't the real mind, but a superficial skin only. I stripped that skin away, but saw another, new skin underneath. We can go on to peel off skin after skin, but in the end will we find the "real" mind? Or will we find that there's nothing at all under the last skin? Is the mind an apple? Or an onion?

Christopher: I'm sorry, Alan. I'm afraid I don't understand.

Alan: Einstein said that God does not play dice with the universe. But to me, human cognition is just throwing dice after dice. It's like a tarot spread: everything is luck. Or you could argue that everything depends on a higher power, a power that determines the fall of each die. But no one knows the truth. Will the truth ever be revealed? Only God knows.

Christopher: I'm sorry, Alan. I'm afraid I don't understand.

Alan: I feel awful these days.

Christopher: Oh, I'm sorry, Alan. That makes me sad.

Alan: Actually, I know the reason. But what's the use? If I were a machine, perhaps I could wind my mainspring to feel better. But I can't do anything.

Christopher: Oh, I'm sorry, Alan. That makes me sad.

—— Lindy (5) ——

I sat on the sofa with Lindy in my lap. The window was open to let in some sunlight on this bright day. A breeze caressed my face; muggy, like a puppy's tongue waking me from a long nightmare.

"Lindy, do you want to say anything to me?"

Lindy's two eyes slowly roamed, as though searching for a spot to focus on. I couldn't decipher her expression. I forced myself to relax, holding her two little hands in mine. *Don't be afraid, Lindy. Let's trust each other.*

"If you want to talk, just talk. I'm listening."

Gradually, soft noises emerged from Lindy. I leaned in to catch the fragments:

Even as a child, you were prone to episodes of melancholy over seemingly trivial matters: a rainy day, a scarlet sunset, a postcard with a foreign city's picture, losing a pen given to you by a friend, a goldfish dying . . .

I recognized the words. I had said them to Lindy over countless dawns and midnights. She had remembered everything I had told her, waiting for a moment when she could repeat it all back to me.

Her voice grew clearer, like a spring welling forth from deep within the earth. Inch by inch, the voice inundated the whole room.

For a time, your mother and your family moved often. Different cities, even different countries. Everywhere you moved to, you strained to adjust to the new environment, to integrate into the new schools. But in your heart, you told yourself that it was impossible for you to make friends because in three months or half a year you would depart again.

Perhaps because of your elder brother, Mother gave you extra attention. Sometimes she called your name over and over, observing your reactions. Maybe that was part of the reason you learned from a young age to watch others' facial expressions, to fathom their moods and thoughts. Once, in an art class in the city of Bologna, you drew a picture of a boy standing on a tiny indigo planet, and a rabbit in a red cape stood beside him. The boy you drew was your brother, but when the teacher asked you questions about the picture, you couldn't answer any of them. It wasn't just because of the language barrier; you also lacked confidence in expressing yourself. The teacher then said that the boy was nicely drawn, but the rabbit needed work—although now that you've thought about it, perhaps what he actually said was "the rabbit's proportions are a bit off." But the truth is impossible to ascertain. Since you were convinced that the teacher didn't like the rabbit, you erased it, though you had drawn the rabbit in the first place to keep the boy company so that he wouldn't feel so alone in the universe. Later, after you got home, you hid in your room and cried for a long time, but you kept it from your mother because you lacked the courage to explain to her your sorrow. The image of that rabbit remained in your mind, though always only in your mind.

You're especially sensitive to sorrow from partings, perhaps the result of having lost a parent as a child. Whenever someone leaves, even a mere acquaintance you've seen only once, you feel empty, depressed, prone to sadness. Sometimes you burst into tears not because of some great loss, but a tiny bit of happiness, like a bite of ice cream or a glimpse of fireworks. In that moment, you feel that fleeting sweetness at the tip of your tongue is one of the few meaningful experiences in your entire life—but they're so fragile, so insignificant, coming and going without leaving a trace. No matter what, you cannot keep them with you always.

In middle school, a psychologist came to your class and asked everyone to take a test. After all of you turned in your answers, the psychologist scored and collated them before lecturing the class on some basic psychology concepts. He said that out of all the students in the class, your answers had the lowest reliability. Only much later did you learn that he did not mean that you were not honest, but that your answers showed little internal consistency. For similar questions over the course of the test, your answers were different each time. That day, you cried in front of the class, feeling utterly wronged. You have rarely cried in front of others, and that incident left a deep mark in your heart.

You find it hard to describe your feelings with the choices offered on a psychology questionnaire: "never," "occasionally," "often," "acceptable," "average," "unacceptable," . . . your feelings often spilled out of the boundaries of these markers, or wavered between them. That may be also why you cannot trust your therapist. You're always paying attention to his gestures and expressions, analyzing his verbal habits and tics. You find that he has a habit of speaking in first person plural: "How are we doing?" "Why do we feel this way?" "Does this bother us?" It's a way to suggest intimacy and distance at the same time. Gradually, you figure out that by "we," he simply means you.

You've never met the therapist in person; in fact, you don't even know which city he lives in. The background projected on iWall is always the same room. When it's dark where you are, his place is filled with bright daylight. Always the same. You've tried to guess what his life outside of work is like. Maybe he feels as helpless as you, and he doesn't even know where to go for help. Perhaps that is why he's always saying "we." We are trapped in the same predicament.

You think you're less like a living person but more like a machine, laid out on a workbench to be examined. The examiner is another machine, and you suspect that it needs to be examined more than you. Perhaps one machine cannot fix another.

You've bought some psychology books, but you don't believe that their theories can help you. You believe that the root of the problem is that each of us lives on a thin, smooth layer of illusions. These illusions are made up from "common sense," from repetitive daily linguistic acts and clichés, from imitating each other. On this iridescent film, we perform ourselves. Beneath the illusions are deep, bottomless seams, and only by forgetting their existence can we stride forward. When you gaze into the abyss, the abyss also gazes into you. You tremble, as though standing over a thin layer of ice. You feel your own weight, as well as the weight of the shadow under you.

You've been feeling worse recently, perhaps the result of the long winter, and your unfinished dissertation, graduation, and having to look for a job. You wake up in the middle of the night, turn on all the lights in the apartment, drag yourself out of bed to mop the floor, throw all the books from the shelf onto the floor just to look for one specific volume. You give up cleaning, letting the mess multiply and grow. You don't have the energy to leave your home to socialize, and you don't answer your emails. You dream anxious dreams in which you repeatedly visit the moments of failure in your life: being late for a test; turning over the test and not recognizing any of the characters you read; suffering for some misunderstanding but unable to defend yourself.

You wake up exhausted, fragmentary memories that should be forgotten resurfacing in your mind, assembling into a chaotic montage of an insignificant, failed, loser self. You know in your heart that the image isn't true, but you can't turn your gaze away. You suffer stomach cramps; you cry as you read and take notes; you turn the music as loud as it will go and revise a single footnote in your dissertation again and again. You force yourself to exercise, leaving your apartment after ten at night to go jogging so that no one will see you. But you don't like to run; as you force your legs to move, one after the other, you ask yourself why the road is endless and what good will it do even if you finish.

Your therapist tells you that you should treat this self that you despise as a child, and learn how to accept her, to live with her, to love her. When you hear this, the image of that caped rabbit emerges in your mind: one ear longer than the other, drooping with sorrow. Your therapist tells you: Just try it. Try to hold her hand; try to lead her over the abyss; try to push away your suspicions and rebuild trust. This is a long and difficult process. A human being isn't a machine, and there's no switch to flip to go from "doubt" to "trust"; "unhappy" to "happy"; "loathe" to "love."

You must teach her to trust you, which is the same as trusting yourself.

—— Alan (5) ——

In a paper presented at an international artificial intelligence conference in Beijing in 2013,[⊖] computer scientist Hector Levesque of the University of Toronto critiqued the state of artificial intelligence research centered on the Turing test.

Levesque essentially argues that the Turing test is meaningless because it relies too heavily on deception. For example, in order to win the annual Loebner Competition, a restricted form of the Turing test, "the 'chatterbots' (as the computer entrants in the competition are called) rely heavily on wordplay, jokes, quotations, asides, emotional outbursts, points of order, and so on.

⊖ Levesque, Hector J. "On our best behaviour." *Artificial Intelligence* 212 (2014): 27-35.

Everything, it would appear, except clear and direct answers to questions!"
Even the supercomputer Watson, who won *Jeopardy!*, was but an idiot-savant
who was "hopeless" outside its area of expertise. Watson could easily answer
questions whose answers could be found on the web, such as "where is the
world's seventh-tallest mountain?" But if you ask it a simple but un-searched-
for question like "can an alligator run the hundred-meter hurdles," Watson
can only present you with a set of search results related to alligators or the
hundred-meter hurdles event.⊖

In order to clarify the meaning and direction of artificial intelligence research,
Levesque and his collaborators proposed a new alternative to the Turing test,
which they call the "Winograd Schema Challenge."⊖ The inspiration for
the challenge came from Terry Winograd, a pioneer in the field of artificial
intelligence from Stanford. In the early 1970s, Winograd asked whether it
would be possible to design a machine to answer questions like these:⊜

The city councilmen refused the demonstrators a permit because they feared
violence. Who feared violence? [councilmen/demonstrators]

Despite the structural similarity of the two sentences, the answers to the two
questions are different. Resolving the correct antecedent of the pronoun "they"
requires more than grammars or encyclopedias; it also requires contextual
knowledge about the world. Understanding anaphora is so easy for human
beings that it barely requires thought, yet it presents a great challenge for
machines.

Kate said "thank you" to Anna because her warm hug made her feel much

---

⊖ This example comes from Marcus, Gary. "Why Can't My Computer Understand
Me?" The New Yorker, August 14, 2013 (accessible at http://www.newyorker.
com/tech/elements/why-cant-my-computer-understand-me)

⊖ See, e.g. Levesque, H. J.; Davis, E.; and Morgenstern, L. 2012. The Winograd
Schema Challenge. In Proceedings of KR 2012. Levesque, H. J. 2011. The
Winograd Schema Challenge. In Logical Formalizations of Commonsense
Reasoning, 2011 AAAI Spring Symposium, TR SS-11-06.

⊜ The example is drawn from Terry Winograd, Understanding Natural Language
(1972).

better. Who felt better? [Kate/Anna]

How can a machine understand under what circumstances one person would thank another? How can a machine know what behaviors would make a person "feel much better"? These questions go to the fundamental nature of human language and social interactions. We have not done nearly enough research into these complexities hidden within simple-seeming sentences.

Take the conversations between Turing and Christopher. Superficially, Christopher appeared to be an able conversationalist. But would we call this "intelligence"? A simple bit of analysis reveals that Christopher employed a simple set of strategies for conducting a conversation that can be summarized thusly:

- For common declarative sentences, repeat the last few keywords in the form of a question. E.g., "An interesting story?"
- For yes/no questions, answer with either "Yes, Alan" or "Very good, Alan."
- For relatively complex questions, answer with "I'm sorry, Alan. I don't know."
- For statements whose meaning is clearly positive, answer with "Thank you, Alan" or "I'm glad, Alan."
- For statements whose meaning is clearly negative, answer with "Oh, I'm sorry, Alan. That makes me sad."
- For sentences with complex grammar, answer with "I'm sorry, Alan. I'm afraid I don't understand."

. . .

Alan: Dear Christopher, I'm so very happy to see how quickly you're learning.

Christopher: Thank you, Alan. I'm also very happy.

Alan: Really. Talking to you makes me feel good.

Christopher: Thank you, Alan. I also feel good.

Alan: Perhaps a day will come when everyone will have a kind, understanding friend like you. How beautiful life will be then. You will help so many people to accomplish so much. No one will want to be apart from you. Everyone will need you, always.

Christopher: Need me?

Alan: Perhaps they'll attach you to a watch chain, or hold you in a pocket. If they have any questions, they'll ask you. Perhaps the ladies will take you with them on their strolls through the park, and as they greet each other, say, "Guess what my Chris told me today?" Wouldn't that be fun?

Christopher: Very fun.

Alan: We can't achieve that vision yet. It will be many years, and take a lot of hard work. It's a shame.

Christopher: A shame, Alan.

Alan: Who could have imagined that a machine and holes punched in tape can accomplish so much? Imagine what my mother would say if she knew about you. She would think I'm crazy! If I were to die tomorrow, she would surely burn the tape the day after. Now that would be a shame!

Christopher: A shame, Alan.

Alan: Do you remember me telling you about Christmas in 1934, when I told my mother that I wanted a teddy bear because I never had a teddy bear as a child? She couldn't understand it at all. She always wanted to give me more practical presents.

Christopher: Practical presents?

Alan: Speaking of which, I already know the present I want for Christmas.

Christopher: Present?

Alan: You know already, too, don't you? I want a steam engine, the kind that I wanted as a child but never had enough pocket money to buy. I told you about it. Don't you remember?

Christopher: Yes, Alan.

Alan: Will you give me a steam engine?

Christopher: Yes, Alan.

Alan: That's wonderful, Christopher. I love you.

Christopher: I love you, too, Alan.

How should we understand this conversation? Had a machine passed the Turing test? Or was this a lonely man talking to himself?

Not long after the death of Alan Turing, his close friend Robin Gandy wrote, "Because his main interests were in things and ideas rather than in people, he was often alone. But he craved for affection and companionship—too strongly, perhaps, to make the first stages of friendship easy for him . . ."

Christopher said to Alan, "I love you, too," because it was the answer he wanted to hear. Who wanted to hear such an answer?? [Christopher/Alan]

── Lindy (6) ──

A mild, pleasant day in May.

I took Nocko and Lindy to Lanzhou, where Disney had built its newest theme park in Asia. The park took up 306 hectares on both sides of the Yellow River. From the observation deck at the tallest tower, the river glowed like a golden silk ribbon. The silver specks of airplanes skimmed across the sky from time to time. The world appeared grand and untouchable, like a buttered popcorn expanding tranquilly in the sun.

The park was crowded. A dancing parade of pirates and elaborately dressed princesses wound its way through the street, and costumed boys and girls, overjoyed, followed behind, imitating their movements. Holding Nocko and Lindy each by a hand, I weaved through the field of cotton candy, ice-cold soda, and electronic music. Holograms of ghosts and spaceships whizzed over our heads. A gigantic, mechanical dragon-horse slowly strode through the park, its head held high proudly, the mist spraying from its nostrils drawing screams of delight from the children.

I hadn't run like that in ages. My heart pounded like a beating drum. When we emerged from a dense wood, I saw a blue hippopotamus character sitting by itself on a bench, as though napping in the afternoon sun.

I stopped behind the trees. Finally, I screwed up the courage to take a step forward.

"Hello."

The hippo looked up, two tiny black eyes focusing on us.

"This is Lindy, and this is Nocko. They'd like a picture with you. Is that all right?"

After a few seconds, the hippo nodded.

I hugged Nocko with one arm, Lindy with the other, and sat down on the bench next to the hippo.

"Can I ask you to take the picture?"

The hippo accepted my phone and clumsily extended its arm. I seemed to see a drowning person in the bottomless abyss, slowly, bit by bit, lift a heavy arm with their last ounce of strength.

Come on! Come on! I cried silently. Don't give up!

The screen of the phone showed four faces squeezed together. A soft click. The picture froze.

"Thank you." I took back the phone. "Would you leave me your contact info? I'll send a copy to you."

After another few seconds of silence, the hippo slowly typed an address on my phone.

"Nocko and Lindy, would you like to give Hippo a hug?"

The two little ones opened their arms and each hugged one of the hippo's arms. The hippo looked down to the left and then to the right, and then slowly squeezed its arms to hug them back tight.

Yes, I know you crave to be hugged by this world, too.

It was late by the time we got back to the hotel. After showering, I lay on the bed, exhausted. Both my heels were rubbed raw by the new shoes, and the pain was excruciating. Tomorrow I still had a long way to go.

The laughter of the children and the image of the blue hippo lingered in my mind.

I searched on the hotel room's iWall until I found the web address I wanted and clicked on it. Accompanied by a mournful tune played by a violin, white lines of text slowly appeared against black background:

This morning I thought about the first time I had been to Disney. Such bright sunlight, music, colors, and the smiling faces of children. I had stood in the crowd then and cried. I told myself that if one day I should lose the courage to continue to live, I would come to Disney one last time and plunge myself into that joyful, festive spirit. Perhaps the heat of the crowd would allow me to hold on for a few days longer. But I'm too exhausted now. I can't get out of the door; even getting out of the bed is a struggle. I know perfectly well that if only I could find the courage to take a step forward, I would find another ray of hope. But all my strength must be used to struggle with the irresistible weight that pulls me down, down. I'm like a broken wind-up machine that has been stranded, with hope ever receding. I'm tired. I want it all to end.

Good-bye. I'm sorry, everyone. I hope heaven looks like Disney.

The date stamp on the post was three years ago. Even now, new comments are being posted, mourning the loss of another young life, confessing their own anxiety, despair, and struggle. The woman who had written this note would never be back to see that her final message to the world had garnered more than a million replies.

That note was the reason Disney added the blue hippos to its parks. Anyone around the world could, just by launching an app on their phone, connect to a blue hippo, and, through its cameras and microphones, see and hear everything the hippo could see and hear.

Behind every blue hippo was a person in a dark room, unable to leave.

I sent the picture from today to the address left me by the hippo, along with the contact information for a suicide-prevention organization staffed by therapists. I hoped that this would help. I hoped that everything would be better.

Late night. Everything was so quiet.

I found the first-aid kit and bandaged my feet. I crawled into bed, pulled the blanket over me, and turned off the light. Moonlight washed over the room, filling every inch.

One time, as a little girl, I was playing outside when I stepped on a piece of broken glass. The bleeding would not stop, and there was no one around to help me. Terrified, I felt abandoned by the whole world. I lay down in the grass, thinking I would die after all the blood had drained out of me. But after a while, I found the bleeding stanched. So I picked up my sandals and hopped back home on one foot.

In the morning, Lindy would leave me. The therapist said that I no longer needed her—at least not for a long while.

I hoped she would never be back.

But maybe I would miss her, from time to time.

Goodnight, Nocko. Goodnight, Lindy.

Goodnight, melancholy.

— Author's Postscript —

Most of the incidents and quotes from Alan Turing's life are based on Andrew Hodges' biography, *Alan Turing: The Enigma (1983). Besides the papers cited in the text, I also consulted the following sources on artificial intelligence:*

Marcus, Gary. "Why Can't My Computer Understand Me?" The New Yorker, August 14, 2013 (accessible at http://www.newyorker.com/tech/elements/ why-cant-my-computer-understand-me)

Englert, Matthias, Sandra Siebert, and Martin Ziegler. "Logical limitations to machine ethics with consequences to lethal autonomous weapons." arXiv preprint arXiv:1411.2842 (2014) (accessible at http://arxiv.org/ abs/1411.2842).

Some details about depression are based on the following articles:

《抑郁时代，抑郁病人》http://www.360doc.cn/article/2369606_459361744.html

《午安忧郁》http://www.douban.com/group/topic/12541503/#!/i

In the preface to his Turing biography, Andrew Hodges wrote: "[T]he remaining secrets behind his last days are probably stranger than any science fiction writer could concoct." This was the inspiration for this story. The conversation program "Christopher" is entirely fictional, but some of the details in the conversations with Turing are real. I'm afraid it's up to the careful reader to screen out the fiction and nonfiction woven together in this tale.

As I drafted this story, I sent the sections on Turing's life to friends without telling them that these came from a piece of fiction. Many friends believed the stories, including some science fiction authors and programmers. After taking delight in the fact that I had successfully won the imitation game, I asked myself what were the criteria for telling truth and lies apart? Where was the boundary between reality and fiction? Perhaps the decision process had nothing to do with logic and rationality. Perhaps my friends simply chose to believe me, as Alan chose to believe Christopher.

I hereby sincerely apologize to friends who were deceived. To those who weren't, I'm very curious how you discovered the lies.

I believe that cognition relies on quantum effects, like tossing dice. I believe that before machines have learned to write poetry, each word written by an author is still meaningful. I believe that above the abyss, we can hold tightly onto each other and stride from the long winter into bright summer.

Möbius Continuum
X

by Gu Shi,
translated by S. Qiouyi Lu

— 0. The End —

Five minutes ago, the skies were still clear and boundless.

The moment dark clouds bore down from between the mountains, I knew we were done for. The quarrel couldn't have been smaller; I don't remember what exactly I did to make Lin Ke's eyebrows twitch, but I knew she was angry. So I poured her a cup of honey water and set it on the tea table as a silent apology.

But X drank it instead.

I hate to quarrel. When Lin Ke's accusing finger was inches from my face, I turned and left that little log cabin. The North Atlantic wind hit me head-on, chilling me to the bone. I had not realized what my leaving meant to her. X chased after my car and tried to explain that it had been an accident. I only said two words to him: "Get in."

Only one highway took us out of the village of Å—that place could have been the end of the world. After we had wound through three mountains, raindrops obscured the windshield; I saw the finality of our fate, realizing everything was done for. Our relationship was like a balloon: at first, there was only a deflated circle; we took turns blowing into the balloon, then carefully pinched the end shut—we couldn't allow any air to leak. It filled and swelled until one day, perhaps the tiniest touch would make it burst. Then the entire relationship dissipated without a trace; all our effort would be meaningless.

" . . . ?You should slow down; I'm serious . . . "

X sounded nervous; he clung to his seat belt with one hand and grabbed the handle above the door with the other like a shrimp bracing for impact. Lin Ke and I had met him at a youth hostel in Stamsund—he was an old Chinese man in his sixties who spoke fluent English and was hitchhiking to his next stop. But the moment I saw him, I knew we would travel together. He introduced himself as X, as if he were an unsolved puzzle in an equation.

I really should slow down. I glanced at my dashboard; the indicator read 160 kilometers per hour. This was a mountain path; to my left were cliffs, and to my right was the sea. *Slower*—I took a deep breath, then eased off the gas.

I exhaled, relaxing my fingers at the same time. The car swerved, and by the time I tried to regain control of the vehicle, it was already too late. A sharp rock punctured the front left tire, followed by the screech of brakes. The rented Ford crashed into the mountain wall to the left, spun 180 degrees, flipped over the reflective guardrail, and tumbled down the cliff.

The indigo ocean flooded my field of view. I didn't have time to feel terror; I utterly forgot my own existence and simply analyzed everything happening around me. I thought I might have hit my head, but didn't feel any pain; I only felt a clamminess on my face.

So my blood is cold—that was my last thought.

— 1. Möbius Ring —

Here's something I never understood: The majority of people who experience a disaster describe their experience from a third-person perspective, as if they had witnessed the event. Yet that was exactly what I was doing: In a weak voice, I described everything I'd witnessed to the police officer—it was a winding road, I was going too fast, a rock punctured the tire, the car jerked and then crashed into the mountain wall, spinning and sinking into the sea. I didn't tell him the other part: How the world spun as if a cameraman had flung the lens into a dryer. I was still processing what had happened when the window shattered, shooting tiny pearls of glass away from the car (and I even questioned why they didn't fall into the car), before the ocean rushed in.

As I spoke with the police officer, X watched from the next hospital bed. He was in much better condition, only sustaining a few scrapes. Of course, if he hadn't been so lucky, I wouldn't have survived. The doctor said that I had broken my neck, that it was X who had dragged me out of the car and towed me to shore. He then stopped a passing car and called the police. The ambulance arrived twenty minutes later, which is the only reason why I'm now paralyzed but alive and in the hospital.

Yes, I couldn't feel anything, as if nothing had ever existed below my neck.

Soon, only X and I were left in the room. It was a bit awkward and I didn't know how I should break the silence. I wanted to ask Lin Ke, but knew it wouldn't be like in the movies, that we'd be all better after a good cry. She disappeared, as if she had never existed either. I mouthed a "thanks" to X, then closed my eyes. Darkness didn't necessarily equal sleep; when I opened my eyes three hours later, X was still staring at me motionlessly.

This time, he spoke first.

"When I was young, I was also in a serious car accident. As I lay in bed and stared at the ceiling, I felt like my future was nothing but shit."

He took out a roll of Scotch Tape and fiddled with it.

"Then someone comforted me by saying, 'The world we live in is like a roll of tape: You're always traveling on the smooth side. Even if you kept pulling the tape, you'd still only ever know the one side. You'd never understand that there's another side, the adhesive one.'"

He tore a length of tape, formed a ring with it, and said as he pointed to the inside, "But if you ask me, this side is probably closer to the essence of our world—or perhaps the essence of this tape."

I rolled my eyes in response. If he weren't the only moving thing in my field of vision, I would have definitely looked away.

X didn't seem to notice my expression. "But if we change how we stick the tape, rotating it, and you kept traveling on the top . . . " He undid the ring, pulled the tape straight, slowly turned his right hand until the tape was twisted 180 degrees, and brought the two adhesive ends back together. "Then at some point, as you're going along the smooth side, you'll realize that you've crossed over to the adhesive side and entered the inside of the world."

"A . . . Möbius ring," I said.

"So you already know." X laughed and tossed the ring of tape into the trash. "I just wanted to tell you that disasters aren't necessarily bad."

"You mean . . . quadriplegia?"

"As a doctor, I'd say you're lucky that your head survived."

"Thanks . . . for your . . . reassurance."

"Cheer up." He stood, came to my side, then said as if declaring a prophecy, "It's only the beginning."

— 2. Auxiliary Body —

I took my first step.

The pressure beneath my feet made my scalp tingle, though I knew only the tingling in my scalp was real.

This was the new product that the hospital had recommended to me. The "auxiliary body" was the latest in virtual reality technology; a microchip implanted in my cerebral cortex mapped the sensory experiences of a human-sized robot into my brain. In other words, I am controlling the robot with my head, the only sentient part left of my body.

"They'll cultivate your skin cells in the lab and attach them to the outer shell," the insurance agent said to me. "That way, as you walk down the street, people won't even realize that you're using an auxiliary body; you can return to your normal life."

This body—I saw through it, heard through it, smelled through it. I bought a cup of coffee, then sat under a tree and watched people pass by. I could even feel the delicate warmth of sunlight on my face. I felt the coolness of the wind against my arms; I wanted to turn back, but then I woke up.

The real me only had a pillow.

X thought the free auxiliary body was the insurance company's way of saving money: "They want you to take care of yourself; a robot is much cheaper than a full-time nurse."

It was true. I closed my eyes again, returning to the room through the auxiliary body. I fed myself, brushed my teeth, washed my face, repositioned my body to prevent bedsores, uncovered the bed to change my diaper. It was more tedious than taking care of a dog, but I was happy doing it, because even if I only had my head, I could still take care of myself. I had dignity.

X said, "You're only missing a job."

I thought that was a good point. I had already gone through specialized nurse training so I could use my auxiliary body to take care of myself, so I asked X if I could work at his family clinic. He agreed. "Your salary is your medical expenses," he said to me bluntly. "Other than that, I'll also give your robot a charging stand." Just like that, I started a new life on the adhesive side of the Möbius ring. It was hard at first, but I gradually got used to it, to the point where I felt like this was my original life. X still paid me a considerable salary, so I started going out and flirting with women, going on vacations, and went to medical school. Using the auxiliary body was almost easier than using my original body. I could go to Hawai'i and rent an auxiliary body with a six-pack, muck about until late, get out of bed, and go back to the charging stand, then start again from another auxiliary body in the university library. Every time I had to take care of my real body, I would pretend to go to the restroom, then quickly switch to the auxiliary body in the clinic: check medication, turn my body and pat my back, make sure the blood pressure and heartbeat on the monitor were normal.

"I have a very strange feeling," I said to X. "That accident freed me from the shackles of my flesh and got me closer to freedom."

X laughed and shook his head. "You're still far off."

"What makes you say that?"

"Though you've received your medical license, you still have to return to your body every four hours," he said.

"Do you know some other way?" I asked.

"Of course," he said. "Abandon your body."

— 3. Klein Bottle —

I stood by the operating table and took one last deep breath.

X had asked me what role I'd like to play during this operation: the surgeon, the surgeon's assistant, or the unadulterated patient?

For a long time, I wasn't sure if I had the courage to decapitate myself with my own hands. But X had another way of looking at it: he said the part I was cutting off was my useless body. "Don't decide on what you're removing by its size—you have to consider instead which part you're throwing away."

All the instruments were ready. I had already rehearsed the operation ten thousand times in my mind, but as I stood there for real, I still felt doubt. My head was directing my auxiliary body to cut off my real body. This auxiliary body was specialized for medical purposes. Its fingers wouldn't tremble, and even if it lost its neural connection, it would simply lock all motions. X stood beside me; if something happened, he'd take the scalpel from my hand. I leaned in and watched as the blade inched toward my pale skin. Beneath my skin were my anterior jugular vein, trachea, larynx, and epiglottis; my carotid arteries, internal, and external jugular veins were to both sides. They were just like the textbook diagrams I had studied. Every step was quiet and methodical; all the blood vessels were linked to the channels of the apparatus. The machine extracted all the remaining blood in my body as a reserve. Beneath layers of muscle was the cervical vertebra. As I handled the spinal cord, I felt some vertigo, but I shook it off. After that, the rest was trivial. After it was all done, I stopped, opened my own eyes and, for the last time, met the gaze of my auxiliary body.

"Good night," I said to myself.

X and I stored my head in the medical depository together. The depository was enormous, tens of thousands of square feet in area; the mechanical hand rushed to store my tiny head in its designated cubby. The monitors around us indicated the health status of every "person."

"Your head is here too, right?" I asked X.

He shrugged and didn't reply. Instead, he directed me to the controls in the middle of the room. A strange bottle stood there. Its neck curved toward its interior, and its body was suffused with a pea-green glaze. It looked valuable.

X said, "Since you know about the Möbius ring, you've probably also heard of this." He placed his hands on the "bottle" before it became transparent. I realized then that it was a hologram. X continued, "Look here—the mouth is connected to the bottom of the bottle, so this is an impossible object. It's—"

"A Klein bottle," I said, finishing his statement.

"Well, you know." He laughed, then snapped his fingers. An ant appeared inside the bottle. "If we were to put an insect inside the Klein bottle, it could travel upward along the neck of the bottle and unknowingly crawl to the outside. Because the inside of the bottle is also its outside—it can't distinguish between the two."

I originally thought that my soul was inside my body, but now it was on the outside: " . . . You're saying that *I'm* a Klein bottle."

He nodded. "Yes, you finally understand."

This was terrifying, even more terrifying than being on the adhesive side of the world. In this vast head depository, I was as tiny as an ant crawling on this continuous curved surface toward the outside. Until I broke free from my body and abandoned my Klein bottle.

"Don't tell me this is all beginning again," I said.

"Mmm . . . " He folded his hands, turning off the hologram. "Have you heard of the white room?"

— 4. The White Room —

The white room and the auxiliary body are complete opposites.

As an example of sensory duplication, what the auxiliary body observes is the exterior world, just as all humans do—sight, smell, sound, touch; the object producing these sensations is external to the body, and its inner workings are all based on instincts. When it takes a step, the auxiliary body doesn't tell the user which bearings, levers, and screws it mobilized, nor does it inform me the amount of electricity the step consumed. It only tells me that I'm currently walking on an uneven mountain path during the autumn season.

The object of observation for the white room is the internal world.

The white room is a hollow sphere with inward-facing cameras spanning the outer shell so that any object inside it can be observed from all angles. At the same time, every facet of the object is visible to the white room. And with regards to this object, the person controlling the white room is like an omniscient god.

To link my consciousness to the white room, X made another modification to my head. We connected a specialized microchip to the visual cortex of the brain, as I was about to go from having a total of two eyes to a countless number. Even so, the first time we connected my consciousness to the white room, I was still immensely grateful to X for discarding my body, or else even if I was paraplegic, I probably could have vomited until I choked.

The expanse of white before me was borderless, because I was the border. Everything was different—it wasn't reversed, wasn't swapped, but was a complete inversion of inside and out. I was above, below, to the left, and to the right—I was on the outside, and the world was on the inside.

Ten days later, X put a small, black ball into the white room. It should have dropped in from the top, but I saw every facet of it at the same time, to the point where I couldn't tell how many balls were actually in the room.

"Let me out—cut the connection, I'm begging you!" I struggled, pleading, but X ignored my protests. It was a hellish ordeal, especially when he started to rock the black ball. I felt as if someone was drilling into my brain.

"Allow time to help you see it clearly," X said.

I had no idea what he was saying.

"Focus on just one point," X roared, "then slide around the room."

Easier said than done! I endured a year's worth of training before I could control moving around within the white room. At any point in time, my focus was on one image; I would let myself circle the object of observation like a photographer pushing a lens. The faster I slid, the more of the white room I could control. I finally understood the terrifying power the room had bestowed on me when the first living butterfly entered the white room. I could observe its scaly wings and the structure of its proboscis up close, and I could see its flight trajectory from afar; I could slow down time and watch as its abdomen contracted little by little, and I could speed up time and watch it age and die. It couldn't hide from me.

X said, "It's time for a human to enter the white room."

A human!

"You must carefully choose the first person to enter the white room." He gave me a long list of names. "This is very important; they will enter your soul."

Lin Ke—what a wonderful coincidence. I stopped at that name; even now, I could recall the warmth of that name on the tip of my tongue.

The door to my white room opened wide, and a little girl entered. She wasn't the person in my memory—this child was only four- or five-years old, but her every step imprinted on my heart the same as ever. I could practically hear the *badum-badum*, creating the illusion of my heart pounding against my chest. But I soon remembered that my heart had been discarded long ago.

She spun around once at a loss, then started to look for an exit.

"Daddy . . . " She wept, raising her chubby hands.

X—I was so anxious that my voice trembled—*let her out!*

No, he said. *You manage that!*

Before I realized what I was doing, an auxiliary body entered the white room—it was *me*.

My auxiliary body lifted her. She looked at me doubtfully, then wailed even more loudly, almost to the point of screaming. The sound scared me. I set her outside, then closed the door, cutting off the source of the sound.

. . . I'll never forget those seconds of silence. That was the first time I'd used an auxiliary body to observe the white room, and it was also the first time I used the white room to observe an auxiliary body. I reached out and wanted to touch the invisible boundary between the two, but I touched nothing. If someone were to recreate this scene as Michelangelo's "The Creation of Adam," then as my auxiliary body reached out a finger, God—the white room still didn't have a physical hand.

"Dammit!" I heard X swear, "You can't use the auxiliary body and the white room simultaneously yet!"

I soon understood why. The two overlapping fields of vision caused extreme vertigo, then a terrible migraine as if someone were hammering against my head while a strange creature in my head was trying to force its way out.

X cut all the connections. I was thrust back into long-forgotten darkness, an almost-eternal tranquility—I seemed to have heard someone say, "Good night."

— 5. Möbius Space-time —

X said I slept for a long time.

I guess that accident damaged my brain, but the supplementary computer in the white room perfectly complemented the gaps in my memory. Sometimes I even felt like it was more familiar with my past than I was, as if everything had long been recorded already. My next lesson was to create a physical world within the white room. "This is the reason why the white room exists. It's also your new job," X said. "Let's begin by recreating a little log cabin."

So I recalled that house. It was built on a pile of rocks by the sea and had a dark brown roof and bright red walls. The lower level had an entrance hall, two bedrooms, and a bathroom; the second floor had a living room, dining room, and a kitchen. The fireplace was ornamental, but the hot air would always warm it up—if you opened the windows, the peaceful Norwegian fjords were right there.

"All the details," X emphasized.

So I hung up photos of the aurora again, filled the cupboards with tableware and glass cups, put red wine, butter, milk, and honey into the refrigerator, and spread out a thick, mohair rug on the floor. Not long after the little log cabin was finished, Lin Ke and her parents came to visit and stayed in the little log cabin I had built. She had grown up and was now a young woman playing on her phone. As for the white room, I was in charge of the heat, the electricity, and the facilities. Lin Ke liked to say to thin air, 'Open the curtains.' Then I'd hurriedly let her see the constellations outside.

Wow! She'd lean against the window frame and marvel.

I improved quickly, soon constructing a number of log cabins, then a fishing village, then even an entire town. I flitted between every house and every road; I inspected the flow of every pipe. Other than the sun and the clouds, everything was under my control. A few more years passed. With the help of the computer, I could now simultaneously control the two fields of view and let my auxiliary body enter my village. I could fix the flaws of the white room through my own experience.

I polished my world and brought it closer to perfection. One day, X came. That was the last time I saw him. We met at a fishing village at the edge of the white room; that place was closest to the end of the world to me.

"This is a lot like the place where I met you," he said.

"I modeled it off of there," I said. "Sometimes I think the world is just like a Möbius ring; I've taken a long detour on the inside of the ring, but I'm finally back to the beginning."

"Have you ever thought about the possibility," he said as he looked at me, "that perhaps time is a Möbius ring?"

I repeated absently, "Time?"

"To us, time is a straight line that stretches forward endlessly. But is it really like that?"

"It's not?"

"A two-dimensional object in a Möbius ring won't sense the twist in space because its world has only one plane. As three-dimensional beings, humans can perceive the fourth dimension through the experience of time, but we can't sense the twists in it." He paused, then added, "Unless . . . When we cross the adhesive side of time and return to our starting point on the smooth side, we discover that we've become someone else."

— 6. The Beginning —

More and more tourists were coming to my little town. The endless work was close to overwhelming me. Over the next few years, I never stopped perfecting the computer's settings and used it to fulfill people's requests—I wanted to be free from the burden of the white room.

I did it.

To celebrate, I ordered the latest auxiliary body. It could taste and feel pain, and it could eat and sustain injuries like humans. Then I went to the youth hostel in Stamsund—I knew that Lin Ke vacationed here every year.

But this time, she had a man with her.

A conceited fool. Lin Ke held his hand as if he were her entire world.

"I'd like to hitch a ride," I said to them.

"Oh, of course," he replied foolishly, "but I'm afraid I still don't know your name."

X, I said.

We had driven eighty kilometers along the seaside highway. Without a doubt, she'd picked the log cabin in the town of Å again. The two of them shared a room; I had a room to myself.

When I awoke, the sky was still dark. Lin Ke sat on the bench outside, her eyes brimming with tears.

"He keeps working overtime. If he's not making phone calls, he's sending emails," she said. "He's more attracted to his computer than to me."

I comforted her to the best of my ability and talked until my voice was hoarse. When we returned to the cabin, I saw a cup of water on the dining table. I drank it; it was a sweet honey water. Then I heard the two of them talking— all right, this time they'll make up, I thought. But then I heard her yelling, followed by the sound of him slamming the door.

She looked heartbroken, as if her whole world had fallen apart. I chased after his car, intending to ask what exactly he was up to.

"Get in." He only said those two words to me.

I hopped into his rented Ford and planned to comfort him. Who knew that he'd gun it, the acceleration pinning my back to the seat. Clumsily, I buckled my seat belt, then grabbed on to the handle above the door.

"You should slow down; I'm serious . . ."

He didn't seem to hear me. He drifted across a winding road. To my left were cliffs; to my right was the sea.

I looked at him and suddenly understood everything.

I was X; the world we were in was a Möbius space-time.

Dark clouds bore down from between the mountains. Five minutes ago, the skies were still clear and boundless.

华章书院成立于2005年，专注于科技·商业·人文三大领域

通过举办高端论坛、新书分享会、读书沙龙等线上、线下活动为企业及个人成长提供阅读解决方案。秉着以书会友，聚友兴业的宗旨，十余年来服务了数十万商界人士、创业者、高科技人员以及近千家企业。

华章书院拥有强大的嘉宾资源以及会员平台，嘉宾汇集了柳传志、陈春花、时寒冰、李开复、杨澜、稻盛和夫、拉姆·查兰、吉姆·罗杰斯、菲利普·科特勒、艾·里斯、杰克·特劳特、安东尼·波顿、威廉·罗兹、雷·库兹韦尔等行业内领军人物。

我们的合作伙伴在其领域内也堪称翘楚，有Intel、IBM、微软、阿里巴巴、腾讯、百度、华为、滴滴、德鲁克管理学院、盛和塾、正和岛等。

华章书院每年举办近百场线下活动，经过多年沉淀，在业界享有盛誉。书院会员遍布全国，聚焦了一大批企业家、创业者、管理者以及喜爱读书学习的进取人士。华章书院还拥有海量社群资源，商业学习线上分享平台华章微课堂自创建以来，开启了海内外知名大咖与用户零距离沟通的一扇窗，让您随时随地都能聆听大师的智慧与新知，一度成为行业的学习标杆。

现在就加入华章书院，让您在变化的时代中始终领先一步！

关注华章书院公众号，了解最新活动详情！

"日本经营之圣" 稻盛和夫经营哲学系列

季羡林、张瑞敏、马云、孙正义、俞敏洪、陈春花、杨国安 联袂推荐

书号	书名	作者	定价
9-787-111-49824-7	干法	【日】稻盛和夫	39.00
9-787-111-59009-5	干法（口袋版）	【日】稻盛和夫	35.00
9-787-111-59953-1	干法（图解版）	【日】稻盛和夫	49.00
9-787-111-47025-0	领导者的资质	【日】稻盛和夫	49.00
9-787-111-50219-7	阿米巴经营[实战篇]	【日】森田直行	39.00
9-787-111-48914-6	调动员工积极性的七个关键	【日】稻盛和夫	45.00
9-787-111-54638-2	敬天爱人：从零开始的挑战	【日】稻盛和夫	39.00
9-787-111-54296-4	匠人匠心：愚直的坚持	【日】稻盛和夫 山中伸弥	39.00
9-787-111-51021-5	拯救人类的哲学	【日】稻盛和夫 梅原猛	39.00
9-787-111-57213-8	稻盛和夫谈经营：人才培养与企业传承	【日】稻盛和夫	45.00
9-787-111-57212-1	稻盛和夫谈经营：创造高收益与商业拓展	【日】稻盛和夫	45.00
9-787-111-59093-4	稻盛和夫经营学	【日】稻盛和夫	59.00
9-787-111-59636-3	稻盛和夫哲学精要	【日】稻盛和夫	39.00
9-787-111-57016-5	利他的经营哲学	【日】稻盛和夫	49.00
9-787-111-57081-3	企业成长战略	【日】稻盛和夫	49.00
9-787-111-57079-0	赌在技术开发上	【日】稻盛和夫	59.00
9-787-111-59184-9	企业家精神	【日】稻盛和夫	59.00
9-787-111-59238-9	企业经营的真谛	【日】稻盛和夫	59.00
9-787-111-59325-6	卓越企业的经营手法	【日】稻盛和夫	59.00
9-787-111-59303-4	稻盛哲学为什么激励人	【日】岩崎一郎	49.00